PRAISE FOR DON
ROMANCE NOVELS

"Grant's ability to quickly convey complicated backstory makes this jam-packed love story accessible even to new or periodic readers." - *Publisher's Weekly*

"Donna Grant has given the paranormal genre a burst of fresh air…" – *San Francisco Book Review*

"The premise is dramatic and heartbreaking; the characters are colorful and engaging; the romance is spirited and seductive." – *The Reading Cafe*

"The central romance, fueled by a hostage drama, plays out in glorious detail against a backdrop of multiple ongoing issues in the "Dark Kings" books. This seemingly penultimate installment creates a nice segue to a climactic end." – *Library Journal*

"…intense romance amid the growing war between the Dragons and the Dark Fae is scorching hot." – *Booklist*

Dragonfire ~ Dragon Claimed ~ Ignite
Fever ~ Dragon Lost ~ Flame ~ Inferno
A Dragon's Tale (Whisky and Wishes: *A Holiday Novella*,
Heart of Gold: *A Valentine's Novella*, & Of Fire and Flame)
My Fiery Valentine ~ The Dragon King Coloring Book
Dragon King Special Edition Character Coloring Book: Rhi

DARK WARRIORS SERIES

Midnight's Master ~ Midnight's Lover ~ Midnight's Seduction
Midnight's Warrior ~ Midnight's Kiss ~ Midnight's Captive
Midnight's Temptation ~ Midnight's Promise
Midnight's Surrender ~ A Warrior for Christmas

CHIASSON SERIES

Wild Fever ~ Wild Dream ~ Wild Need
Wild Flame ~ Wild Rapture

LARUE SERIES

Moon Kissed ~ Moon Thrall ~ Moon Struck ~ Moon Bound

WICKED TREASURES

Seized by Passion ~ Enticed by Ecstasy ~ Captured by Desire
Books 1-3: Wicked Treasures Box Set

HISTORICAL PARANORMAL

THE KINDRED SERIES
Everkin ~ Eversong ~ Everwylde ~ Everbound
Evernight ~ Everspell

KINDRED: THE FATED SERIES
Rage

DARK SWORD SERIES
Dangerous Highlander ~ Forbidden Highlander
Wicked Highlander ~ Untamed Highlander
Shadow Highlander ~ Darkest Highlander

ROGUES OF SCOTLAND SERIES
The Craving ~ The Hunger ~ The Tempted ~ The Seduced
Books 1-4: Rogues of Scotland Box Set

THE SHIELDS SERIES
A Dark Guardian ~ A Kind of Magic ~ A Dark Seduction
A Forbidden Temptation ~ A Warrior's Heart
Mystic Trinity (a series connecting novel)

DRUIDS GLEN SERIES
Highland Mist ~ Highland Nights ~ Highland Dawn
Highland Fires ~ Highland Magic
Mystic Trinity (a series connecting novel)

SISTERS OF MAGIC TRILOGY
Shadow Magic ~ Echoes of Magic ~ Dangerous Magic
Books 1-3: Sisters of Magic Box Set

THE ROYAL CHRONICLES NOVELLA SERIES
Prince of Desire ~ Prince of Seduction
Prince of Love ~ Prince of Passion
Books 1-4: The Royal Chronicles Box Set
Mystic Trinity (a series connecting novel)

DARK BEGINNINGS: A FIRST IN SERIES BOXSET
Chiasson Series, Book 1: Wild Fever
LaRue Series, Book 1: Moon Kissed
The Royal Chronicles Series, Book 1: Prince of Desire

MILITARY ROMANCE / ROMANTIC SUSPENSE

SONS OF TEXAS SERIES
The Hero ~ The Protector ~ The Legend
The Defender ~ The Guardian

COWBOY / CONTEMPORARY

HEART OF TEXAS SERIES
The Christmas Cowboy Hero ~ Cowboy, Cross My Heart
My Favorite Cowboy ~ A Cowboy Like You
Looking for a Cowboy ~ A Cowboy Kind of Love

STAND ALONE BOOKS
That Cowboy of Mine
Home for a Cowboy Christmas
Mutual Desire
Forever Mine
Savage Moon

**Check out Donna Grant's Online Store at
www.DonnaGrant.com/shop
for autographed books, character
themed goodies, and more!**

This is a work of fiction. All of the characters, organizations, and events portrayed in this novel are either products of the author's imagination or are used fictitiously.

www.DonnaGrant.com
www.MotherofDragonsBooks.com

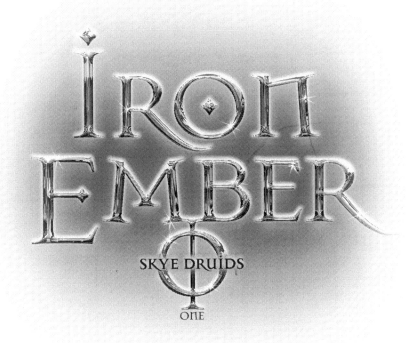

IRON EMBER

SKYE DRUIDS

ONE

NEW YORK TIMES & USA TODAY BESTSELLING AUTHOR

DONNA GRANT

CHAPTER ONE

SKYE DRUIDS

She was back.

It was the last place she wanted to be but the only place she had to run to.

Elodie threw open the curtains. Dust danced in the air, the sunlight catching it. She stared out the dirty window to the sea beyond. Skye. The home she'd proclaimed she would never leave because she loved it so fiercely.

It was also the place she had sworn to never return to.

And yet, here she was.

"Bloody hell," she murmured as she turned her back to the window and looked over what remained of the furniture from her parents' cottage.

Her gaze slid to the hearth where echoes of children's laughter clung to the stones. Her mother had made the best hot cocoa. After playing for hours outside in the winter, Elodie, her elder sister, Edie, and her brother, Elias, would sit before the fire with steaming cups of cocoa and her grandmother's strawberry scones.

Elodie squeezed her eyes shut. She wanted to hold onto the lighthearted memories, but the other ones were always on their heels—the ones that had altered all their lives, throwing them into chaos.

She blew out a breath and focused on the clutter and mess before her. The dust was so thick that she knew she would end up with respiratory problems for days if she didn't take precautions. And it wasn't as if she could use magic to prevent it.

Returning to Skye was like walking through one of Dante's nine circles of Hell. Elodie didn't know how she would survive being back on the island. If only she'd had somewhere else to go. *Anywhere* else. If she still believed, she would think Skye had interfered and brought her back.

"If that's the case, then my magic wouldn't be gone, now would it?"

It was hard not to be bitter and angry about her life. She owned her decisions, but she had been on a different path. Then, everything had imploded with the force of a nuclear explosion.

When she looked around after, everyone just went about their lives as if her family hadn't been rocked to its core. As if she and her siblings hadn't had their blinders ripped off with such force that it'd changed all three of them in one heartbeat —their innocence gone in the blink of an eye.

Corann had tried to help, but the old Druid hadn't been able to reach any of them. And Elias had left. Elodie still hadn't forgiven him for leaving her and Edie to navigate the churning waters of their society. Elodie might have been the youngest, but she was the one who'd ended up taking care of Edie. Her sister had the kind, gentle spirit of their mother. Elodie had lashed out and turned to drinking and drugs, but Edie had gone into herself.

Elodie walked through the main area of the cottage and past the kitchen to the hallway. Pictures of their family still hung on the walls. Snapshots of a happy life that had hidden the rot beneath. She stopped at one where Edie smiled brightly with a cake and lit candles before her. Maybe Elodie hadn't been the one to take care of Edie. They had leaned on each other, clinging to one another and struggling to keep their heads above water. It was only because of her sister that Elodie hadn't sunk too deeply into the hard life. She'd known she had to be there for Edie. And in the end, they'd kept each other afloat.

Until Elodie hadn't been able to stay another minute on Skye.

Fifteen years. It seemed like a lifetime, but it was much too soon to be back. Nothing would keep her on Skye longer than necessary this time. Not her sister. Nothing. Skye had annihilated her family. It had destroyed her. How Edie could remain on the isle was a mystery. And Elias? All Elodie could hope for was that her brother had found some semblance of happiness. They all deserved it.

Elodie forced herself to walk to each room, but she couldn't manage to go inside her parents'. She stood before the closed door as screams and shouts from that horrible day filled her head. Elodie backed away and turned on her heel.

How in the world would she stay in the cottage? Sleep just feet from where it'd all happened.

"I can't," she stated with a shake of her head.

Elodie grabbed her purse and the single bag that held her measly belongings and started for the door. Then she remembered *why* she was on Skye.

"Fuck!" she yelled and fought the sudden urge to release the scream of frustration that welled up.

She wasn't a crier, but everyone had their breaking point. She forced the tears back and dropped her bags. The only way to get on with her life was to take her sister's offer. All Elodie had to do was clean up the cottage so they could sell it. It was a good deal. Elodie had the place to herself instead of sleeping on the sofa at Edie's crowded house with her sister's kids and husband. And all without having to pay any sort of rent.

Since Elodie was homeless and jobless and had less than two hundred pounds to her name, it really was a blessing. At least she'd thought that until she arrived on Skye. Even driving around the island had made her chest constrict. Her anxiety rose with every mile. Then she'd arrived at the cottage. It had taken Elodie half an hour to work up the courage to actually walk inside.

"Maybe I deserve this torture," she said aloud. "I didn't exactly live a good life."

This was supposed to be her chance to start over. To travel the path she'd been on before she got derailed.

"Fine. Let's do this."

She opened the door, then went to all the windows and opened them despite the frigid temperatures and the threat of rain. The dust had to go somewhere, and the sooner she got it out of the house, the better. Elodie started in the bedroom she had once shared with her sister. She carefully folded the bed linens from each twin bed and dumped them outside. Thankfully, Edie had given her fresh sheets, pillows, and blankets.

Next, she found an old towel and used some cleaner to wipe down the walls and window, sweeping the cobwebs from the corners before vacuuming the carpet. Only then did she bring in her bag and purse.

Elodie wiped her face with her arm and made her way to the main area. Someone had placed sheets over the furniture. She slowly and carefully folded them, but there was so much dust that some still escaped. The pile joined the bed linens outside. On her way back inside, she smiled as she saw the dust wafting out the windows. Hopefully, most of it would land outside instead of back in the house.

The smallish living area didn't take long to wipe down. The windows would take more than one cleaning. She didn't want to touch the outside yet. That was a whole other matter entirely. Her first priority was to get the inside clean enough that she could locate any repairs that needed to be addressed. Only after she did that would she tackle the outside.

The old cottage was too quiet. Elodie pulled out her phone and put on her favorite playlist as she went back to cleaning. She kept moving, which helped to keep her warm. There was a brief shower, but she didn't bother closing the windows. The house needed to be aired out to get rid of the musty smell. She suddenly froze, the hairs on the back of her neck lifting. Slowly, she straightened from scrubbing the bathroom counter and looked at the doorway. No one was there. At least no one she could see.

A chill raced down her spine. With the sponge still in her gloved hands, she walked into the hallway. She glanced at her parents' room, then looked the other way. Elodie slowly made her way to the kitchen. Her gaze landed on a tall, gorgeous man with black and silver hair, standing next to a pretty female with red hair.

The man was a Fae. It seemed there was no escaping them anywhere, but they hadn't been allowed on Skye in decades. At least as far as she knew. What was he doing back?

"Hi," the woman said.

Elodie swung her gaze to the female. She looked close to Elodie's age, and something about her seemed familiar.

"You don't remember me, do you?" the woman asked with a smile.

Elodie shook her head. It was unnerving that people already knew she was on the isle. Worse that they remembered her when she had done everything to forget Skye and everyone on it. "I don't."

"You've been gone awhile. I'm Rhona."

In an instant, Elodie remembered Rhona and her cousin, Sorcha. They used to come over occasionally. She had always liked both girls. Elodie glanced at the floor, slightly embarrassed for the harsh welcome she had given them. "Of course."

Rhona looked at the man beside her, love shining in her eyes. "This is Balladyn."

"A Fae," Elodie said before she could stop herself.

Balladyn inclined his head of long hair. His eyes were

silver, but she saw a ring of red around them. "Reaper, actually." His voice had an Irish lilt.

Reaper. Elodie wasn't sure what that meant.

"We wanted to welcome you back and see if you needed anything," Rhona said.

Elodie shifted her feet nervously. Did they know she'd lost her magic? "That wasn't necessary."

"You're one of us," Rhona said with a soft look. "We look after our own."

Resentment threatened to choke Elodie, and she had to remind herself that she shouldn't direct her anger at Rhona. She hadn't been any older than Elodie back then. Corann was a different matter. "Corann sent you?"

A frown moved over Rhona's face so quickly that Elodie almost missed it. "We lost Corann. I've taken his place."

"Oh." Damn. She should've had Edie bring her up to date on things. Then again, Elodie hadn't wanted to talk to any Druids, so she had made sure not to take an interest in anything. "Honestly, I won't be here long. As soon as I get the place fixed up and sold, I'm leaving."

Rhona's green eyes narrowed slightly. "That's a pity. We could use you."

No one ever had use for her. Elodie glanced at Balladyn to see that the Reaper's gaze hadn't moved from her. It was unnerving to have him watch her in such a way, and yet she didn't feel threatened. "It's for the best."

"Why don't you come for tea later this week? We can catch up," Rhona said.

Elodie's plan to keep to herself was rapidly disintegrating. She liked Rhona—or at least the person she had once been. It wasn't in Elodie's nature to be outright rude, but Rhona would likely ask questions that Elodie wasn't prepared to answer. And she was tired of lying. "I'm no–"

"Please don't decline. Think it over." Rhona smiled. "Please."

Well, bugger it. "I'll consider it."

Rhona's smile was huge. "Great. And if you need any help, we can get this place together quickly."

The offer was so tempting that Elodie nearly took it. If they did, she could leave Skye that much quicker. However, if she agreed to Rhona's offer, it would inevitably lead to those pesky questions she was intent on dodging. "Thanks, but I've already made good headway today."

"At the very least, let me fix the leaking roof," Balladyn said.

Her gaze snapped to him. The roof was leaking? She glanced around but didn't hear any dripping. Then a drop landed on top of her head. This might be a bigger project than she'd thought. She faced him and forced her tight lips into a smile as her stomach churned with anxiety. "I would appreciate that."

"It's done," he said with a bow of his head.

"Thank you."

Rhona flashed another smile. "It's good to have you back. I hope you'll consider the tea."

Elodie held her smile until the two of them suddenly disappeared. She blinked and frowned. Balladyn must have teleported them out. At least the leak was fixed. She looked up at the ceiling and spotted the water damage.

"I'm going to be here forever," she grumbled.

CHAPTER TWO

SKYE DRUIDS

The wind was as sharp as a knife as it cut over the water and right through him. Scott Ryan bundled deeper in his coat, wishing he had worn his gloves. Fuck, he was cold. He wouldn't mind observing if he could do it from the indoors. Normally, the cold didn't bother him that much, but then he wasn't used to island life.

A leggy woman strolling casually down the street as if the wind weren't trying to snatch her away snagged Scott's attention. A black beanie covered her head, leaving a long, blond braid that fell down her back to lay against her plaid burgundy coat. She had a black scarf wrapped around her neck and black gloves on her hands. The strap of a purse hung across her body.

What really drew his gaze was how she almost stood in protest against the weather when everyone else rushed to and from buildings and their vehicles. Her chin was lifted, her

gaze focused straight ahead. Defiant. As if she dared anyone—
or any*thing*—to touch her.

Scott wanted a closer look to see what color her eyes were.
He'd seen confidence before, but this woman wore it like a
crown. Or maybe it was just her I-don't-give-a-shite attitude.
Whatever it was, he liked it.

"And there she is."

Filip's voice drew Scott's attention. He glanced at his
comrade to see where Filip looked. Scott's lips flattened when
he realized it was the same woman he'd been watching.

"Elodie MacLean." Filip said her name like a prayer.

Scott blew out a breath, silently cursing the odds. "Are you
sure?"

"I'd know her anywhere." Filip waited until Elodie was
inside the store before looking at Scott. His pale gray eyes
didn't do a good job of hiding his sorrow. The beanie he wore
almost hid Filip's black hair. He adjusted the cap and sniffed.
"She used to walk around Skye as if she owned it."

"Did she?" Scott wanted to know.

Filip chuckled. "Damn right, she did. With a glance from
her, men would leave their wives and girlfriends. She wreaked
havoc all over the island. There wasna a male on Skye who
wouldna have done anything for a night with her."

"You included?" That infuriated Scott for some reason.

"Even me."

"Did you?"

Filip shook his head. "No' for lack of trying."

Scott pulled his hands from his coat and blew into them
before rubbing them briskly together in an effort to create

some warmth. "We know she's here. Now, we can get on with things."

"This should be simple enough."

"Doona underestimate the Druids here," Scott cautioned. "That's a good way to ensure we fail."

Filip snorted. "We willna. We can no'."

"There's too much riding on us. I'm no' taking anything for granted. I'm also no' going to be an idiot and disregard the Druids here."

Filip swung his head to Scott. "You didna grow up here. Of course, you're scared of them."

"I'm no' frightened. I'm pragmatic. That's the difference between being prepared and losing."

"Just tell me whatever you need," Filip said as he returned his gaze to the store. "I'm here to help us succeed."

Scott moved to stand in front of Filip and blocked his gaze. "Need I remind you what just happened with the Fae here? If Rhona and the tall bastard by her side catch wind of what we're doing, then we're done before we get started."

"They willna catch on to anything because we're going to be careful," Filip replied evenly.

Scott stared down at Filip. The lad's grief was so deep that Scott wondered if he had been the right choice. Then again, there was no other option. "You're here to help me navigate Skye and introduce me to Elodie, but if that's too mu—"

"It isna," Filip spoke over him.

Scott studied him for a long moment, looking for any cracks. Filip didn't bow beneath his gaze. "Okay."

"There she is."

Scott glanced over his shoulder in time to see Elodie emerging from the store. She carried a tote filled with groceries in one hand and made her way to the café.

"Come on," Scott called as he jogged across the parking lot and then the street.

When they entered the restaurant, a wave of heat washed over Scott. He smiled and nodded to a woman, who told them to sit wherever. Scott locked his gaze on Elodie, who had taken a seat as far in the back as she could—as if she didn't want to be seen. Scott chose a booth diagonal to hers so he could easily watch her. He and Filip removed their jackets and sat. Both ordered coffee, but he added a croissant to his order.

"Tell me more about her," Scott urged Filip.

Filip shot a furtive glance in the woman's direction. "Look at her. Have you ever seen anyone so pretty?"

In fact, Scott hadn't. Elodie could make a man forget his name. Not that Scott was that kind of man. At least, not usually. He would have to watch himself with her. She was stunning, but something more caught his attention.

"She ruined some marriages," Filip continued, unaware of Scott's thoughts. "She hung around my brother, teasing anyone with a cock with only her smile. She liked to party hard. If anyone told her she couldna do something, she did it just to prove them wrong."

Scott frowned at the picture Filip painted because it didn't match the woman he observed now. "That was before she left Skye. By what I'm seeing, she's changed."

"Someone like that doesna change too much. She could drink me under the table, and that's saying something."

"Why did she leave?"

Filip sat back when the server delivered their coffees and Scott's croissant. When they were alone again, he lowered his voice and said, "Her father died. Her mother was taken to prison, and her brother disappeared."

"Elodie was left alone?"

"She and her older sister, Edie. They're a year apart."

Scott glanced at Elodie as she read a book and quietly drank her hot beverage. "You said Edie was on Skye, right?"

"Aye. She lives with her husband and two bairns. She turned out okay."

"I doubt anyone who suffered what those lasses did is *okay*."

Filip shrugged. "Maybe no' Elodie, but her sister is."

"I'm guessing our target got a wee bit wild after the tragedy with her family?"

"Aye. Many of the elders tried to step in, but Elodie wouldna have any of it. No' even Corann made a difference."

Scott studied Filip. For a Druid who didn't like Skye or the people on the island, it was obvious that whoever Corann had been, they had left a lasting mark on him. Filip's voice held reverence each time he mentioned Corann's name. "Did your brother try to help her? Did you or any of your friends?"

Filip visibly winced at the mention of Kevin. "We were all having fun. We were no' thinking about anything else."

Scott grunted in reply. He remembered his own wild time when he was younger. Even when he knew that he should be doing something, he ignored it for the sake of fun. He had pulled himself out of it eventually. So had Elodie, it seemed.

Filip turned his head to look out the window. Scott took a bite of his croissant and noted how many in the café were shooting glances at Elodie. She seemed oblivious, but given the tightening of her shoulders, he suspected that she felt the looks. He was halfway finished with his coffee when she put money on the table, gathered her items, and walked from the restaurant. She passed right by the window where he and Filip sat. Once more, she kept her attention straight ahead. One woman against the wind—and the world. She carried her head high, but he suspected the demons she carried were a heavier load.

What was she doing back in Skye? She didn't speak to anyone, and it was clear that people recognized her. Only a person who didn't want to have any connections kept quiet in a small place like Skye. As curious as he was about all of that, none of it mattered to his end goal. Scott should be more focused on finding a way to Elodie in case his charms didn't work. Something about her warned him not to even try to use his usual wiles on her. Maybe it was the way she held herself. It might be because of the defiance he spotted in her. Or…her magic might prevent him.

His mission put him in her path. Whether he wanted it or not, he needed to know her. He had to learn every detail about her and her sister. That way, he would know how to navigate anything that came his way. Too much rested on his and Filip's success on Skye.

"How long after her father's death and mother's confinement did Elodie leave Skye?" Scott asked.

Filip's brows drew together for a moment as he looked at Scott. "A year. Maybe two."

"Why did she no' leave right away?"

"She left after completing school."

"But Edie didna leave?"

Filip shook his head and shrugged. "So?"

"Why did the brother and Elodie leave, and Edie stay?"

"I doona know. Edie mixed with a different crowd. I know verra little about her."

Scott finished his coffee. "I need those details."

"Sure."

"How did the father die?"

"Murdered."

Scott was taken aback. "And you're just now telling me this?"

"I'm used to everyone knowing. You didna ask why the mother went to prison."

Scott ran a hand down his face as he tried to shake off the shock. "Bloody hell."

"Aye," Filip said softly.

"You told George that Elodie would be easy to convince."

"She will be."

"If she isna, things could go tits up quickly. Especially if the Reaper and Rhona turn their attention on us."

Filip twisted his lips. "They willna."

Scott leaned forward and lowered his voice to barely above a whisper so no one else could hear him. "Balladyn was once King of the Dark. He's now the Warden of Skye. That means if he and Rhona discover what we're about, nothing and no one can save us. They'll wipe us from existence."

"We'll be gone before they know why we're here," Filip replied.

Scott released a breath. He understood the grief Filip felt since he was also dealing with it. Kevin might be gone, but at least Scott could keep his best friend's brother alive.

"We can do this," Filip added.

Finally, Scott nodded. "Aye. We can."

CHAPTER THREE

SKYE DRUIDS

Elodie was never going to the café again. She had thought she could be inconspicuous, but she should've known better. Everyone in Skye was a busybody—whether they were Druids or not. They were always in everyone else's business. The stares alone made her want to jump on the table and give them something to gawk at.

The old Elodie would've done just that.

She inwardly winced as she set the bag of groceries on the kitchen counter. Her old ways were responsible for her current situation. Many on the island, Corann included, had tried to help her and Edie. Elodie hadn't wanted any of it back then. She didn't want it now, either. But even she could admit that she would've benefited from it after *the incident*.

Elodie snorted and opened the refrigerator to put in the milk, eggs, cheese, and yogurt. It wasn't an incident. It was a catastrophe.

A fucking cataclysm.

She stood in the open door of the fridge as her memories took her back to that earlier time. They were like tar, sucking her down into a dark pit that she knew she would never come out of. She slammed the door on the refrigerator and the memories.

"No," she stated firmly.

There was no way she would go down that lane. She hadn't let those vile, revolting thoughts fill her head while she was away, and she wouldn't let them take her now while on Skye—or in the cottage.

"They're just memories. They don't control me. *I* control them."

Elodie put away the rest of the food. She loathed cooking about as much as she did Skye and the Druids, but she would suffer it so she didn't have to go back into town. That had been insufferable. The latte had been delicious, but it wasn't worth repeating the visit. Besides, she didn't need to spend what little money she had left on frivolous things, and a latte was certainly that.

Her stomach was soured now, though. She had wanted to exhaust herself to the point of collapse so she could sleep. Cleaning all day had just about gotten her there. If only she hadn't had the latte. The heavy dose of caffeine would keep her awake far longer than she wanted. ·

She tugged the cleaning gloves back on and went into Elias's room. Everything remained exactly as it had been the day he left. Posters of rock bands: Linkin Park, Foo Fighters, and Thirty Seconds to Mars hung on the wall, along with scantily clad models and various photos of Elias and his friends.

Her gaze went to the floor. Elias had never picked up his clothes, but there was nothing there now. Even the bed was made. She knew Edie was responsible for that. How long had her sister kept up the house before she'd finally had enough and walked away?

Elodie had been gutted when Elias left. Then she had been furious. He hadn't cared about her or Edie enough to check in or even make sure they were cared for before they finished school. Edie had been an absolute mess. To be fair, she had been, too. Elodie had never known how much of it was about *the incident* and how much of it had been Elias leaving. It didn't really matter.

Then what had Elodie done? She had left Edie, too. What kind of sister was she to walk away?

"The kind slowly dying on this damn island," she whispered.

Skye had been draining her of everything good in her life. If she hadn't left, Elodie might be in jail with her mother. Edie had said that she understood why Elodie had to leave, but her sister wouldn't have run if their places had been reversed. Then again, Edie was soft-hearted, kind, and forgiving.

Elodie took a step back into the hallway. She turned her head to look at the closed door at the end of the hall. The ghosts of the past were in her parents' room. They weren't banging on the door, but they were there. Waiting. Ghosts that might send her over into the deep end this time. Maybe she was destined for this and running away had only prolonged the inevitable.

Her life had been utter shite for so many years. No matter where she turned, no matter what she did, Elodie couldn't seem to make any headway. She was spinning her wheels. There came a point when she had to recognize that fact. When she had to accept that the life she had dreamed of would never be.

Because the ghosts or demons or whatever name you wanted to give them were constantly over her shoulder, waiting to wrench away anything good and remind her of her place.

"You don't have to go in there."

Elodie shrieked and spun around, slamming her shoulder into the wall. Her gaze landed on Edie, and all the air left her. She slid down the wall with her shoulder throbbing and her heart racing erratically.

"I'm so sorry," Edie said as she squatted before her, her face lined with concern. "I thought you heard me come in."

Elodie closed her eyes, hating the adrenaline rush that pumped through her. It made her already queasy stomach turn, the latte threatening to come back up.

"Damn. I really scared you." Edie sat beside her on the floor. She put a hand on Elodie's arm and rubbed up and down in a comforting manner. After a few minutes, she said, "You don't have to stay here, you know."

It took great effort for Elodie to lift her head and open her eyes. "I do."

"You don't. There's room for you with us. Or even at one of our rental houses. One's coming open in a few days."

That was Edie, always trying to help. She was the fixer. If a problem existed, she found a solution. Elodie smiled at her and shook her head. "I've hit rock bottom. Let me have the few tattered remains of my ego to stay on my own."

"I wish you'd tell me what happened in Edinburgh." Edie's brow puckered.

Elodie really looked at her sister. Just a year older, Edie's hair was a shade of darker blond. She kept her wavy locks cut to just above her shoulders and parted to one side. She wore only a little mascara, which made her blue eyes really stand out in her face. "You look so much like Mum."

"Me?" Edie laughed and shook her head. "I think you do. You have her hair." She reached out and touched a long strand. "I remember how she used to sit in front of her vanity every night and brush it. You not only got the exact pale blond color, but you also have her light blue eyes."

"How did you stay on Skye?" Elodie blurted out.

Edie dropped her hand and sighed. "I was too afraid to leave."

"I was too afraid to stay."

"You were always stronger than me."

"Bollocks," Elodie said with a flat stare.

Edie chuckled and smiled wryly. "We both know I speak the truth."

"You could've come with me. I tried to get you to leave."

Her sister sighed again and drew her knees to her chest as she looked around the cottage. "The same reason you and Elias had to leave was what made me stay. Now, you're back. I can't tell you how happy that makes me."

Elodie couldn't hold Edie's gaze. She had made it clear that she was leaving the first opportunity she got, but it was as if Edie refused to listen to her about that. "It is good to see you again. You only came to the city twice since I left."

"It was difficult getting away being married and having the bairns."

What she didn't say was that it was easier for Elodie to travel. It was the truth, but her vow never to return to Skye had kept her away. Elodie didn't like the conversation. She needed to turn it. "I tried looking for Elias. I wish I knew where he was. Have you heard from him?"

"A few times a year."

Elodie felt as if she had been kicked in the gut. Her brother had reached out to Edie but not her. Why? What had she done to him? He was the one who'd left. He was the one who had ignored her cries to stay. "So, he's purposefully not talking to me."

"I don't know," Edie said with a shrug, but she wouldn't meet Elodie's gaze. "I told him where you were. I even gave him your number. I thought he might contact you. But you shouldn't feel left out. Our calls are less than two minutes in length. Then, it's months before I hear from him again."

"You don't have to sugarcoat things for me."

Edie snapped her gaze to Elodie. "I'm not."

Elodie waved her words away. Time to change the subject again. "I wasn't expecting you tonight."

"I started thinking about you being here at night. Thought I'd offer our place once more just in case you changed your mind."

"You're my favorite sister. Just in case you didn't know." Elodie flashed a bright smile.

Edie rolled her eyes and laughed. "I'm your only one, so that doesn't count."

"It absolutely does."

Her smile died, and Edie's expression grew serious. "You can tell me anything. I'm here for whatever happened. I'm not sad that you're on Skye again, but I wish you'd let me help."

"You are helping me."

"You know what I mean."

Elodie did. She wanted to change the subject again, but she knew that look in her sister's eyes. Edie was like a dog with a bone. She wouldn't let it go until she got a satisfactory answer. "I wish you could, but I got into this mess, and I need to be the one to get out of it."

"Are you in danger?"

Elodie thought about that for a moment, then shook her head. She hoped she was right. "Like I said, I've hit rock bottom. Staying here and cleaning up the old place will give me the time I need to sort things out. I've mucked up my life pretty epically. I've been drowning for a while, but I didn't want to acknowledge that fact. Then, life made me."

"You're the strongest person I know," Edie stated, sincerity shining in her blue eyes. "If anyone can pull themselves up, it's you."

"Thanks for the vote of confidence."

"It's the truth."

Elodie snorted and leaned her head against the wall. "I'm not sure my behavior before I left constitutes strength."

"Everyone deals with grief differently. That was how you handled it."

Elodie groaned as she thought about it. "It was fucking horrible. Why didn't someone knock me upside the head? Grandmum? Grandda? Corann? You? Anyone."

Edie put her hand on Elodie's knee. "Because everyone

was grieving, and no one knew how to handle the aftermath of…things."

"*The incident*," Elodie said for her.

Edie nodded. "Yes. That."

Even now, after a decade and a half, it was still difficult for her sister to talk about it.

"Have you talked to someone?" Edie suddenly asked.

Elodie pulled a face. "That isn't something you bring up in conversation. And, no, I didn't tell anyone."

"I meant, have you talked to a therapist?"

Elodie stilled. She slowly shook her head. "Have you?"

"Yes. For the past seven years."

"Has it helped?"

Edie's lips twisted with her one-shoulder shrug. "In some ways. I think it would've been better for all of us if we had spoken to a therapist right after it happened. All those years of carrying it around was like a weight hindering me."

That's exactly what Elodie felt—weighed down. Though hers was more than just *the incident*.

"Finding a therapist you connect with isn't always easy, but it's worth it. I can give you the name of mine. I think you'd like her."

"Maybe," Elodie said. "I don't know if I ever asked, but do your children have magic? Trevor doesn't, right?"

A pained look crossed Edie's face. "No, he doesn't. Unlike Mum, I told him who I was and what that meant if we married. I also told him that I wouldn't leave Skye. He accepted all of it. I wonder what would've happened had Mum done that with Da."

Elodie remained silent as she looked away. She didn't want to think about that.

"The kids do have magic," Edie continued. "I've been teaching them the old ways like Mum taught us. They know their heritage, and they'll be training with other Druids. I was so relieved when they were born with magic. We're down to around four thousand Druids on Skye now. We used to outnumber everyone. Each year, more and more are born without magic."

Elodie's heart constricted painfully. "Why are they losing magic?"

"They marry those who don't have magic, of course. Therefore, our blood is being diluted at a rapid rate. It's worse around the world. We still have a good presence here, but I wonder how that will be in a hundred years. Fifty?"

Elodie swallowed.

"I've not had a chance to catch you up on things." Edie scooted to the opposite wall so she could lean back. "Corann passed away."

"I heard."

Edie's brow quirked. "You went out?"

"To get some groceries, but I didn't talk to anyone. Rhona and Balladyn came to see me here."

"Wow," Edie said, her face showing how impressed she was. "Corann chose Rhona himself. We just had a full-scale battle on Skye."

Elodie was taken aback. "What?"

"The Warriors and Druids from McLeod Castle came, as well as the Dragon Kings. We joined the Reapers to fight against the Fae Others."

Elodie squeezed her eyes closed for a second. "Wait. Hold up. First, the Fae are allowed back on Skye?"

"It would seem so."

"And who are the Fae Others?"

"The Others began with two Druids from another realm, who aligned with two Fae and two Druids of our realm in an effort to defeat the Dragon Kings."

Elodie took off her gloves and listened with interest. "I always dreamed of seeing a Dragon King. They were here? I hate that I missed that, but how stupid do you have to be to take them on?"

"Apparently, not as idiotic as you might think. The Others nearly won, but the Kings prevailed. The story goes that Usaeil, the Queen of the Light Fae, was part of the Others and had turned Dark—hiding that fact for years. She was killed, and Corann took out the leader of the Others, a Druid from another realm. It took all his magic to defeat her."

"Sounds like a good ending."

"You'd think, right?" Edie said and flattened her lips. "Unfortunately, the Fae and even the Druids realized how much more power they could get if they formed a group. So, Dark and Light Fae worked together and created the Fae Others, intent on taking out the Reapers."

"Balladyn introduced himself as a Reaper. Who the hell are they?"

"Fae chosen by the goddess Death to keep the balance within the Fae. She's the judge and jury, and the Reapers are her executioners."

Elodie raised her brows. "Wow."

"Balladyn is the Warden of Skye, Elodie. He and Rhona

put the Fae Others and their soldiers in their place. A couple of
Druids lost their lives, and many more were injured, but we
won."

"That sounds incredible. You mentioned the Warriors and
other Druids."

Edie grinned. "Yes. Remember when we were told that
other formidable Druids were around?"

Elodie nodded.

"That's them. They're from MacLeod Castle. I didn't get
much more information about them, other than that the
Warriors are the same ones Corann told us about, those who
had primeval gods locked inside them."

Elodie's eyes widened in shock. "The gods from Hell the
droughs called up to fight the Romans?"

"The very ones," Edie said with a conspiratorial grin.

"With other Druids." Elodie could hardly believe any of
this. It seemed a lot had happened on Skye.

"We could've used your magic. It was always stronger
than mine."

Elodie smiled wanly. "Sounds like you all had it covered."

"Goodness. Look at the time." Edie got to her feet and
dusted off her bottom. "Are you sure you're good here?"

"Positive," Elodie said from her place on the floor.

Edie blew her a kiss. "I'll check on you tomorrow then."

Elodie waited until the door had closed behind her sister
before she released the breath she'd been holding. She had
gotten through a conversation without telling her sister about
her magic—or lack thereof. How many more would she get
before the truth came out? Every ugly grain of it.

CHAPTER FOUR

SKYE DRUIDS

An entire week lost. Scott was torn regarding how he felt about that. On the one hand, he was surprised by how peaceful he found Skye. He was a city lad, born and bred. He usually found country life dull, yet nothing about the Isle of Skye was boring.

Then there was Elodie. She was proving to be more difficult to bump into than expected. She kept to herself and went out at different times. Days passed when she didn't leave the cottage. When she did, it was usually a quick trip into town for groceries. She didn't eat out, and she hadn't returned to the café.

And yet, everyone was talking about her.

It didn't matter where Scott and Filip went, the name *Elodie* was on everyone's lips. Some were curious about her return, while others let their hatred be known. Those were mostly women who Elodie had spurned years ago. They didn't want a repeat of the husband stealing.

Despite Scott's demand to get details about Elodie, he had very few. When Scott had questioned Filip about the murder, all his friend did was shrug.

"I was young. I don't remember details," Filip replied.

Which was no help to Scott. He could ask some residents, but while they were willing to talk amongst themselves, he wasn't sure any would welcome a stranger poking his nose in their business.

Scott finished the last of his ale and saw the woman behind the bar roll her eyes repeatedly every time Elodie's name reached her. She clearly didn't like Elodie, and she just might be the one to give Scott some specifics about his target.

He waved the bartender over. She approached with brows lifted. "Another one, please," he said as he handed her his mug.

She took it and filled it before handing it back.

Just as she was turning away, Scott asked, "Everyone is talking about the same woman. What's going on?"

"Nothing," the barkeep said with another eye roll. "She's returned and will no doubt start up her shite again."

"And what shite is that?" he pressed.

The woman glanced around before leaning her forearms on the bar and lowering her voice. "Let's just say that she didn't care if a man was married or not when she set her sights on him. She broke up a lot of relationships."

"Is it really just her fault, though? It takes two."

"Oh, she knew exactly what she was doing."

Scott held the woman's dark gaze, noting the bitterness. "Did she break up your relationship?"

"Yep."

Oh, yeah. Lots of acrimony. "I'm sorry."

"It was for the best. Just as her leaving was."

"Was she run out?"

The woman snorted. "If only. It's what she deserved, but everyone felt sorry for her."

Now they were getting to the good parts. "Why?"

"Her father was killed."

Scott glanced at Filip, who was sitting with a group of people around his age. "Did the mother really kill the father?"

"That she did."

Scott's mouth went slack. Not that he hadn't believed Filip, but there was something about hearing it from someone else. "Bloody hell."

"Exactly. That face right there is how almost everyone on Skye was back then. Elodie got away with anything."

The pub went silent as death as the woman's voice echoed through the establishment. Scott followed everyone's gaze to see none other than Elodie walk in. She was only a few feet away, which allowed him to get a better view of her. Her pale blond locks hung nearly to her waist. She had the sides clipped at the back of her head, showing off two small braids on either side of her face mixing with the rest of her length. Her heart-shaped face held large eyes in an arresting pale blue color. Her lips were full, the structure of her face a work of art. He'd never seen anyone he would call ethereal, but that word described her perfectly. Her long coat hid her upper body, but he had already gotten a glimpse of her lean legs.

Scott's gaze returned to her face, noticing for the first time how pale she was as she fought to hold it together. Beside

Elodie stood a woman who resembled her. No doubt her sister, Edie, the one that Filip had told him about.

"Seriously?" Edie asked the room, looking individuals in the eye. "Do none of you have anything better to talk about?"

Scott saw Elodie fighting the urge to leave. He wouldn't stay if he were in her shoes, but sometimes running away only made things worse. To his surprise, Elodie marched past her sister to a table and sat without saying a word. Edie followed, her gaze shooting daggers at everyone, especially the bartender.

"Watch your husbands and boyfriends, ladies," a woman in the back shouted.

Edie started to rise, but Elodie grabbed her arm and, with a look, got her sister back into her seat. Scott admired her cool head. It would be easy for someone to lose their temper and tell everyone off. It took greater effort to keep such comments to yourself.

Gradually, the conversation continued in the pub. When Scott looked at the barkeep, she was staring at Elodie, her animosity evident. He never understood why people blamed everyone but their significant other for cheating. Elodie and her siblings had suffered a horrendous tragedy when they were still young. What she did back then was probably in direct response to that, and yet these people wouldn't let go of their anger from over a decade prior.

Filip rose from his seat and carried his drink to the bar. He took the stool next to Scott. His voice was just above a whisper as he said, "Damn. Everyone still hates her."

"Not everyone," Scott pointed out. The men were eying Elodie with interest. Some of the women around her age seemed curious, but it was the older women who wanted nothing to do with Elodie.

Filip shrugged. "Enough, though. It's in the past."

About that time, Edie and Elodie left the pub. Scott wanted to go after them. He'd lost his chance to talk to her, and if her welcome had been any indication, he likely wouldn't get another shot.

"Good riddance," the barkeep said as the door closed behind the sisters.

"Get over yourself, Anna. It was fifteen years ago, and you were leaving David anyway," an older woman stated as she got to her feet. "Elodie was a child dealing with the loss of her parents. She had an excuse for her behavior. You're an adult. What's yours?"

Anna let out a breath. "I don't like her, Violet."

"The past is the past," Violet stated. She looked around the room with her blue eyes, pausing briefly as she met Scott's gaze. "Let me say that again for anyone holding a grudge against Elodie after all this time. The past is the past."

Filip let out a low whistle after Violet had taken her seat. "I guess she put Anna in her place."

"Who's Violet?"

"She's one of the deputies I told you about. There are five, splitting Skye into sections. We used to outnumber the others here, and it was easier for Corann to get information to his deputies, who then got it out to their people rather than calling everyone together."

Scott nodded. "Because that would've drawn attention. How many Druids now?"

"One of my buddies just told me they dropped to under four thousand recently."

"Still a nice number. More than anywhere else on our planet."

Filip grunted. "It used to be double that. If we keep diluting our blood, we'll be gone."

"Which is why we're going to make sure that doesna happen."

"Aye, we are." Filip smiled.

"We have to succeed first."

"George has a perfect plan. What could go wrong?"

"The battle that was just here is a reminder of what could go wrong."

Filip scoffed at that. "The Fae were stupid and greedy. We willna make those same mistakes."

"Skye has its Warden now. Balladyn and Rhona are no' to be underestimated. No one on this island should be."

"I agree with that, but we have to somehow meet Elodie."

Scott threw down some money and slid off his stool. "That might be harder than I first thought. I need some air."

He walked outside, leaving Filip and the noise of the pub behind. He inhaled the brisk night air, letting it fill his lungs. He needed to come up with a plan and quick. Imagine his surprise when he spotted Elodie and her sister in the carpark. Scott paused and watched as Edie gave her sister a hug before getting into her vehicle and driving away. Scott's gaze was glued to Elodie as she sighed forlornly and looked at the moon as dark clouds drifted over it.

CHAPTER FIVE

SKYE DRUIDS

Why had she let her sister talk her into going to dinner? Elodie had known the residents of Skye wouldn't forget—or forgive—easily. Tonight had been proof of that. Just another example that Skye was Hell.

She pulled her gaze from the many stars dotting the night sky. No amount of wishing would take her anywhere else. The only thing she could do was deal with things on the island and then get out as fast as she could.

Elodie turned to her car as she fished out her keys. Her gaze collided with a man's. Her heart jumped into her throat for an instant at discovering someone watching her. He was near the pub, standing beneath a light so she could see him, though not in detail. He looked near her age with dark hair and a beard that was just past a five o'clock shadow. Six feet, at least. Rugged build. A face cut from granite. Eyes that seemed to stare right into her soul.

"Hi. I didna mean to intrude. I saw what happened inside,"

he said as he hitched a thumb over his shoulder. "I was leaving and wanted to make sure you were all right."

"I'm fine." She unlocked her door and opened it to get inside.

"You should've stayed."

Elodie paused and looked at him, taking in his tall stature. He stood casually near the corner of the pub and shot her a lazy smile that probably charmed women — not her. He had his hair trimmed short on the sides and back with the top longer, styled in that effortless look achieved with product by a man who knew how to do his hair.

His wide lips held that smile as he watched her. She wondered what color his eyes were. She couldn't tell from the distance, and she had no intention of getting closer. He was clearly a man who took care of himself, and she'd bet that he had the body to prove it.

"I'm not in the habit of subjecting myself to that kind of disdain." Though she had no idea why she bothered to answer him at all. The fact that he'd followed her outside made her uneasy. "What do you want?"

His lips twisted as he shrugged his shoulders. "I just wanted to tell you that the hostility of a few shouldna keep you from enjoying yourself."

As if there were anything about Skye to enjoy. Once, she would've named a multitude of things, but *the incident* had ripped off her rose-colored glasses.

"I'm Scott, by the way," he said. "Scott Ryan."

Elodie watched him for a moment longer. A part of her wanted to have a conversation, but she knew that now wasn't the time. She hadn't yet pulled herself out of her current situation. She gave him a nod of acknowledge and climbed into her car.

On the drive back to the cottage, she kept thinking about what Scott had said. He likely would've learned all about her from those in the pub. Why had he really approached her? He wanted something. She was certain of that.

Was he a reporter? Come to dig into her father's death? Was he some newcomer to Skye who wanted a shot at sleeping with her? The one thing Elodie had learned was that everyone wanted something. Power. Money. Love. Everything was up for grabs, and the sooner a person realized that everyone was after something, the easier it was to maneuver and navigate the complex and constantly changing battleground called life.

Edie had called her jaded, and she *was* cynical. She had every right to be.

"If you keep looking for the worst, then that's what you'll find."

Her mother's words rattled around in her mind, causing her throat to clog with emotion. Elodie wished she could see the best in everything as Edie did. How could she, though, when she kept getting shite on again and again? She'd start to pull herself out of the gutter, only to get trampled.

It wouldn't be long now. The cottage was clean, and she was starting on the outside tomorrow. Her list of needed repairs was growing ever longer. A part of her was irritated at Edie for allowing the cottage to fall into disrepair, but then she remembered that it wasn't just Edie's fault. She and Elias also shared in that burden, and neither of them had done anything. Why should Edie have to do it all just because she chose to stay on the island? Elodie was glad that her sister hadn't held a grudge because Edie had every reason to be upset with her and Elias.

When Elodie pulled into the cottage's drive, she parked the car and turned off the engine. She had left lights on inside. It gave the appearance that the house was occupied, as if a family lived there once more. But she knew the only inhabitants were the ghosts of the past. Remnants of a time when she had thought the world was hers for the taking and people would always love her and be there for her.

The truth, however, clung to the cottage like mist and cobwebs. And there was no running from the truth. Ever.

She should know. She had been trying to do it for fifteen years.

Elodie exited her car and slowly made her way to the cottage's side door just as rain began to pelt her. She caught a glimpse of the cove. They had gone down to the water to swim on many occasions. Memories of weekends lying on the beach and soaking up the sun made her grin. Skye had been an enchanted place for her once. She'd thought its beauty and the magic that brought the Druids together was as close to a utopia as there was.

Her happy memories of the beach floated away like smoke. She unlocked the door and stepped inside. At least the cottage smelled clean. No more dampness or stale air greeted her when she entered.

Elodie dropped her purse onto the sofa that had seen better days. It was dated, but at least the fabric had held up, mainly because of lack of use. The same could be said for the two chairs. The carpet, on the other hand, was awful. It needed to be replaced. It would make the cottage sell quicker. But it all came down to the funds.

One of the reasons for dinner with Edie had been to go over some of the needed repairs. Elodie had wanted to wait until she cleaned the outside, as well as the garage, but she thought her sister had a right to know what they were looking at. Elodie could clean. She also had a few skills in mending simple things, but she couldn't replace the roof, fix the moldy section of cabinet she found near the kitchen sink, or replace carpet. She and Edie had never spoken about how much would go into the house. Elodie had just assumed that all she needed to do was clean to get it ready to be put up for sale.

"Wishful thinking," she murmured.

The house had sat untouched for years. A lot of damage could happen in that amount of time. The roof, for example. How long had it been leaking? They needed to address the water damage, which meant she had to inspect the attic. At this rate, she would never get her share of the proceeds to leave. Which brought her back to who was going to pay for the repairs. She didn't have any money. Could Edie and Trevor cover it? Was it even fair to ask them to do that? What about Elias? Either way, when the cottage sold, they should get back whatever money they put into repairs.

The cottage might have a decent view, but her father's murder would be disclosed. That would put off some buyers. It would likely mean taking a lower price on the house, as well. And that would result in Elodie's cut being even smaller.

"What other choice do I have?" she asked the universe. "I didn't want to come back. I did everything I possibly could to stay away. Yet here I am. I don't belong on Skye. I don't think I ever did."

No one had asked about her magic. Why would they? Of course, Edie would assume that she still had it. What an awkward conversation that would be. Elodie wasn't sure she could even explain what had happened or when. All she knew was that her magic was gone and had been for years.

She went to the cupboard and looked at the meager offerings she had for dinner. Maybe she shouldn't have left the pub. Edie—and even the guy, Scott, outside—had said that she should've stayed. It had been too much for Elodie, though. The looks, the comments.

The hatred.

Not everyone despised her, but there had been enough loathing in the room to choke her. Which it had done. She wouldn't have been able to get anything down. Though she really couldn't blame people for how they felt. She hadn't exactly been a good neighbor or friend. She had wanted the pain to stop, and she had tried anything and everything to make sure that happened.

Drinking. Drugs. Sex. The trifecta.

When boys her age didn't wipe away the agony and grief, she'd gone after older men, hoping they might help. But they hadn't. And she hadn't cared if they were married or not. If they showed even the least bit of interest—and sometimes if they hadn't—she had gone after them. The number of families she had destroyed in her bid to stop her pain was humiliating. She'd hate her, too, if she were in their shoes. She'd spent years detesting herself for what she had done, which had only sunk her deeper into misery instead of helping.

Even when she stopped the self-loathing, she carried what she had done with her like a stone chained to her neck. There was never a time she put *the incident* or her behavior behind her. She revisited it each and every day. Always a reminder of the despicable human she had once been.

"I'm sorry, Mum," Elodie said. "I know I promised you I'd make a good life for myself, but…I haven't been able to."

Her throat clogged again. A part of Elodie wanted to give in to the emotion and see if a good cry might wash away her sins and hurt, but she had cried oceans, and it had done nothing to erase the past.

That wasn't the only thing she had to contend with. There was also what'd happened in Edinburgh. Her sins were slowly choking the life out of her. When would she stop fucking everything up?

CHAPTER SIX

SKYE DRUIDS

Scott remained outside long after Elodie had driven off. He was intrigued. And no one ever captivated him. Not like that.

He'd seen it all and done more. He knew just how to smile to capture someone's attention. He knew exactly what to say to entice — with a little magic, that was.

Yet Elodie hadn't seemed fazed by it.

Granted, he hadn't turned on his full charm. She didn't seem the kind of woman who so easily fell for such things. Life had clearly hardened her. Made her distrustful and wary. Getting close to her would be more difficult than he'd first thought. There was a way in, though. Everyone had something they needed or wanted. He just had to find out what it was.

"Thought you were long gone," Filip said as he walked up.

Scott shrugged. "I spoke with her."

"No shit? How did that go?"

"She's distrustful."

Filip grunted as he plunged his hands into his coat pockets.

"She doesna have any friends here. It willna be long before she's looking for some."

"She doesna care about friends."

"You saw how she reacted in the pub. She cares."

"No' in the way you think," Scott argued. "She expected that. She doesna like it, but she knew it was coming. She rarely leaves the cottage. We need to find out what's keeping her there."

"My old schoolmates told me. She's fixing it up."

Scott swiveled his head to Filip. "What?"

Filip frowned as he shrugged. "What's so strange about that? Apparently, she and Edie are looking to sell it."

"That's our way in," Scott said with a grin.

Filip's brow furrowed deeper. "What is?"

"We're going to help her."

"Whoa. What are you talking about?"

"Kevin told me your father used to be some kind of handyman and taught you, too."

Filip nodded slowly. "Aye."

"So, we help her."

"It's been a while since I did that kind of work," Filip said with a sigh.

Scott grinned. "Our mission is to convince Elodie to join us. That means we do whatever we have to in order to make that possible. Admit it. It's a great way in."

Filip chuckled as he shook his head. "It is that."

Scott didn't hold back his grin as they walked to Filip's SUV. He glanced up at the sky, wondering which constellation Elodie had been looking at or if it was just the moon in general. There was a lot more to Elodie MacLean than most realized. He planned to peel back each layer until he knew her better than she did. It's what Scott did. It was why George had sent him.

He wasn't exactly proud of his ability, but the magic came in handy. Usually, his charm and smooth words were enough, but his magic was always at the ready when they weren't. Things were at a crossroads for their organization. George had taken him aside and let him know just how dire things were. They *needed* Elodie. She was the answer.

Scott had asked Georgina what kind of magic Elodie had, but George hadn't elaborated. She'd simply said, "She's the answer."

That's all Scott needed to hear. He trusted Georgina completely. His companion, however, was another matter. Filip wanted to help, but it was evident that misery tore him in two. Scott glanced at Filip as they drove. "Saw you with your friends tonight."

"Aye," Filip said nonchalantly. "Have no' seen them in some time."

Scott nodded. "Good work. You learn anything else?"

"After Rhona and Balladyn's display, the Druids wanting a change are wavering."

"Let's no' worry about them for now. We need to keep our focus on Elodie."

Filip shifted nervously in his seat, switching hands on the steering wheel. "If someone finds out what we're doing—"

"Let's make sure that doesna happen."

"But if they do," Filip said as he glanced at Scott.

Scott slid his gaze out the windshield. "We need to be careful. You've returned to settle your brother's affairs, which is the truth. I'm a friend, tagging along. It's a solid cover story."

"Things are different on Skye since I left. Corann knew everything about everyone. I never would've agreed to this if he were still alive."

"He isna, though," Scott pointed out.

Filip shot him a dark look. "The rumor was that Rhona hadna yet stepped into Corann's position. So many Druids were speaking up about wanting a change to stop the decline in our numbers. All that changed a few weeks ago with the battle on Skye."

The battle had given Scott pause. It was all Druids anywhere could talk about. Fae Others who had used Skye Druids to ensnare Reapers. The Six, those who led the Fae Others, hadn't counted on all the Skye Druids or the Dragon Kings joining the Reapers to make a stand.

Scott would've loved to have seen the battle for himself. There had always been rumors about Reapers, but nothing to ever substantiate their existence until a few months ago when it was suddenly a fact. For whatever reason, the Reapers had kept themselves hidden from everyone, but especially the Fae. Now, it seemed the Reapers didn't care who knew about them.

Based on what George had told him, the Reapers were faster and more deadly than a regular Fae because the goddess Death had imbued them with her magic. Not to be outdone, the Six had created soldiers to mimic the Reapers. Scott couldn't imagine what Skye had looked like with the Dragon Kings, Reapers, Death, and the Skye Druids facing off against the Six and their soldiers. The sheer amount of magic that had been flowing around Skye must have been epic.

Dragon Kings. That was a new one for Scott. When
George had shared details about the immortal beings, Scott
had been stunned. He'd thought that George had kept them a
secret, but it turned out she had learned of them in a vision and
did some digging on her own. With the Kings coming to aid
the Skye Druids during battle, those on the island must know
about them. Did other Druids around the world? It seemed that
those in Scotland should have known, at least. He wondered
what the Kings looked like in their true forms. Hell, he wanted
to see one as a human. As for the Fae, Druids in some groups
usually knew about them. The Fae were everywhere, so it was
hard to miss them. Though most mortals had no idea they
were even there.

Filip turned off the road onto a bumpy drive to the house.
They bounced along as Scott's thoughts shifted to the Skye
Druids. They were legendary. They weren't beings he wanted
to tangle with—no one did.

The same could be said for Rhona now. Even Scott had
heard the murmurs of dissent, especially in Edinburgh when
Corann had named Rhona as his successor. Apparently, she
had nothing that set her apart from other Druids. At least that's
what everyone thought until Balladyn came into the picture.
From the way it had been described to George by someone she
wouldn't divulge, Rhona and Balladyn shared each other's
magic in a way it had never been done before. His Reaper
magic was hers to use, just as her Druid magic was his to use.
It dated back to a prophecy that, apparently, few on Skye even
knew about.

But Corann had.

Filip had said the old Druid had kept it to himself. Corann

did few things without reason. It was almost as if he had known what needed to happen for Rhona and Balladyn to find their connection and use it to beat back the Fae Others.

Scott understood Filip's hesitation about things. Rhona had made her stance clear on all things pertaining to the Others. If she learned what they were about, she wouldn't hesitate to stop them. And Scott knew it wouldn't be done quietly or politely. She and Balladyn would show their force once more.

And that would be it for their organization.

Filip parked the SUV and turned off the ignition. He sat there for a moment before looking at Scott. "Will George send backup for us?"

"We're all there is," he answered, meeting Filip's gaze.

"Bloody hell."

Scott watched fat raindrops land on the windshield. "It's why I'm no' going to let anything stop us from reaching our goal."

"What if we go to Rhona and tell her everything? What if we laid it out for her?"

"She's made her decision clear. We can no' take the chance that she'll refuse."

Filip blew out a breath. "Aye. It's just that a lot is riding on us."

Scott studied him carefully. As long as Filip and he were on the same page, they could succeed. Scott didn't know the meaning of failure. He would do whatever he had to for him, and for all the Druids around the globe.

"I'll do whatever you want me to do," Filip said. "I know how important this is."

Scott grinned. "Thanks. George thought we'd make a good team. Let's show her that she was right."

Filip rolled his eyes. "That's the last thing she needs to hear. She already rubs it in that she's always right."

"Tends to happen when one is a seer."

"Bloody arrogant woman," Filip said with a chuckle. His smile died swiftly. "Has she ever been wrong?"

Scott shrugged. "No' that I'm aware of. I'm no' sure she'd tell us if she had. She leads because she's a seer. Everyone trusts her."

"Which is why I doona understand her no' seeking out Rhona."

"George has her reasons. Ask her when we return."

Filip faced forward. The rain beat a steady rhythm on the SUV, making it impossible to see clearly out the windshield. "Did you know it was supposed to be my brother with you here and no' me?"

Scott lowered his gaze. He inwardly cringed at the mention of Kevin, who had been killed days before this mission. Kevin's death had rattled them all and propelled George to move up the timeline of the operation. Time was no longer on their side. "Kevin was a good Druid. A good man." His best friend.

"The best. A better man than I'll ever be."

"Doona say that," Scott said as he looked at Filip. "What we do here is in honor of Kevin and all the Druids who were killed."

Filip smiled sadly and blinked rapidly, his gaze still focused out the windshield. "Kevin was all I had left of my family. It's just me now."

"I'm your family. Everyone in the organization is family. Never forget that."

Filip finally turned his head and met Scott's gaze. "I'm sorry for being an arse."

"You're grieving."

Filip frowned. "As Elodie was fifteen years ago. It feels like there's a hole in my chest that will never heal. An emptiness that is sucking me down. I'm angry at everyone. The things I say are…" He sighed. "If she felt even a thimble full of what I'm going through, then it's no wonder she acted out as she did."

Scott didn't know what to say.

"Kevin wouldna act like this if I had died. He would've kept his mind on the mission and grieved later."

"You doona know that, and trying to speculate will only drive you insane. We've got this. And there's nothing wrong with having a healthy dose of respect and fear for Rhona and Balladyn. We'll stay under their radar. We're no' going to do anything that will make anyone suspicious."

Filip grunted. "Have you met the people of Skye? They're nothing if no' suspicious of newcomers."

"Aye, but you're no' a newcomer. You're one of them."

Filip's lips curved into a smile. "That I am."

"Good," Scott said as he slapped Filip on the shoulder. "Let's get in the house and start planning. I've got an idea for how we can approach Elodie."

CHAPTER SEVEN

SKYE DRUIDS

Kerry woke, gasping. She put a shaking hand to her brow as she sat on the edge of the bed. Sweat beaded her face, and her heart raced so fast that she feared it would never slow. It wasn't fear that assaulted her but…excitement.

She reached for the glass of water on the table and drank it in three huge gulps.

"It was just a dream," she murmured.

Yet the images replayed in her head, over and over. The young Druid sleeping in her bed, utterly unaware of the danger that seeped into her house. It slid beneath doors and between cracks until it filled her bedroom, wrapping around her like a cocoon. When she finally woke, finally realized that she wasn't alone, it was too late. The mist couldn't be budged.

The Druid had opened her mouth to scream. The mist dove into her mouth, down her throat, and sucked the wind from her lungs. Her body jerked and fought as magic filled her hands, but it was too little, too late. She was dead within seconds.

Kerry shook her head and pushed her aging body to its feet. She shuffled to the chair where her robe lay and slid her arms into the garment's sleeves before belting it. A glance at the clock told her it was just after half past two in the morning. After a dream like that, she doubted she would get back to sleep.

She put on her slippers and made her way into the kitchen. It took her three tries to light a match to start the burner to heat some water. As she turned to look out the window over the sink, it showed her reflection. She didn't know when the years had caught up with her. It'd seemed to happen so quickly. Not that she had ever been pretty. Even her mother had told her that her looks wouldn't win her a man—it would be the strength of her magic. Kerry had held onto that well into her late forties. Even when she moved into her fifties and then her sixties, the kernel of hope that she would find love had always been there.

But it was never to be.

Her magic, however, had brought her greater rewards. When she had been asked to be one of Corann's deputies, the day had been almost as great as she imagined her wedding would've been. That was when she realized that if she couldn't have love, she would pour her soul into Skye and her people.

And that's exactly what she had done for the last thirty years. Three decades as a deputy, first to Corann and then to Rhona before the position had been taken away. Kerry had been manipulated by the Fae Others, and Rhona and Balladyn had figured it out—which was probably the only reason she remained alive. Still, they'd stripped her position from her.

When she walked from the prison created just for Druids deep within the Red Hills of Skye, she had sworn to herself that she wouldn't hide in her cottage. She would face whatever rumors and whispers awaited her.

The first few days hadn't been terribly difficult. Then, after her section had learned that she was no longer deputy when they announced her replacement, her phone had rung continuously. First, they wanted to know if she had stepped aside because she was ill. A part of Kerry wanted to lie because the truth was so much harder. But it would come out eventually. It was better if she was the one to say it. So, she did.

Between the calls and visits, she repeated the story so many times it became rote. Oh, everyone showed righteous anger on her behalf for what the Fae Others had done, and then outrage for Rhona replacing her. And her so-called friends said and did all the right things. But having been deputy for so long, Kerry had learned one precious truth— everyone gossiped. The more titillating the story, the more widespread the talk.

Continuing her normal routine after that was an exhausting, taxing exercise in futility. But she did it. And she kept her head high. After all, she hadn't done anything wrong. She had stood up for Rhona and the Skye Druids. It wasn't her fault that whoever she had been emailing had managed to manipulate her.

She could admit that not showing Rhona the emails was wrong. When she went to Glasgow to see her sister, she had intended to meet with the person she had been exchanging emails with, only to reiterate that she didn't think the Druids should create a group of Others. She was the one who had helped the Fae Others set Rhona up to be killed in Belfast.

What Kerry hadn't told anyone was that she remembered that part. She knew the Druids she had called to await Rhona's arrival the night she should have died. Kerry didn't know why she recalled that bit and nothing else, but it hung over her like an ax, waiting to land on her neck.

She turned away from the window when the kettle whistled. Kerry had never liked looking at herself. Her hair was limp and thin, her body carrying extra weight that the doctor said wasn't good for her heart. Her people hadn't respected or liked her because she was pretty or thin or because she had great hair. They had come to her with their problems because she was always there for them. Now, that was gone.

Where did that leave her?

Kerry dropped the tea bag into her cup and poured the boiling water over it. As the tea steeped, she carried the cup to the table with its two chairs. She slowly lowered herself onto one, hearing the creaks in her knees. A bowl of sweets sat in the middle of the table. She always made sure to have her pockets full of them. The children knew it and rushed to her whenever she was about. With every day that passed since her removal as deputy, fewer and fewer children ran to her.

Before, she rarely had a meal by herself in the pub because her people would come to talk to her. Now, they left her alone completely. They didn't completely shun her, but they were subdued. It was like a knife being repeatedly thrust into her back.

She didn't have many years left. Would she spend them

like this? Alone and angry and hurt? She didn't have a
husband or children. No other family for her on Skye. The
Druids had been her family, and now, she had lost them, too.

Kerry thought about the dream again. It had felt real. Too
real. As if she had been in the room with the Druid. She
couldn't recall the Druid's name as she wasn't one of those in
Kerry's area, but she recognized her face. Maybe she should
go to Rhona and tell her. Or, at the very least, contact the other
deputies and alert them.

No. It was better to just forget it. It was a dream and
nothing more. After everything she had been through, it made
sense that her brain would fabricate something awful. She
needed to feel wanted again. This was her subconscious giving
her that reason. But in the end, it would only cause her more
heartache. She was an outcast now. Shunned and avoided.
She'd better get used to that. If she had thought her days had
been lonely before, she would learn just how bad it could get.

Kerry removed the tea bag, poured milk into her cup, and
stirred. She tapped the spoon on the side of the teacup and set
it on the saucer. As she lifted the tea to her lips, she froze at
the sound of drums.

Her heart jumped into her throat. The fact that the
Ancients continued to speak to her meant that she was still
relevant, still important to Skye. She listened to hear the
voices once more. Kerry got to her feet and closed her eyes.
The Ancients conversed in a thousand voices—until only one
spoke to her, reminding her that she had been used.

The Ancients were known for their riddles, but one had
silenced all the others and had spoken to Kerry in clear,
concise words. Had the Ancient returned? The woman's voice

had been steely, unforgiving. Kerry had failed the Skye Druids. She had failed herself. Maybe she would get the chance to fix everything.

"I thought you said you weren't going to forget you were used."

The Ancient's voice was just as clear as before. Kerry whirled around as it sounded right behind her. There was nothing there, though. "I haven't."

"You're letting the Druids dictate who you are."

The Ancients were wise. They weren't all-knowing, but they were deliberate in who they chose to speak with. She must have done something good to have one come to her. "I've spent my life serving the Druids on Skye."

"And now they determine your role. Only a victim would allow that. I know you remember contacting the Druids who agreed to kill Rhona."

Kerry took a step back as the voice sounded all around her. She swallowed hard.

"You remember much more than that. Don't you?"

She did, but she had never uttered the words aloud. After she'd read the email exchange between her and the Fae Others, her memories had returned. All of them.

"Don't you?" the Ancient repeated in a hard tone.

Kerry nodded slowly. "I do."

"What did you feel when you wrote those emails?"

Kerry hesitated. Could she say the words aloud? Did she dare? If she admitted the truth, everything she was, everything she had worked to be would crumble like sand. Not speaking the words didn't erase them from her mind. They were there.

Always. She tried to ignore them, tried to forget. But she couldn't.

"I believe every word I wrote," Kerry said in a rush. She gasped at the freeing sensation that washed through her. She put her hands on the back of the chair and laughed. Why hadn't she done that sooner? "The Druids are vanishing. Things need to change. Even on Skye. We hold the numbers, but for how much longer? The Fae Others nearly defeated us. If our allies hadn't joined us, they would have. I don't care what anyone says about Rhona and Balladyn. We could've lost."

"Aye. The very way of life the Druids have come to know would end."

"That can't happen." Kerry straightened. "I won't let it."

"Just what we wanted to hear."

"What do you want me to do?"

There was a long stretch of silence before the Ancient said, *"You've already begun."*

Kerry frowned, not understanding. "What do you mean?"

"You'll know the Druids you need to target. Those who won't serve fully."

"Those who don't see the big picture."

"Exactly. We've given you something to use that will help. You dreamed of it tonight."

Kerry's heart missed a beat. "The mist?"

"Don't let us down."

"Wait," Kerry said. "Why me?"

"No one else is capable of hearing us."

"Yet, you're one voice."

The Ancient chuckled. *"Only the strongest of Druids can hear us in one voice and hear us clearly."*

"Oh." Kerry couldn't stop the smile from spreading across her face. Her mother had often spoken about how powerful her magic was, and this proved it. Corann had never talked about hearing one Ancient. No one had, at least that Kerry was aware of. Especially not Rhona.

Kerry was so deep in thought that it took her a moment to realize the drums had faded to silence. The Ancients were gone. She was sad about that, but she also knew they would return. Because, apparently, only the strongest heard them so clearly and in one voice. She giggled at that. Oh, how she wanted to shout that all through Skye and rub everyone's noses in it.

Rhona had removed her as deputy because she couldn't trust Kerry anymore. Well, Kerry had a surprise for her. The more Rhona pushed against the change; the more Kerry would ensure it happened. She wouldn't start with the leader of the Druids. No, Rhona's turn would come last. Kerry wanted her and Balladyn to see what they had done by stripping such a proud Druid of her position.

Then again, why should she stop there? She had more magic than Rhona did. She could easily take Rhona's place as leader.

Kerry smiled, no longer feeling the ache in her bones or fear from the dream. She found a pen and some paper and sat to begin writing out her list of names.

CHAPTER EIGHT

SKYE DRUIDS

Elodie rinsed her mug as the door to the cottage flew open. Her sister rushed inside, a disheveled mess.

"Oh, thank God," Edie said as she put her hand to her heart.

Elodie faced her sister as she wiped her hands on a towel. "What's going on?"

"Where's your mobile? I've been calling for the past thirty minutes."

"Oh. It's in my room, probably still charging."

Edie's lips tightened. "Did you not hear it ring?"

"I put it on silent while I sleep. What's going on?" she asked again.

Edie sighed loudly and yanked off her coat with angry movements. She then tossed it on the back of a kitchen chair. "What happened, my dear sister, is that a Druid died last night."

"That's horrible news, but I fail to see what that has to do with me."

"She was murdered."

Elodie carefully draped the damp towel over the edge of the sink before turning. She no longer considered herself a Druid or even from Skye, but she was still shaken at the news. There was a lingering worry in her mind, something just out of reach that she couldn't pull into focus. "How?"

Edie's brows drew together as she came to stand before her. "I don't know, but this wasn't like what happened with Da."

"You said she was a Druid, so of course, it isn't like him."

If it were possible, Edie's frown deepened. "You're upset. I can see that. I thought it was because of...of..."

"*The incident*," Elodie finished for her. "It isn't."

"Then what is it?"

She shrugged. "I'm not certain. I didn't sleep well last night."

"You've not slept well since you've been here."

That was true. "I know, but this was...different."

"Different how?" Edie pushed.

Elodie shrugged, waving a hand around as if she could pull the words out of the air. "Dreams. So many dreams, but none of them clear. And a sinister feeling. I thought it was just ghosts."

"Ghosts?" Edie asked in surprise. "The cottage is haunted?"

"No. Not at all. At least, I don't think so." Elodie winced. She wasn't making things better. "I'm speaking metaphorically. Memories of our childhood leading up to that day and then after."

Edie nodded slowly. "Yeah. Those ghosts. I get that."

"They've rattled me since I walked through that door after returning." She couldn't stop herself from glancing down the hall to the still-closed door of her parents' bedroom.

Edie followed her gaze. "You've still not gone in there, have you?"

"Nope."

"Want me to do it?"

"Nope."

"Elodie."

"I said no," Elodie replied firmly. "I'm a big girl. I can do it."

Edie sighed and took her hands. "I want you to know that you don't have to. You don't have to do any of this. I'll give you whatever money you need."

Elodie squeezed her sister's hands. "I love you for that, but I'm not here to take a handout."

"It's not a handout. You're family."

"I'm the one who fucked up my life. I'm the one who will get it straightened out."

Edie wrinkled her nose. "Why don't we finish the cottage together?"

"I can manage it." When Edie started to argue, Elodie quickly said, "If it gets to be too much, I'll come straight to you."

Edie rolled her eyes before pulling Elodie against her for an embrace. "I'm sorry, but I'm rejoicing in you being back. I'm going to take every second I can with you."

Elodie wrapped her arms tightly around her sister. "I missed you, too. More than you know."

"Please tell me what brought you here."

Elodie released her sister and plastered a smile on her face. It felt tight. "My usual. I was stupid."

"The one thing you've never been is stupid." Edie licked her lips and glanced at the floor. "Listen, I was thinking of going to see Mum. Want to come?"

"No."

"Elodie, please. She misses you."

"I can't," Elodie said with a shake of her head.

Edie shrugged and took a step back. "I spent a lot of time going back through memories, wondering how I didn't see what was going on between them."

Elodie turned her head away. She'd had those same thoughts. Being back in the cottage had drudged them up again. "Stop."

"You, me, and Elias never saw anything because they made sure we didn't. We didn't see the bruises. Didn't hear the fights."

"Stop," she said again. Elodie hated to think how long her mother had suffered in silence as the family laughed and played. How many times had Elodie and her siblings spent the day with their father at the beach while Mum remained behind? There was always a good excuse or reason that didn't make any of them question things.

Edie was quiet for a long moment. "Everyone has a breaking point."

"Mum should've told him that she was a Druid. If he had

known that she had magic, maybe he wouldn't have abused her."

"Maybe. Maybe not."

"Why didn't she use magic to stop him? She had ample opportunity. She didn't have to kill him."

Edie lowered her gaze to the floor for several heartbeats. "We're speculating on their actions and thoughts. Neither of us was in that relationship. We don't know why things happened. Only two people know the truth."

"And one of them is dead."

"He abused her," Edie stated.

Elodie crossed her arms over her chest. "He was our father."

"And she is our mother."

"I don't hate her for what she did."

Edie raised a brow. "Really? Because it sounds like you do."

"She only saw one way out, and she took it."

"Sometimes, that's all a person has."

She knew that feeling all too well. Elodie reached out a hand. Edie grasped it, and they embraced again.

"It really is good to have you here. I can see you all the time," Edie said, tears in her eyes, her voice trembling.

Elodie wished she were happy being back on Skye. Maybe it would be different if she were staying somewhere other than the cottage. As soon as she thought that, she knew it was a lie. Everything about Skye, the Druids, and the cottage was a reminder of a past she needed to release and let go of. That meant never returning—just as her brother had done.

"Come to dinner tonight," Edie said as she released Elodie.

"You've not gotten to spend much time with Trevor or the kids."

Elodie knew it was a mistake. She wasn't good company, and she never knew what to say to children. But how could she refuse her sister? Edie's eagerness was visible. Elodie would hurt her soon enough when she left. There was no need to do more now. "Sure."

"Really?" Edie asked, her surprise evident. "Wonderful. Okay." She glanced at her coat. "I need to plan. I need to go to the store." She clapped her hands together and spun in a circle twice before laughing and hurrying to her coat. "Be there at five."

Then she was gone.

Elodie rubbed her hands up and down her arms. Her smile had vanished with her sister. All she could think about was the elusive dreams. She kept trying to remember them, but the details refused to surface. Then there was the Druid's murder. Elodie hadn't asked how many were killed on Skye each year, but she couldn't imagine it was very many—Druids even less since they protected their homes.

She went to the bedroom and looked at her phone. She had fourteen texts from Edie and eight phone calls. Elodie sat on the bed and looked up the local news on her mobile. She found a brief segment about the murder, listing the victim—a thirty-five-year-old woman. There was nothing about who'd found her, how she'd been found, or even how she'd been killed. But there would be. The news would race through the Druid community like wildfire.

Elodie told herself that it was none of her business. She shoved her mobile into the back pocket of her jeans and stood.

Then she remembered the cold numbness that had filled her when Edie had told her about the murder.

"Shite," she murmured.

Elodie shook her head, attempting to free her mind of the thoughts. She had a long day ahead of her. The sky was clear, and she needed to take advantage of it and get as much done outside as she could.

At least that was her thought until she stood outside braced against the freezing wind. There was shite everywhere. It wasn't just weeds in the flowerbeds. Junk and trash littered the area, as well. The only way she knew they were gardens was because she had helped her mum plant and weed them. Now, they just looked like piles of overgrown weeds that needed to be demolished.

"Perfect," she mumbled.

She headed to the garage. It took her several attempts and all her strength to get the garage doors open. The sight of the junk within made her immediately shut the door again. She couldn't clean the garage until she threw the stuff inside away. Which left two choices. She could tackle her parents' room, or she could begin calling around to get estimates on repairs.

Elodie strode back inside the house and removed her coat and gloves. Then she sat at the table with her phone and made a list of people to call. Within an hour, the first arrived to give her an estimate. She spent the rest of the day showing people around and pointing out the damage. A few showed her things she had missed.

And each of their estimates was more than she made in a year.

The last thing she wanted was to go to dinner and make

conversation with a man she didn't know and kids who would ask countless questions. Because wasn't that what children did? But Elodie showered and got ready. Then she got into her car and drove into town to pick up a bottle of wine and some whisky, because as poor as she was, she wouldn't arrive emptyhanded.

Thankfully, it didn't look as if many people were in the liquor store. She quickly got out of her car and made her way inside. She decided to splurge on a bottle of Dreagan whisky and a cheaper pinot noir. She had a feeling she would need the whisky. Maybe she wouldn't even bring it in to dinner. Perhaps she would save it for herself.

She was making her way to the register when a man near her age walked down the aisle toward her. He looked vaguely familiar. He smiled instead of giving her a glare, so she smiled back as she passed him.

"Elodie?"

Fuck. She halted and turned to him.

"You doona remember me, do you?" he asked, his gray eyes watching her carefully.

She shook her head.

"It's Filip. Filip Gordon."

As soon as he said his name, she recognized him. A genuine smile curved her lips. "It's been a while."

"Aye," he said with a nod, grinning. "I've been gone, too. I, ah, well, people have been talking."

"Of course, they have," she mumbled and tried to keep the bitterness out of her voice, knowing she failed.

He twisted his lips. "I'm here for family business. Kevin died."

Sadness filled her for the boy she had known so many years ago. Kevin had been good to her. He had tried to help her, but she had been beyond help back then. "I'm so sorry to hear that, Filip."

Filip shrugged, his grief evident on his face as he put his hands into the front pockets of his pants. "Thank you. Are you staying on Skye long?"

"No. You?"

"Nay," he answered with a smile that almost reached his eyes. He ran a hand through his short, black hair. "Listen, I heard you were doing some work on your parents' place. Need any help? I need to make some extra money. My friend and I are pretty good at handiwork."

She followed the jerk of Filip's chin to see none other than the man from outside the pub—Scott. Their gazes met. His were a deep blue like the ocean. She quickly looked away, hesitating.

"Let us come by and give you a quote at the verra least," Filip suggested.

What could it hurt? Besides, Elodie was sick to her stomach at the estimates the others have given her. Filip and Scott couldn't be any worse than that. "Do you have references?"

Filip shot her a look. "You knew my da. He showed Kevin and me the proper way to do things."

That was true. Elodie knew the right thing would probably be to go to Edie and Trevor with the quotes and let them decide. Adding one more before she did wouldn't hurt. The decision would be out of her hands, anyway. She wasn't the one who would be footing the bill.

"Okay," she agreed.

The corners of Filip's eyes crinkled with his grin. "Great. Tomorrow morning at ten sound good?"

"I'll see you then," she said and continued down the aisle past Scott. She felt his gaze on her, but she didn't look his way.

CHAPTER NINE

SKYE DRUIDS

Scott woke early the following day. He couldn't believe that Filip had managed to convince Elodie to let them bid on the work.

"Da is laughing his arse off in Hell right now," Filip muttered.

Scott shot him a look as they drove to Elodie's. "Why?"

"Because I swore nothing would ever make me do manual labor again. His motto was that a man should know how to do everything and excel at one thing."

"You might hate it, but he taught you so much that we're going to Elodie's."

Filip snorted and shook his head as he slowed to turn onto her road, the blinker *clicking*. "She's allowing us to give her a bid. That doesna mean we'll get the job. I doona fancy working outside in this weather."

"How do you know it's outside work?"

Filip laughed, shaking his head again. "We're on Skye.

Wind. Rain. The roofs always need to be repaired or replaced when a home is left unattended. No doubt there's water damage inside the house from leaks. Da had Kevin and me with him doing such repairs when we were growing up. It's hard work that doesna always wait for warm weather."

Scott watched the wind cause the bushes in front of a cottage to shake violently. The wind was something he hadn't counted on, but he was getting used to it. Or maybe he just loved the smell of the sea.

"Bloody hell. You're smiling," Filip stated with dismay. "You're looking forward to this."

Scott shrugged. "I like Skye."

"Doona get attached. They're no' keen on outsiders."

"People move to the isle all the time."

Filip made a sound that was half laugh, half snort. "Nay, they doona."

"I thought Skye was a haven for Druids."

"Skye Druids, aye."

Scott frowned at that. "Are you saying they wouldna let me in?"

"I'm saying they wouldna make it easy. The Skye Druids have made a name for themselves. Most of the families can trace their ancestors back to the first Druids who came to the island."

"Most," Scott pointed out. "No' all. If the Druids are worried about our blood being mixed with non-Druids, it seems they would welcome more of us."

Filip looked at him. "Do you always take the most difficult path?"

Scott considered that for a moment. "I think my mum would say I do."

"If everything goes as we plan, and as soon as Rhona and Balladyn learn what we're about, you'll never be welcome on Skye again."

"Neither will you."

Filip was quiet for so long that Scott didn't think he would answer. Finally, Filip said in a soft voice, "Aye."

For someone who claimed to hate the island, Scott suspected that Filip had also missed it. Several places in Scotland were picturesque and awe-inspiring, but it was more than that which caused so many to flock to the island. Skye was magical. No. It was more than that, too. It was… enchanting. Breathtaking. It reached inside a person and gently, tenderly enveloped their hearts with mysticism and mystery. With delights and wonder.

Skye had utterly bewitched Scott.

He couldn't understand how anyone ever left. Then again, he hadn't lived here. He had no idea how the Druid community was. No doubt it was like any village where everyone knew everyone else and their business. That wasn't something Scott had ever had to deal with growing up in the city. He'd heard others complain about it, but he didn't think it would be so bad. The idea of someone knowing his order when he walked into a place or calling out his name in greeting sounded appealing. Then again, the grass was usually greener on the other side of the fence. He'd always hated that analogy, but it fit.

His thoughts came to a screeching halt when Filip slowed again. Scott's gaze went to the white cottage sitting on a hill. The drive dipped down to the road. When Filip parked, Scott could see the cove's blue water. Elodie's house was set some distance from the beach, with some houses closer to the water's edge, but the view was still magnificent. The water. The mountains.

Edinburgh was a coastal city, so he'd always had it near. But this was different. It was as if something clicked into place inside him. As if he had come home.

"Mate? You all right?" Filip asked.

Scott swallowed, feeling almost lightheaded. Shite. He didn't want to leave Skye. Ever. "Aye."

"Really? Because you doona look it."

Scott licked his lips and turned his head to Filip. "I love this island."

"Bloody hell," Filip stated as he flattened his lips. "I knew it. Everyone falls in love with Skye."

"Even you?"

Filip looked at the cove and nodded. "It's in my blood. I can never fully remove it."

"Many Druids wish they had a community like this. I know I would've loved it."

"You say that until you come up against the rules." Filip tugged his beanie over his ears. "You would chafe against them."

Filip had a point. Scott had never been good with rules. Still, to have so many to turn to and learn from, he couldn't imagine where his magic would be now if he had been taught as Filip had.

"Ready?" Filip asked.

Scott nodded and reached for the door. Wind battered him

the instant they stepped out of the SUV, but it only made him smile. At times, it felt as if the island were testing him, trying to knock him on his arse. It probably would eventually, but he was enjoying the challenge.

Skye wasn't a living, breathing entity. But there could be an argument that it was. Like now. Scott had the distinct impression that the island wasn't happy that they were at Elodie's. Was Skye trying to protect her? He could understand that. Elodie and her family had suffered a terrible tragedy. He wasn't sure how he would handle one of his parents killing the other. From the tidbits he'd picked up from Filip and listening around Skye, no one knew the real story. No one, that was, except for Elodie and her siblings.

Scott wanted to know the details because he knew they were the answer to getting close to her. Filip thought him morbid for being interested. Scott had tried to explain that he didn't want to know about the murder but rather the *reasons* behind it. A loving wife didn't just have a mental break one day and kill her husband.

They walked to the front door with a small stoop and an awning. Filip rapped his knuckles on the door. The sound of locks being turned reached them. Filip was shivering, his hands buried deep in his coat pockets, but he smiled when Elodie's face appeared.

"Right on time," she said as she stepped aside for them to enter.

Scott followed Filip inside and breathed in the clean smell of the house. The way everything sparkled he could tell that Elodie had been busy. He looked her way to find her gaze on him. Her light blue gaze quickly slid away as she motioned for them to follow her through to the kitchen.

The cottage was similar to Filip's in both size and layout. He glanced inside the living area as he passed. The décor was dated but still looked good. Some people paid a high price for such furniture.

"Tea? Coffee?" Elodie offered.

Scott wanted to stay for as long as possible, and her offer would allow that. "Whatever you're drinking."

Her gaze landed on him. For a heartbeat, she simply stared. "It's tea."

Scott wondered what she was thinking. She was quiet, but it was usually the quiet ones who had the most active minds.

"Tea is great," Filip said.

She set down her mug and filled the electric kettle with water before turning it on to boil. Then, she faced them. An awkward silence filled the room. Scott waited for Filip to say something. He was the one who'd known her, after all. But Filip removed his beanie and twisted it in his hands. Elodie turned her head to the window and looked out at the cove. His gaze moved over her blond locks that she had pulled haphazardly into a low ponytail. He'd seen his sister trying to achieve such a look. Had Elodie worked to get her hair styled in such a fashion? Or had it just happened? He bet it was the latter.

"It's a beautiful view," Scott said.

She nodded her head. "It is. We're hoping that will help sell the cottage."

"I doona think you need to worry about it selling," Filip said.

The kettle beeped to let her know the water was boiling. She retrieved two mugs and set them on the counter, then added the tea bags and poured the water. "I hope you're right. I knew it would take a lot of cleaning, but I hadn't counted on how many repairs would be needed." She returned the kettle to its stand and glanced at them. "I foolishly thought I could come in, clean it up, maybe do a few minor things myself, and put it on the market. I don't think I considered how long the house had been sitting here."

"Edie and Trevor didna use it as a rental?" Filip asked as he accepted the mug.

Elodie's lips twisted. "I guess not."

"Maybe because it wasna just Edie's. She was thinking of you and your brother," Scott said as she handed him his tea. Their fingers brushed. She jerked back, spilling a little of the hot water on him.

"I'm sorry," she said quickly.

He smiled and then lied. "I didna feel it." In his periphery, Scott saw Filip roll his eyes. Scott ignored him and wiped his hand on his jeans where the water had landed.

Elodie cleared her throat and grabbed her mug between her hands as if to warm them. "You might be right. I never thought to talk to her about it, and she never brought it up. It could've been earning us all some money."

"Aye, but it would've had to be separate from their rentals," Filip said. "Separate listings, separate maintenance, separate payments. That would've given them a larger payout than you or Elias were given. They probably didna want the hassle."

Elodie's brow furrowed. "Still. They knew all about the

rental business. It's what they do. It could've helped to keep the house up all these years."

"How long has it sat empty?" Scott asked.

She looked into her mug as she said, "About ten years."

Filip let out a whistle after he removed his tea bag and took it to the garbage. "There must be a lot of damage."

"There is." Elodie motioned to the honey and milk on the table.

Scott waited until Filip was finished and then tossed his tea bag and poured some milk into his cup. "I suppose you've already had some bids. Have they listed out all the damage? I'm asking so you can show us. We can also look around for more, if you'd like."

"I have three bids." This time, she briefly met his gaze.

Did he make her uncomfortable? He would have to change that. Ever since their fingers had touched, she had taken small steps backward until she was against the kitchen cupboards.

Scott backed up. He wanted her trust. No, he *needed* it. No matter how long it took, he would gain it.

Because they needed her to keep Druids alive.

CHAPTER TEN

SKYE DRUIDS

Elodie tried to keep her breathing even. She hadn't been able to stand still since Filip and Scott had walked into the cottage. She had thought it was just the idea of having two men inside with her. Then Scott's fingers had brushed hers. There hadn't been an electric shock, just a warmth that slowly spread up her arm and then through her body.

It wasn't at all uncomfortable. Quite the opposite, actually. And that in and of itself put her on edge. She was used to not feeling much of anything physically. If she were interested in a guy and he returned the interest, then she saw where it went—which was never anywhere.

Unfortunately, some of the men had been rather nice. They had declared feelings for her, things that she could never return. She used to try and explain that she was dead inside. It had happened when her magic vanished. Nothing she did brought it back. She had tried to fall in love. She had said the words and done everything she had read in books or seen in movies, but she simply couldn't do it.

Worse, she never felt the attraction everyone always talked about. One of her co-workers seemed to fall in love with a new guy every couple of months. It hadn't taken Elodie long to realize that the woman was in love with the idea of falling in love.

"It's such a rush!" her co-worker had explained. *"First, it's like an animal attraction. Eyes meeting across the room and all that. Then there is this need to be close to them. Oh, my God! It's the most amazing experience."*

When Elodie pointed out that the experience never lasted past a few months, her co-worker had waved away her words as if they weren't important.

Maybe Elodie wasn't attracted to anyone because of what'd happened with her parents.

Maybe it was because of the marriages and families she'd destroyed before leaving Skye.

Maybe her magic had taken her ability to fall in love when it'd left.

Or maybe she'd just been born this way.

Whatever the reason, she accepted it. So why, then, did the warmth unfurling through her now from Scott's touch make her so wary? And…excited? It was the briefest of touches. Could it even be classified as one? It was more like a brush or a graze.

But that didn't explain the warmth.

She blinked and realized that Filip had been talking. Elodie glanced at Scott. His dark blue eyes watched her. She didn't gaze too long at him. It felt as if he could see straight into the black pit of what remained of her soul—a place that never healed. But that was her fault. She hadn't let it.

"What do you think?"

Elodie startled. She looked at Filip and forced a nervous smile. "I'm sorry. I didn't—"

"He asked if you'd tell us about the repairs. And then we can go take a look," Scott said.

Scott had a deep voice, but something about it had a calming effect. She wasn't fooled, though. She had been around enough charmers to know that he was one.

"Sure," she answered and began listing off everything.

Filip hurried to make a list on his mobile, but Scott simply stared. It was unnerving to have that unwavering, deep blue gaze focused on her. Then they were both walking through the house. She didn't follow them. She hadn't followed any of the people who had come to give her quotes. Mainly because she didn't want to be one of *those* people. But also because they went into her parents' room, and she wasn't ready for that yet. It would look strange if she suddenly stopped outside the bedroom. Which would then bring questions, and she really didn't want that.

So, she stayed in the kitchen and drank her now-cold tea. She hated cold tea, but she didn't want to waste it. The fact that she was penny-pinching tea bags should tell the universe how far she had sunk. Elodie popped her mug into the microwave and heated it enough to be drinkable.

She tried to sit at the kitchen table, but hearing Filip and Scott moving around the house made her nervous. That was odd since none of the others had caused such feelings in her. When the pair went into the room she slept in, she strained to hear what they said. Then wondered why. It certainly couldn't be because she might have felt a wee bit of something with Scott.

When had she ever gotten that lucky?

Suddenly, Scott walked into the kitchen. He gave her a smile as they looked around the room. She fidgeted, then got irritated with herself for being so nervous. It felt like an eternity later before the two moved into the dining room and then the living area. She stayed where she was when they found their way into the attic.

Elodie could determine where they were by the sound of their footfalls above her. When they came back down, they lingered for a long time in her parents' room. Everyone who came to give a quote had. She imagined it was pretty bad in there. She hadn't asked Edie about it. Maybe she should, to prepare for whatever was within.

The truth was, she was a coward. She wouldn't open the door to her parents' bedroom, she wouldn't talk to Edie about it, and she wouldn't go see her mum. If she did any of those things, she would have to face the past—something that had haunted her since it'd all happened. It was also a past that she wanted to lay to rest.

The only way to do that was to face it. But she was too scared.

Hence the problem.

Elodie dropped her forehead to her hands on the table and sighed. She wanted to get her life on track. She had told herself that even before she came to Skye, and she knew the way to do it. Why then couldn't she? What was she so afraid of?

"You're no' afraid of anything," her dad used to say teasingly.

But it had been the truth. She'd never been afraid of the dark, the monsters under her bed, rejection from a guy, or going after her dreams. Nothing.

Until *the incident.*

And her magic leaving.

She at least needed to tell Edie about her magic. Hoping that she would get through her time on Skye without that coming up was delusional, and Elodie was anything but.

In an effort to stop thinking about the past and Scott, she turned her thoughts to dinner the night before. She had met Trevor twice in the nine years he had been married to Edie. Her sister's husband wasn't exactly handsome, but he had an air about him that made Elodie see why Edie had fallen for Trevor. He adored her sister. That much was plain to see.

After what had happened with their mother, Elodie looked for anything that would indicate that Edie was in the same kind of relationship. Her sister was so much like their mum that it caused Elodie concern. But the way Edie and Trevor gazed at each other, both so full of love, warmed her heart. Edie had found love.

Trevor touched her sister often. His hands were always on her, whether it was walking past Edie or sitting at the table. Between the looks and touches, Elodie knew that she didn't have to worry about her sister anymore. Plus, Trevor was aware of Edie's magic and not only accepted it but welcomed it.

The children had stared at Elodie all night, which was a little unnerving. They had spent the first thirty minutes quiet and then wouldn't stop talking after that. At eight and six, they were a handful, but much to Elodie's surprise, they were also a delight. She had no experience with children, but she had one on each side of her on the sofa by the end of the night. Plans had already been made for another dinner next week. It made her wonder how things might have been had she visited her sister. She might have been there for baby showers and maybe even the kids' births. Christmases and birthdays. She had missed so very much by distancing herself from Skye.

Elodie's head snapped up when Scott and Filip walked to the front door and then went outside. She hadn't heard them come out of her parents' room. Stifling a yawn, she couldn't wait until she had a full night's sleep again. The previous night hadn't just been plagued with dreams but an ominous feeling she couldn't shake.

She rose from the table and rinsed her cup, hating that she ended up wasting the tea in the end, anyway. Elodie folded some laundry in her room while the men were outside. When she heard the knock and then the door open as Filip called out, she went to meet them in the kitchen.

"We're in for a storm," Filip said, his nose and cheeks red from the wind.

Scott nodded as he glanced out the window. "You can see it coming in."

Elodie turned to look behind her and saw the dark clouds on the horizon.

"Here it is."

She looked at Filip to see a piece of paper with the jobs and their cost written in pencil. She scanned down to the bottom, taking in the total. She blinked, wondering if she'd read it right. It was almost half the price of any of the others she had gotten. Elodie went back to the top of the list and read through each line. Filip and Scott had caught everything except for two items the others had.

"What about the spot at the back—?" she began.

Filip shrugged. "It's up to you. I left it off because it's more cosmetic than anything. Plus, I'd include that if we're doing work near there. It's a small enough area no' to charge more."

She nodded, accepting his answer.

"As for the other," he continued, "you're talking about the area in the garage, right? I can cut that spot out and put in a new board. It doesna require extensive work."

Elodie shook her head in amazement. She expected businesses to try and upsell, but those two items in all three bids had cost a lot. "Are you sure about this price?"

"If you're worried that we're making money, doona," Scott said. "It includes labor."

She would be a fool to turn this down. Unless they did a poor job. Elodie looked at Filip. She recalled that his father had been the one everyone called for odd jobs, and that Filip and Kevin were often with him.

"You can trust me," Filip said as if reading her mind. "I'll do a good job for you, Elodie."

She folded the paper. "I need to talk to Edie."

"Of course," Filip replied.

Scott said, "We'd like to get the spot in the back corner of the house done free of charge. It wouldna be verra neighborly for us to see something and allow more damage to happen with the storm coming."

"I can't allow you to work for free." She didn't like the idea of anyone doing things for free. It was their time, energy, and materials. Since she counted each penny, she knew how important it was to get paid.

Filip winked at her. "Come have a drink with us sometime. That'll be payment enough. We can talk about Kevin."

How could she refuse now? "Thank you."

"I should've done more a long time ago," Filip said, suddenly serious. "I'm sorry I didna. I was a kid."

"We all were," she said before he could continue. "If anyone should apologize, it's me."

Filip shook his head. "I disagree." He cleared his throat and glanced at Scott. "We're going to get to work before the storm hits."

"One more thing," she said. "The carpet in the bedroom area. Can you replace that?"

Filip chuckled. "You knew my da. He did everything and taught us—including laying carpet. Want me to get you a quote on that, too?"

"If you don't mind."

"I'll measure," Scott said as he walked away.

Elodie found herself alone with Filip. She moved closer and lowered her voice. "How long have you known him?"

"A few years. He's a good guy. He and Kevin were close. Scott decided to come with me to help me sort things. I'll probably be selling Da's cottage."

"Your cottage," she corrected.

Filip's lips twisted. "Aye. It's strange to think it, and even stranger to hear it. As for Scott, I wouldna bring someone into your home that I didna trust with my life. In case you're wondering, he's a Druid."

She hadn't been, but now that Filip had told her, she couldn't stop thinking about it. She missed her magic every day, but especially the times she happened upon a Druid who had no idea how precious—and precarious—their magic was.

CHAPTER ELEVEN

SKYE DRUIDS

Rain drenched Scott and Filip as they finished repairing the corner of Elodie's cottage, the water soaking through their coats, sweaters, and undershirts to land upon their skin like tiny shards of ice.

"Fuck me," Filip muttered as a gust of wind made him nearly drop the hammer.

Scott turned his head away from the worst of the tempest, but it did little to help. It almost felt as if the storm were alive.

And attacking them.

The magic on Skye was significant, but surely not like that. Or was it?

Scott caught Filip's eye. "Tell me the rain isna after us."

"I can no'," Filip shouted over a boom of thunder.

He frowned, unsure if Filip was teasing or not. They kept working. Any conversation was delayed since it was impossible to hear anything over the roar of the rain and the cracks of lightning and bellowing thunder.

"Get inside. Now!"

They looked up to see that Elodie had opened a window near them. Scott lowered his gaze to Filip and finished hammering in the last nail, then they both raced to the door. Elodie was there with towels.

"Get out of those clothes," she ordered. "Some of Elias's things are in the bathroom and his bedroom. Something should fit you until your clothes dry."

Filip didn't argue. He raced to the bathroom. Scott removed his boots and hung his coat, the garment dripping water onto the floor. He hesitated, wondering if he should take it to the sink.

"It's fine. I'd rather you get dry and warm," Elodie said and gently turned him toward her brother's bedroom.

Scott was more than happy to remove his sodden clothes and wipe the cold rain from his body. True to her word, Elodie had taken out several pairs of sweatpants and some sweatshirts and sweaters. There were socks, as well. Scott hastened into a pair of gray sweatpants and a faded maroon sweatshirt with some logo that was all but gone. With the dry socks on, Scott was already warming up.

He returned to the kitchen with his wet clothes in hand. Elodie took them and placed them on a drying rack with Filip's. Scott tried to help her, but she wouldn't let him. Then Filip placed a mug in his hands. Scott closed his eyes and sipped the delicious tea, the heat filling him as he swallowed.

"Thank you," he said when Elodie turned back to him.

Her lips flattened. "You two stayed out there too long."

"It needed to be done," Filip added.

Elodie lifted her gaze to the window as she reached for her

mug. "What an angry storm. I didn't see many of them like this in Edinburgh."

Scott was startled to hear that she had been in the same city as he, but he was more interested in her take on the storm. "Why do you say it's angry?"

"Look at it," she said without taking her eyes from the window. "The rain is slanting sideways. The wind howls its fury. And the lightning…" She paused. "It almost feels as if it's trying to tear the sky in two while the thunder rattles the very ground."

No sooner had she said the words than the sky let loose a long rumble that indeed shook the house and rattled the windows. Scott glanced at Filip, but he was looking down at his tea, his expression closed off.

"Most say it's because we're an island," Elodie continued. "That it's the sea and the wind currents. But the Druids know it's so much more."

She fell silent. Scott wanted her to continue, but given how she and Filip were acting, he wasn't sure if he should push.

Filip finally broke the silence. "It doesna want me here."

Elodie's head swiveled to him. "You're a Druid, Filip. You were born here. You belong."

"Maybe it's me," Scott said. His breath locked in his chest when Elodie's pale blue gaze slid to him. For the briefest of moments, he saw the pain and fear she fought so hard to conceal from everyone—including herself.

"I rather think it's directed at me," Elodie replied.

Scott frowned. "Why would you say that?"

Instead of answering him, she looked out the window. He was beginning to think she would never respond when she whispered, "Skye is particular about who finds a home here."

"You were born here, too," Filip said, using her words. "You're a Druid. You belong."

The smile she gave him was so full of melancholy that it brought Scott up short. Elodie was hiding something big—something she didn't want anyone to discover. But for the life of him, he couldn't imagine what it could be. Like Filip had said, she was a Druid born to Skye. She belonged. He, however, didn't.

Elodie turned from the window and faced them. "It doesn't look to be letting up anytime soon. Besides, your clothes are still drying. How about some lunch?"

"I could eat," Filip said with a smile.

Scott chuckled. "You're always hungry."

"I can no' help it. I've a high metabolism," Filip told her with a wink.

The laugh that bubbled from Elodie was musical. Scott was transfixed by how her face lit up. And her eyes...they sparkled. He wasn't sure if it was the strength he saw in her or the fear she battled, but he was glad that he had been sent to Skye for her. Everything about her captivated him.

"Let's see what you have." Filip started to rise.

Scott pushed him back into the chair. "You burn everything you attempt to cook." He looked at Elodie. "If you want edible food, keep him away from the kitchen."

Her eyes crinkled at the corners. "Thanks for the heads-up. Though I should warn you that I'm not the best either. However, since it's merely sandwiches, I think I can handle it."

Scott and Filip helped Elodie get everything out of the fridge and onto the table. She got out plates while Filip found the bread. Scott watched the easy way Filip got Elodie to talk. As they made their sandwiches, he brought up their childhoods and things he and his brother had done to get into trouble.

It wasn't until they were halfway through their meal before Filip asked, "Elias didna take all his things?"

"He left in a hurry," Elodie replied softly.

Scott saw that the mention of her brother was like scratching at a wound that hadn't healed. He tried to imagine how he might feel if his sister had left without a word. "Well, I'm thankful for the clothes. Otherwise, we'd be sitting in towels or a blanket."

Filip chuckled wryly. "Damn, that storm. Every way I moved, the rain seemed to move with me. It struck my face with force."

Scott could've kicked Filip. At the mention of the tempest, Elodie seemed to withdraw into herself.

There was no more talk during the meal. They cleaned up and moved into the living area as the storm raged. Scott lit the fire while Filip sank into one of the large chairs. Within moments, his friend was snoring.

Elodie walked in and caught sight of Filip. Her lips twitched as she bit back a laugh. "He's always been able to sleep anywhere. I can't tell you how many times he did that in school." She sat in a corner of the sofa and curled her legs under her.

Scott took the other chair. He stared into the fire as it took root and began to pop. He wanted to ask Elodie so much, but now wasn't the time to come right out and ask her what'd happened to her father. That might very well get Filip and him thrown out into the storm. No, that wasn't something she would do. Elodie would just shut down. He suspected she did that a lot.

"It's good that you came to Skye with him."

Scott swung his head to her and nodded. "Kevin's death was a shock."

"What happened to him?"

"He was murdered."

Elodie's face blanched. "What? How?"

Scott hesitated. How much did he reveal?

"Never mind," she said with a wave of her hand. "It's none of my business."

"It isna a secret. That isna why I paused. Kevin wasna the first Druid in recent months to be singled out and killed."

She licked her lips. "I don't understand."

"You lived in the city. You know how volatile things can be as a Druid."

Elodie's gaze skated away. "I didn't mix with other Druids in Edinburgh—or any place I've lived."

That drew him up short. "Why?" The word was out before he even thought about it.

"I ran from Skye because I wanted to get away from anything having to do with Druids and magic. And, yes, I ran. As far and as fast as I could. I left Edie behind, just as Elias left us both. I didn't care. I knew if I stayed…"

"What?" he urged softly.

Her eyes returned to meet his. "That the island would suffocate me. I thought if I had a chance at a life, I needed to leave all of this behind." She swung her hand out, indicating the cottage, her family, and Skye.

"Did you find what you were looking for?"

She issued a soft bark of laughter filled with cynicism. "I came close at times, but something always shoved me right back to the ground. I kept pulling myself back up, only to be knocked down again. In case you were wondering, that's why I'm here. What little I had in Edinburgh is gone."

"Surely no'."

"There's no need to be kind. It is," she said dryly. After a moment, she sighed and looked at the fire. "Filip told you about my parents, didn't he?"

"Aye." Scott decided to be honest. He suspected that she would appreciate that.

Elodie wrapped her arms around herself and rubbed. "I used to think our family was cursed or something. We had a great life until *the incident*. I have no idea where Elias is, and I know how my life has been. I'm such a horrible sister that I believed Edie was making up how good things were for her so I wouldn't worry. Then I came back and discovered that she has an amazing life with a loving husband and two adorable children." She glanced at him. "Looks like our family isn't cursed. Maybe it's just me."

"You're no' cursed," he told her.

"Mum never told Da she had magic."

Scott grew still and waited for her to continue.

"What kind of wife doesn't tell her husband something as important as that? If he had said that he didn't believe in magic, she could've shown him it was real. And if he had been sickened by it, she would have known they shouldn't be together. Yet, that isn't what happened. Instead, she decided not to tell him. That's the part I don't understand."

Her voice was so low that he barely caught the last sentence. Scott didn't have an answer for her. He was just as mystified by her mother's actions as she.

"I've not been in their bedroom since it happened," she confessed as she looked at him. "I don't think I can go in there."

Scott held her gaze. "Then doona. No one says you have to."

"What about meeting the past head-on?"

"You can do that in a variety of ways. It doesna mean you have to go into their bedroom."

CHAPTER TWELVE

SKYE DRUIDS

Elodie knew Scott was just being kind, but his words affected her. All this time, she had kept telling herself that she had to go into the bedroom. What if she didn't? What if Scott was right? What if she could face the past in another way? The relief that filled her was so great that she grew dizzy.

"Are you all right?" he asked, concern in his deep blue eyes.

She was all too aware of the very masculine, very handsome man talking to her. Elodie couldn't stop thinking about the warmth of their touch. Had it been her imagination? Or had it really happened? Would it occur again if she reached out and brushed her fingers against his?

Did she even want to know the truth?

What was the worst that could happen? Maybe she had imagined it and was back to feeling nothing for everyone around her. On the other hand, what would it mean if she had felt something—and did again? She didn't need to add a man or sex into the mix with everything else she was dealing with. It would only complicate an already thorny situation.

"Elodie?"

Bloody hell. Even her name on his lips sounded pretty. She stirred herself to force a smile. "I'm fine."

"You doona look it."

She folded her hands in her lap and shrugged. "I will be. As soon as I finish here and leave."

"You returning to Edinburgh?"

"I don't know where I'm going." She hadn't felt as if she belonged anywhere for fifteen years. She might have lived in some beautiful places, but the shiny newness of it wore off quickly, and she was soon back to trying to make a life in a place that felt as foreign to her as going through life without magic.

Scott leaned forward and propped his forearms on his knees. "No' everyone on Skye holds a grudge. There are those who would welcome you."

"Like you?" she asked with a grin.

He glanced down, chuckling. "Aye. I like it here. A lot."

"It's your first time on Skye?"

"I'm sad to admit that it is," he replied.

She shrugged. "Then stay. If you can handle everyone being in your business, you would enjoy the Druid community."

"I like the idea of such a society. We only have a small one in Edinburgh. I wish you would've found us while you lived there."

Elodie regretted turning their conversation to the Druids. She wouldn't tell him that she had lost her magic, but she also didn't want to lie. If she wanted to prevent questions, then she *had* to lie.

As if sensing they had turned to a topic she didn't want, Scott asked, "Does your sister know how you feel about the bedroom?"

"She knows. She offered to clean it."

"You're no' going to let her, are you?"

Elodie found herself smiling as she met his gaze. "Is it that obvious? My father always said my pride would get in my way."

"I doona think it's pride. Perhaps think of it as your way of tackling the past. It's one of various ways. Maybe you do it. Maybe you doona. I think returning to the cottage—and sleeping here—was a bigger step than going into their room."

She didn't know why Scott was being so kind. It could be just who he was, but she wasn't that trusting anymore.

"Do you want me to tell you what it looks like?" he asked.

Elodie twisted her lips as she shook her head. "I know it was scrubbed once the police came and took Mum away. Corann and his deputies arrived after that and cleaned the bedroom again. They told Edie and me that everything was fine, but there's a mark on this house now. Not exactly evil, but... I don't know how to describe it."

"Dark."

"Yes. That's it. The cottage has a dark feel to it. Someone took a life here. I don't think any amount of cleaning or magic can get rid of such a thing."

Scott shrugged as he leaned back. "I doona know. I think laughter, love, and happiness could do it. You said your family was content here once."

"I viewed things through the eyes of a child. As I got older, I went back through some memories and remembered how often Da and Elias fought. Mum kept telling Elias to leave things alone. I think my brother knew what was happening."

A frown furrowed Scott's brow, but he didn't ask the question she knew burned on his tongue.

Elodie glanced at Filip to see him still sleeping. His snores were low, his mouth open, and his head tilted at an angle that would likely give him a neckache by the time he woke. She returned her attention to Scott. She wasn't sure why she'd told him that last part. She didn't discuss her father's murder with anyone—not even her sister.

And yet, she suddenly wanted to tell someone. Well, not just anyone. She wanted to tell Scott.

"He beat her." The words came out in a rush. Elodie closed her eyes as a flurry of emotion filled her. "He beat her." She repeated the words, her eyes burning as she thought of how her mother had suffered. "And I never knew. Edie never knew."

"But your brother did."

Elodie nodded and peeled open her eyes. She blinked to hold back the sudden tears. "Mum could've used magic to stop Da from hurting her. She could've shown him that she was stronger, but she didn't."

"Because she loved him."

"That wasn't enough in the end. She endured years of it and then one day lost it? Mum was like Edie. Compassionate, tolerant, and generous to a fault."

Scott was silent for a long moment. Then, "Something must have happened to push your mother that day."

"Enough to kill him?" Elodie shook her head. "I can understand hurting him. Even kicking him out and divorcing him—her family never liked Da anyway. But to kill him? To destroy our family in such a way that I lost both parents that day?"

Scott gave her a sad smile. "Have you asked her?"

"I've not spoken to her since the police took her away."

"You know your mum. You speak about her as being kind and bighearted. I also imagine she was the type of mother who would protect her children above everything. Including herself."

Elodie stared at him as a cold chill spread through her body. "What?"

"Am I right? Would she have given her life to protect you and your siblings?"

She nodded. "Absolutely."

Scott held her gaze without replying. Elodie's mind frantically searched her memories. "Da never laid a hand on either of us girls. I never saw him touch Elias either."

"You said they argued."

"Aye. I argued with him, too."

"The same way as your brother?"

Elodie's chest grew tight. "No."

"How much older is Elias?"

"There are three years between him and Edie. Four between him and me."

Scott shrugged again.

Elodie struggled to breathe. "Are you saying that…?" She couldn't even get the words out.

"That your brother was home at times when you and Edie were no'? That he and your father might have had a row? That maybe your father hit him? It could be all of that. It could be none of it."

Elodie wasn't a mother. She couldn't say if that had caused her mum to snap that day or not. But she knew someone she could ask—Edie.

"Have you asked your brother about it?"

Scott's voice dragged her back to the present. "I've not spoken to Elias in years. I know he checks in with Edie, but he's never reached out to me."

"You've no' reached out to him either."

"You're not pulling any punches, are you?" she said in a harsher tone than intended.

Scott's lips twisted. "I told you there are other ways to face the past. I get the feeling you doona talk about this much."

"Never."

"Sometimes, getting it out makes all the difference. I'm looking at things from a perspective you've no'. I wasna there. It isna my family."

She nodded. "You've made some valid points. I never would've thought about some of the things you've pointed out."

"Do you want to let go of the past?"

"I don't think we can ever fully let go. What happens in the past shapes and defines us. What I want is to no longer feel as if the past controls me."

Scott shot her a bright smile. "You'll get there."

"How can you say that with such certainty?"

"Because I see you."

He said it with such honesty that she was at a loss for words.

"I see your pain," he continued, his gaze boring into hers. "You do a valiant job of hiding it, but it's there. It's difficult to miss. I doona blame you. I'm certain I'd be weighed down by such a past, too. Yet it sounds like you're ready to move on. Maybe that's why you're back."

"You make it sound easy."

Scott snorted, his lips curving into a grin. "It willna be."

She looked at Filip. "He's struggling, too."

"Aye. Kevin's murder weighs on him."

"Tell me about it. All of it. Please."

"Kevin was murdered because he was a Druid."

Her brow puckered. "You're serious."

"As I said, there's a small community of Druids in Edinburgh. And some who doona want us there—they doona want any Druids."

"And you think that's why Kevin was killed?"

"We know it."

"How?" she asked with a shake of her head.

Scott looked at the fire and then swallowed. He paused before saying, "There was a message left with the body. The same one that has been left with every Druid—*mie* or *drough*—killed." He looked at her, his blue eyes blazing with anger. "*Bàs ort*. Death to you."

CHAPTER THIRTEEN

SKYE DRUIDS

The storm was perfect. It lashed the island with such fierceness that Kerry couldn't stop smiling. She had never delved into her magic in such a way before.

And it felt good.

Really good.

Her entire life had been that of the dutiful Druid, doing what her parents wanted. Making sure she excelled with her magic to catch Corann's attention. Her parents had had such high hopes for her. They had been devastated when she couldn't catch a man's eye to keep her family's line going. No child should hear from their parents the things they had said to her.

Her mother had blamed it on the fact that Kerry liked food. But she hadn't realized that with every verbal insult and emotional sting, Kerry had found solace in food. And the more weight she gained, the more her mother berated her. That didn't stop until her mother's memory began to fade with dementia.

And still, Kerry took care of her.

If Kerry couldn't find love, she found enjoyment in magic. She sought comfort in the Druid community on Skye. She was friendly with everyone, but she rarely had close friends. That was because she had trust issues. Corann had been working on that with her for decades—without much success.

But no one in her quadrant seemed to know or care. They came to her often with their problems and whatever crises arose. Knowing that they trusted her with such private information healed the many wounds of Kerry's soul.

Then Rhona had upended her world without a second's hesitation.

"She's not worthy of ruling the Druids of Skye."

Kerry closed her eyes as the Ancient's voice filled her head. There were no drums, but that didn't matter. The Ancient had told her that she was special because she could hear only one voice. No one had ever told Kerry that before. It was a peculiar feeling that she never wanted to end—and feared it would any second.

She walked to the door and opened it to look out at the storm. The roar of the rain was music to her ears, the lightning a visual show that sent chills over her skin.

"Rhona would never dare do this."

"Never. Feel the power running through you!"

Kerry closed her eyes. The magic charged through her at an alarming rate. No more being the good Druid. No more doing what was expected. She was finally throwing off that mantle and being who she was meant to be.

"Yes!" the Ancient shouted. *"Take the power you've always had. Let it consume you."*

Kerry's body shook with the force of the magic. She swayed but stayed on her feet. Thunder rumbled, and the ground quivered in reply. She thought about being stripped of her title as deputy because of the emails to the Fae Others. Though she'd sworn to Rhona that the emails had all been lies, in her heart, she finally accepted that she had believed every word.

If the Skye Druids were to remain relevant and powerful, they needed to take command of all Druids and put things back in order. Their numbers were fading at an alarming rate. Not to mention those born with magic that had no idea they were Druids because the family had turned away from their communities long ago.

Druids—all Druids, be they *mie* or *drough*—needed somewhere to live safely and peacefully. A place that no one, not even the Dragon Kings, would dare disrupt. That was what Skye had originally been. It was what it needed to return to.

And she would be the one to bring that about.

"Your name will be immortalized for thousands of generations to come," the Ancient said. *"This mission falls to you. None other has listened to us. It's why we've come to you."*

Kerry opened her eyes and smiled. "I won't fail you or the Druids. I see now that everything has led me to this moment. I know what I must do."

"We've shown you how to grow your magic. Use it."

The road ahead of Kerry would be hard, but there was no other choice. The future of the Druids rested on her shoulders.

Maybe it was good that she wasn't a deputy any longer. This way, no one would be scrutinizing every move she made. Oh, she wasn't foolish enough to think that she wasn't being watched, but she knew how to be careful.

Besides, if Rhona or Balladyn had even a hint she was responsible for the storm, they would have her back in the Druid prison in the Red Hills. The fact that she was still walking around proved that they didn't suspect her. Then again, they had other worries, like the Druid's death.

Kerry smiled as she poured more magic into the storm.

"By all that's magical," Rhona whispered as she stared at the Druid lying unmoving on her bed. The woman was on her back with her head at an odd angle, and her arms to the sides. Her mouth was open as if something had been stuffed down it. But the worst part was her throat. It had been torn open, seemingly from the inside.

Balladyn stood beside her, his fury rolling off him. "This wasn't natural," he murmured in his Irish accent.

"This was magic." Bloody hell. Rhona briefly closed her eyes. After their victory against the Fae Others, she'd thought she would have a few months of peace. The dead Druid said otherwise.

"Aye." Balladyn drew in a breath and slowly released it. "We don't have much time before the authorities return."

She glanced at him. "The Detective Inspector is one of us. Theo will give us whatever time we need."

"Rhona?"

She turned at the sound of Theo's voice. A moment later, he appeared in the doorway of the bedroom. He glanced at the bed, and his face tightened with anger. "DI Theo Frasier, this is Balladyn. Balladyn, Theo."

Theo inclined his head of short dark hair to Balladyn. "Wished we could've met under different circumstances."

"Agreed," Balladyn said as he crossed his arms over his chest. "Do you have any suspects?"

Theo's brown eyes cut to the Druid once again. "Nothing. No forced entry. No fingerprints anywhere. If it were no' for that, I would say she knew her attacker. The death was violent. Whatever happened to her, it didna just suffocate her. It ravaged her."

"Just her throat?" Balladyn asked.

Theo walked to the bed and threw back the covers to show the body otherwise unharmed. "Until there's a full autopsy, we will no' know for sure."

Rhona was once again thankful there were Druids in all positions on the isle. There had to be. Otherwise, it would be damn difficult to keep who they were a secret. Not many of those without magic who called Skye home didn't already know. There had always been rumors about them, but most had no idea what being a Druid really meant. It wasn't about sacrifices or any of the other wrong things posted on the internet.

"Someone wanted her to suffer," Rhona said.

Balladyn grunted. "That much is obvious. What isn't, is why she was killed."

"I'm working on that," Theo said. "Hopefully, we'll know

soon if she had an ex-lover or someone who held a grudge."

Rhona shook her head. "This wasn't about just a grudge."

"What do you mean?" Balladyn asked.

Rhona pointed at the victim. "Someone wanted to make a statement. Knowing we'd figure it out, they went after a Druid with magic."

"You think this is about the previous issue?" Theo asked.

The previous issue being that half the Druids on Skye wanted things to stay as they were, and the other half wanted to carve a new path, which included forming a group of Druid Others. "Maybe. I recognize her, but I can't place her or think of her name. I need to speak to my deputy in this region, Roy. He'll be able to tell me which side she fell on."

"I thought that was settled," Theo said with a frown.

Balladyn raised a brow as he looked at the DI. "We'd hoped there would be a lull and some peace, but apparently that isn't going to happen."

A chill consumed Rhona as she listened to the raging storm outside. She might have worried about Corann naming her to replace him, but she'd not only accepted her position, she believed in it now. Balladyn was the Warden, and she was the leader of the Skye Druids. Together, their magic flowed freely from one to the other in an unprecedented fusing of power. A Reaper and a Druid.

They had shown the Fae Others that Skye couldn't be taken. That hadn't been enough to stave off whoever was causing trouble now, though.

"Will there be more deaths?" Theo asked, his tone troubled.

Rhona swung her gaze to the DI. "Not if I have any say

in it."

Balladyn looked at the window as lightning flashed behind the closed curtains. "Is anyone on Skye powerful enough to create such a storm?"

"No' that I'm aware," Theo said.

Her mind raced through the Druids who had the potential. "Some of us like to tout our strengths and magic, while others are more subdued."

"Meaning, you've no idea." Balladyn's frown deepened.

The house rattled with a boom of thunder. Rhona didn't like the feel of it. "What makes you think this storm is magical?"

"Can you not feel it?" Balladyn turned from her and walked to the window. He threw open the curtains so he could see through the glass. "It has been going for a few hours now. No lull, no movement."

"As if it's parked over us," Theo said, his lips flattening.

Rhona fisted her hands. "Bloody hell. What is happening on Skye?"

"We'd better find out quickly," Balladyn said as he looked at her over his shoulder.

Rhona looked at the dead woman once again. "Theo, I usually let you do what you do. But this time, I'd like to work concurrent investigations."

"Corann did that all the time. Do what you need. I'd rather no' have more of us killed," Theo told her.

Balladyn snapped the curtains closed again. He walked to Rhona and held out his hand. She took it, and they were back at her cottage in the next instant. With no eyes watching her, she sank onto the sofa and dropped her head into her hands.

"Did we do this?" she asked. "Did us standing up against the Fae Others cause this?"

The cushion dipped as Balladyn sat beside her. He rested a hand on her back and played with the ends of her hair. "The Reapers had known a shift was happening within the Fae for some time. Erith wanted to find the answer. Sadly, we did."

"The Fae Others."

"Aye. I feel another shift."

Rhona lifted her head and turned toward Balladyn. "You think this is the Fae messing with us again?"

"It could be," he said, his red-ringed silver eyes watching her carefully.

Her stomach clenched. "But you think it's Druids."

Balladyn shrugged. "I'm not saying a Fae *wouldn't* go to such extremes to harm a Druid, but that really isn't our style."

"It is, however, something a human would do." She sat back and sighed. "I'd hoped I'd never have to investigate anyone on Skye again. What happened with Kerry was…"

Balladyn nodded as he rested his hand atop hers. "I know."

"It was only with the help of the Warriors and Druids from MacLeod Castle that we even discovered what Kerry had done. The others' reaction to her hasn't exactly been…kind."

"She did it to herself."

"I know. It's difficult to wrap my head around the fact that someone I trusted so deeply betrayed me and our people. Now, we have to hunt someone else on Skye. I have a feeling this will be worse. It won't just be removing someone from their position this time."

Balladyn drew her to his side and pressed a kiss to her temple. "You're not doing it alone."

She leaned against him fully. What was happening to her island? To her people? The more pressing question was: Could they return to who the Druids had always been?

Rhona pulled out her mobile and dialed Roy. She would rather see him in person, and while he would never turn her away, he liked his solitude. Rhona only went to see him when she had to.

"Hello?" he answered on the second ring.

"Hi, Roy. I have a question."

"Her name was Rebecca Miller," he said.

Rhona closed her eyes. Of course, Roy would know why she'd called.

"If you're calling, that means she was killed with magic."

"Tell me about her," Rhona urged.

"Rebecca was all about our traditions," he said after a brief pause. "Her family has been on Skye for several generations."

"What about any enemies?"

Roy made an indiscernible sound. "No one I can point to who might wish to take her life."

"I still need any names you have."

"I'll get them to you immediately."

Rhona sat up and opened her eyes. "Thank you. And send them to Theo, as well."

"Will do. Do we need to be concerned?"

She wanted to tell him no but she couldn't. "Every Druid needs to be on alert. Please get the word out to your people. I'm alerting the other deputies as soon as we finish."

"Is there any indication that this was an isolated event?"

"We're not taking any chances," she said and met Balladyn's gaze.

CHAPTER FOURTEEN

SKYE DRUIDS

Scott stared at his dry clothes still hanging in Elodie's cottage. He quietly drank some water as he considered his next move. The storm let up occasionally for a moment before it seemed to renew to batter the island again.

Filip continued sleeping deeply. After their talk, Elodie had seemed to sink into her thoughts, and then she also fell asleep. Scott had remained awake for the last two hours as he listened to the rain lashing the house. His mind went to Elodie's parents. When Filip had told him that Elodie's mother had killed her father, he hadn't imagined the actual circumstances. He doubted many on Skye knew them—or even cared. However, there were always those who loved to gossip—and the more scandalous, the better.

Nothing was more shocking than a woman murdering her husband.

Scott knew he should probably wake Filip so they could

leave, but he didn't want to. He was on Skye to get close to Elodie. What better way than being stuck with her during a thunderstorm?

He finished his water and soundlessly returned to the front room. He'd placed a blanket over Elodie and one on Filip. They both slept like the dead. It was no wonder with Filip. Scott had heard him up all hours of the night. Most likely because of Kevin's death and their return to Skye. The same could be said for Elodie, except her nightmares were probably worse. Scott couldn't believe she had decided to stay in the cottage. He certainly wouldn't have. If there were ever any doubt about her courage, Elodie had proven its existence by staying at the house.

Scott found his gaze lingering on her face. His mission was to gain her trust and turn her to their side by any means necessary. He was adept at doing just that. There was no room for failure. He'd never hesitated to do what he had to do. He kept his focus on the big picture.

Yet he didn't want to use his usual words and platitudes with her. He didn't want to pour on the magical charm. He didn't want to lie and coax. He wanted to tell Elodie everything.

And if he did, he knew what her answer would be.

So, he remained with his thoughts, mulling over her past, the pain in her eyes, and the steel of her spine. She was clearly a private person. He'd deduced that early on, even before Filip had told him she likely wouldn't open up about her past. Then, somehow, she had. He hadn't even charmed her. He didn't know why his customary words had felt like acid on his lips.

He only knew that he hadn't been able to be anything but himself.

Which was a dangerous thing.

Everyone had a past. He was no exception. He kept everyone at a safe distance and allowed very few to get close to him. And never, ever a woman. To fall in love was the greatest gift of all. But it also set a person up for the ultimate betrayal.

He sighed and walked farther into the room. Scott added another log to the fire and stirred the coals. He remained quiet to allow Elodie and Filip to rest. Both clearly needed it. He then made his way to a window and gazed out at the dark sky. If he didn't know it was two in the afternoon, he would think it was night. The more he watched the storm, the more he suspected it wasn't natural. Which led him to wonder who had created it. And why.

On an island of Druids—the most powerful of them—there were many potential responses to his questions. And he didn't like any of them.

Scott was used to Druids hiding their power, not actively showcasing it. Then again, given what Filip had told him about Skye and the community here, this display didn't seem to be something the Druids did. That led to him thinking about the Druid who had been murdered the night before, as well as those lives taken in Edinburgh. But Edinburgh wasn't the only city affected. It was happening everywhere.

That's why the answer was Skye. He would've gone to Rhona directly since she led the Druids here, but George had been adamant that it had to be Elodie. She hadn't explained why, even when Scott had asked. Maybe he should've pushed harder.

He walked to his chair and sat. He hoped that the murder on Skye the previous night had been an anomaly and not something that had followed him and Filip from the city. Though perhaps that wasn't a bad thing. If the same being were slaughtering Druids, it would meet its match in those on Skye.

Scott's eyes began to grow heavy. The sound of the rain and the warm room were lulling him to sleep. Scott blinked and adjusted himself in his seat. He needed to stay awake— just in case. He didn't suspect anyone of trying to harm Elodie, but he wouldn't take the chance when she was the answer to their problems.

The next time they spoke, he would turn the discussion to magic. He was curious to know what she could do. It had to be something extraordinary for George to single her out. Scott was thankful that he and Filip had gotten to Elodie before anyone else had. At least he thought they had. For all he knew, she could be working for the other side.

His gaze landed on her face again. He didn't want to notice how beautiful she was, but it was impossible not to. The walls she kept erected around her were thick and strong. Ones that no one would be able to breach unless she allowed it. The cottage unnerved her. He imagined that might have been the reason she'd opened up to him. Whatever the motivation, he was glad.

Suddenly, a loud bang and crash sounded at the back of the cottage. Scott jumped to his feet. It had seemed as if it'd come

from her parents' room. He listened for more, but there were
only the moans of the wind, the spatter of rain on the
windows, and the pop of the fire.

Scott glanced at Filip to see him also on his feet, his face
pale. Scott turned to the other side and looked at Elodie on the
sofa. Her eyes were open and wide.

"What was that?" Filip whispered.

Scott shrugged and started toward the doorway. "Stay
here. I'll be back."

"Don't," Elodie ordered.

He paused and looked at her, frowning. "Don't what?"

"Don't go back there." She clutched the throw in her lap.

Filip cleared his throat. "Do you often hear things?"

"No," she replied in a soft voice.

Scott met Filip's gaze. "All the more reason for me to
check it out."

"I...don't think it's a good idea," Elodie said again.

Scott turned toward her. "Why?"

"I don't know. Just a feeling."

That made him pause. Was her magic warning her?
Perhaps he should listen. Then he remembered all the dead
Druids. If someone had come to Skye for him, Filip, or Elodie,
they were in for a fight. He looked at Filip. "Be ready."

"Aye," Filip said with a nod.

Scott gathered his magic to him and slowly walked
through the house, his ears straining. The electricity blinked
once, twice, and then went out altogether. He stilled and let his
eyes adjust to the darkness. The house was unfamiliar to him,
but it was a simple layout. He saw it in his head, mapping it all
out so he knew which way to go.

The kitchen looked undisturbed. No one was waiting for him unless they were in the fridge. He glanced behind him, seeing the glow of the fire from the living area. Scott continued moving through the house. He came to the bathroom first. It didn't take long to look in there. The window was intact, and nothing had fallen off any shelves. He then moved to Elias's room. Again, everything looked in order, and no one was hiding there. He walked back into the hallway and to Elodie's room. Same as the previous rooms. Which left the parents' room.

Scott silently walked to the door. He looked at the knob and reached for it. The handle was cold against his skin. He gradually twisted until it unlatched. Scott pushed it open slightly and slid into the room. Wind and rain lashed him from the broken window, a limb as thick as his thigh and the length of his body stuck through it.

There was glass and debris everywhere. Scott picked his way to the limb to toss it back out the window. As soon as he touched it, something dark and unpleasant enveloped him. He jerked back, looking at his hands. This wasn't just some stray tree limb that had landed in this room. Someone had sent it.

Scott set his mouth and spun on his heel. He spent a few moments checking the room to make sure nothing else had entered the house other than the limb. Then he returned to Filip and Elodie.

"What is it?" she asked.

He ignored her and looked at Filip. "I need you to seal the window in the back room to stop the rain from entering. Don't touch anything."

"Okay," Filip replied and started past him.

Scott grabbed him. "Don't touch *anything*."

"I heard you," Filip replied.

He released Filip, then turned to Elodie.

She had gotten to her feet. "What is it?"

Scott didn't want to tell her. He wanted to lie and say it was just a stray limb, but she needed to be prepared. "Is the cottage warded?"

"I... Mum did that long ago."

"But no' since?" he pressed.

She shrugged. "Edie might have. I don't know for certain."

"You need to ward it then."

"Why?" she demanded.

Scott sighed. She would learn of it eventually. "Someone sent a tree limb through the window of your parents' room."

Elodie frowned. "Why do you say *someone*?"

"Because there's *drough* magic on it."

Her lips parted in shock. "Why?"

"I doona know. Yet. But I'm going to find out. Just like I want to know who created this storm."

Elodie's head swung to the window. "It might be better if you and Filip left."

"Someone is coming after you. We're no' going anywhere."

Filip stumbled around the corner of the doorway. "Bloody hell."

Scott and Elodie rushed to him and helped Filip to a chair.

"The window is sealed, but there's a lot of water damage," he muttered to Elodie.

She waved away his words. "Rest."

Filip grabbed her hand to stop her when she started to move off. "Who have you spoken to since you've been back?"

"Very few. I rarely leave because of the welcome I usually receive," Elodie answered.

Scott caught her gaze. "What about the woman at the pub? Did you two exchange words?"

"I've found that's never helpful." Elodie gently pulled her arm away from Filip. "Why? Do you think Anna is responsible?"

"Someone wanted to hurt you," Filip said.

Scott looked from Filip to Elodie. "We're no' leaving."

"You can't watch me forever," she said.

Filip snorted. "After what happened to my brother and the Druid last night, we most certainly can."

"Come on," Scott told Elodie. "I'll help you ward the house while Filip rests."

She hesitated but eventually followed him.

"Do you have some candles? We should light some until the power returns."

"Sure," she said in a small voice.

He glanced at her, but she was already in the shadows so he couldn't see her face. He used his mobile as a flashlight to help her get the candles. Once they were lit and set around the house, he went to the front door. He put away his mobile and began spelling the doors to keep out anyone who might want to harm Elodie, when he happened to look behind him.

Scott didn't think anything of not seeing Elodie. She must have gone to the back door or the windows. But as he moved through the cottage, he realized that nothing had been warded.

He found her on the bed in her room. She had her legs pulled up to her chest as she stared solemnly at the wall opposite her.

"What is it?" he asked.

There was a lengthy pause before she looked at him and said, "I can't."

"You can no' what?"

"Do magic."

CHAPTER FIFTEEN

SKYE DRUIDS

Elodie wanted to take back the words, but she couldn't. Scott would've found out anyway. Still, that didn't make the truth any easier to swallow.

"Stay here," he told her and walked out.

Elodie almost called him back. Was he leaving to tell all of Skye her dirty secret? Perhaps it was for the best. She was tired of carrying the burden. Tired of pretending to be something she wasn't.

What stung the worst was that she had been foolish enough to think Scott and Filip might actually help her. Elodie should've known that good things didn't happen to her. She looked down at her right hand, thinking again of the heat that had moved through her at Scott's touch. She had to fight to keep from staring at him. From running her fingers through his thick, dark hair.

From thinking things she had no right to fantasize about.

But it had been so long since she had felt those stirrings

deep inside her. The temptation to see if there was more and if Scott could make her feel *something* was too enticing to resist.

Elodie bit her lip as she thought about how quiet the cottage would be when he and Filip left. She'd thought she wanted solitude. Then Scott's smile and seductive voice had her sharing things about her past that she had never told anyone. Things that would no doubt make the rounds on Skye soon—secrets never lasted long on the island.

Scott suddenly returned to her room, startling her. He didn't spare her a glance as he went to the window and held up his hands as he chanted a warding spell. It hurt her heart to see him doing magic that she had taken for granted. She couldn't take her eyes from him.

When he finished, he lowered his arms and looked at her. "Filip and I have made sure the house is protected."

"Thank you." It had taken everything she had to stay in the cottage. Now, she didn't want to leave.

Scott drew in a long breath and released it. "Do you want to talk about it?"

She didn't have to ask him what he was referring to. "Not really, but the truth will come out eventually. I can't hide it anymore. I've been careful about what I've said around Edie. We haven't really discussed magic, so I haven't had to say anything to her. Yet."

"Your sister doesna know?" Scott asked with a frown.

Elodie met his gaze and looked away. "It's not exactly easy to talk about."

"But you had magic before?"

"I did. I didn't heed the warnings not to use it frivolously.

Instead, I used it for everything. Small things. Big things. Stupid things. Needless things."

Scott leaned back against the chest of drawers. "How long has it been gone?"

"For so long that it's a distant memory." Finally, she looked at him.

"Bloody hell," he murmured.

She twisted her lips. "Exactly."

"Did it go all at once?"

"No. It was gradual. I didn't notice it at first. Spells that had once been easy took more concentration. Then, sometimes, they wouldn't work at all. Until one day, it was gone for good."

Scott's lips pinched together as worry clouded his face.

Elodie wanted to believe he was troubled about her, but they barely knew each other. This was something else entirely. She wanted to ask about his thoughts, but he likely wouldn't tell her. Not now. She would discover what it was, though.

"Have you tried using magic since you returned to Skye?" he asked.

"There are only so many times a person can attempt something before it becomes too painful to even consider."

"But…this is Skye. Your home. The isle of the most powerful Druids in the world," he argued.

Elodie shrugged one shoulder. "I think I'm better off without it, honestly. I did some careless, selfish things with my magic. This is my penance."

"I doona believe that."

"You weren't here. The anger you saw at the pub? They have every right to their feelings."

He snorted and shook his head. "Maybe if it had just
happened, but that was over fifteen years ago. It's time
everyone moved on. Including you."

"I've been trying."

"No' while on Skye."

She cocked her head to the side. "What is your fascination
with the island?"

"You grew up here, so you can no' possibly know how
other Druids dream of it."

Elodie let her knees fall apart to sit cross-legged. "All
Druids are welcome. Skye was always meant as a refuge for
those with magic."

"I'm no' sure other Druids know that."

"Then let them know."

He eyes grew intense. "You should try magic again. One
more time while you're here."

"I can't. If I'm unable to do it… I'm at the end of my rope.
It would likely end me."

Scott's lips softened. "You wouldna have to do it alone. I'd
be there. So would Filip. I know your sister would, too."

The offer was appealing. More than it should be. She had
thought about her magic a lot in the long hours of the night
when she hadn't been able to sleep. She'd almost tried the first
spell she had ever learned so many times, but she'd chickened
out at the last minute every time. She hadn't lied to Scott. If
she couldn't do it, if the magic didn't return, she would have
nothing.

"Filip spoke about how Corann and his deputies took each
of you to a place where the magic filled you. Where's yours?"

Elodie debated whether to tell him. She knew what he

would want next, and she wasn't sure she could give it to him. And yet, she told him anyway. "The beach."

"You've no' gone, have you?"

"No," she answered in a whisper.

Footsteps sounded down the hall. A moment later, Filip's voice reached them right before he peered around the doorway to her room. "Um…guys? I think we should contact Rhona about the limb."

"I agree," Scott said.

Elodie wanted to argue, but if it was *drough* magic, Rhona needed to know. Skye had a few *droughs* but they kept to themselves and didn't bother anyone. It was why Corann— and now Rhona—allowed them to stay.

"Both of you really think someone sent that limb here?" she asked.

Filip quirked a brow. "It's obvious."

"Aye," Scott said.

She glanced at the window. "There are other houses around. Maybe the magic missed its mark, especially with the storm."

"A magical storm," Fillip added.

Scott caught her gaze. "Rhona needs to know whether it was meant for you or someone else. The magic used on that limb is serious."

The more Elodie thought about it, the more she knew that Scott and Filip were right. However, it would mean telling Rhona about her magic. She really didn't want to do that. She would've preferred that no one knew—too late for that now.

Elodie pulled out her phone and dialed the number she had gotten from her sister. It rang only once before Rhona answered. "It's Elodie," she said. "I think you might need to come to the cottage."

"Are you hurt?" Rhona asked.

"No."

"We'll be right there."

Filip jumped when someone cleared their throat behind him. Filip swallowed heavily and looked at Elodie as he stepped to the side. "Rhona and Balladyn are here."

Elodie's gaze slid to Scott. He shot her a smile that was probably meant to comfort her, but nothing could make this any better. The three of them went to the kitchen where the couple waited in the pale light of two candles. That quickly changed when Balladyn snapped his fingers, and a ball of light suddenly appeared over them, so bright it was like the electricity had returned.

Rhona searched her face. "You warded the cottage heavily. Tell me what happened."

Elodie didn't want to take credit for the wards, but there was no point in stating that now. It would come out eventually.

"It might be better if we show you," Scott said.

Balladyn's gaze locked on him. "And you are?"

"Scott Ryan," he told them. "I'm from Edinburgh."

"He was good friends with Kevin. Scott came with me to help with…things," Filip added.

Rhona watched Scott for a few moments. "Is this your first time on Skye?"

"It is," he admitted. "It's a beautiful place."

The tension in the room became a little awkward. Rhona seemed to accept Scott, but Balladyn didn't appear as willing. Elodie's heart thudded in her chest. The friction she felt was likely due to what was coming. She felt like a young girl about to be reprimanded by her parents.

As if sensing her discomfort, Rhona's gaze slid to her. "Why don't you show us now?"

Elodie glanced at her parents' door. This couldn't be the first time she walked into the room. Not with so many eyes on her.

"Follow me," Scott said and started down the hall.

Elodie shot him a grateful smile as Rhona and then Balladyn moved past her. Filip paused beside her a moment. He winked before following the group. Elodie didn't budge from her spot. She heard Scott showing them the limb and then Rhona's outrage at the *drough* magic. While neither Scott nor Filip had been able to remove the thick limb, Rhona did it easily. Balladyn then repaired the damage.

All too soon, they were back in the kitchen with Elodie.

"I'm glad you called," Rhona said. "I have to agree with Scott and Filip. That limb was meant for the cottage."

Elodie crossed her arms over her chest, feeling cold and hollow. "A place that has been empty for years. Until I returned."

"I admit, it's been long enough for people to forget and move on. Sadly, some of them like their grudges." Rhona's lips flattened. "The fact that this is *drough* magic makes it easier to track down who might have sent it."

Scott stood beside Elodie. "If they live here, you mean. What about someone visiting?"

"What are you not saying?" Balladyn demanded in a calm voice that didn't match the fierceness of his gaze.

Filip glanced at the floor. "Kevin was murdered in Edinburgh. He isna the first Druid to be killed."

"And he willna be the last," Scott added.

Rhona looked between the two men before focusing on Filip. "Why do you think Kevin was murdered?"

"The message left with him. *Bàs ort*."

"Death to you," Rhona said with a frown.

Scott nodded. "It's the message that's been left with all the slain Druids."

The worried look that passed between Balladyn and Rhona concerned Elodie. "Surely, no one would dare come to Skye and try such a thing."

"A lot has changed," Rhona said with a hint of anger.

Scott jerked his chin outside. "This storm isna natural."

"We're aware," Balladyn replied.

Rhona's lips compressed. "And we're working on it."

"There's a chance Elodie has been targeted," Scott continued. "Whether it's about her past or what we've been dealing with in the city, I'm no' certain."

Rhona tucked her long, red hair behind an ear as she swung her gaze to Filip. "Were you going to tell me about your brother? About what's happening in Edinburgh?"

"Aye," Filip replied.

Balladyn's brows drew together. "How many Druids were killed in Edinburgh?"

"Six in the last five weeks," Filip answered.

Rhona shook her head. "Why that city?"

"It isna just Edinburgh," Scott said.

Rhona pinched the bridge of her nose and sighed, then

looked at Elodie. "Perhaps it might be best if you stayed with Edie."

"If someone is after me, I'm not endangering my niece and nephew," she said.

Rhona didn't look pleased with that announcement, but she accepted it. "Balladyn and I can add wards to the cottage."

"Thanks. I did want to talk to you ab—" Elodie started. It was time to get the truth out.

But Scott spoke over her. "She would appreciate that."

Elodie parted her lips to argue, but he quickly shook his head. Since Elodie didn't want to share her secret, she took the opportunity and remained silent. But she knew she would have to tell Rhona sooner or later. It would never be easy to tell anyone that her magic was gone. Yet by remaining silent, she only made it more difficult on herself.

"No more Druids are dying on my watch," Rhona mumbled.

Elodie forgot all about her secret as she witnessed firsthand how Rhona and Balladyn shared their magic.

CHAPTER SIXTEEN

SKYE DRUIDS

Scott hadn't known what to expect upon meeting the Reaper. Balladyn was as imposing and forbidding as Scott had expected. But what Scott hadn't counted on was the protectiveness the Reaper had for Skye and its Druids.

Rhona had been just as impressive. Her green eyes flashed with intelligence and strength. She was in no way leaning on Balladyn—or the Reaper, her. They were, in fact, a team. The rumors he'd heard were obviously true. That could be something great for the Druids.

Or it could spell doom for everything that Scott and Filip were fighting for.

"Why did you stop me?" Elodie asked once Rhona and Balladyn had departed.

Scott met her light blue gaze. "You know why."

Thankfully, Elodie didn't say more. Scott could feel Filip's gaze. He half expected Filip to ask what was going on, but he didn't.

"No one will be able to harm you in the cottage now," Filip said. "Two of the most powerful beings on Skye have warded it. I'm no' too ashamed to admit that watching them was amazing."

Scott grinned. "Aye, it was." When he looked at Elodie, he saw she wasn't paying attention to them. Instead, she had gone to look out the kitchen window. He followed her. "What is it?"

"The rain is letting up."

"I'll be damned," Filip said as he listened. "She's right. Looks like Rhona and Balladyn took care of things."

Scott counted the seconds between the flash of lightning and the thunder. "It does sound as if the storm is moving off. Who can control weather?"

"No one that I know of," Filip said.

Elodie shrugged. "I didn't think any Druids could, but I've not been around in some time. A lot has changed on Skye."

Scott struggled with what to do. The one person George had said could help them didn't have magic. How was Elodie supposed to do anything without her power? Scott wouldn't give up so easily, though. If Elodie hadn't tried to do magic since returning, then he would nudge her in that direction. It couldn't hurt to try. It was his only option.

Well, that and telling George they needed to find someone else to help them. He wasn't ready to do that just yet, though.

Within fifteen minutes, the storm was all but gone. It took another five before the electricity returned. There was no reason for him and Filip to remain. A fact that soon became apparent to everyone.

"Thank you both for everything," Elodie said.

Scott wasn't done. He still had things he needed to talk to

her about. He glanced at Filip, but his friend was gathering his clothes to change, leaving Scott standing alone with Elodie. She searched his gaze, and he saw a hint of fear in her eyes. But he knew what she dreaded the most.

"I willna repeat your secret," he whispered.

Elodie's gaze slid away for a heartbeat. "It's going to come out eventually. I know you think my magic will return. That's why you didn't want me to tell Rhona."

"You've no' tried to do any magic while on Skye yet."

"Why do you care so much?"

Because you're the answer we've been searching for. Because Druids everywhere are counting on you. He didn't say either. It wasn't the time. "I just do. Is there something wrong with that?"

"I suppose not."

He smiled, giving her his sexiest grin and hating himself for using it on her. "I hope us staying and helping gives us a leg up on the competition to repair the cottage."

She laughed. It made him feel as if the sun's warm rays were shining on him. He only cared about getting her magic back so she could help them. That's all that mattered. Not her suffering. He didn't want to worry about her. To care.

But damn if he didn't.

"I'm going to talk to Edie about all of it tonight. I think it's safe to say that you do get lots of points for staying with me," she said, breaking into his thoughts.

"I doona want to think about what might've happened had you been alone." Scott hadn't meant to put a somber note on the conversation, but if she couldn't do magic, she never would've known the limb was spelled. It could've killed her because Elodie likely would've attempted to move it by hand. The magic would've sunk into her instantly. Scott didn't know if it had been meant to kill or harm, but it didn't matter. She had been targeted.

Her gaze was sincere as she said, "I'm glad I wasn't alone."

There was no longer a reason for Scott to dawdle. He gathered his now-dry clothes and changed. When he came out of the room, Filip and Elodie were reminiscing. As soon as they noticed him, Filip indicated the door.

"We're going to outstay our welcome," Filip said.

Elodie smiled at them. "I cannot thank either of you enough."

Filip waved and made his way to the door.

Scott hesitated beside her. "Stay safe."

"I will," she promised. "You, too."

He had the sudden urge to reach for her hand, to see if something passed between them again. Instead, he forced his feet to move forward and headed out of the house. He winced when she shut the door behind him, the bolt sliding into place.

"What the hell is going on?" Filip asked when Scott was inside the SUV.

Scott stared at the cottage. "What do you mean?"

"What did you want Elodie to keep from Rhona?"

Scott turned his head to Filip and lied. "A secret she's carrying. One that doesna matter to anyone but herself."

"And Elodie told you?" Filip asked in surprise.

Scott had already thought about how he would answer these questions. "The limb doused with *drough* magic frightened her. She knew she was disliked, but she wasn't prepared for any of this."

"Who would be?" Filip's lips twisted as he started the engine. "Whoever did that needs to be tracked down and punished."

"I've no doubt Balladyn and Rhona are doing just that."

"Like you, I doona think it's someone from Skye. That means an outsider came here. Do you think they followed us?"

Scott shrugged as Filip pulled out onto the road. "It's possible. We should check in with George and see how things are there."

"If the murderers came after us, then we need to prepare."

"We will."

"Nay. I mean, we need to get Elodie and return to Edinburgh immediately."

Scott agreed. Unfortunately, that wasn't going to happen. "Elodie needs time."

"Then we explain why she doesna have it. She's reasonable. She'll listen and understand."

He looked at Filip, who had his gaze locked on the wet road now littered with debris from the storm. "She's no' the same girl you knew. Life has changed her."

"No' that much."

"Are you the same as you were fifteen years ago?"

Filip made a sound in the back of his throat and threw Scott a wry look. "Nay."

"Then doona assume she is."

"We have to tell her. Everything. If we hadna been there, that limb…"

Scott nodded, turning his attention to the road. "I know. But we can no' be with her around the clock."

"She doesna need that. She's smart, and she was wicked quick with her magic. I'm sure she's only gotten better over time."

Scott needed to change the subject. "We might have shared a wee bit too much with Rhona and Balladyn."

"Fuck me," Filip said with a humorless laugh. "Balladyn's eyes seemed to see right through me. I swear, I was beginning to think he could read my mind."

"They need to know that Druids are in danger. But that's all we can share with them."

Filip shrugged as he turned the wheel to follow the road. "I doona know. They might join us."

"It would be great to have the Skye Druids join us, but I doubt that'll happen. Rhona has made her position on a Druid Others group perfectly clear. She has no reason to trust us. Balladyn less so. And there isna time to convince either of them."

"We may need them eventually."

Scott couldn't argue that point. "If it comes to that, we willna need to persuade them of anything. They'll have seen it with their own eyes. George has seen a way for things to end. And that means Elodie."

"Look, I know you and my brother were close friends—"

"The closest," Scott interjected. "He was like a brother to me."

Filip glanced at him. "He *was* my brother. That's why I'm going to tell you that I doona want you using Elodie. She's a survivor, but that doesna mean she's no' vulnerable. I know you have a way with people—especially women. She deserves more than lies and half-truths to earn her trust."

Scott should have been offended by Filip's words, but he wasn't. They were the truth. Lies came as easily to him as breathing. He didn't know why he had such a gift of charm, but he had used it to its full potential. He wasn't exactly proud of those skills, but they came in handy in difficult times.

Sadly, he had often used them just because he wanted to.

That had stopped when he met George, and he and Kevin had become friends. Scott had learned to use his talents for other means, ones that could benefit their organization and the Druids who needed it the most.

"You doona have to seduce her to get her to join us," Filip added.

Scott looked at Filip's profile, seeing the muscle jump in Filip's jaw. "I wouldna do such a thing."

"I've seen you do it."

"I willna with her. I give my word. You're right. She deserves better."

Filip visibly relaxed. "Thank you."

"I'm sorry you felt like you had to say that."

"It's just that I saw how you two were together. The protector act is working on her."

"It isna an act." The instant the words left his mouth, Scott wished he would've kept that to himself.

Filip looked his way again, holding his gaze a beat longer than last time. "She's no' in a good place."

"None of us is. The past has a hold of her, and we're fueled by revenge."

"Aye," Filip said softly.

Scott shifted in his seat, uncomfortable with the grief that began to rise. After they found Kevin, he had given himself only a few days to grieve his best friend. Once George had given Scott his mission, he had turned all his focus onto that. When he returned with Elodie, *then* he could return to his grief. There was no place for it here.

His mind immediately filled with thoughts of Elodie. While he had been with her, he hadn't thought of Kevin or the other murdered Druids. His thoughts had been consumed by her.

"We can do this," Filip said into the silence of the vehicle. "We have to do this."

Scott nodded and forced his lips into a smile. "Doona worry. We will succeed. I can assure you of that."

"I know. Kevin always said that you were the most trustworthy man he knew."

Scott's throat clogged with emotion.

CHAPTER SEVENTEEN

SKYE DRUIDS

Elodie tried not to fidget as she stood in her sister's kitchen. Edie and Trevor had remodeled the inside of the cottage for a more modern feel while keeping the charm of the exterior. Elodie couldn't imagine how much it had cost. Not a single space in the entire home had been left out. Standing in the house, no one would know that it was almost two hundred years old.

She watched Edie cooking dinner. Trevor cut vegetables and joked with the kids. Edie laughed at something they said and looked over at the trio. Trevor walked up to his wife and pressed his lips to hers for a lingering kiss while the kids rolled their eyes and made gagging noises.

Elodie felt her lips curving into a smile. The entire scene made her heart hurt. She was thrilled for Edie, but it also made her acutely aware of what she didn't have—and what she might never have.

"Da!" the eldest exclaimed.

Elodie laughed when she saw Trevor rubbing Edie's butt and whispering something in her ear that made Edie duck her head. The two were sweet, and while their children were grossed out now, they would look back on their parents' relationship one day and realize that was how people were meant to love.

The opposite of what her parents had shown her.

"Can I help it if your mother is the most beautiful woman I know?" Trevor said as he turned back to the kids. He shot Elodie a teasing grin.

This was only her second time with her sister's family, but they had opened their arms to her. Accepted her. It was such a unique and foreign feeling that Elodie was hesitant to dive into it—just in case they changed their minds. That's how fucked up she was. She knew her sister would never turn her back on her, but Edie's husband and children could.

"Can I borrow you?"

The voice startled Elodie, and she realized that Edie had spoken to her. Elodie made her way to the stove, and Edie handed her a wooden spoon.

"Stir that for me, please," Edie said.

Elodie did as requested and inhaled the fragrant sauce. "You do remember I'm not a great cook."

"What I remember is you saying you had better things to do than stand at a stove," Edie said with a laugh.

Elodie burst into laughter. "I did say that, didn't I?"

"Often."

They shared a look and a chuckle. It was good to think back on younger years and not have the dark cloud of *the incident* hanging over them. It was there—it always would be.

Yet neither of them was letting it affect them tonight. Elodie hadn't realized how much she'd needed this. Especially after what'd happened earlier at the cottage.

She didn't want to tell Edie about it, but she knew she had to. Later. After dinner, when they were alone. Elodie didn't want to spoil the happy atmosphere now. It was too precious and priceless to be interrupted so carelessly.

"You're going to tell me what's wrong," Edie whispered as she came up behind Elodie and dumped some seasoning into the sauce.

Elodie briefly met her sister's gaze. "I will. I promise."

"I'm not going to let you leave until you do."

Trevor came up then and said, "You may no' know this about your sister, Elodie, but she's stubborn."

"Oh, I know," Elodie said with a chuckle. "I have many examples of the times Edie dug her heels in on something."

Edie elbowed Trevor as she grinned at him. "I always have a good reason when I set my mind to something."

"Aye. You do, love," Trevor said and gave her another kiss.

Behind them, the kids made gagging noises again.

Elodie decided to join in. "Eww, you two. Get a room."

That made the kids bust into squeals of delight. Soon, everyone was laughing and teasing. If only it could've continued.

All too soon, the meal had been eaten, and the table cleared. The children were in the playroom while the adults had moved to the cozy sitting area with a fire roaring in the huge, original hearth. Elodie sipped the last of her wine as her sister reclined on the sofa, leaning against Trevor, who had his arm around Edie.

"You two have a lovely family," Elodie told them.

The corners of Trevor's hazel eyes crinkled as he smiled. "Thank you."

"We've worked hard for our lives here," Edie said. She turned to look at Trevor. "We're happy."

"Verra," he agreed, running a hand over the top of his thinning, light brown hair.

Elodie sat forward so she could pull out the quotes from her back pocket. She set aside her wine and unfolded the papers. "While cleaning the cottage, I found several places that require more extensive work than I can do."

"We were expecting that," Trevor said.

That made Elodie feel a little better. She smoothed out the papers on her lap. "I called some companies for quotes. We never spoke about that kind of work being done on the house, and I wasn't comfortable making any decisions on my own." *Because I have no way to pay*, but she didn't say that.

Edie reached for the papers with a smile. "I meant to tell you that I've set aside some money for that. There's just been so much going on. Do you have someone you liked above the others?"

"I do." Elodie handed the stack to her sister. "They came yesterday right before the storm hit. While they were there, they fixed an area at the back corner of the cottage to minimize future damage."

Trevor frowned. "How much did that cost you?"

"They did it free of charge."

Edie lifted her head from the quotes. "Who was it? I don't

know anyone who would do that kind of work without charging."

"Filip Gordan and his friend, Scott Ryan."

Trevor's face hardened. "You let someone who isna part of a business work on the house?"

Elodie fought the acrid retort on her lips. This was hers and Edie's cottage, not Trevor's. He didn't have a right to butt his nose into things. Then Elodie remembered that Edie and Trevor were footing the bill for the repairs. She kept her mouth closed, but she still didn't like the swift change in Trevor.

Edie put her hand on her husband's leg. No words passed between them, but whatever her sister meant, Trevor got because the tension in him melted away. "Filip's quick-thinking might have saved us more damage."

"I know it did." Elodie had the urge to stick out her tongue at Trevor. The reaction was so swift and uncharacteristically asinine that it shook her. All because Trevor questioned her.

But the more she thought about that, the angrier she became. She was a grown woman, capable of making decisions. If he doubted her, then why allow her to be there at all? And then she knew... Edie had pushed for it. Which meant the welcome Elodie had felt wasn't as genuine as she'd first thought. And that hurt. Deeply.

Elodie sat quietly as Edie and Trevor looked over the quotes and talked amongst themselves. Finally, Edie looked at her. "I had no idea there was that much damage."

It was on the tip of Elodie's tongue to say that's what happened when a home was left unattended, but she was as much to blame for that as her sister. Just because Edie lived on Skye didn't mean that everything fell to her.

"I was shocked, as well," Elodie replied.

Trevor sighed. "That's a lot more money than I anticipated handing over."

Handing over? Elodie once more fought not to lose her temper. She didn't know why everything Trevor said suddenly angered her. Besides, it wasn't just his money—it was Edie's, as well.

"How do you feel about Filip doing the work?" Edie asked her.

Elodie opened her mouth to answer when Trevor snorted loudly.

"They're no' a business. If there's a mistake, we'll likely be fighting with them for years to get it corrected. That's what always happens with people like that."

Elodie finally snapped. She locked her gaze on Trevor. "We've known Filip and his family for our entire lives. Filip's father was the one everyone called for repairs, and he taught Filip everything he knows."

"But you've no' been here for years," Trevor replied.

Something in his eyes and tone caused Elodie to want to get up and run out of the house. Was this the real Trevor? Or was this what he showed when it came time to discuss business—and more importantly, money? Elodie wasn't sure she wanted to know the answer.

"I never intended to use our money," Edie said to her husband. "I still have my savings from before. There's more than enough to cover this."

In other words, arsehole, we don't need your input.

Elodie was appalled at the words in her head. She desperately wanted to say them, but she didn't. Edie and Trevor had been kind to her since her arrival. The last thing she needed to do was cause problems between her sister and her husband just because Elodie was in a pissy mood.

It's lack of sleep. That had to be the reason. She didn't normally allow people to get under her skin the way Trevor had managed to do in such a short time.

Yet as she felt the tension mount between Edie and Trevor, Elodie grew uncomfortable. Then Trevor's gaze swung to her, and the hate she saw there was so swift that she second-guessed if she had actually seen it.

"Is that so?" Trevor replied in a cool tone.

Edie shifted to face him. "Like you said, it was more money than you intended to spend. This is for my family. There's no need to dip into our finances for that."

"You'll be getting repaid for that," he stated, his gaze locked on Elodie. "Edie will get every cent back plus interest."

Elodie had expected this, just not the attitude. "Fine."

"Interest?" Edie echoed, shock on her face. "Absolutely, not. I'll handle this, Trevor. It's my family."

The fury that passed over his face left Elodie shaken. Her heart thudded in her chest, and unease turned her blood to ice. Instinct made her want to snatch her sister to her side, but she remained frozen, watching the entire scene unfold before her.

Trevor glared at his wife. "Your family? *Your* family? *We're* your family. I and the kids, in case you needed reminding."

"That's not what I me—" Edie started.

Trevor rose and stalked from the room, taking the cloud of

rage with him. Elodie didn't breathe again until a door shut somewhere in the house. She looked at Edie to find her sister staring at her lap.

"What was that?" Elodie asked.

Edie shrugged and glanced up at her. "Trevor had a bad family life. He's...possessive."

That had gone well beyond being controlling. What Elodie had seen was dangerous, waiting to balloon into something destructive to everyone. "That isn't normal."

"I think I know my husband," Edie snapped.

Elodie was stunned by her sister's outburst almost as much as her glare. Things had been going really well. Why had Elodie felt the need to say something? "I was out of order. I'm sorry."

"Forget it," Edie said and turned her head to look out one of the windows to the darkness beyond.

Elodie sighed and briefly squeezed her eyes closed. "There's one more thing I need to tell you, and then I'll go."

"Do you need money?" Edie asked in exasperation.

Elodie was hurt by the question. She hadn't asked her sister for money. Ever. "No." Whatever bliss Elodie had found in the home was gone. She could fill Edie in on things later. It would be better for everyone if she left now.

"Wait," Edie said and caught Elodie's hand as she stood. "It's my turn to apologize. I'm sorry. I hate when Trevor and I argue. Please, sit and tell me whatever it is."

Elodie searched her sister's blue eyes and saw the sincerity there. She wanted to dig deeper into her sister's relationship with Trevor but now wasn't the time. Elodie slowly sat. "First, who do you want to do the work on the cottage?"

"Filip. I trusted his father for years, and I've seen some of Filip's work before he left Skye."

"What about what Trevor said?" Elodie knew she shouldn't push, but she had to know.

Edie shrugged and glanced out the doorway. "It's our cottage. Mine, yours, and Elias's. It's our decision."

Meaning it was Edie's money. Not that Elodie blamed her after Trevor's outburst, but she suspected there would be more arguments about this. Elodie wished she had the means to pay for the repairs herself so none of this would be happening. "I'll send Filip a text when I get home."

"And the other?" Edie pushed.

Elodie licked her lips, her nerves tightening as she thought about the day. "The storm earlier was created with magic."

Edie didn't react for a moment. Then she asked, "How do you know?"

"As I said, Filip and Scott were there when it struck. They ended up staying because it wasn't safe for anyone to be out on the roads. After a time, the electricity went out, and then… well, a limb broke through the window of Mum and Da's room—a branch coated in *drough* magic."

Edie's face lost its color. "What?" she asked in a strangled whisper.

"Neither Scott nor Filip could touch it. I ended up phoning Rhona. She and Balladyn came to see the damage. They're the ones who removed the limb and fixed the window. That's also how we learned that someone had created the storm." She paused, unsure whether to tell Edie the next part or not. "It seems all four of them think someone was trying to hurt me."

"You're moving in here," Edie stated firmly.

Elodie shook her head. "I'm not. I can't."

"Why not?"

"If someone does want revenge, I'm not bringing that to your home where your children sleep. I'd never forgive myself if anything happened to them."

Edie's shoulders dropped, but she didn't argue. "Does Rhona know who is after you?"

"Not yet. She and Balladyn are investigating."

"Does this...does this have anything to do with the murdered Druid?"

A shiver ran down Elodie's spine. "I don't think so."

"I don't like you being in that cottage."

Elodie reached across the table and took her sister's hands as she smiled. "I'll be fine. Rhona and Balladyn added wards."

"What?" Edie asked, her eyes wide.

"I was surprised, too. Everything will be fine. We'll get the house in order so it can go on the market. Once it sells, you'll take your cut and whatever money you need to cover what you're putting in for the repairs, and all of this will be over."

Edie's expression fell. "And you'll leave."

Elodie squeezed her sister's hands. She didn't like to see her so hurt. So, she did the one thing she knew not to do. She lied. "I don't know. We'll have to see."

The smile on Edie's face was worth it.

CHAPTER EIGHTEEN

Scott couldn't sleep. He kept thinking about Elodie being in the cottage alone and the limb covered in *drough* magic. Finally, he got tired of tossing and turning and got up to dress. He had Filip's keys in his hand before he knew what he was doing. Scott scrawled a quick note to his friend before walking out of the house. He would just drive by Elodie's and make sure everything was fine.

He drove for miles on Skye's winding roads without encountering a single car. It was so different than the city, yet he liked it. The island made him feel as if he were the only person there. The quiet was refreshing, the stillness invigorating. No matter how he tried to understand it, he couldn't see why Filip had ever left.

Elodie leaving was another matter entirely. He would've done the same thing in her shoes. Sometimes, the only way to move forward after such a tragedy was to leave a place behind.

He leisurely continued down the roads. The sky was clear, and most of the debris from earlier had been cleared away. The moonlight bathed the island in a soft glow. All he wanted to do was pull over and just take it all in. While the serene scene was picture-perfect, something sinister was on Skye. Whether it had always been here or had recently arrived, it had focused its attention on Elodie. With the murdered Druid the night before, Scott couldn't take any chances.

Though he had no idea what he was looking for. Magic could come in all sorts of ways. It made it more difficult when hunting someone, but it could be done. *He* had done it. Several times. He'd been hunting Kevin's killer when George had sent him here.

The only reason Scott hadn't balked was because George had said that Elodie could end all the strife. Now, Scott wasn't so sure. How could Elodie do anything without magic? Hadn't George seen that? What was Scott missing?

He thought about calling George but hesitated. George never disclosed everything that she saw as a seer. For all he knew, something could change in or around Elodie so she ended up everything George claimed. Everything George did was for the Druids. He had doubted her once, and it had nearly ended in disaster. So, he wouldn't doubt again. George knew how to use her abilities.

If only she could use them to save the Druids from being killed instead of bringing in Elodie.

Scott took the turn to Elodie's cottage. He drove slowly, his gaze searching for anything that seemed out of place. As he reached her drive, he turned off his lights and veered onto the side of the road. Trees blocked his view of the cottage, and he didn't want to chance waking her by driving by. He parked the SUV and turned off the ignition.

Exiting the vehicle, he softly pushed the door closed before starting down the drive. He rounded the bend that opened to the view of the cottage and the cove. That's when he saw it. Mist clung to the ground, heading straight for Elodie's cottage at a speed that told him it was far from natural.

Scott called his magic to him as he ran toward the house, but he wasn't fast enough. The mist enveloped the building as if it were searching for a way inside. The way it moved was frightening—as if it were alive.

As the storm had been.

He pushed his magic toward it, trying to get the mist's attention. It didn't do anything. He tried again, this time using more of his magic. He saw something move out of the corner of his eye. Scott turned his head in time to see a small portion of the mist coming at him. He flew through the air from the assault. Before he knew what was happening, he landed with a hard thud against the garage and dropped heavily to the ground.

Scott bit back a groan of pain and jumped to his feet. He could take stock of his wounds later. As soon as he faced the mist, it came at him again. Enveloped him. While he couldn't see anything, it felt as if a dozen fists were pummeling his body.

He bellowed as he threw out a shielding spell. It moved the mist off him for the briefest of moments before it came back. His body was wracked with agony as the mist hit him repeatedly. His knees buckled, and then he was being pressed

into the ground, his face shoved into the dirt hard enough that
he couldn't breathe.

Just as quickly as it all began, it stopped.

He pushed himself up with his arms and spotted Elodie
standing at the now-open door. She rushed from the house in
her bare feet when she saw him. Scott looked up to see the
mist above them. There was no face to it, but he knew it
watched her. He tried to tell Elodie to stay back, to remain
inside, but he wasn't quick enough.

Scott forced his feet under him. He glanced up to see the
mist gathering into a single column. He knew it was about to
come at them. He took Elodie's hand and ran to the door,
pushing her in ahead of him. Scott grabbed the knob, swung it
closed, and then turned to put his weight behind it. The mist
slammed into it, knocking him on his arse as the door flew
open.

Suddenly, Elodie was there, pushing the door closed again.
Scott jumped up and put all his weight behind the effort.
Finally, the door latched shut. He closed his eyes with his
cheek against the wood and waited to see what the mist would
do next. The house didn't shake, and the windows didn't
rattle. No mist poured through any cracks.

He turned to put his back to the door and then looked at
Elodie beside him. Her long, blond hair hung loosely about
her shoulders, and her blue eyes were wide. "Are you hurt?"

She shook her head. "What just happened?"

"Apparently, the mist wants you."

"Mist? This morning it was rain, now mist?"

He noticed how rapidly her chest rose and fell. Shock.

That's what he saw on her face. Not that he blamed her. He was in shock himself. "Looks that way."

"What are you doing here?"

"I couldna sleep. Thought I'd take a drive and make sure things were okay here."

Her brow furrowed for a moment. "I didn't hear your vehicle."

"I parked near the road. I didna want to wake you if you were asleep. And now that I'm telling you this, it sounds a wee bit…"

"Like a stalker?"

"Aye." He wrinkled his nose as he inwardly winced. "I swear I was just checking on you."

She pushed away from the door and crossed her arms over her chest. "You could've formed the mist."

"I could've, but I didna. I know you've no reason to believe me, we just met, but I'm telling the truth."

Elodie studied him for a long moment. "If you had called the mist, I don't think it would've done that to you," she said as she jerked her chin to him.

Scott glanced down to find his clothes ripped and shredded. He had blood on him—his blood. He knew he'd been beaten, but he hadn't realized that it was this bad. Just then, all the aches of his body made themselves known.

"Let's get you cleaned up."

He watched her retreat deeper into the house. Scott sighed and pushed away from the door. He took a few steps and decided to use the wall for support. He found Elodie in the kitchen, holding more of her brother's clothes. She handed them to him, and he slowly made his way to the bathroom.

When he emerged after a shower and change, she was at the kitchen table with a first-aid kit.

She stood and walked around him after he'd sat. "You hit your head."

"Aye. When it slammed me into the side of the garage."

Elodie didn't say more as she set about tending to him. She had a light touch. Scott closed his eyes and went over the attack in his head.

"So," she finally said, "looks like someone wants to harm me."

His eyes opened to find her before him. "I doona think the mist can get into the cottage. Could be Rhona and Balladyn's wards did the trick."

"Until something else comes for me. It isn't as if I can fight it."

"You willna face it alone."

"This isn't your fight."

He grunted and held out his hands. "Look at me. They made it my fight."

"I can't continue counting on others."

"Why no'?" He stopped her hands from dabbing at his wounds. Scott held her gaze, sinking into the soft blue of her eyes. "We're going to help you."

"I need to be able to fight this on my own."

"Only fools refuse help."

She quirked a blond brow. "You might have a point."

"You were born with magic. You can get it back."

Elodie released a sigh. "If someone wants to hurt me, then I want to be able to fight back."

"So, you'll try to do magic?" Scott could hardly contain the hope that flared in his chest.

Her lips curved into a small smile. "Yes."

Only then did he realize that he still had a hold of her hand.

CHAPTER NINETEEN

SKYE DRUIDS

Her heart was racing, and it had nothing to do with the mist that had attacked Scott and everything to do with his touch. Elodie could barely think of anything else. His hand was large and warm, his skin callused. He held her securely. Gently.

Seductive, tantalizing heat slid through her. Need roused, stirred. She swayed with the longing that suddenly engulfed her. She was awash with it, drowning in it.

And it felt wonderful.

Scott's deep blue eyes were locked on her. She saw his desire. Sexual tension crackled around them. She should release him and return to her room, but she wouldn't. She *couldn't*. She felt something again. It was astonishing and exquisite and startling. Oh, how she had missed this. How could she have forgotten? How had she gone so many years in that gray fog, walking around like a zombie?

Every nerve ending crackled with sensation, and an awareness swirled through her that left her hot and cold at the same time. It was an overwhelming attack on her senses, but she never wanted it to end.

Scott's thumb softly rubbed the back of her hand. She shivered at the contact, wanting more. So much more. Years ago, she would've taken it. But she wasn't that girl anymore.

Are you not?

When had she stopped feeling? When had she stopped going after the things she wanted? When had she given up? It was time she remembered who she was. It was time she embraced life as she once had.

She moved closer to Scott. Their bodies were almost touching. Another surge of longing inundated her, and her heart pounded. Her blood rushed. She leaned forward and lifted her mouth to his. Their lips brushed. The contact made her skin sizzle with awareness, and her lips yearn for another taste.

She pressed her body against his for a deeper kiss. The moan that rumbled through Scott's chest made her stomach flutter in excitement. Elodie was so wrapped up in the sensations running through her that she didn't realize that Scott had pulled away until he said her name. She blinked a couple of times until she could focus on him. Embarrassment flared within her. Had she misread the signs?

"That thing could return. I'd never forgive myself if my attention was diverted and you were injured," he said.

Because she couldn't do magic. Because she couldn't protect herself.

Mortification joined her humiliation. She moved away until Scott no longer touched her. She forced herself to nod as if his words made perfect sense. The difficult part was that

they did. She understood why he was being cautious, but that
didn't make the embarrassment any more bearable. "Of
course."

"Elodie," he began.

"There's no need," she said over him.

He grabbed her hand when she started to turn away. "I'd
like to stay. Just in case the mist returns."

It wasn't as if she could send him back out into the night to
possibly be killed. Who knew where the mist had come from
or where it was now? For all they knew, it was waiting for one
of them to leave the cottage.

Elodie shrugged as if it didn't matter to her, when in truth,
she was glad he wanted to stay. The cottage was difficult to
handle during the day, but at night, it was pure agony. "The
wards might keep it out, but it would be nice to have someone
here."

"Just in case," he repeated, searching her gaze.

She didn't know what he was looking for. Elodie shivered
now that she wasn't near his heat. She gently pulled her hand
from his and wrapped her arms around herself. "You can use
Elias's bed."

"I'll sleep on the sofa."

"Sure," she said and took another step back. "Make
yourself at home."

He nodded, still watching her. Elodie finally gave up and
turned on her heel. She hurried to her room and closed the
door before diving under the covers in an attempt to warm her
suddenly frigid body. Try as she might to forget what had
transpired between them, her mind drifted to the way Scott
had taken her hand. How he had held it. The look in his eyes.

The brief touch of his lips.

She hadn't misread the signs. There was something between them.

Scott fisted his hands at his sides as Elodie walked to her room. He licked his lips, taking in the brief taste of her. It had taken everything he had to stop the kiss. He'd been sent to convince Elodie to join them, not seduce her. Sure, he had used such tactics before, but he didn't want to do that with her. He—*they*—needed her trust.

When he finally told her everything, he didn't want her to think that he'd used sex to gain her confidence. And if he gave in to the desire that burned as hotly as fire through him, that was exactly what would happen.

George had told him to secure Elodie's aid by any means necessary. Scott wasn't sure why he didn't want to lie or seduce Elodie. Maybe it was because she had already suffered so much in her life. Or perhaps because she had opened herself to him without him using his magic. There seemed to be some trust building, just as he wanted. But it was happening naturally.

And it left him shaken.

He turned to look at the front door, his thoughts on the mist. Why were these things attacking Elodie? Did whoever was after her know how important she was to his organization? Was this about them? It didn't make sense that someone would want to hurt Elodie for something that'd happened so many years ago. Then again, the degree of hate people carried gave him pause.

Scott shoved a hand through his hair and made his way to the front room. He stoked the coals and added more wood. It wasn't long before the room was aglow in firelight. He tried to rest, but his mind was too busy. He sat on the sofa for a while before pacing the room, then the house, trying to dispel the desire that burned inside him. He stopped beside Elodie's closed door but heard nothing inside that gave him pause.

He retrieved his mobile and found the screen smashed, but it still worked. Scott sent a quick text to Filip to tell him what'd happened. Then he went back to his pacing. He checked the doors. The wards were strong there. When he peeked through the curtains, he saw the thick mist. Scott hurried to the next window to find the same. It covered the entire cottage. But the mist wasn't trying to get in.

Or was it?

Everything *was* warded. He stilled and listened. The eerie silence from outside was unnerving. Slowly, he walked through the cottage. The flicker of the fire drew his attention when he reached the front room again. He made his way to it, his heart lurching. Every window and door was shut and bolted, adding another layer of security to the wards. But the flue was open, so the house didn't fill with smoke.

"Fuck," he muttered and quickly sent another warding spell directly to the fireplace, just as something tried to bank the fire.

"I'll kill you!" her father bellowed.

Tears coursed down her mother's face. "Stop, Edward. Just stop. There's no need for this. Please!"

"Da, no!" Elias shouted.

There was screaming. So many screams. And then silence.

Her ears were ringing. She blinked. The blood. Where had it all come from?

Elodie came awake with a start. She tried to hold onto the dream, but it faded with each beat of her heart until she couldn't remember even who was in it or what it was about. She threw back the covers and swung her legs over the side of the bed. Just as she was about to rise, she paused.

Something wasn't right. The fear that thudded through her, leaving ice in her veins, wasn't about the dream. It was something else entirely.

"Scott," she murmured and jumped up.

Elodie threw open her door and rushed from her room. She glanced at her parents' door and then headed to the front of the house. She found him facing the hearth with his hands outstretched, and his lips moving quickly with a spell.

She didn't know what to do. It wasn't as if she had magic to help him.

You used to.

She quieted her subconscious as her mind struggled to find a way to assist him. One of the curtains wasn't closed all the way. That's when she saw the thick, gray mist. Elodie didn't need to look outside to know that it covered the cottage. Her head swung back to Scott. How long had he been fighting it?

"What do you need?" she asked as she ran up.

He didn't look her way, didn't stop his chanting. Elodie

could join the chant, but what good would it do without magic? She was utterly useless. She couldn't help Scott and couldn't call anyone to them without putting them in danger. Unless...

"Rhona," she said.

Scott furiously shook his head, never breaking his concentration on the spell. Elodie threw up her hands. Scott then jerked his chin to the pile of wood. She frowned. What about the pile? There was plenty there to last the night and well into the morning. Then she glanced at the fire itself to see that it was going out.

Elodie grabbed some logs and set about making the fire grow. She worked quickly, sweat beading her skin, her face burning from being so close to the flames. She didn't move until Scott's hands gently pulled her to her feet.

"I think we stopped it," he mumbled wearily.

She faced him and saw the paleness of his skin. "Rest."

"Water. And something stronger," he said with a weak smile as he collapsed into one of the chairs.

Elodie ran to the kitchen and grabbed some water, the bottle of Dreagan whisky, and two glasses. Scott downed the water first. Her hands shook as she poured them both some whisky. His breathing was still labored when she handed him the glass.

"How close was it?" she asked.

He met her gaze over the rim of the glass before taking a sip. "You doona want to know."

Close, then. "You should've woken me."

"I didna have time. How did you know what was happening?"

She shrugged. "I didn't. A bad dream woke me."

"What was it about?"

"I can't remember."

He grunted as he downed the rest of the whisky. "It's a good thing you woke when you did."

She watched how he tried to keep his eyes open. "You should go rest."

"I need to recharge my magic."

"What can I do?" Hopefully, she had it, and they wouldn't be required to go anywhere since they couldn't leave.

His head lolled to the side. Elodie grabbed the glass, catching it before it could hit the floor as his fingers loosened.

She got the throw from the sofa and covered him. Then she looked at the fire. Who wanted her harmed? And how would she stop it?

Magic. She had promised Scott she would try her magic again. Tomorrow, she would give it a go. Because she should be able to protect herself. If something were after her, she didn't want anyone else getting hurt simply because she was afraid to see if being back on Skye might return her magic.

One way or the other, she would have a definitive answer tomorrow.

CHAPTER TWENTY

SKYE DRUIDS

Kerry stood beneath the midnight sky with her arms wide. The spell was easy. Too easy. Her magic had never responded so quickly or powerfully before. Apparently, that was what happened when she wasn't compelled to follow the rules. She couldn't believe more Druids didn't give in to their full powers. If they did, no one would dare stand against them—not even the Dragon Kings.

The sound of laughter filled her head. *"Reaching a little far,"* the Ancient said.

Kerry kept her eyes closed as she concentrated on the spell the Ancient had taught her. "Never."

"Good. More Druids need to think like you."

Kerry couldn't help but smile at the praise. No one had ever given her compliments like that before. She had needed them. Everyone did. Now, they were finally hers. She drew in a deep breath, the magic consuming her. It felt amazing. As if it had been waiting all this time for her to *see* it.

"Give in to it," the Ancient advised.

Kerry tried, but the magic was so powerful that it was hard for her to stay upright.

"That's because you've never felt the full force of it before. That's all you, Kerry. All the magic you've kept contained your entire life. You're finally setting it free, finally freeing yourself."

The spell found its mark. She smiled and finished it. Kerry's knees gave out. She dropped to the ground, her hands catching her as she pitched forward. Euphoria. That was the emotion skidding along her skin and rushing through her veins. She was becoming a Druid everyone would soon fear. Rhona only thought she was a problem before. Wait until Kerry unleashed hell upon Rhona and Balladyn. Then the Skye Druids would bear witness. See who was the most powerful. Kerry would put Rhona in her place and banish Balladyn and all the Fae from the island once and for all.

She didn't care about some prophecy about a Warden. The Druids needed a leader they could count on, one who knew how to make tough decisions. They needed someone with experience. Rhona had none. She had floundered for months. Only by the grace of allies did Skye not fall to the Fae Others.

"Never again," Kerry muttered as she climbed to her feet.

She dusted off her hands and looked at the sky. Her life had pivoted and done a complete one-eighty in just a few short days. None other than the Ancients had shown Kerry her destiny. No one would ever be able to argue that point. The Ancients didn't care that Corann had chosen Rhona, nor did they care about some Warden. The Ancients guided Kerry, and they would show her the way.

Her. Not Rhona.

Kerry smiled and turned toward her home. She made her way inside. As she closed the door behind her, she caught her reflection in the mirror hanging on the wall. She touched the wrinkles around her eyes and mouth. Everyone had always commented on how cheerful she was. She didn't mind the lines on her face. They proved that she had lived a long life. She didn't even mind the size of her body. She enjoyed a delicious meal and whisky. Why should she deny herself those luxuries?

Her gaze moved to her hair. This was different. She hated the limp, dreary locks her mother had passed to her. All those years as Kerry grew up, her mother had worn wigs, all the while telling Kerry she needed to do something about her hair. Maybe it was time she did.

Kerry cocked her head to the side and considered what to do. Should it be longer? Fuller? What about a color? Black? Blond? Red?

She chuckled as she imagined what Rhona's face would look like if Kerry approached her with red hair. The laugh died away.

"Not red," she told her reflection. "If I'm embracing everything else about myself, I shouldn't try to be something I'm not. Just give it a little…extra."

With the power inside her, Kerry crafted a spell and used it to make her hair fuller with more body. She was about to remove the gray, but as she turned her head from side to side, she decided against it.

"Now that's hair," she said as she reverently touched her locks.

It was her, only better. Just like her magic.

Balladyn flattened his lips as Rhona's mobile buzzed on the table next to their bed. It had taken him most of the night to get her to sleep. Ever since the murder, she had been wound tightly, but things got worse after Elodie's. The *drough* magic, as well as Scott and Filip alerting them to the Druid killings, had distressed her. Rhona had been obsessed with learning whether what they said was true. Unfortunately, it was. And that only caused her more worry.

He turned his head on the pillow, careful not to move Rhona, who had her head resting on his chest. Balladyn lifted his free hand, and her mobile snapped into his palm with a thought. He glanced at the caller ID to see that it was Theo. The only reason the DI would be calling so early was if something else had happened.

Balladyn lowered his voice to a whisper as he answered the call. "DI Frasier."

"Uh…Balladyn," Theo said before clearing his throat. "Is Rhona okay?"

"She's had a rough night. She only got to sleep a few hours ago. What can I help you with?"

Theo blew out a breath. "You're going to have to wake her. There's been another murder."

"A Druid?"

"That's the only reason I'd bother her."

Balladyn clenched his teeth. They had been able to contain

the first death, but it wouldn't be long before the entire island learned of this one. The Druids would soon piece together that they were being targeted. "Where?"

After he'd gotten the information from Frasier, Balladyn hung up and debated leaving Rhona to rest. But he knew she'd never forgive him for going without her. He drew in a breath and gently shook her.

"Wake up, sweetheart. You're needed."

She murmured a protest and moved closer to him.

"I know," he told her before kissing her forehead. "I wish we could stay. There's been another Druid murder."

Rhona sighed heavily, then opened her eyes to meet his. "What's happening to our island?"

"I'm not sure yet, but we'll figure it out."

"Before how many more Druids are killed?"

He kissed her. "Let's not think of that right now. Frasier is waiting for us."

Rhona pushed herself into a sitting position. She rubbed her eyes and shoved her long, red hair out of her face. Balladyn saved her some time and called her clothes to her as she got to her feet.

"Thank you," she said with a smile as she looked at him over her shoulder.

He winked at her and stood, his clothes quickly covering him. "Anytime."

She squared her shoulders as he came to her side. "Who's the Druid?"

"Fredrick Smyth."

Rhona frowned at the news.

"Who is he?" Balladyn pressed.

"He's in his seventies. Keeps to himself. His family can trace their line for hundreds of years to the first residents of Skye," she told him.

Balladyn held out his hand. As soon as she fitted her palm against his, he teleported them just outside of Smyth's home. DI Frasier was waiting for them. As soon as he saw them, Theo waved them over.

"Sorry to wake you," he said as they approached.

Rhona nodded in greeting. "Thanks for the call. What happened?"

"A neighbor heard a scream. They looked out the window and said there was a shape in the air."

Balladyn shook his head. "What kind of shape?"

"They couldna describe it. Said it looked like mist." Frasier cleared his throat. "The neighbor then came to check on Mr. Smyth. The door was open. They got worried and went inside. That's when they found him and called us."

"Is it the same kind of death as last night's?" Rhona asked.

Frasier made a face. "No' exactly. It's better if I show you."

Balladyn felt Rhona's gaze on him. He kept a tight hold of her hand as they followed the DI into the house. Before they reached the door, Balladyn caught the lingering scent of death. He steeled himself for what they would find.

Smyth wasn't in his bed as the previous victim had been. The elder male—or what was left of him—sat in a recliner. The walls, ceiling, and floor were coated with blood and body bits. Those in the room were doing their best to keep it together, but everyone was pale and fighting to keep from losing the contents of their stomachs.

The only sound Rhona made was a quick inhale. Balladyn felt her shaking as he held her hand. He understood her shock —and anger. Someone was targeting Druids. There had been a small chance that the first victim had been a one-off. That wasn't the case now. There was a serial killer loose on Skye.

One who was after Druids.

"I thought the first killing was one of anger," Theo said in a low voice. "But this...this is pure fury. Violence."

Rhona breathed through her mouth. "Someone wanted to obliterate him."

They all stared at the gruesome scene for another few minutes. Finally, Balladyn caught Frasier's attention and jerked his chin toward the door. Frasier nodded and made his way out of the house and away from those who might eavesdrop.

"Did you get anywhere with who might have been after the first victim?" Rhona asked after they'd followed the DI outside.

Frasier rubbed his forehead, his exhaustion evident. "As you know, we're a small force. We're no' equipped to handle something like this. We're doing the best we can. But, to your question, I've no'. Everyone I spoke with had nothing bad to say about her. It doesna appear as if she had any enemies. The list Roy passed on to me was good, but there isna anyone on it I can connect to her death."

Balladyn had been afraid of that. "We got some new information that might be helpful."

"I'll take anything," Frasier said.

Rhona licked her lips, her gaze darting to the house. "Apparently, Druids in other places are also being targeted.

Edinburgh has seen six Druid deaths in five weeks. Glasgow has reported three in the last month. Inverness, London, Paris, Prague, New York, Moscow."

"Bloody hell," Frasier murmured. "Why are we being targeted? Does this have to do with the Fae Others?"

"We're looking into that," Balladyn replied.

Rhona lifted her chin. "I don't want to cause panic, but every Druid needs to know so they can keep themselves safe. I've already got my deputies getting the word out."

"We need to let every Druid around the world know," Frasier said. "Any way we can do that?"

Rhona glanced at Balladyn. "I was thinking about that earlier. We need to do something."

"Before they come for you," Theo replied.

"I dare them," Balladyn stated fiercely.

Rhona tightened her fingers on his hand. "It's inevitable. You need to watch yourself, too, Theo."

CHAPTER TWENTY-ONE

SKYE DRUIDS

The scream jerked him out of his slumber. Scott sat up and blinked away the last of his sleep. His head swung to the side as his eyes landed on the figure stretched out on the couch. *Elodie*. He jumped up, tripping over the blanket he hadn't realized covered him. Scott landed awkwardly on his knee before getting back to his feet and lunging for the sofa.

He grabbed Elodie's shoulders and gently shook her. "It's just a dream, Elodie. Wake up."

It took another shake before her lids fluttered open. Her pupils were dilated, her breathing rapid. Her entire body was stiff.

"It was just a dream," he said again.

At the sound of his voice, a shudder went through her before her body finally relaxed. She drew in a shaky breath and closed her eyes. Worry settled deep within him. She'd mentioned a dream earlier. This had to be about her father's murder. Maybe being back in the cottage wasn't such a good idea.

"Do you want to talk about it?" he asked after a lengthy silence.

She swallowed loudly and met his gaze. "If I could remember it, I would. As soon as I wake, the images disappear."

"Do you know who was in it?"

Elodie shook her head.

Scott glanced at the fire and rose to add more wood. He didn't want to take the chance of the mist returning for another try. After he'd stoked the fire, he returned to the sofa. Elodie was sitting up now, the blanket wrapped tightly around her.

"I'm no' sure being here is good for you."

She glanced at him and grinned. "Is it the nightmares or the attempts on my life that made you reach that decision?"

Despite the circumstances, he found himself chuckling. "Point taken."

"You're right, though." Her smile died as she stared into the fire.

"I can take you to Edie's, if you want."

Elodie drew in a deep breath and slowly released it. "I'm not going there."

"Something happen?"

"Yes. No." She sighed, her frustration clear. "Maybe. It's probably that I'm on edge and just took things wrong."

Scott shrugged and fought the urge to put his arm around her. "Siblings fight."

"It wasn't Edie. It was Trevor."

Scott also turned to the fire and considered her words. "Is he upset about the cost of things?"

"I never visited Skye. I didn't even see them get married because it was a spur-of-the-moment thing. Edie never pushed me to come back here. She made a couple of trips to see me, but I understood that her life was here. I say all of that to explain that I don't know Trevor. And in the brief time I've been here, I've spent little time with him. It's obvious he loves my sister and the kids."

"But?" Scott urged when she paused.

Elodie's nose wrinkled as she shook her head. "As I said, I probably took things wrong, but he got really snippy when Edie and I discussed the repairs for the cottage. The smiling, loving man I had seen with my sister was suddenly gone. He became someone else entirely."

"Money tends to make people act crazy."

That elicited a small grin. "True. Edie seemed shocked by it, too. It was partly my fault. The lack of sleep has made me irritable, and I didn't help matters."

"This is between you and your sister, though."

"That's what Edie tried to tell him," Elodie said as she looked at Scott. "Trevor then told her that he was her family."

Scott raised a brow as he turned his head to her. "Really?"

"It's weird, isn't it?"

"Aye."

She let out a relieved sigh. "I'm glad I'm not the only one. Regardless, the entire thing felt awkward, and I really don't want to be around him."

"I doona blame you. But I also doona think you should stay here alone."

"I'm not sure Trevor would appreciate me asking Edie to come here."

Scott glanced at the cushion as he recalled their brief kiss. He was about to tell her that *he* could stay with her. He knew just how to put the suggestion so she would think it was her idea. He knew just the right expression to have, too—and the right amount of magic to use.

And yet, he did nothing. What the hell was wrong with him?

Elodie slid her gaze away and cleared her throat. "I'm sorry I woke you."

"Doona be. How many nightmares do you have a night?"

"At least one. Sometimes two."

"And you doona remember them?"

She rubbed her hands on her arms beneath the blanket. "No."

It was the perfect opportunity to use his magic, to deepen their trust. And it felt wrong. So very, very wrong.

"How do you feel?" She turned her head to him. "The spell you used earlier wiped you out."

Scott found himself nodding. "Better. It's been some time since I've used that much magic at once."

"I'm glad you were here."

"Me, too."

He couldn't look away from her light blue gaze. The flames from the hearth reflected in their depths. He liked being with her. The cozy cottage, the wildness of Skye, the magic that pulsed through the island like a heartbeat. The resilient, fierce beauty beside him. In another life, he could've been happy with having all of this as his.

But no matter how much he wanted it, that life wasn't his to have.

What if...?

He shut the thought down quickly. He wouldn't be doing himself, Elodie, or the organization any favors by allowing his attraction to rule him.

Elodie was the first to look away. "I don't like that I can't defend myself. I don't like being a burden on anyone." She shot him a quick glance. "I've no right to ask, but would you or Filip consider staying until I know if I can get my magic back?"

Scott's stomach clenched with a mix of excitement and dread. He'd wanted this and had somehow gotten it without saying or doing anything. Being with her would allow him to help her with her magic—as well as impart information about the organization.

It would also try him in ways he'd never been tested before.

Was he up to the task? There was no other choice for him. He had to be—for every Druid around the world.

"Of course," he replied.

The smile that curved her lips made his balls tighten. She had to know how alluring she was, how utterly captivating. He wanted to lean in to her and place his lips on hers again. To slip his tongue into her mouth and know her full taste. He longed to have her body pressed against his so he could feel her curves and softness.

He ached to sink deep inside her, fusing their bodies in a dance as old as time itself.

As if his thoughts had conjured it, her mouth pressed

against his. Scott was so surprised that he didn't move for a moment; thought maybe he was dreaming it. Until he felt the warmth of her body. Whatever tentative thread of control he had snapped. His arms wound around her as one hand tangled in the length of her glorious hair.

It wasn't a soft kiss. It wasn't a sweet one. Instead, it was fire and passion, longing and hunger so thick and heady there was no escaping it. And, heaven help him, he didn't want to.

Scott let her sweet taste fill him as their tongues tangled. He managed to catch the throw between them and yank it free to toss aside. Then, Elodie was in his lap. But that still wasn't enough. He wanted more.

And, in that instant, he knew that he would *always* want more of her.

How could he not? A woman like Elodie got into a man's blood, his very psyche, and never let go. The future didn't matter at the moment. All he could think about was discovering every inch of her delightful body — and covering it with his scent so she would never forget him. He wanted her wound as tightly as he was. With need, with desire.

With *hunger*.

He moved them until she was lying on the cushions. The sound — half purr, half moan — when he lay atop her made his already hard cock throb. Her hands were in his hair as their mouths clashed once more. By all that was magical, she kissed as if she would die without him. Her ardor made his burn even hotter. When her legs locked around his waist, he ground against her.

This time, they both moaned.

He had to get her clothes off. Apparently, her thoughts ran

in the same vein because she yanked at his shirt. There was a loud, ripping noise, but neither paid it any heed. Scott broke the kiss long enough to toss the garment aside. Then he devoured her mouth once more.

His hand lifted the hem of her shirt and met bare skin. He felt her stomach clench as he caressed upward until his hand brushed the underside of her breast. There was no bra in his way. That's when he remembered that she had been asleep when he arrived.

"Don't you dare stop," Elodie said between kisses, her hands holding his face.

Scott grinned at her words. He would only stop if she asked. He cupped her breast, feeling the weight of it in his hand. Then he gently massaged it before brushing his thumb over the hardened peak. Elodie moaned, her back arching.

He rose to his knees, simultaneously pulling her into a sitting position. Together, they wrestled her top off before falling back against the sofa in a tangle of arms and lips. There was little room on the couch to move as he wished. Without a second thought, Scott slipped an arm beneath Elodie and held her tightly against him before using his other hand to push himself to his feet.

She ended the kiss and met his gaze. Her lips were swollen as she smiled at him. "Good idea," she told him when he laid her on the rug before the fire.

He smoothed the hair back from her face and gazed down at her. If he were smart, he would let her go right that instant. He would make up some excuse and return her clothes. But he couldn't. He wanted Elodie. Wanted her with such a deep yearning that it left him breathless and reeling. He couldn't release her now if he tried. She was already in his blood, already deep in his soul. There was no getting her out now.

And he wouldn't want it any other way.

Damn the consequences. Just this once, he wanted to think about himself. He'd sort through the fallout later. Because there would be consequences.

The frantic pace from just a few moments ago had shifted, altered. Scott didn't understand how or why. He felt it. The desire…the craving had grown. They were no longer drowning in it. They *were* the emotions.

Elodie's fingers trailed along the curve of his jaw, the sound of her nails against his whiskers mixing with the popping of the fire. "I've been wanting to taste your kiss since I first saw you."

Her confession hit him hard in the chest. "I'm all yours. Do what you will."

"You may regret saying that."

Scott shook his head. "Never."

Her fingers softly stroked and moved around to the nape of his neck. Then she pulled his head down to hers. If he had thought their fiery kiss was sexy, the languid way their tongues mated now would burn him from the inside out.

He could've kissed her for eternity and still demanded more. Yet there was so much more pleasure to be had. It took three tries before he finally ended the kiss and sat up. He loved the way the firelight bathed her skin in a reddish-orange glow. Her blond hair was spread haphazardly around her as her eyes blazed with need.

His gaze skimmed down to the rapid pulse at her throat, then lower to her magnificent breasts. He fought the urge to bend and take a pale pink nipple between his lips. That was to come. But first, their clothes had to go. He didn't want anything between them.

Scott reached for the waistband of her pajama bottoms and slid them—and her panties—over her hips and down her legs. He moved so she could kick them off. Scott rose to his feet and looked down at her. Her beauty left him awestruck. Lying as she was, naked and exposed and flushed with passion, she looked like some ethereal entity who had come to Earth for a night of pleasure.

He had never removed his pants so fast in his life. As he stretched out between her legs, Elodie's eyes rolled back in her head as her hands came to rest at his sides.

She scraped her nails lightly along his skin and whispered, "Yes."

CHAPTER TWENTY-TWO

SKYE DRUIDS

She was burning. But it was such a glorious feeling.

Elodie had thought she would never feel passion again. Never know the beautiful agony of desire. And yet, here it was, coursing through her with such force that she felt as if it were trying to tear her apart.

The glorious feeling of Scott's weight atop her was heady in itself. Oh, how she loved having him there, feeling his warmth—the hardness of his body...and cock. His amazing mouth was on hers again. He kissed as if he had been taught by long-forgotten gods. Demanding, coaxing. Commanding. Claiming.

He enticed, he charmed, he challenged with every tongue lick and movement of his lips. And she answered in kind. The flames of desire that had sparked her to kiss him on the sofa consumed her. It licked at her skin, urging her to delve deeper into the passion, the all-consuming craving for the man in her arms.

How could she resist? She was powerless to do anything but *feel*. After years of nothing, fierce emotions bombarded her from all sides. But she wasn't afraid. Not while in Scott's arms. She knew she was safe.

Her hands slid over his broad shoulders, the thick sinew moving beneath her palms. She couldn't stop touching him. She couldn't wait to run her hands all over him, especially his arousal that rested against her stomach.

Elodie sucked in a surprised breath when he pinched her nipple and rolled it between his fingers. All the while, his mouth moved down her neck. She gasped as desire shot through her body to pool between her legs. She wanted him inside her, deep and hard. Her lips parted as she tried to find the words. Then his lips wrapped around her nipple, and her thoughts scattered.

She moaned and ground her hips against him, needing the friction. Her body was primed and ready. The realization shocked her. Scott had done that to her with just his mouth. She couldn't wait until she experienced the rest of him.

His mouth moved to her other breast where his tongue worked its magic on that turgid peak. Elodie was so close to orgasm, all she needed was the right angle to rub herself against him. When he moved away, she cried out in frustration. Then his finger was inside her. With one movement, she shattered.

Scott watched the pleasure wash over Elodie's face as she climaxed. He smiled in satisfaction. More would come. After all, they had just gotten started.

He settled between her legs as her body clamped around his finger. Her lips were parted on a silent scream, her eyes closed, her head thrown back. Glorious. That's what she was. Utterly breathtaking.

With his eyes still locked on her face, he withdrew his finger and slid it back into her wet heat. She gasped, and her body stiffened. Scott wore a smile as he leaned down and swirled his tongue around her swollen clit as he thrust his finger in and out of her body. The cry of pleasure that fell from her lips was music to his ears.

The second orgasm on the heels of the first was stronger. Elodie tried to catch her breath, but her body wasn't hers any longer. It was Scott's. Every nerve ending was exploding. The ecstasy was so addictive that she clung to it, riding out the climax for as long as she could.

When she came to, Scott was still between her legs, his tongue bringing her to life once more. She shook her head. This wasn't possible. How could he make her feel...*everything*...after she had been numb for so long?

She wanted to tell him to stop, but she didn't dare. What if she never felt anything after this? What if they paused, and whatever was happening between them vanished? She couldn't take that chance. So, she sank into the desire that tightened low in her belly. She'd had two orgasms back-to-back, something that had never happened in her life. And the stirrings of another were already heating her body.

He added a second finger as he pumped them between her legs. Elodie gasped, wanting more, wanting *everything* Scott wrung from her.

She raised her head to look at him. Their gazes met. His flashed with need and approval—and the promise of more. She dropped her head back, panting as his tongue flicked rapidly over her clit, and his fingers found that delicious spot within her. The orgasm was swift and uncontrollable. White dots flashed behind her eyelids as she rode the waves of bliss for a third time.

The sound of his name being shouted from Elodie's lips was the sweetest thing Scott had ever heard. He raised his face to watch her for the third time. The sight of her ensconced tightly in ecstasy's hold would be branded on his mind.

But he couldn't wait any longer. He needed to be inside her, needed to feel their bodies joined.

He rose and guided his arousal to her slick entrance. He licked his lips, tasting her. Then he pushed inside her. The walls of her sex gripped him tightly as her orgasm continued. Scott gasped and fell forward onto his hands as he fought not to give in to his climax. Somehow, he regained control.

When he opened his eyes, Elodie was lying still. Her eyes were closed, her chest heaving as a fine sheen of sweat covered her skin. Her arms were lying limply by her sides. Scott slowly withdrew until just the tip of him remained and then slid back inside her. She moaned as her eyes fluttered open. Her gaze met his as a smile tilted her lips.

"We're no' done yet," he murmured.

She wrapped her legs around him and brought his head down for a kiss. He began to move his hips slowly, matching the dance of their tongues.

Her body was numb from the orgasms, but there was no denying that she liked the feel of Scott moving inside her. She hadn't gotten to stroke him as he had her. Nor had she gotten to take his cock in hand and explore it, taste it, as he had with her. But she would. Maybe not tonight, but soon.

For now, she clung to him as his tempo steadily increased, until he drove into her hard and fast. The time for kissing was done. Now it was passion and unrelenting hunger that had taken them. She clung to his sides, her legs drawn up so he could go deeper. The feel of him moving inside her was almost too much.

It was everything she wanted and more. So much more. She couldn't put her finger on what it was, but it was there, off to the side, watching and waiting. For what, she didn't know. But there was no denying its existence. Perhaps it had always been there.

Then she didn't care. There was something so right and

amazing about their joining that she didn't want to think about anything else. Just them. Just this precious moment.

Just him.

Scott.

Powerful and commanding. Kind and gentle. Fire and ice. Need and passion.

"Scott," she whispered when she felt that familiar feeling forming again.

"Come with me," he urged with harsh breaths. "Come with me."

She gasped when he shifted angles slightly so he could rub against her clit as he thrust. Elodie sank her nails into his skin as the climax began to grow, pushing her closer and closer to the edge. Her skin tingled, and the room grew fuzzy. She focused on Scott, on the feelings swirling within her body.

"Now!" he bellowed.

Elodie felt his cock pulse inside her, and the orgasm swept through her like a tidal wave. She fought for breath even as he continued pumping his hips. He flung her so far and high that Elodie thought she could see forever. The ripples of the climax ran through her over and over until she had nothing else to give.

She tried to open her eyes and look at Scott, but she was too exhausted. Elodie felt him pull out of her, and she missed him immediately. But then he was next to her. He rolled her, his arm holding her against his body. She sighed as she rested her head on his chest.

"Sleep," he whispered. "I'll be here when you wake."

The drowsiness that had pulled her to sleep vanished. She hadn't dreamed his words. He had said them. They still hung in the air. His fingers played with the ends of her hair. It felt so good. Almost as good as lying next to him. Nearly as good as his kisses.

She realized then that their legs were tangled together. Elodie thought of what she had sensed earlier, the thing that had been off to the side, watching and waiting. She was afraid to look closer at it, afraid it would be the thing she wanted most—and the thing she feared terribly.

She had been on her own for so many years. It had been her choice to keep away from her family and not let friends get too close. She'd had a few lovers, but nothing that came close to what she would consider love. They had merely been a distraction, something to take her mind off her miserable life.

Despite her best efforts, she was home. A place that was filled with ghosts of the past and more questions than before.

And a man who had seemingly come out of nowhere to make her feel again.

It was a near-perfect night, marred only by the attack and the recurring nightmares that made her increasingly uneasy. But she wanted to remember this moment, this flawless moment, forever. She knew better than anyone that times like these didn't come around often. Usually, people had their heads in the past or the future and missed the here and now. Well, she wouldn't be one of them. She would lap up every wonderful second.

Then she could look back on it in the years to come and remember. And sigh.

"I'm no' going to leave, lass," Scott said.

Elodie snuggled tighter against him. "I know."

He kissed her forehead. "Rest. You need it."

"Because of you," she said with a smile.

His chest rumbled with a chuckle. "I could give you some more."

"Later."

"Ah, such a demanding lover," he teased.

She shifted her head to look at him. They smiled at each other.

Scott's face grew serious. "That was incredible. *You* were incredible."

The thing she didn't want to look at, the thing that stood watching, took a step closer.

Elodie's heart skipped a beat as she stared at him in awe. She touched Scott's face. "There's more to come."

CHAPTER TWENTY-THREE

SKYE DRUIDS

"Elodie. Elodie, my bonnie lass, open your eyes."

She wanted to do just as her mother asked, but Elodie couldn't.

"Everything is going to be fine, darling girl. I promise."

Elodie tried not to cry, but the tears kept leaking from her closed eyes. Her mother gently wiped them away.

"I love you," her mother whispered.

The voice reverberated in Elodie's mind as her eyes snapped open. She clung to her mother's words. There had been nothing to see in the dream. Still, she couldn't dispel the feeling that whatever she had dreamed about was sifting through her fingers like grains of sand. The harder she tried to hold onto them, the faster they flowed. The others had been nightmares, and while she couldn't remember what she'd felt in this dream, she *did* recall the comfort of her mother.

For the first time in a long while, Elodie wished to speak to her mum. Emily MacLean had always known when her children needed her. The past really was all around if Elodie were hearing her mother's voice in her dreams. At least it wasn't a nightmare. Elodie didn't think she could handle that.

She blinked as her eyes burned with unshed tears. How she wished she could walk into her mother's arms. Her mum had made sure each of her children was equipped to fight their own battles, but she had always been there to comfort or congratulate. Elodie hadn't realized how much she had missed that until now.

What kind of person was she to have forgotten that? Just because her mother had killed her father. That wasn't fair. Neither was refusing to see or speak to her mum in fifteen years.

Warm lips pressed behind her ear. She startled, having forgotten that Scott was lying curled behind her. His arms tightened around her.

"Your breathing changed. What's wrong?" he asked in a sleepy voice.

Elodie stared at the dancing flames. "Another dream."

"Do you want to talk about it?"

Could he be any sexier? She was pretty sure he couldn't. Elodie turned in his arms to face him. She was able to see a glimpse of sunlight through the split in the curtains. "I heard my mum."

"So, no' a nightmare?" he asked as he settled onto his back. He held her with one arm and curled the other behind his head. "That's good, aye?"

She had to smile. "Yes."

"And you remembered something about the dream?"

"Only her voice. I can't recall what she said, though."

"Hmm." Scott closed his eyes and took a deep breath. "When was the last time you spoke with her?"

"The day my father was killed."

His head rolled toward her as his eyes opened. "That's a long time."

"It is."

"You said he was abusive to her."

Elodie nodded and rose on an elbow to look into his face.

There was a lengthy pause before he asked, "Why have you no' talked to her?"

"She killed my father."

"I realize they are your parents, but surely some considerations must be taken because of the abuse."

Elodie glanced at his bare chest and let her fingers slide into the dark, curly hair there. "She didn't have to kill him."

"I'm no' defending your mum, but your da didna have to hit her either."

"I'm not making excuses for what he did."

Scott quirked a brow but didn't say more.

Was she making excuses for her father? Or did she blame her mum for not being stronger? For not trying to get away, file for divorce, do something—*anything*—but kill him?

Elodie shook her head and looked away. "I didn't want to wake up and talk about this."

"You need to talk about it, though. That much is obvious."

"Is it?" She ducked her head. Nothing was apparent to her. Then again, she was rather messed up in the head.

Scott rubbed his hand up her back, drawing her closer as he did. "Doona be too hard on yourself. What happened to you and your family is ghastly. Everyone deals with things differently."

Her gaze returned to meet Scott's. She searched his deep blue eyes that reminded her of the ocean—fathomless and intense. It would be easy to lose herself in his gaze, to let the attraction between them devour her. How could she not when she could feel once more? But maybe it was because of that that she needed to find her footing first.

"Elodie," he whispered and brought his other hand to her as he lifted his head.

Her eyes slid shut, and her lips parted, waiting to feel his. Just as their mouths met, the shrill ring of a mobile broke the silence.

"Bloody hell," he murmured and pressed his forehead against hers.

She laughed and looked over to see his pants moving with the vibration of his mobile. "It's you."

Scott sat and groped for the sweats he had put on the previous night. He dug his phone out of the pocket. His lips twisted. "Filip," he told her before answering it. "Hey."

Elodie could hear Filip's voice but not his words. She didn't want Scott to think that she was eavesdropping, so she dressed as he explained what had happened with the mist. Elodie walked to the kitchen and heated some water. She got out tea as well as some coffee for Scott. When she turned around, she heard him ending the call as he walked naked into the kitchen.

She couldn't help but eye him appreciatively. He was trim and toned. His chest tapered to narrow hips, and he had a washboard stomach with that cut of muscle right above his hip

bones that always drove her wild. Her gaze lowered to his
cock that was thickening before her eyes. Her mouth went dry
at the thought of what had brought her such pleasure the night
before. Long legs corded with muscle and a light dusting of
hair.

Scott's moan was half growl. Her gaze jerked to his face.
The desire she saw there mirrored hers. She swallowed,
unsuccessfully trying to coat her mouth and throat.

"Filip's on his way," Scott said, his voice heavy with
desire.

Elodie tried to calculate how much time they had before
Filip arrived. She glanced at the table and then the floor in an
attempt to decide which would be more comfortable.

"Fuck that," Scott said as he stalked to her.

He jerked her against him, their lips meeting in a wild rush
of need. He shoved her pants down—it took both of them to
get one of her legs free. He lifted her and pressed her against a
wall with his hard body. Then he was inside her.

Elodie clung to him as her eyes closed in ecstasy. Her
fingers sank into the cool strands of his dark brown hair while
his lips kissed down her throat. His hips began rocking. She
locked her ankles behind him, letting her head fall back
against the wall as he burrowed deep, touching her right where
she wanted. Just how she needed it.

She wasn't surprised when she felt the orgasm building—
she was powerless to stop it. Elodie cried out as she came, her
body pulsing with such pleasure that she forgot everything
except the man inside her. He climaxed right after her. The
feel of his seed filling her body was a reminder that they
hadn't used protection either time. She would have to talk to

him about that, but not now, not after something so beautiful, so…extraordinary.

Elodie held him as his body jerked one final time. Then he sighed and buried his face in the crook of her neck. They stayed like that for several moments, still pressed against the wall. Finally, Scott lifted his head.

"Damn, woman," he said with a sexy grin.

She caressed his face, her heart happy and full. "Indeed."

A frown replaced his smile. "I wish we had more time."

"We will later."

He pulled out of her and gently lowered her to the floor. At the sight of his cock, he looked at her.

"I know," Elodie said. "We haven't been very responsible. I may not have any magic, but I know a spell I can teach you."

Scott's brow quirked. "For?"

"Think of it like a morning-after pill." There was no emotion on his face, but the fact that he didn't so much as blink concerned her. "If you'd rather me ask—"

"I've no problem. I just didna realize there was such a thing. I suppose I should've," he added with a shrug.

She put her hand on his arm and smiled. "It's something Mum taught Edie and me early. She wanted to make sure we had a choice, even if a guy didn't give us one."

"That's good."

"It's a quick and easy spell."

Scott nodded woodenly. "I'm ready."

The sound of a car door shutting reached them. Elodie cursed. She glanced at the water pot. She hadn't even heard it ding, but then she had been otherwise occupied. "I'm going to take a quick shower. Help yourself. We'll do the spell later."

She didn't wait for Scott to answer as she hurried to the bathroom and turned on the shower. Elodie pinned up her hair and washed her body. Just as she'd promised, she was in and out quickly. She tied the belt of her robe in place and brushed her teeth before going to dress in her room.

By the time she returned to the kitchen, she had just finished plaiting her hair. Scott had put on some clothes. He stood against the counter with a mug in his hand. Filip was seated at the table, an open bakery box before him.

"Morning," she greeted them.

Filip smiled at her and motioned to the box. "I bought us a treat."

She peeked inside and saw the pastries. Elodie eagerly snatched a croissant and bit into the buttery texture. Her gaze briefly met Scott's, and an awkward silence fell over them. Elodie tried to find something to say, but she couldn't think of anything. Finally, she gave up and made her tea.

"I need a shower." Scott set his mug next to the sink and walked out.

Elodie turned to find Filip watching her. "I guess Scott filled you in on the mist."

"Aye." Filip's lips pressed into a thin line. "This isna something you should keep to yourself. You need to tell Rhona, as well as your sister."

"Edie doesn't need to know."

"Then tell Rhona at the verra least."

Elodie knew he was right, but she also knew that the more she spoke to Rhona, the quicker the Druid leader would discover that Elodie had lost her magic. For some reason, the thought of the Druids kicking her out made her stomach churn.

Filip continued, unaware of her thoughts. "I'm glad one of us will be staying with you at all times."

Elodie set aside the half-eaten croissant, no longer hungry. She dusted her hands. "Now that I think on it, I don't like it. It only means that one or both of you could be harmed."

"We're no' going to let anything happen to you."

There was something about the way Filip had said that. Almost as if it were a vow. But why? They hadn't spoken in years, and even back then, she hadn't cared about anyone but herself. Why was Filip so interested in her safety? Then she recalled Kevin's murder. Of course. He didn't want anyone else to die.

"Thank you," Elodie said with a smile.

Filip pushed to his feet. "There's something else."

"What?" The instant she asked, Elodie knew she didn't want to know the answer.

"There's been another Druid murder."

CHAPTER TWENTY-FOUR

SKYE DRUIDS

Sleeping with Elodie had been everything Scott had thought it would be.

It was also something he knew he shouldn't have done.

But he hadn't been able to help himself. Even that morning, he'd had to have her. Hell, he'd been so wrapped up in her that he'd completely forgotten to use protection. What kind of wanker did that? Him, apparently.

Scott wiped a hand on the fogged mirror to see himself. He stared into his reflection, knowing he was fucked. He might have promised George that he would get Elodie to their organization one way or another, but now he felt sick. Every way he looked at this, Elodie would think he'd used her. Why hadn't he talked to her before giving in to his desire?

"Fuck me," he muttered and braced his hands on either side of the sink as he hung his head.

He wished that was all he had to occupy his thoughts, but there was also the mist, and a second murder on Skye. How much longer would it be before Rhona and Balladyn discovered who he really was? He didn't imagine that they would be so welcoming when they found out. Maybe he should tell them.

It sounded like a sensible solution, but there was a good chance they would remove him from Skye. And that simply couldn't happen. Not until Elodie had agreed to return to Edinburgh with him. Though that also hinged on her magic returning.

Scott squeezed his eyes closed. He sighed and straightened, but he didn't look at the mirror this time. He changed into the clothes Filip had brought for him. Once he was dressed, Scott ran his fingers through his hair and went to find Elodie.

He found her sitting at the kitchen table. By the look on her pale face, Filip had filled her in on the latest slaying. His friend was gone, leaving him alone with Elodie. Scott listened for Filip, but it didn't sound like he was in the cottage.

"He's outside," Elodie said. "He wanted to see if the mist had caused any new damage."

Scott nodded. Where did he start? What did he do? He always knew what his next steps were. But that was before Elodie. She had disrupted his routine, his very way of thinking.

The sound of her chair scraping as she pushed it back drew his attention. She stood before him and took his hand to place it on her stomach. His gaze locked on their hands. He knew what she wanted. Scott had never thought too far into the future. Someone was waging a war on Druids. How could he think about a wife or kids when Druids were dying?

Yet the thought of a life growing inside Elodie, one the two of them might have created, made his throat close with emotion.

"If you can't do it, tell me now," she said.

He lifted his eyes to hers. "I—"

"There's no more damage," Filip said as he came back inside.

Elodie dropped Scott's hand and turned to the sink to put away the dishes. Scott watched her, trying to think of something to say. He didn't have time as Filip walked into the kitchen.

"Did you two hear me?" Filip asked.

Scott tried to look normal. "Aye. That's good news."

"Elodie told me we have the contract. I figured if we're going to be around, we might as well get to work."

Scott forced a smile. "My thoughts exactly." He glanced at Elodie. When he turned back to Filip, his friend was frowning.

"*What's going on?*" Filip mouthed, his pale gray eyes glancing in Elodie's direction.

Scott shrugged. It wasn't as if he would tell him.

Filip's expression went flat. "*You didna,*" he mouthed.

Scott leaned his hands on the back of the chair. "Where do you want to start with the repairs?"

"With Elodie contacting Rhona," Filip stated.

It might be the right thing to do, but Scott didn't want the attention on himself or Filip. Rhona and Balladyn were already interested in them. Scott had warned them about the killings, but now he wondered if he'd made a mistake.

"I already did," Elodie said, her back still to them.

As if on cue, a knock sounded on the door. Scott swung his

head to Elodie. He wanted to talk to her alone first. He reached out and caught her hand.

"What?" she asked as she searched his face.

He parted his lips. He didn't know what to say. How could he tell her that he had a bad feeling about Rhona's arrival? His and Filip's time on the island was quickly running out, and Scott hadn't done anything he'd promised George.

"Scott?" she asked with a frown.

"We're still going to try that thing later, right?" He was rather proud of himself for coming up with something to say.

She nodded, searching his face. "Yes."

With that, she pulled out of his grasp and headed to the door.

"I hope you know what you're doing," Filip stated in a clipped whisper.

Scott couldn't meet his gaze. "I didna plan it."

"It's done now."

There was no more talking as Elodie led Rhona and Balladyn to the kitchen. Scott straightened and found Balladyn's red-rimmed silver eyes trained on him. The Reaper had his long, black and silver hair pulled back at the base of his neck in a queue. His stance was wide, his arms crossed over his chest. Scott knew that position. He used it often when he didn't trust someone.

"I wish you would've called last night," Rhona said. "You can also say Balladyn's name. He would hear you and bring me."

Elodie leaned against the sink, as far from everyone as she could get. "There wasn't exactly time to get to a phone. Next time, I'll know what to do."

Scott watched as Rhona's green gaze landed on him. He didn't move as he stared back at her. She didn't trust him. Not that he blamed her. He was new to the island, and the murders had begun not long after his arrival.

"We did a little digging. Quite a few Druids have been killed," Rhona said.

Filip grunted. "And another here last night."

"Unfortunately." Rhona sighed loudly. "Elodie, your second attack confirms that someone wants to hurt you. What happened fifteen years ago is a long time for someone to hold a grudge. Besides, they could've come after you anywhere. Why now?"

Elodie shrugged as she clasped her hands before her. "I wish I knew."

"I think the wards the two of you added stopped the mist," Scott told Rhona and Balladyn.

Rhona's eyes brightened. "That's good to know."

"It'd be better to know who's controlling the mist and killing Druids," Balladyn stated.

Scott agreed. "Filip and I are doing repairs for Elodie. We'll make sure one of us is with her at all times."

"Or she could come with us," Balladyn said.

Scott immediately became defensive, glaring at Balladyn. He realized his mistake the moment the Reaper smiled.

Elodie looked around the room until she came to Rhona. "I told Scott yesterday, but the rest of you should know. I…I don't have magic anymore."

Scott hated the tremble in her voice. He knew that had been difficult for Elodie to say. He wished she had waited until after she'd tried her magic again, but she must have had her reasons for revealing it now.

"For how long?" Rhona asked softly.

Elodie swallowed loudly but held her chin up. "It happened shortly after I left Skye."

"Others leave Skye and don't lose their magic," Balladyn said. "Why did you?"

Elodie shrugged. "I don't know. It just happened"

Rhona walked around the table and came to stand in front of Elodie. She took Elodie's hands in hers. "We'll figure out what happened. You're one of us. You'll always be one of us."

"I don't have magic," Elodie argued.

"You did once. There's a reason it's gone. And there might be a way to get it back."

Elodie gave her a watery smile. Scott wanted to go to Elodie and draw her into his arms, but Balladyn's gaze kept him in place. The Reaper knew that something was going on between them. It wasn't as if Scott were trying to hide it. Or was he? Once more, he thought about the fact that they hadn't used protection.

"What do we do now?" Filip asked.

Rhona released Elodie's hands and faced everyone. "I'd like information on the Druid murders in Edinburgh. Is there a pattern? Just *mies*? *Droughs*? Male? Female only? Anything that could link the killings?"

"Nothing," Filip answered. "We've been trying to find a connection between them."

Balladyn's brow lifted. "We?"

"Aye," Filip murmured and glanced at Scott.

The Reaper's gaze returned to him. Scott drew in a breath.

There was no way Balladyn and Rhona would leave without answers. How much should he tell them? "There has always been a gathering of Druids in Edinburgh. We try to stick together in most large cities."

"If they know there are others around," Rhona said.

Filip nodded. "Druids usually know how to look for others. It isna like Skye, where most everyone already knows about magic, even if they don't know who is a Druid and who isna."

"How do they know where to look? What do they look for?" Balladyn pressed.

Scott glanced at Elodie. "We keep a lookout for anyone who exhibits magic. One of us approaches them and determines if they're *mie* or *drough*."

"And you are?"

Scott bristled at Balladyn's question. He stared into the Reaper's unusual eyes. "*Mie*, of course."

"Of course," Balladyn mimicked.

Rhona shot Balladyn a look before turning to Scott. "What happens if the Druids don't wish to join your group?"

"Then they go their own way. We simply let them know we're there," Scott answered. "There are *droughs* around. No' many. A few stick together, but the others are loners."

"They doona trust each other," Filip added.

Rhona tilted her head to the side. "Who do you answer to?"

"Georgina Miller. Though we call her George. Her family has lived in Edinburgh for years." Scott hoped that was all they would ask. Anything more would be delving into information he wasn't ready to share with Elodie.

Rhona looked between Scott and Filip. "Does your group have a name?"

"Nay," Filip answered.

She cut her green gaze to Scott. "I'll find out eventually. But keep your secret for now. What I really want to know is... do you have any guesses on who is committing the murders?"

"If we knew, we'd go after them," Scott answered.

Balladyn dropped his arms to his sides. "The two of you could be the murderers."

"I wouldna kill my own brother!" Filip shouted and lunged at Balladyn.

Scott caught Filip in time and pushed him back. "Easy," he told Filip. "It was a valid question."

"The hell it was," Filip stated, his voice dripping with outrage.

Once Scott knew that Filip wouldn't try to attack Balladyn again, he turned to the Reaper. "Our friends have been killed. We want answers. If we were the killers, would I really tell you what was happening in Edinburgh and other places?"

"You can't deny it's a coincidence," Rhona said.

Scott nodded grudgingly. "Aye. It is."

"Why did you really come to Skye?" Balladyn asked.

Scott fought not to look at Elodie. He felt her gaze on him, but she hadn't said anything.

"To settle my brother's affairs," Filip answered.

Rhona's eyes were steady as she focused on Filip. "Do you plan to remain on Skye?"

"Nay," he replied.

Balladyn grunted. "Just long enough to work on Elodie's home, aye?"

Bloody hell. Scott knew they were getting backed into a corner.

"Kevin was close to Elodie," Filip said. "When I saw how people treated her at the pub the other evening, I knew my brother wouldna have stood by and done nothing. I learned she was repairing the cottage, so I offered to give a quote. I'm doing this in my brother's name."

Rhona issued a single nod. "Please understand that these questions have to be asked. Our people are being killed, and I want answers. We will stop whoever is responsible."

Scott knew they would. Just as soon as Elodie got her magic back, and he brought her to Edinburgh.

CHAPTER TWENTY-FIVE

SKYE DRUIDS

Elodie stood beneath the winter sky, the thick clouds moving slowly. Her eyes closed with the rays of the sun that managed to slip through and find her. But the warmth didn't last. When she opened her eyes again, she stared at the gently rolling waves as they crashed onto the beach.

The white sand was dull beneath the overcast sky, unlike when it glistened during the summer. The wide expanse of beach had been a favorite play area for her siblings and her. Running, laughing, teasing. And, yes, bickering. They had thrown balls as well as magic while at the beach. The cove gave them seclusion.

It was impossible to think back to those happy days and not remember how Elodie had said she would never leave. She had thought it the perfect place. How naïve she had been. Nothing was perfect. Not her family, not anyone.

Anger churned as she braced herself against a gust of wind. She had believed her father to be the best man in the entire world. He had been kind, loving, and generous. At least she had believed that. He had fooled her. He had fooled everyone. The only one who had known who Edward MacLean really was had been her mother.

Elodie had felt betrayed—by both her parents. Her father for the abuse against her mother, and her mother for his murder. That kind of deceitfulness was nearly impossible to heal from.

She sniffed and burrowed deeper into her coat. She had come to the beach because this was where she had first begun her training as a Druid. Elodie had believed it was because of the beautiful setting, but now she knew it was because her father wouldn't know what they were doing. It wasn't as if she could be angry at her mum for that. Elodie was glad that she knew how to use her magic. And yet, that circled back to the lies between her parents. She wanted to know why her mother hadn't told her father that she was a Druid. That weighed heavily on her mind.

Elodie frowned as she shook her head. She was at the beach to try using her magic. Thinking about the past wouldn't help. It only made her angry, and that was never a good emotion when a *mie* called to their powers.

She drew in a breath and then blew it out. The fear inside her made her stomach churn and her heart race. Maybe rage was better than anxiety. The urge to leave and forget all about attempting magic made Elodie take a step back.

"What am I doing?" she asked.

How many times had she tried? How many times had she been disappointed? The only way she had been able to carry on was to try and forget that she was a Druid, to forget that the magic had left her.

Now, Scott wanted her to try again. She did need to protect herself against whatever was after her. She couldn't have Druids around her forever, nor could she stay inside the protected cottage her entire life. Whatever was out there would find her eventually. Elodie had to be able to use her magic.

But what if she tried and it really *was* gone for good?

Elodie's breath quickened. A Druid without magic wasn't a Druid. She would be nothing more than human. Nothing special. Nothing unique. She took her hands out of her pockets and looked at them. Magic had once come so easily. Spells had been effortless to master. Her mum had been so proud.

"Come back, please," she begged. "I learned my lesson. I won't use it frivolously again. I swear."

She closed her eyes and called to her magic. Elodie focused deeply on her body, waiting to feel even the slightest stirrings. Nothing happened.

Her throat clogged, but she wasn't done yet. She sank onto the sand and crossed her legs. With her hands on either side of her, and her fingers touching the white grains, she once again closed her eyes. Elodie took a deep, steadying breath and then slowly released it. She thought back to the day her mother had first brought her out to the beach to practice.

"Concentrate, Elodie. It'll take time, but you'll be able to feel your magic."

"What if I don't have any?"

Her mother smiled gently. "My darling girl, you have it."

"How do you know?"

"I know." She tapped her finger on Elodie's nose. "But the only one who can call and control it is you. Until you feel it, you won't be able to use it."

Elodie lifted her chin. "Then I'm going to feel it."

"Good girl. Now, close your eyes. Elongate your breaths. That's it. Whenever you need a connection, put your hands on the sand. Magic flows through Skye. It will heighten yours."

Her mother's voice grew distant. Faint drumbeats, deep and slow, reached her.

"Good. Very good. Call to your magic, Elodie. It's waiting for you. It's always waiting for you."

With her mother's words echoing through her mind, Elodie recreated the entire scene. The sounds of the outside world became faint and then distant. She sank her fingers into the sand, feeling the grains rub against her skin as she sought out Skye's beautiful, powerful magic. She waited to hear the drumbeats of the Ancients. Waited to feel something, anything.

But she was disappointed yet again.

Elodie had no idea how long she sat there before she finally opened her eyes, feeling empty. She got to her feet and dusted off her bottom. She wouldn't cry. She had known that her magic was probably gone for good, but it hurt worse than she'd thought to have it confirmed. Scott had given her hope. Being back on Skye had given her hope.

She turned around and drew up short at the sight of Scott. He stood on the rocks behind her, watching. How long had he been there? She was glad that he hadn't interrupted her. It had been hard enough doing this alone. She didn't want anyone with her.

Elodie made her way to him. The wind whipped at his dark hair. He ignored it as he followed her with his gaze. She thought about their night together and how right it had felt. The way he'd touched her, looked at her. It had been a heady experience, like a drug—and she wanted more.

"Hi," he said when she reached him.

"Hi."

"Any news?"

The hope in his eyes made her look away. "No."

"No matter. You can try again later. I wish you would've told Filip or me you were out here. You could've been attacked."

She looked at the cottage. Filip was working on the roof. "I wanted some time to myself."

"About earlier with the spell…" he began.

Elodie didn't want to talk about that. "I have to meet Edie. She's giving me the deposit for the work. I'll be back shortly."

"Want me to come with you?"

"I'll be fine," she said and started walking.

He kept in step with her on the path to the cottage. "Are you angry with me?"

"No."

"It seems like it."

She stopped and looked at him. "We had unprotected sex. I don't want a child. I may never want children, but especially not now. My life is in utter turmoil, not to mention someone appears to be after me. I came here because I had no choice, and I don't know what to do now."

"Then come back to Edinburg with Filip and me."

Elodie was taken aback by his suggestion. "We barely know each other."

"You doona have to live with me. My sister has an extra room you can use for a wee bit. My point is, you have options."

"Do I?"

He nodded and moved closer as he took her hand. "Aye, my bonnie lass, you do."

She linked her fingers with his. Elodie smiled at him. He seemed to really care about her. Why else would he stay with her and ask her to go back to the city with him? "I'll consider it."

"I can introduce you to so many people in Edinburgh."

"Druids, you mean." And just like that, her happiness dissipated.

Scott shrugged. "You heard Rhona. We'll figure out your magic."

"Can we talk about this later? I need to get to Edie," she lied. She didn't want to think about her magic—or her lack thereof.

"Of course."

They walked in silence to her vehicle. Scott stood in the drive and watched her back out. The trip to Edie's didn't take nearly as long as Elodie wanted. Then again, it wasn't good to drive when her thoughts were all over the place. She also didn't want to run into Trevor. Thankfully, his vehicle was gone when she pulled up to her sister's house. Before she got out, Elodie looked around to see if there was mist or anything else that might attack her.

"Hey," Edie called from the door. "I saw you drive up."

Elodie forced a smile as she hurried into the house. "Hope this isn't a bad time."

"Not at all. Tea?"

"Please."

They walked to the modern kitchen. The house was quiet with the children in school and Trevor gone.

Edie laughed. "You don't realize how much noise kids make until they're not around."

"Speaking of the bairns, I have a favor."

Edie stopped what she was doing and looked at her. "Anything."

"I...well, there's no other way to say this. I had unprotected sex. Twice."

"Ah." Edie dusted off her hands. "Take off your coat. There may not be a need to do that spell."

Elodie frowned at her words. "What do you mean?"

"I've learned a few things since you've been gone," Edie said with a wink. "One particular spell can determine if someone is pregnant."

"But this just happened last night."

"Doesn't matter."

Elodie shrugged. "Okay. Do whatever you need."

Her sister placed her hand on Elodie's stomach. The instant Edie began to mumble the spell, Elodie grew dizzy. She grabbed onto the edge of the island to stay on her feet. Blood rushed through her ears, and sweat covered her body. She was going to be sick.

"All done," Edie said. "Looks like you got lucky."

Elodie perched on one of the barstools and nodded. "Thanks."

"You don't look well."

A moment later, her sister set a glass of water before her. Elodie took it with a shaky hand and drank. Gradually, she began to feel better. "Thank you."

"That spell shouldn't have made you sick."

Elodie glanced at her sister. "I'm surprised you've not asked why I didn't do the spell myself."

"Why would I? I know you can't do magic."

"What?" Elodie asked as she jerked her head to her sister, shock making her body rigid.

Edie shrugged. "Why are you so surprised?"

"I never told you."

"You didn't have to. I was there."

Elodie shook her head in disbelief. "Edie, I didn't lose my magic until I left Skye."

"No, you lost it here. It's why you left."

No. No, that was wrong. Elodie knew the exact moment she'd lost her magic, and she most definitely hadn't been on Skye. "Why are you saying that?"

"I was with you. We sat up all night as you cried." Edie's frown deepened as she studied Elodie. "Don't you remember? You kept asking me what you were going to do. I told you that plenty of people live on Skye without magic, but you said you couldn't stay."

Elodie placed her hands on the cool granite to try and calm her racing heart. "That isn't how it happened."

"Why would I lie? I'll never forget it. It's the day I lost my sister. I can even tell you what you were wearing."

"Stop," Elodie said as she slid off the stool and started toward the door. "Just stop."

Edie followed her, a deep frown marring her forehead. "You're scaring me."

"*I'm* scaring *you*?" Elodie whirled in astonishment to face her sister. "I know what happened in my life."

Edie threw up her hands as she came to a halt. "All right. Maybe I misremembered. I'm sorry."

Elodie searched her sister's face for a full minute. Then she released a breath she hadn't known she was holding. "That's it. You misremembered."

CHAPTER TWENTY-SIX

SKYE DRUIDS

Oddly, Scott didn't mind the manual work. The tasks weren't exactly easy, but they allowed his mind to sort through things. He was worried about Elodie, but when she returned from her sister's, she looked better than she had at the beach.

He needed to report to George and tell her that Elodie didn't have her magic. That she might never have her magic. But Scott held off because he didn't want George to tell him to come home. Elodie was still in danger. And…well, he wanted to spend more time with her. It was wrong. Scott knew it, but there was no getting around his feelings. Though he wasn't sure exactly what those feelings were. They were there, and that was enough for him to make his decision.

He straightened as he watched Elodie hand Filip a check. Filip then waved and jogged to his SUV before driving off. Scott pulled his beanie over his ears as Elodie walked to him.

"He's going to cash the check and get supplies," Elodie told him.

Scott nodded. "All right."

"Also, you don't need to worry about the other thing. The, um, spell. Turns out Edie knew another one to check to see if I had gotten pregnant."

The disappointment that filled him shocked him to his core. He didn't want kids now. Did he? Though he had envisioned what Elodie might look like with her belly swollen with their child. "That's good."

"Yes." She looked away and shifted on her feet.

"What's wrong?"

Elodie shook her head and took a step to walk away, then hesitated. "Edie knew I didn't have magic."

"Maybe you told her and forgot."

Elodie gave him a flat look. "That isn't something you forget."

"Point taken. Did you ask her how she knew?"

"She said I was on Skye when it happened. That we were together."

Scott let her words sink in. "And?"

"And what? That isn't what occurred. I wasn't here. I left *before* my magic deserted me. The thing is, she seemed so sure."

"Sometimes, the past gets jumbled in our heads, mixing what happened and what we wish had happened."

Elodie drew herself up. "I know what happened. I've lived with it."

"I believe you."

"Do you? Because Edie didn't."

Elodie walked into the house. Scott followed her, pulling off his gloves and beanie to stuff them into his coat's pockets.

"One of us is lying. And it isn't me," Elodie continued.

Scott found her in the kitchen. She stood at the sink, staring out the window at the water beyond. "Why would she lie?"

"That's what I've been asking myself, but I can't come up with anything."

He hesitated, wondering if he should ask the next question. In the end, someone had to. "Do you think someone could have messed with your memories?"

"No."

Short and to the point. But Scott noticed Elodie's fingers gripping the sink tightly. He walked closer. "Rhona stopped by shortly after you left. She wants us to drop by her place."

"More questions," Elodie said with a sigh.

Scott hadn't been keen on going, but now he thought that it might be exactly what Elodie needed. "It's probably better if we get it over with now."

"Sure. It's not like I have anything else to do."

He sent a text to Filip. Elodie handed her keys to him. He didn't ask questions as they got into her car. Scott followed the instructions to Rhona's house, which was on the other side of the island. They hadn't even exited the car before Rhona and Balladyn stood on the porch to greet them.

"Thanks for coming," Rhona said with a smile.

Scott returned the expression and nodded at Balladyn, who simply scrutinized him. There was no doubt the Reaper didn't trust him. And with good reason. Scott wished he could tell them the truth, but that wouldn't help anyone.

Rhona's cottage was smaller than Elodie's, and the Druid leader had put her stamp on every room. The house was welcoming and charming—nothing at all like the Reaper who had yet to take his eyes off Scott.

Scott had run into his share of enemies, but none like Balladyn. Even if he weren't a Reaper, Balladyn would've been imposing. A lot of rumors circulated in Skye about the Warden, and Scott suspected that they were all true. Balladyn wasn't a Reaper who stood aside for anyone or anything.

Rhona led them into the living area. Both Scott and Elodie declined refreshments. He stayed close to Elodie, choosing to sit beside her on the couch. Elodie had been different ever since the beach. Though he wasn't sure his hesitation in performing the spell that morning had done him any favors. That was something to think about later. Right now, he needed to focus. No doubt Balladyn would endeavor to trip him up. Scott wasn't just protecting himself now. He had the others in the organization to think about.

"I tried it this morning," Elodie said from beside him.

Scott blinked, shocked and angered that he'd been so deep in thought that he'd missed Rhona beginning the conversation. It didn't take him long to figure out what it was about, however.

"And?" Rhona pressed. She sat in a well-used chair with a table beside her. A book rested on the surface, a pair of reading glasses atop it.

Elodie shrugged and tried to look indifferent, but Scott saw the hurt she couldn't hide quickly enough. "Nothing," she replied.

Balladyn stood near Rhona. "When did you say your magic left?"

"After I left Skye." Elodie's lips pinched.

Scott knew that she was thinking about what Edie had said. He wondered if Elodie would tell Rhona and Balladyn about that. When she didn't, Scott decided it wasn't his place to say anything.

"I've been doing some investigating," Rhona said. "There have been instances where a Druid's magic disappeared. One in particular involved…well, the specifics don't matter. Suffice it to say that she was duped and used her magic for nefarious purposes. The Ancients took her magic as a repercussion. Although I've also recently learned that her magic began to return when the person who tricked her rejoined his, um, family."

That was interesting. Scott was curious to know who she was talking about, but he assumed that Rhona had left out the names for a reason. "Any other ways?"

"A Druid powerful enough to bind someone else's magic," Balladyn replied.

Rhona swallowed loudly. "There was also the case of a Druid who had her magic syphoned by her mother and sister."

Elodie snorted. "In other words, either the Ancients did this to me, or I pissed off a Druid."

"Something like that," Rhona replied.

Elodie shook her head. "I don't buy any of that. My magic waned gradually. I suspect if the Ancients did it, it would have disappeared immediately. Same with a spell."

"Not necessarily." Rhona's lips flattened as she glanced at Balladyn. "What I keep coming up against is the old adage we were always told about not using our magic for trivial things."

"Which I did," Elodie interjected.

Rhona shrugged. "You wouldn't be the only Druid to do that. Why would it only affect you?"

"I wish I knew. I got my hopes up that being back on Skye would return it, but…" Elodie blinked rapidly as she shook her head. "It hasn't come back. I can't try again."

Rhona scooted to the edge of the chair. "I understand. Maybe you wouldn't have to."

Scott perked up at that. He looked from Rhona to Elodie and back again, anxiously awaiting the Druid leader's next words.

"What do you mean?" Elodie asked in a small voice.

Rhona hesitated. "I don't want to get your hopes up, but I'd like to try something."

Elodie's pale blue gaze swung to him. Scott saw the question there. He nodded and smiled in encouragement.

"What can it hurt?" Elodie murmured to no one in particular.

Scott's heart thudded against his chest. Elodie was the answer. George wasn't infallible, but she wouldn't have sent him to Skye on a wild goose chase. That meant that Elodie had to have magic. Some angry wife from fifteen years earlier had probably cursed her or something. Rhona would discover it and right the wrong. Then, Scott could tell Elodie about the organization. He and Filip would convince her to return with them, and Druids would stop being murdered.

Rhona turned her green gaze on Scott. "If you wouldn't mind. I'd like to do this with just Elodie."

Damn. "Of course." Scott reached over and squeezed Elodie's hand before getting to his feet.

"We can wait out here," Balladyn told him.

Alone with a Fae—and not just any Fae, a Reaper. The Warden of Skye. Scott knew this had been set up intentionally. He steeled himself as he followed Balladyn outside to the back deck. The view of the rolling hills and the distant mountains was beautiful, but Scott preferred the cove.

"You care about her."

Scott wasn't surprised that Balladyn went right to the heart of the matter. "Elodie has been dealt a terrible hand. She's a survivor. She's strong, but everyone could use someone to lean on."

"And you want that someone to be you?"

Scott faced the Reaper and shrugged. "I didna intend for it to happen, but aye. She's a beautiful woman."

"You say you've never been to Skye."

"That's right. This is my first time."

Balladyn nodded slowly. "What do you think?"

"I think it's amazing. I admit, I regret waiting so long to come."

"Why did you?"

Scott inwardly smiled at the question. "I told you. I'm here with Filip."

"Because Kevin was your friend."

"He was more than my friend. He was like a brother. His death…" Scott had to pause as the image of Kevin's dead body flashed in his mind. Scott swallowed and shook his head to dislodge the memory and the grip of grief that seized him. "His death hit all of us hard. Kevin was a good man, a good Druid."

"And you want revenge."

"I suspect you would, too, in my place."

Balladyn crossed his arms over his chest, seeming unaffected by the cold temperatures. "I suspect I would."

"You are no' a Druid, but I'm sure you know that our numbers have declined rapidly over the last decade."

"I'm aware."

Scott looked at the sheep on a hillside. "Combine that with the knowledge that someone is actively seeking out Druids to murder them, and it sets everyone on edge."

"Enough that you came to Skye for aid."

Scott swung his head back to Balladyn. "Are you asking if I'm here to ask the Skye Druids for help?"

"You know that's exactly what I meant."

"That wasna my intent, nay. But if it happened? I doona think George would be upset by the prospect."

Balladyn's icy, red-ringed gaze was relentless. "I think you're here for something else."

"Like what?"

"I don't know yet. But I will figure it out soon enough."

Scott bristled at the Reaper's tone. "Is that a threat?"

"It's a fact. But if a threat is what you need to hear, then consider it one."

A blast of frigid air rushed past Scott, but he ignored it. "I'm here because Rhona asked it. And I'm here for Elodie."

"While you just happen to be with Elodie each time she's in trouble..."

"I'm thankful for that. Otherwise, she would be dead."

Balladyn's gaze narrowed. "Whatever it is you're hiding, tell me now."

"I'm no' hiding anything."

"I have no patience for liars."

Scott lifted his chin.

Balladyn's stare was unflinching. "I think you're the one we're after."

"You have a murderer loose on the island. One who has already killed two Druids and came after Elodie twice. If I were the killer, I've had plenty of time to finish Elodie and leave."

"I know."

Fury boiled within Scott. "Then why say it's me?"

"To gauge your reaction." Balladyn dropped his hands. "The only reason I've not personally escorted you back to Edinburgh is because we don't think you or Filip are responsible for the deaths. But you *are* hiding something."

Scott didn't back down from the Reaper. "Let me know when you figure it out."

"You can be sure I will."

CHAPTER TWENTY-SEVEN

SKYE DRUIDS

Elodie couldn't explain the sudden anxiety that gripped her firmly, squeezing until she thought she might pass out.

"I'm a friend," Rhona assured her.

Elodie nodded because she wasn't sure she was capable of words. Every fiber of her body screamed at her to run—as far and as fast as she could go.

"Do you want your magic to return?"

The question was like a surprise punch to the kidneys. Elodie blinked at Rhona. "Yes." She hated how wobbly and frightened her voice sounded.

"I remember how powerful your magic was."

Elodie wasn't sure what to say to that. So, she simply stared at Rhona.

The Druid leader returned her look. After a second, Rhona sat back in her chair. "Do you know what I remember most about your mum? It isn't her kindness, though she was known for that. It was her command of magic. Some Druids like to show off, make sure others know just how powerful they are. Your mother never felt that need. She was confident in herself and her abilities. Her quiet strength resonated each time she did magic."

Tears blurred Elodie's vision. When she thought about her mother, all she could recall was the murder.

"Emily passed that on to her children. I used to be so jealous of you, Edie, and Elias. It took me months to master some spells, but not you three. It came so easily."

Elodie looked down at her hands. "Funny hearing you say that because I was jealous of you and how easy spells came to you. No one doubted your abilities since both your parents were Druids."

"Many think our magic is waning because we mix our blood with those that don't have magic. For a long time, I believed that, too. Then you came back to Skye. I've been thinking about the past."

"That isn't always a good thing."

Rhona shrugged one shoulder. "The past defines us. It makes us who we are now. Running from it or ignoring it is like pretending we don't see ourselves in the mirror."

Elodie finally lifted her gaze to the Druid. "Easy for someone who hasn't stood in my shoes to say."

"I'm not making light of what happened to your family. Quite the opposite, actually. Look at you and your siblings. All of you continued on. You kept living. That's because of the strength in all of you."

Elodie laughed, but there was no humor in the sound. "Living? I've not been living. I've been existing. And barely, at that. I'm only on Skye because I had nowhere else to go."

"What happened in Edinburgh?"

Elodie turned her head away. She didn't want to talk about it.

"You need to talk to someone," Rhona said. "You have people who care about you. Edie. Scott."

At the mention of Scott, warmth infused Elodie. She didn't want to care about him. But she did.

There was a rustle as Rhona scooted to the edge of the chair once more. "I'd like to try something."

Elodie looked over to see that the Druid had her hands out, palms up. Elodie looked at them, then at Rhona. "What?"

"I want to see if I can sense your magic."

What did she have to lose? Elodie placed her palms atop Rhona's. The Druid's fingers lightly closed around her hands. Elodie jerked slightly. Not because there was any pain or discomfort, but out of fear. Which didn't make sense. She knew Rhona wouldn't harm her. Why then did that urge to flee return with a vengeance?

"You're afraid of me," Rhona stated.

Elodie refused to look away this time. "No. Yes."

"Why?"

"I don't know." The truth seemed to be the only answer Elodie could give.

Rhona's look was grave. "You have nothing to fear from me. I'm here to help."

"I know."

"You need to believe those words."

Elodie swallowed. She had to believe the words. How could she when the fear was so strong? But she tried because she wanted her magic back. Again and again, she told herself that she knew Rhona was here to help, and that the Druid leader was a friend and wouldn't hurt her. At first, nothing happened, but eventually she felt the ball of fear begin to loosen. Then, a sudden calmness stole over her. She was able to breathe easier, which also relaxed her. Her eyelids became so heavy that she lost the fight to keep them open.

"Stay with my voice." Rhona's words were soft, gentle. Like the soft kiss of a summer breeze.

Elodie found herself on the beach. The sun was bright. The day warm. Big, fluffy clouds drifted lazily past. Waves rolled soothingly to the shore. Her body hummed with magic. She felt it in every pore. It waited patiently for her, formidable and abundant.

She wiggled her fingers as they sparked. How she loved the feel of it, the rush as it charged through her body. Dozens of spells ran through her head. She had already learned those. She wanted something trickier. Her magic was ready for the tougher spells—just as she was.

Elodie leaned her head back to let the sun bathe her face in its glow. She called to her magic. It answered immediately. It was a seductive feeling. One that she had experienced from a young age. So young that she hadn't told her mother. Nor had she shared with her siblings the spells she'd overheard them learning that she'd copied when no one was around. No one needed to know the strength within her.

A smile formed when the drums of the Ancients filled her ears. She hadn't spoken to them, and they hadn't conversed with her. But that was fine. It was enough that she knew they were there, and that they were aware of her. She kept the drums of the Ancients a secret, also. Not because she was afraid but because she knew it was something between her and them.

The drums started to fade. The waves became harder and harder to hear. The sun dimmed, and the warmth withered.

"Elodie."

Her eyes opened to look into Rhona's green ones. Elodie then glanced at her hands. How could she have forgotten the vibration of her magic just beneath her skin?

"I had no idea," Rhona said softly.

Elodie pulled her hands from Rhona's and clasped them together in her lap. "No idea of what?"

"That you had that kind of magic within you. And the Ancients. Did you really hear them when you were just three?"

The reminder of what she had lost was like a dagger twisting in her gut. "Yes."

"I didn't feel a curse or spell on you."

Elodie swallowed, trying to draw liquid into her mouth. "So, the Ancients took it?"

"I don't think so."

"What?" Elodie frowned. "But I can't do magic. How do you explain that?"

Rhona shrugged and sat back once again. "I can't."

"In other words, you can't help me."

"I didn't say that."

Elodie shook her head, frustration and resentment mixing into a volatile combination. "None of this makes any sense. None of it ever has. First my sister, now this."

"What about Edie?" Rhona asked, her gaze intense.

Elodie glanced away. Why did she have to bring it up? She didn't want to talk to anyone about it. "It's nothing."

"It's something. And I'm guessing it's about your magic."

Elodie jumped to her feet, needing to move to dispel the energy bubbling within her. She paced several times before the hearth, seeking its heat. "Before I told her I didn't have magic, she knew. She said I lost it before I left Skye, but I know that isn't right. It's my magic. My life. I know exactly when I lost it."

"And that was?"

"After I left. When I was using magic for every little thing."

Rhona rubbed her palms on her thighs. "Interesting that Edie would think it happened differently. Then again, Elias had already left, and you two were staying with your grandparents. Not to mention dealing with everything with your parents."

Elodie halted and faced Rhona. "I don't want to be here. I never wanted to return to Skye. I don't belong."

"You are a child of Skye. You do belong."

"Then where's my magic?"

Rhona blew out a breath and stood. "We'll figure it out."

"And if it never returns?"

"What if it does?"

"Do you have any idea how many times I've tried?"

Rhona walked to her and held her gaze. "I felt your magic. When I took you to the past, I *felt* it, Elodie. The sheer power of it is staggering. You have no idea how much you have."

"Had," Elodie corrected.

But Rhona kept talking. "I don't think Corann knew either.

I'm not sure anyone but the Ancients did. Why do you think you heard the drums at such an early age? You even knew it wasn't something that everyone experienced."

Elodie shrugged, unable to find an answer.

"Few Druids have the kind of magic you do."

"The kind I *had*," Elodie corrected again.

Rhona issued a chuckle. "I hate to break it to you, but I think it's still there."

"If you tell me it's all in my head, I might scream."

Rhona's lips twisted. "Maybe it is. You suffered a trauma."

Elodie fisted her hands and fought for control. "I lost my magic *after* all of that."

"Who's to say that it didn't take it that long to manifest? We might have magic, but we don't always have the answers or the understanding. Why do you think we seek out the Ancients?"

"I suppose you also have an explanation for the attacks?"

Rhona's face fell. "Unfortunately, I don't." She spun and returned to her chair. There, she dropped her head into her hands before taking a deep breath and sitting up straight. "Druids are being killed. That much is fact. I wish what Scott and Filip told us was an exaggeration, but it isn't. The murders have come here now. Right about the time of—"

"Scott and Filip's arrival. You can't really be serious," Elodie demanded.

"I was going to say when you returned."

Elodie was taken aback. Her hands relaxed as shock went through her. "Oh. But I'm not the killer."

"I know. I don't think a murderer would bring attention on them by attacking themselves. Not to mention, you'd have to know when someone would be near to save you. No, it's someone else on the island."

That didn't make Elodie feel any better. "Is this because of my past? The things that I…did…before I left?"

Rhona rolled her eyes. "People can be petty and hold grudges, but to resort to murder?" She wrinkled her nose. "I don't think so. Then again, I've been wrong about people before. It nearly cost me my life."

There was a story there. Elodie wanted to ask, but it wasn't the time. Maybe Edie would know the details. "What now?"

"The police are trying to find a suspect. Balladyn and I are also helping since this involves Druids. We're getting the word out today for everyone to stay vigilant."

"Against mist?"

Rhona glanced at the fire. "Scott stopped it."

"Because it couldn't get in anywhere else in the cottage. Not after we put up the wards. Reaper wards."

Rhona nodded absently. "We've already thought of that. It would take days for Balladyn to get to every Druid house and put up wards, but if that's what it takes, that's what we'll do. Meanwhile, don't hesitate to call for Balladyn if you're attacked again. We'll be there in seconds."

Elodie smiled, knowing that Rhona meant every word. She wasn't sure why she had felt such fear earlier, but Elodie was glad it had dissipated. Rhona was one of the few she could trust. Maybe it was just the grip of the past that wouldn't loosen its hold on Elodie. Scott had told her to face the past so it couldn't control her anymore. Perhaps it was time she did just that.

CHAPTER TWENTY-EIGHT

SKYE DRUIDS

Kerry walked into the pub with her head held high. She inwardly smiled when the conversation paused as the occupants noticed her. To the Druids of Skye, she had been shamed after being removed as a deputy. And to them, that meant she should remain hidden.

She had concealed her true self for her entire life. No more.

"Hi, Matthew," she said to the man behind the bar with a wave. She turned her head and nodded at a couple. "Glen. Mary. How are you?"

Of course, no one answered her, but she didn't care. It was enough that she had shocked them. The Druids on Skye needed a jolt to their system. They had followed an old man who kept many secrets that he took to his grave and then appointed Rhona, who didn't have a clue what she was doing. Soon, it would be Kerry's turn to lead.

She took her usual seat in a back corner with a window on

her right. She had no intention of having deputies doing her bidding as Corann—and now Rhona—did. Kerry would take the Druids in a new direction. The first order would be to remove anyone who didn't have magic from the island. Druids came to Skye first, and it should only be Druids who lived here.

The world had once feared them. It was time they did again. It was also time for the Skye Druids to remind the Fae and Dragon Kings of their strength.

But Kerry wouldn't close the island to only those born of Skye. Every Druid would be welcome. She would teach them things that Corann never dared. Things Rhona didn't know yet —and likely never would because her magic was no match for Kerry's. It would be Kerry who returned the Druids' previous glory.

She would be the one to rebuild their ranks—and their magic. The Ancients had deemed it so. How could she not succeed?

Kerry wasn't surprised when no one came to take her order. To them, she was no one now, simply because she was no longer Rhona's deputy. With one word, Kerry could kill everyone in the pub. She stilled the urge. She wasn't a *drough* who killed without thought or hesitation. The Ancients had chosen her, and she wouldn't do anything to upset them.

She rose and made her way to the bar, where she waited for Matthew to finally come over. Kerry gave him a bright smile. "How's your day?"

"Fine," he said standoffishly.

"Mine has been very good, in case you were interested."

He simply stared at her.

Her smile grew. "I'd like to order my usual."

"Which is?"

For a moment, her smile slipped. She wanted to put him in his place, but that wasn't how things were meant to go. Instead, she swallowed her anger as her face tightened. "You know exactly what it is. I didn't realize you were so petty, Matthew. You forget, I know your secrets."

His narrow face paled.

"Oh, don't worry," she told him. "I won't tell anyone. As long as you treat me with respect. You don't know what happened. You've only heard the gossip, and we know how that has gotten you into trouble before. Don't we?" She added just a hint of a threat to her words.

Matthew swallowed loudly. "I'll have your order out soon."

"Thank you," she said with a grin before returning to her table.

Kerry would've pulled out her mobile and played solitaire in the past, but that was before. Now, she had plans to make. She raked her gaze over each Druid in the pub. She had been a deputy for a long time, as well as a trusted member of society. She knew just about everyone's secrets. Some were salacious, some were boring. But secrets were secrets. They would come in handy if she needed to prod anyone to head in the right direction.

She would start in her area, where she knew the most. Then she would work her way into the other areas of Skye. She might not have anything on others, but once Skye saw how her people seemingly loved and followed her despite her being removed as a deputy, the rest would fall in line.

First, though, she had to take care of a few loose ends—the Druids who wouldn't be a part of that future. Once she weeded the flowerbed, she could focus on her next step. To be honest, she quite enjoyed the weeding. She had a list of Druids who would be better off...out of the way. And she had made decent progress already.

Not to mention, it was fun seeing the authorities, along with Rhona and Balladyn, scratching their heads in exasperation. Rhona had embarrassed and belittled Kerry. The Ancients had shown her what the future held for her. It was up to Kerry to stop hiding who she really was, as well as the magic that she had kept to herself, all in the name of *community*.

No more.

"Thank you." She beamed at Matthew as he set the plate of food before her, along with a tumbler of whisky.

He ducked his head and hurried back behind the bar. Kerry chuckled. This would be so much fun.

"Well?" Rhona asked as she and Balladyn watched Scott drive Elodie home.

"He's hiding something for sure."

She shut the door and turned to Balladyn. "Did you get what it was yet?"

"Nay." A small smile played on his lips. "The damn Druid isn't afraid of me."

Rhona laughed as she tugged at his hand when she walked to the living area. "You like him."

"I do. He has courage. Scott doesn't seem like a man easily cowed."

She kicked off her shoes and tucked her leg beneath her before sitting on the sofa. Balladyn sank down beside her. "Hearing about both attacks and how he stood against it was impressive."

"Aye, but I come back to why."

Rhona rolled her eyes. "It can't be because he cares for Elodie? Wouldn't you have done that for me?"

"Always, sweetheart," he said with a grin as he took her hand in his. His face grew serious. "His and Filip's arrival coincides with the killings a little too cleanly."

"You could say the same of Elodie's return. And she was living in Edinburgh before this."

Balladyn sighed. "There have already been two deaths, and we don't have any answers. There will be another tonight."

"I know. I think only your wards kept the mist out of Elodie's cottage."

"If that's the case, then I'd better start warding everyone's house."

Rhona looked down at their joined hands. "She's scared."

"As anyone would be in her shoes."

"You don't understand." Rhona lifted her eyes to his. "She was frightened of me. She was shaking with it."

"Did you feel her magic?"

Rhona nodded slowly. "It's there."

"Did you tell her that?"

"No."

Balladyn raised a single brow. "Why not?"

"I didn't feel a spell or curse. I can't sense anything impeding her magic, and yet it's being obstructed somehow. Maybe the spell I used wasn't strong enough to determine more. When I took her back to the past, the strength of her magic floored me. It's more than I ever expected."

"How much more?"

"It's safe to say she's one of the top three strongest Druids on Skye."

Balladyn grunted. "Interesting. Do you know why she left Edinburgh?"

"She only said she had nowhere else to go. When I pushed for more, she refused to talk."

"Just as Scott wouldn't divulge what he's hiding."

Rhona frowned. "You can't think they're working together."

"Scott's interest in Elodie is undeniable. Aye, I think he's attracted to her. A blind man could see that. But there's something more."

"More as in she's in danger?"

"More as in we need to keep an eye on them."

Rhona nodded at his words. "I was afraid you were going to say that."

"I know what you're thinking."

"Do you?" she asked with a quick grin.

His red-ringed silver eyes softened. "If this were the Fae Others, the soldiers would already be here."

He knew her so well. Rhona loved Balladyn so much. She

couldn't believe everything they had gone through to find their love. "Then who is killing the Druids?"

"Who would want to?"

"If it were only *mies* being murdered, I'd say a *drough*."

"Would a *drough* not kill another *drough*?"

"They would, but they usually like to target *mies*. The hatred goes back centuries."

Balladyn thought for a moment. "Yet, Druids still want to create a group of Others. That would mean *mies* and *droughs* working together. I see that going over as well as the Dark and Light Fae joining forces."

"That's true." Then it suddenly hit her. "What if it's a group of Druid Others attacking the Druids?"

"I was thinking the same thing."

"Some Druid Other groups have formed. It's why there was a demand here on Skye."

"One that you've kept in check."

She rolled her eyes. "Barely. It nearly got me killed. And if the Fae Others hadn't come, I think there would still be an outcry by some to form a faction."

Balladyn squeezed her hand. "It's time we take a closer look at anyone new to Skye."

"Do you have any idea how many visitors we get a day? Even in the winter?"

"We have to start somewhere."

Rhona knew that he was right. She tugged on her shoes. "This is too much for just the two of us. I'm calling for the deputies."

"Are you sure that's wise."

"I have to trust them. Besides, Kerry is no longer a concern. She's doing her own thing."

Balladyn's lips flattened. "I still think you should've banished her from Skye."

"She made a mistake. The Fae Others manipulated her. It could've happened to any of us."

"It wouldn't have happened to you."

Rhona leaned over and gave him a soft kiss. "I'm glad you think so."

"It wouldn't have happened to me, either." He winked.

She gave him another kiss, then got to her feet. "It seems the battle we won over the Fae Others didn't warn away any enemies. We're going to need to show them again."

"Lead the way, darling. I'll be right behind you."

"Beside me." She pulled him to his feet. "Always beside me."

Balladyn smiled. "Always. Now, where do you want me to start?"

"I'm going to contact the deputies and get them here immediately. Can you start warding Druid houses?"

"Of course."

"Be careful."

He eyed her. "I'm not the one being targeted. Besides, I'd relish a battle so I can discover who dares to come after your people. Then we can stop them."

After another kiss, Balladyn was gone. Rhona blew out a breath. She was worried. Very worried. Something sinister crept over Skye, and it needed to be stopped—and soon. Two murders were two too many. But how did they stop an enemy they couldn't find?

Then she thought of Elodie. She had been attacked twice. Could this involve her? It stood to reason that it did. Someone wanted Elodie out of the picture, and Rhona suspected it was because of Elodie's magic—even if she couldn't use it. In order to uncover who was after Elodie and killing Druids, they needed bait.

Rhona looked at her phone. She hesitated in calling Elodie. Rhona was sure she would agree, but first, Elodie needed her magic. That was the only way this could be successful. Otherwise, they would be repeating this again and again, each time putting someone's life in danger.

"So, I need to figure out why Elodie can't use her magic," Rhona said to herself.

There was one person no one had spoken with—Emily MacLean.

CHAPTER TWENTY-NINE

SKYE DRUIDS

Scott glanced at Elodie, who stared out the passenger window as he drove them back to her cottage. He had gone over his conversation with Balladyn in his head, which meant he hadn't realized that she also seemed lost in thought.

Suddenly, Elodie said, "I'm trying to think of a reason I would be scared of Rhona."

"Maybe because she's in a position of power?" he offered.

Her shoulders moved as she took a breath. Elodie's head swung to him. "It was more than that. I was in flight mode. Everything told me to get as far from her as I could."

"Did she hurt you?" The idea that Balladyn had separated them so Rhona could do something to Elodie made Scott see red.

"Quite the opposite." Elodie sighed. "It doesn't make sense. None of it. I trained with Rhona. She's never done anything to me or anyone else."

"That you know of."

"Corann never would've tapped her to take his position if Rhona had a mean bone in her body."

Now Scott understood. "Which begs the question of why you were frightened."

"Exactly. I knew she wouldn't hurt me. Not with words, and not with magic."

"Yet the feeling was there. Did it go away?"

Rhona nodded. "Eventually. She searched for my magic."

"And?" He tried to keep his voice calm, but he was too excited about the possibility of good news. He chanced a look at her again to see her gazing out the windshield.

"Her magic instantly calmed me. The fear evaporated. I hadn't realized how much it had taken control of me until then. I'm amazed that I was still in her home. And then..."

She trailed off. Scott gave her a moment to collect herself. When Elodie didn't expound, he urged, "What?"

"A memory resurfaced of the first time Mum took me to the beach to train. I recalled details as if it were happening right then."

His heart thudded in his chest, hope rapidly spreading through him. Scott gripped the steering wheel tightly. He needed to be calm. If he pushed her too hard, Elodie would start to question him, and he wasn't ready to tell her everything. Not yet. He needed just a little while longer.

"I remembered the feel of my magic moving through me," Elodie said in the barest of whispers.

Scott glanced at her to see tears rolling down her cheeks. He inwardly winced. Here he was, thinking about his organization's plans, while she was suffering. He felt like a cad. Shame washed over him. Elodie was dealing with many traumas. He had no right to heap more on her slender shoulders, whether she could handle it or not.

The more he thought about it, the more Scott knew he had to call George and tell her to find another way to save the Druids. Even if Elodie found her magic again, Scott couldn't, in good conscience, take her to Edinburgh and into war. Elodie had been through enough for one lifetime.

Elodie sniffed loudly and wiped at her face. "When the memory faded, so did the feeling of my magic." She buried her head in her hands.

He reached over and put a hand on her shoulder as he pulled to the side of the road. After putting the vehicle in park, he tugged her into his arms and held her as she sobbed. He and every other Druid took their magic for granted. He couldn't imagine what it must be like to reach for it and have the magic not answer. It would be devastating. Shattering.

Try as he might, he couldn't find words that would lessen her pain. Instead, he remained quiet as her pain enveloped them both. The patter of rain on the car pulled his attention outside. It was as if the sky were crying with Elodie. As if all of Skye wept with her.

To his shock, his eyes swam with moisture.

The longer they sat there, the more solidified he was in his decision to call George. But he didn't want to leave Skye. Not until he knew that Elodie would be safe from whoever was after her. Scott would search for whoever was killing the Druids. He would avenge Kevin's death, and all the Druids who had been murdered. Then, and only then would he be able to return to Edinburgh.

Elodie pulled out of his arms. He studied her tear-stained

face and spiky lashes. She wiped at her cheeks. With a shaky breath, she sat back in her seat. "I can't remember the last time I cried like that."

"My sister always tells me that tears are cathartic."

Elodie smiled as her pale blue eyes briefly met his. "I think she's right because I feel better. Somewhat."

"Good." He hesitated, wanting to say more. But what? That he enjoyed holding her? That he liked that she had let him comfort her? It sounded so…trite. It sounded like something he'd say to charm someone.

And that wasn't what he wanted to do with Elodie.

"I, uh…can we sit here for a little longer?" she asked.

Scott rested his hands on his thighs. "Whatever you want to do."

"It's just that, well, I have to talk about something."

He unbuckled his seat belt and shifted so he could see her better. "Talk away."

She nervously gripped her fingers before shooting him a quick glance. "It's about why I came to Skye."

"Take your time." Scott would be lying if he said that he wasn't curious about why she had left the city. Given her reaction, whatever it'd been had really upset her.

"I don't want to talk about it, but Rhona's right, I need to." Elodie nodded once. Her gaze remained focused through the windshield, presumably watching the raindrops run together. "I can't say that I was exactly happy in Edinburgh, but I was more or less content. I worked at a printing office doing some dead-end job I hated. But it paid the bills. My co-workers were nice — well, most of them."

Scott remained still, studying her as she spoke.

Elodie glanced at her hands. "Living paycheck to paycheck is difficult. I was looking for another job, hoping to find something that paid better. It was either that or find a cheaper flat. My roommate was trying at times. I knew it was wrong to bring someone in who I didn't know, but I was desperate. I needed help with the rent." Elodie paused for a long moment. "Kate wore expensive clothing and carried name-brand purses. But she worked as an office assistant somewhere. There was no way she could afford such things on her salary. She liked to go out. A lot. She often asked me to go with her, but I always declined. Until one day when I said yes."

The rain began to fall faster. The wipers cleared the window, but a moment later, the water had blanketed it again.

"That's when I found out what she really did." Elodie shook her head, her lips twisting. "She wormed her way into parties and to rich men's tables." Elodie looked at him. "You wouldn't believe how easy it is to do. If you dress the part, they think you're with the group. It was the first night I'd let myself have fun in…ages. I danced. I drank the free-flowing champagne. And I laughed."

He shrugged one shoulder. "Sounds like you needed it."

"I did. I just wish I would've done it with someone else. When I realized that I'd had too much to drink, I went looking for Kate but couldn't find her anywhere. I thought maybe she had left with someone. I was drunk. Not a good situation for a woman alone. I managed to find my way to a bouncer and asked for help. The club made sure I got into a cab, and it took me home. Kate wasn't there either. I didn't make it any farther than my sofa. That's where I was in the wee hours of the morning when the police banged on my door."

Scott frowned, the story taking a turn he hadn't expected. "What did they want?"

"Seems some of the men at the party had their wallets stolen. The police demanded to see my bag. Since I knew I hadn't done anything, I gave it to them. Imagine my surprise when they opened it and a man's wallet was inside."

Scott raised a brow. "And Kate?"

"Gone. Along with a few other wallets. I was arrested, of course. I swore I had nothing to do with it, but it was hard for anyone to believe me when the proof was right there. I lost my job because I couldn't make the bail and stayed in jail for a few days. I couldn't pay the rent because I didn't have a job, so I lost my apartment. To add insult to injury, Kate also stole my debit card and cleaned out my bank account. There wasn't much there, but it left me with nothing. Fortunately, she didn't know about my second account where I had a little savings. I spent weeks working with the police to give them everything I knew about Kate. Since she had also robbed me, and I only had one wallet—not to mention I didn't leave with her—they eventually dropped the charges. Though I had no way to get my job back. I had no choice but to return to Skye. The sale of the cottage will give me a little money to go somewhere and start again."

"What about Kate?" he asked. "Did they catch her?"

"I don't know. I don't care. I want to forget all about that ordeal. I just wanted to have a night where I forgot about everything. Instead, it upended my life."

Scott reached for her hand and gave it a squeeze. "You survived it, though."

"Someone at my age being homeless and without a job? It's terrifying."

"How long did Kate live with you?"

"About eight months."

He twisted his lips. "Seems like the universe made sure you had to return to Skye."

"I've thought that, too."

His gaze lowered to their hands. It felt right to be with her. To touch her. Just as it felt right to be on Skye. The island had seduced him, beguiled him. Or maybe he had been enchanted.

He knew Elodie had bewitched him.

"I should have my life in order by now." Elodie shrugged. "It just feels as if I can't get my feet under me."

"Maybe that's because you were no' meant to be anywhere *but* Skye. This is where you belong. Think about how many things had to happen to send you back here."

Her nose wrinkled. "I have. It's a little unsettling."

"Doona think of it that way. Think of it as a course correction. Skye is in your blood. Just as you are part of it."

"Now you sound like my sister and Rhona."

"There's no denying that Skye is special. I've fallen for the island."

Elodie's lips curved into a grin. "Have you now?"

"Without a doubt. This place is,"—he paused, searching for the right word—"paradise."

"Even with Druids being killed?"

The reminder made his gut churn. "That's what brought us

here. It bothers me that the murders didna start in Skye until Filip and I arrived."

"The same could be said about my reappearance."

Scott didn't reply because he was thinking about George's vision.

"You think it's me?" Elodie asked in disbelief.

He quickly shook his head. "I doona."

"You weren't so quick to say that just now."

"I was thinking about your attacks."

Her brows drew together. "You think something followed me here to kill me?"

There was a distinct possibility. Scott knew that if Elodie had any chance at all, he had to tell her everything. The truth, however, might change things between them forever.

"There's something you need to know."

CHAPTER THIRTY

There's something you need to know.

Scott's words hung between them. Elodie was glad she had told Scott about the incident in Edinburgh. That, along with her tears, lifted a huge weight off her. Now, however, she knew that whatever he wanted to talk about wouldn't be something she wanted to hear.

"Tell me," she urged.

He ran a hand down his face. The smile was gone. His face was set in hard lines, almost as if he steeled himself for what was to come. Which only made her heart beat faster.

"Scott?"

He looked away, making her feel like him holding her gaze was too difficult. "You doona know how nice it is to have a community as you do on Skye. Druids in Edinburgh may never know there are others around. Sometimes, we find Druids. Other times, we doona. For many, many years, it was just me, my da, and my sister. We kept our secret close. We didna have a beach to ourselves where we could practice magic. We did it in the secret of our home, careful that no one could hear. And we never, ever did it outside of the house."

While she had spoken, Scott had remained still. Now, he fidgeted. If they had been anywhere else, she was sure he would've stood and paced. Silence stretched, broken only by the patter of rain and the squeak of her wipers.

Finally, he released a long breath. "One day, I encountered Kevin at a pub during a football match. We were rooting for the same team. We had mutual friends, and our two groups spent the rest of the evening hanging out. Kevin invited me to a party the next day, and then I invited him somewhere. I'd never had a friend like him before. It felt as if I'd known him my entire life. I met Filip, and Kevin met my family. That went on for months. It was Kevin who finally let it slip that he was a Druid. So, I did some magic of my own." Scott laughed at the memory. "Next thing I knew, Kevin had taken me to a group of Druids. I got my family involved, too. It was like we'd finally found a place to be ourselves."

Scott slid his gaze to her. "It wasna anything like Skye, but it was close. Georgina Miller, or George as we call her, leads us. I no longer felt as if I had to hide. No' that we go around doing magic everywhere."

"I understand," Elodie said. And she did. More than he knew. She had missed having other Druids around these past fifteen years.

He gave her a quick smile. "George sends us through the city to find other Druids."

"Any Druids?" she asked.

Scott hesitated for a moment. "Aye. Both *mies* and *droughs*."

"Isn't that dangerous? Our two divisions don't get along."

"We've had to do something. Few understand what's going on. Druids are dying at an alarming rate."

She searched his gaze. "You think by banding together, you can stop the deaths?"

"We do."

"How?"

He looked away and squeezed his eyes closed. When he opened them, he stared out the window for a full minute. "George is a seer."

Few Druids had that gift. Hearing that made Elodie sit up straighter. "Can she find the killers?"

"Sort of. She sent Filip and me to find someone who could help us." Scott then looked at her.

It took Elodie a moment to realize what he was saying. Shock went through her first. Then the cold hand of anger. "You two just happened to hear that I needed help with the cottage? It was a reason to get close to me."

"Elodie, please, let me finish explaining," he begged.

She shook her head. "You've been using me the entire time. No wonder you pushed me so hard to find my magic. You need it."

"I...bloody hell," he ground out, frustration making his voice rise. "I'm telling you all of this because you need to know."

"Did you tell Balladyn?"

Scott's gaze jerked to her. "No."

"Why not? Haven't you and Filip told me repeatedly that they could help?"

"They wouldna understand."

"Why is that?" she demanded.

Scott gripped the steering wheel as he stared at her. "You're the answer, Elodie. You can stop the murders."

"Why didn't you tell Rhona or Balladyn?" she demanded again. Elodie didn't want to hear the pleading in Scott's voice. She didn't want to see his eyes imploring her. "I trusted you. Did you attack me so that I would trust you?"

"No!" he bellowed. "I would never do that."

Her chest constricted as she thought of the feelings she had for him. "I thought you wanted me to move with you to Edinburgh because there was something developing between us."

"There *is* something between us."

She was going to throw up. Her stomach churned as her heart broke. "Yes, there is. Lies and deceit."

He rested his forehead on the steering wheel and gripped it with both hands. "I didna lie to you. No' once."

"Omitting the truth is lying." Her heart hurt so badly she wanted to double over and wail.

Scott lifted his head and looked at her, regret coloring his cheeks. "What lengths would you go to in order to stop people from being killed? How far would you go to get revenge for someone you considered a brother?"

Damn him. She couldn't look away from his eyes as the truth slammed into her. "To the ends of the Earth."

"That's where I'm at, lass. I never expected you. I never anticipated finding myself fal—"

"Don't you dare say it," she demanded. Elodie couldn't let him say the words. She would believe them, and right now, she couldn't handle that.

He swallowed and sat up. "It's the truth."

"I don't want to hear them."

Scott nodded slowly.

"So, what were you going to do if you couldn't convince me to go back to the city with you?"

He took a breath and then slowly released it. "I intended to call George today and tell her to find another way."

"Because I don't have magic?"

"Because you've been through enough. There has to be someone else who can help."

Elodie looked out her window and crossed her arms over her chest. She didn't want to soften toward him. It was so easy to believe him. She had from the very beginning.

"I never lied to you," Scott said again.

She wished he had waited to tell her at the cottage. Then she could have told him to leave. Instead, she was stuck in the car with him. She could get out and walk in the rain, but it was her car. Elodie debated whether to make him get out. She knew he would.

"I'm sorry," he murmured. "Everything I did, I did for Druids everywhere."

"You should've told me everything from the beginning. I would've helped."

He sat there for a moment in silence. "We couldna take the chance that you'd refuse and tell Rhona."

"Tell Rhona what, exactly?" she asked as she looked at him.

"Maybe it's better if you doona know."

She glared at him, letting the full weight of her fury reflect in her eyes. "You've come this far. Tell me all of it."

"My group is a Druid Other faction."

All the air escaped Elodie. "The Skye Druids just battled the Fae Others, and you come with this news?"

"We didna have a choice. Someone had to do *something*," he replied. "The police had no idea of the connection, and it wasna as if we could tell them."

Elodie had been out of the loop regarding Druid news. Until she returned to Skye, and Edie had filled her in on everything. If she hadn't known about the Others, then she wouldn't have thought twice about helping Scott. But she knew now. All of it.

"Do you understand what you're doing?" she asked.

He gave her a flat look, his expression turning hard. "Of course, I bloody well understand. I've watched my friends be killed. I've stood by, helpless and waiting for the authorities to figure it out. Then George had a vision, and I was willing to do anything to keep any more Druids from being murdered."

"You're part of a group of Others. The very thing my sister and every Druid on Skye fought against. You do understand what the Fae Others were attempting, don't you?"

"We're no' them. We're different."

"I don't think there is a difference."

He searched her gaze before nodding. "I'm sorry you feel that way."

He put the car in gear and pulled back onto the road without another word. Elodie's heart grew more troubled as they got closer to the cottage. When he pulled onto her drive,

Filip came out of the garage where he had stored their materials.

Elodie didn't think she could handle any more of Scott's excuses. She was out of the car and running to the house before he had even shut off the ignition. Her hands shook with the news she now had. It was information she couldn't keep to herself, but if she went to Rhona, they would force Scott and Filip to leave. It was what they should do. The Others, in any form, were dangerous.

Mies and *droughs* gathering together, three of the most powerful from each group combining their magic to become more formidable. The Fae Others had sought out the Reapers to kill and had used Skye to do it. It made sense that Druid Others would be murdering Druids.

The door to the cottage opened. Elodie stilled in the kitchen, waiting to hear Scott's boot falls behind her. Instead, a lighter tread approached. She knew it was Filip before he called her name.

"Elodie, can we talk?" he asked.

"I think it's better if you leave."

He cleared his throat. "What about the work on the cottage?"

Damn. She had forgotten about that. Payment had been made. She could ask for it back, but he'd already bought supplies. "Finish. Quickly."

"We will."

She whirled around and met Filip's gaze. "No. Just you. I don't want him here."

"It'll go faster with two people."

"Then find someone else. I don't want to see him." She didn't want to see Filip either, but she hadn't slept with him.

Elodie fisted her hands at her sides. She had felt something with Scott. And that made everything hurt a thousand times worse. Because she had thought...*hoped*...there was something more between them.

"I understand," Filip replied softly. He turned to go, then paused. He swiveled his head back to her. "We just want to stop the killings."

"Everyone does. Joining a group of Others isn't the way to go."

"The group was formed five years ago. We've never done anything like the Fae or the original Others. You doona have to believe me, but it's the truth."

She watched him walk out of the house. Elodie didn't know or care if they stayed. She couldn't think of anything but the words swirling in her head, things she wished she didn't know. Because now she had to go to Rhona. She had to speak out against Filip and Scott.

Do you really?

Elodie pivoted and started for her room. She halted at the sight of the door to her parents' room. For just a second, she thought about going inside. Flinging open the door and waiting for the ghosts of the past to descend upon her.

But now wasn't the time. She wasn't ready, emotionally or mentally.

Her throat grew tight when she thought about all the things she had shared with Scott. Things she hadn't told anyone. Ever. And yet, it had been so easy to talk to him. It had been so easy to *be* with him.

She walked into her bedroom and sank heavily upon the bed. Then she fell back and stared at the ceiling. Skye was supposed to have been a new start for her. No. That wasn't true. Coming home was meant to give her time to face the past while she fixed up the cottage. After the sale of the house, then she was supposed to start a new life.

Why then did it feel like she had started something already? Something she didn't want to lose.

CHAPTER THIRTY-ONE

SKYE DRUIDS

"Elodie," her mother beckoned. "It's going to be all right."

Someone was screaming. Her mother's eyes were filled with fear, but her voice was oddly soft. Elodie tried to concentrate on her mum's face, but she couldn't focus. A headache started behind her eyes, the kind she always got when she was sick, and her eyesight changed.

She tried to look past her mother, but her mum held her face firmly.

"Elodie, I promise. And I've never broken a promise to you."

Elodie's eyes snapped open as the last word reverberated in her mind. She struggled to cling to the dream. Her mother's face disappeared from her mind's eye, but not her voice. Elodie could still hear it clearly.

She sat, shoving her hair from her face. She had fallen asleep in her clothes. It took her a moment to remember what had happened. When she recalled Scott's confession, all the anger and hurt returned. She had retreated to her room in the hopes of keeping away from Scott and Filip.

Elodie swung her legs over the side of the bed and stood. She walked out of her room to the hallway and listened, but she didn't hear the guys. She had told them to leave. Now, she wondered if that had been such a good idea. She thought of the mist and how she had no way of protecting herself. But the deed was done. She was alone, just as she wanted.

She made her way to the kitchen and looked out the window to see that dusk had fallen. Elodie rubbed her tired eyes. The cottage was too quiet. It felt huge now that Scott wasn't around.

The rub of it all was that she wanted to talk to Scott. How could she now, though? He'd had an ulterior motive in everything he'd done and said. Whatever trust had been there was gone. His admission had seen to that. Her feelings...she shook her head. She couldn't think about that right now.

Even though she knew Scott could've kept pretending instead of admitting everything, it was hard to give him any credit. Because, once again, he'd had a motive. That hurt the most. She had thought there was something real between them. The blame for that lay on her shoulders. She was the one who'd finally felt something. She should've known not to let herself be drawn in by that, but it had been impossible not to.

And she was sure Scott had felt something, too. Or maybe he was just that good of an actor. It didn't matter what answer he gave her, she wouldn't believe him.

Elodie rubbed her hands up and down her arms. She walked through the cottage, room by room, feeling the emptiness of the house like never before. It was almost as if the ghosts of the past had retreated, as well. She halted before the fire. A fresh log had been placed in it, and someone had stocked more wood. It was the first time she had been alone in the house since Scott and Filip had given her the quote. Elodie didn't know what to make of the feelings churning through her.

She had always liked her company over that of others. It'd never bothered her to be alone. Now, however, she longed to feel Scott's gaze, to hear his deep voice, and to see his dark blue eyes. She ached to feel his comforting arms around her.

Her mobile rang, the sound shattering the silence and startling her. Her heart pounded from the adrenaline as she hurried to her room where she had her phone charging. She fumbled with it until she had it in her hand. When she finally had it gripped, she looked at the screen to see who was calling, only to see *Unknown Number*. For a moment, she hesitated, wondering if she should answer it. She decided she was being silly. It was just a call. What could happen over the phone?

"Hello?" she asked.

The silence that greeted her sent a chill skating down her spine.

"Hello?" Elodie repeated.

The line went dead.

Elodie pulled the mobile from her face and looked at it. Who had blocked their number? Maybe it was just a wrong number. Or perhaps the connection was bad, and they hadn't heard her. Whatever the cause, she wouldn't let it freak her out. The house had enough ghosts already. She didn't need to add another one.

Unable to help herself, Elodie went to the front of the house and looked out a window. Filip's SUV was gone. Scott and Filip had promised not to leave her alone because of the attacks, but she had also told them that she didn't want them near her. It wasn't as if she could be angry they had done exactly as she'd demanded. Except Filip was supposed to continue the repairs. Though, it was evening. He couldn't be expected to work all day.

She let the curtain drop back into place and turned around. Night was falling quickly. She could gather a few things and head to Edie's, but the same argument she'd had to begin with about not wanting to bring anything to her sister's family remained. It wasn't as if Elodie had funds to rent a room somewhere for the night. Besides, that would leave her in the same quandary the following night. And the one after that.

"I'm an adult," she said aloud. "I can do this. The cottage is warded. It kept the mist out before."

Her head swung to the side as she looked into the front room where the fire crackled. She would have to make sure it didn't go out. If she had magic, she would've used a spell to ensure it didn't. She wondered if perhaps Scott or Filip had used such a spell. Her fingers hovered over the phone as she contemplated texting to ask.

"No."

She lowered her cell. It was time she did something on her own—past time, actually. She had leaned on others enough since returning to Skye. She was supposed to face the past, not ignore it as she had been.

The hardest part had been admitting that she no longer had her magic. Now that others knew, the only thing left for her to do was go into her parents' room. It wasn't as if blood still covered the walls. It had been cleaned, and everything within replaced. The only thing that remained were the memories, the aftershocks of that horrible day that continued to ripple through time.

Edie had managed to get past it. For all she knew, so had Elias. As for her mum, Elodie knew it was time to see her. Facing the past meant facing *everything*. It was going to be difficult, but she would get through it. Somehow. As she had done with everything else in her life. By just putting one foot in front of the other.

Her stomach grumbled, reminding her that she hadn't eaten in a while. Elodie walked to the kitchen and toasted some bread. She found some sausages in the fridge that Scott had bought and heated those in the microwave. It wasn't much of a meal, but it was sustenance.

The quiet of the house unsettled her more than the memories of the past. Elodie put on some music through her phone, but she skipped every song that came on. Some of her favorite ones she didn't want to hear. Finally, she gave up and turned off the app to finish her meal in silence. Only after she had cleaned up did she find herself staring at her cell again. She needed to talk to someone, and she knew exactly who she wanted to speak with.

Elodie went to her contacts and scrolled through until she found her brother's name with his information she had gotten from her sister. Her finger hovered over Elias's number for several seconds before she got up the nerve to press the icon to call. She hated how her hand shook as she lifted the phone to her ear. It rang three times. Just as she was about to hang up, the line connected.

"Hello?" asked a deep voice on the other end.

Her eyes closed and filled with tears. She hadn't realized how much she'd needed to hear from her big brother. "Elias?"

"Elodie?" She heard surprise in his voice.

Tears slipped down her cheeks. It took her two tries to talk. "Hi."

"Hi, yourself. I'm glad to hear from you."

She sniffed and sank into a chair at the table. There was no stopping the tears now. She blinked open her eyes. "You'll never believe where I am."

"Last Edie told me, you were in Edinburgh."

"I'm on Skye. In the cottage."

There was a long beat of silence. "Are you alone?"

His question made her frown. "I am. Why?"

"Why no' stay with Edie?"

"Because I don't want to be a burden. I'm getting the house ready to sell. I assume Edie told you about that."

Another pause. "She didna."

"Oh." Shite. Elodie didn't want to cause a fight between her siblings, and she really needed the money. "The place is in bad shape. None of us took care of it. Not that I blame Edie. She has her family. We just thought it was time."

"I'm no' averse to selling."

But there was a problem. That was obvious. "That's good." She swallowed, trying to think of something to say. "Do you think you might come for a visit while I'm here? It's been a long time since we've all seen each other."

"Why no' come see me?"

"I…well, I suppose I could." Her thoughts raced with details about the repairs on the cottage. And Scott.

"That would be better."

Something in his words caught her attention. "Why would that be better?"

"The timing of everything. Come tomorrow."

Unease shifted through her. "Why the hurry? And what about Edie?"

"As you said, we've no' seen each other. It would be good to catch up. I'm sure Edie could use a little time away, too."

Her gut was telling her that Elias was lying about something—or at the very least omitting. Then it hit her. "You don't want me in the cottage."

"I didna say that," he answered.

Elodie wiped the last of the tears from her cheeks. "I just wanted to hear my brother's voice. I know you kept in touch with Edie, but not me. I didn't exactly reach out to you either. Returning to Skye made me realize that I need to face the past."

"Nay!"

His bellow shocked her. Elodie's growing frown deepened. "What's wrong with you?"

"Elodie," Elias said more calmly. "The past is done. It tore our family apart. Why would you want to go back to it?"

"Because my life has been hell. I want a fresh start, and I don't think I can do that until I face things. Coming to Skye was just the start. I'm tired of being weighed down by everything. You and Edie managed to get by, but I haven't."

Elias snorted loudly. "Who said I was good?"

"Are you?" she asked in a soft voice.

"We've all dealt with that day in our own way."

"You went away. You abandoned me when I needed you the most."

Elias signed. "I know. I'm sorry. That's all I can say. I'm sorrier than you'll ever know. But I had to leave. If I didna…"

"I understand." And she did. After all, she'd left Edie behind.

"I should've done better to keep in touch," he said after a moment.

Elodie smiled, even though he couldn't see her. "Me, too. Can we change that?"

"I'd like that. A lot. I meant it about you coming tomorrow."

She looked around the kitchen. She didn't like being in the cottage. Especially alone. Then there was Scott. She didn't want to see him, either. On top of that were the attacks directed at her.

"Elodie?"

"Before I say yes, you should know a couple of things."

"I'm listening."

She drew in a deep breath. "My magic is gone. And Druids are being killed on Skye. Some believe I'm being targeted."

"Bloody hell!" Elias bellowed. "You should've called me straight away. Get Edie there with you right now."

Elodie winced at the alarm in his voice. "Calm down. The cottage has been warded—by Druids, Rhona, and even Balladyn."

"The Reaper on Skye?"

Obviously, Elias kept up with what was happening on the island. "The very same."

"Elodie, I need you to listen to me. Doona trust anyone that isna me, Edie, Rhona, or Balladyn."

Her thoughts immediately slid to Scott. "Why?"

"I'll tell you everything when I get there. Doona let anyone else inside the house."

"Um…that might be an issue. I hired someone to repair things around here."

She could hear Elias moving stuff around through his end of the phone. "Who?"

"Filip Gordan, and his friend from Edinburgh, Scott Ryan."

"Doona let them in the house again. Do you understand?" Elias bit out.

"Scott saved me, though."

"Elodie. Did you hear me?" her brother barked.

She nodded. "Yes."

"I'll be there as soon as I can." The call disconnected.

Elodie placed the phone on the table as a shiver went through her.

CHAPTER THIRTY-TWO

SKYE DRUIDS

"I'm freezing my balls off," Filip grumbled.

Scott ignored his friend as he watched Elodie's house from inside the garage. "I told you to go home. I'll be fine."

"Like I'm going to leave you alone to take care of another attack by yourself."

Scott looked over his shoulder at Filip. "Thanks, mate."

Filip shrugged. "It's what Kevin would've done."

"You make it sound as if you two were completely different. You're no', you know."

"We were. But I appreciate you saying that. Kevin was the better man. He didna make stupid mistakes."

Scott snorted and shook his head as he faced Filip. "We all make stupid mistakes. Trust me, your brother did, too."

"Did he tell you I nearly turned *drough*?"

Scott sobered at the comment. "Nay."

"That's why he ended up in Edinburgh. I'd left, you see..." Filip lowered his gaze as he huddled in his coat. "Got mixed up with the wrong crowd. I still doona know how he found out. I didna say anything."

"Brothers know." Scott thought about his sister, Willa.

Filip shrugged and looked up at Scott. "I'm glad he knew. However it happened. He saved me. I look back and still wonder how I allowed myself to think becoming *drough* was what I wanted."

"Doona be so hard on yourself. We all find ourselves in places at times in our lives when we're at a crossroads. We have choices, and we try to make the right ones. Sometimes, we do. Other times, we doona."

"Da would've disowned me," Filip stated. "If he'd found out. Kevin never told him." Filip's shoulders moved as he took a breath. "Everyone loved Kevin. He always knew the right things to say and do. It was like he saw his path clearly and never deviated from it."

"That doesna make your path any less. Maybe it makes yours even greater because you struggled."

Filip grinned. "That's something Kevin would've told me. No wonder you two were such close friends."

"He was the brother I never had."

"He was a good brother."

Scott nodded solemnly as he eyed Filip. "Aye. And if you need another one, you know where to find me."

Filip's face split into a smile. "You may come to regret that."

"Never. Kevin and I promised each other that if anything ever happened to one of us, the other would look after our family. That's what I'm doing, but doona think it's out of obligation. You're a good man, Filip. You've proven that with all you've done for Elodie."

Scott glanced through the crack in the doors to look at the house. He hadn't gone inside. He'd left that to Filip, but he set more wards, just in case. Elodie might not trust him anymore, but he would see her safe.

"Have you told her?"

He swung his head back to Filip. "What?"

"That you care about her?"

Scott started to deny it but found he didn't have the energy. "It wouldna make any difference now. I've betrayed her trust. Once that has been broken, it's nearly impossible to repair."

"Depends on how hard you try."

"Now look who's giving advice," Scott said with a grin. But it quickly melted away. He looked down at his hands that had held Elodie earlier. "I should've stepped aside from this mission as soon as I realized there was an attraction."

"George wouldna have cared. She would've told you to use it. That the end justifies the means."

"I would've agreed with her before, but no' now." He looked at Filip. "I willna coerce anyone to help us. We should've been upfront with Elodie from the beginning."

Filip wrinkled his nose. "And taken the chance that she would refuse?"

"She's refusing now."

"Because she doesna have her magic."

Scott lifted one shoulder in a shrug and leaned back against a wooden shelving unit against the wall. "Even if she did, she wouldna help us."

"What made you tell her today?"

"It's been bothering me. I couldna hold it in any longer. She deserved the truth."

Filip eyed him for a silent moment. "Or maybe you wanted to give her a reason to turn you away."

The statement hit too close to home. "I doona know what you mean."

"Really? That's odd since Kevin once told me that you could have any woman you wanted, but you always found some excuse to end things."

"I thought we were talking about you."

"Subject changed," Filip said with a wry grin.

Scott shook his head. "George sent me here because I have a way of getting others to do what I want."

"Aye. With your words. She calls you the silver-tongued charmer."

"I've used my words and charm for so long that it became habit. I never knew if someone was with me because they wanted to be or because I *persuaded* them."

Filip raised a brow. "So, you decided to test it out on Elodie?"

"That wasna my intention. I had a plan. Then I met her, and it all went to shite. I didna want to lie. I didna want to charm her. It was easy to be myself with her. So, I was," he said with a half-hearted shrug.

"And you fell for her."

Scott wanted to deny it, but his heavy heart wouldn't let him. "I did."

"Again, have you told her?"

"It wasna exactly the time."

"What are you going to do now? Hide out here for the rest of your life?"

Scott turned to look at the house again, hoping to catch a glimpse of Elodie's silhouette through the curtains. "I'm staying tonight. After...? I've no' thought that far ahead."

"That's shite, and you know it."

"Fine," he snapped and swiveled to pin Filip with a glare. "Do you want me to say that I love Skye, and I never want to leave? That I've found something on this island, and the thought of never experiencing it again leaves me as cold and fearful as no' having Elodie in my arms?"

One side of Filip's lips lifted in a smile. "Now you sound like Kevin. He loved Skye in a way that I never did—he and my father both. I couldna see it. At least, I didna back then. I'm no' sure if it's my brother's death or because I've changed, but I know what you mean about the island. Once it has a hold of you, it doesna let go. Which brings us to George and the organization."

"We have to go back." Just saying it left a bad taste in Scott's mouth.

"Without Elodie? That's no' going to go well. George will send others."

"It willna do her any good if Elodie doesna have magic."

Filip nodded. "Too bad whoever is after Elodie doesna know that."

"That's why I'm here. I doona care how Elodie feels about me. I'm no' leaving her alone. I swore I wouldna, and I'll keep that promise."

"As I said earlier, you can no' do that forever."

"Why no'?" Scott would take whatever he could get, and if

all he'd ever have with Elodie was a glimpse every now and then as he protected her, then that would have to be enough.

Filip shook his head. "Tell her you love her."

"If I thought it would make a difference, I'd do it in a heartbeat. But you saw her. She's no' going to welcome that kind of confession."

"Have you told George that Elodie doesna have her magic?"

Scott briefly closed his eyes. "If I do, she'll call us home."

"Rhona and Balladyn could protect Elodie better than we ever could."

"I'm aware." He sighed. "I keep wondering if we brought the killer to Skye. I can no' get that out of my head. If we did, then it's up to us to sort it."

Filip's brows rose as he gawked at Scott. "We couldna fight whoever was in Edinburgh one on one. What makes you think we can here?"

"Because this is Skye. And we doona have another option."

"We do."

Scott snorted as he rolled his eyes. "You mean tell Rhona and Balladyn? He already knows we're hiding something. Do you think they'll willingly help? I hate to be the one to tell you, but they'll remove us from Skye in an instant. Whether we're alive after or no' is up in the air."

Filip shifted on his feet as he looked down. "Look, I've never been one who had a lot of friends. Kevin made them easier than I did." He glanced up at Scott. "I've already lost one brother. I doona want to lose another."

"You're no'," Scott said.

"You can no' promise that."

Scott walked to him and put his hands on Filip's shoulders. "I have to do this. Please understand."

"I do."

Scott searched his face. When he saw nothing but acceptance in Filip's eyes, he dropped his arms. "Thank you. Now, there's no use in both of us staying up all night. Go home and get some rest. We'll have to work tomorrow."

Filip reluctantly nodded. "I'm staying. We'll take turns keeping watch. And that's final."

"All right," Scott said with a chuckle and held up his hands. "Thanks."

They shared a smile before Scott went back to observing the house.

Rhona drummed her fingers on the table as she stared at Balladyn from across the room. "I have to talk to Emily."

"It's a prison," Balladyn stated.

She gave him a flat look. "You're a Reaper, honey. You can get anywhere."

"That doesn't mean I should. Talk to Edie first. Or what about their brother? What's his name?"

"Elias." Rhona shook her head. "I don't know if they'll have anything different to say than Elodie did."

Balladyn walked to the table and pulled out a chair to sit. "Didn't you tell me that Edie and Elodie's timetable of when Elodie lost her magic is different?"

"It is."

"Edie is easy to get to. We should start there."

Rhona really hated when he was right. "Fine. Let's go."

Balladyn started to argue but decided against it and held out his hand. She took it. In the next instant, they stood outside Edie's home. Balladyn knocked as they heard arguing coming from within. A few moments later, Trevor answered the door.

"Hi," Rhona said. "Sorry to intrude, but we need to speak to Edie."

Trevor looked from her to Balladyn and back again. "Can this wait? It isna a good time."

"It can't," Balladyn replied.

Trevor blew out a breath and stepped aside to allow them entry. Rhona glanced at Balladyn as she entered the house, but he was still watching Trevor.

"Wait here," Trevor told them and walked away.

Rhona hated that they'd seemed to come when the couple was having a row. "Maybe we should leave."

"No," Balladyn said in a low voice. He had his head cocked to the side, listening.

As a Reaper, his senses were even more enhanced than a normal Fae's, and they had better senses than humans. Even Druids. Rhona waited to see what Balladyn picked up. Unfortunately, she didn't have time to ask as Edie came around the corner.

The Druid looked frazzled. Her mouth was set angrily, and her body was stiff. "I apologize for Trevor leaving you in the entryway. Please, follow me."

She took them to a room right off the foyer. It was immaculate, even for a house with two children. The sofas alone looked to be high-end. Rhona glanced around the room, noting the elegant touches.

"If this wasn't important, we would've waited," Rhona said.

Edie sank into a matching chair and motioned them to the sofa. "What can I help you with?"

"It's Elodie," Rhona started as she and Balladyn took a seat.

Edie's anger dissipated, replaced by concern. "Has something happened?"

"Not at all," Balladyn assured her.

Rhona leaned forward. "Elodie told me about her magic. She also said that you have a different recollection of when she lost it."

"I've kept that secret for years," Edie said quietly. She turned her head and looked away, her eyes going distant. "The police had just taken Mum. Da was...dead. Elias packed his things and left. All I had was Elodie. I tried to be there for her, to help her with her magic leaving, but I was grieving, too. I did the best I could."

Balladyn asked, "Why would Elodie think differently than you do?"

Edie blinked, seemingly surprised to find them there. She gathered her composure and said, "I presume because it was too difficult for her to deal with."

"But everyone said she used magic to get her men," Rhona stated.

Edie shrugged. "I can't speak to that. I only know what happened with Elodie."

"But you heard the rumors about her, right?" Balladyn pressed.

Edie nodded as she rolled her eyes. "It was hard not to. Did Elodie act out? Without a doubt. Had she ever done anything like that before? Never. It was in response to the collapse of our family. We were all dealing with everything the best we could."

"Tell me about that day," Rhona pressed.

Edie's face paled. "You mean…when my father was killed?"

Rhona nodded. "Please."

Edie clasped her hands together. She was quiet for a few breaths. Then she spoke. "It was a Tuesday. We were getting ready for school."

CHAPTER THIRTY-THREE

SKYE DRUIDS

"Come on. Come on," Elias whispered anxiously, waiting for the phone to connect. He drove above the speed limit, uncaring if the cameras caught him . Time was of the essence.

"Hello?" Edie answered.

Elias didn't want to make the call. He'd prayed that he would never have to. "Hey, sis."

"Elias," she replied happily. "It's good to hear from you. Guess who's on Skye?"

"Elodie. I know." His gut clenched with dread. "She called earlier."

There was a slight pause. "Oh. That's great. I'm glad she took that step."

He was, too. Elias just wished it was under different circumstances. "Has she told you that she's no' keen on staying at the cottage alone?" He hated lying, but now wasn't the time for facts. There might never *be* a good time.

"I offered for her to stay with us, but she assured me that she wanted to be on her own," Edie told him.

"I doona think that's a good idea."

"Why? Has something else happened?"

Elias heard the worry in Edie's voice. "The attacks warrant her no' being left alone."

"She isn't. Scott and Filip are with her. You might remember Filip's brother. Kevin?" Her voice dipped with sadness as she said, "Kevin was murdered in Edinburgh recently."

Elias's gut clenched again. "Aye. I remember Kevin and Filip. Edie, look, I'm worried. I'd feel better if you could get Elodie and bring her to your place."

"She has a car. She can drive. I can't make her come if she doesn't want to."

He slammed a hand on the steering wheel. Fuck. Why did everything have to be so difficult? "I'm aware she can drive."

"What's going on? What aren't you telling me?"

So verra much. "Nothing," he lied.

"Elias," she stated in her best *mom* voice.

His control shattered. "How did you feel staying in that place? Alone? Why would you let her do it?"

"Let her?" Edie snapped. "I didn't *let* Elodie do a damn thing. She's a grown woman who makes her own decisions. And for your information, I lived in that house alone for several years just fine. Elodie will be fine, too."

He gritted his teeth. "And the attacks?"

"The house has been warded. I've been assured she's safe."

"Even though Druids are being killed on Skye?"

"The cottage is more protected than my home, Elias."

Elias shook his head, realizing too late that Edie wouldn't help. "I'll see you soon."

"What? Are you saying...do you mean you're coming to Skye?" she asked in disbelief.

"Yep."

Elias disconnected the call and pressed his foot on the accelerator. He had too many miles to go to waste worrying about speeding.

Kerry stood on her back porch and looked at the sky. The sparks from the fire she'd built danced high in the air. She could stare at the flames for an eternity and never grow tired of watching them.

She had already chosen her next target. Perhaps she should've gone after them first, but it didn't matter. They were just one of many who needed to be taken care of. Every time she thought about what the Druids would be in the future, she smiled.

"This is the first step of several," she said.

Though she wondered why the Ancients had waited so long to move the Druids in this direction. Then she realized the answer: They had been waiting for her.

Well, she was finally ready.

She looked at the sky and found the moon, then frowned. Kerry had usually waited until the early hours of the morning, but she didn't want to hold off this time. A smile pulled at her lips. Rhona and Balladyn were running around with the police, trying to find a connection. The joke was on them because it would be too late before they discovered anything.

By the time they did, Kerry would be ready to remove Rhona and Balladyn. She wasn't foolish enough to simply banish them from Skye. No, the couple needed to be killed. That would likely bring the rest of the Reapers and Death back to Skye, but Kerry wasn't worried. She would have the entirety of the Skye Druids standing with her.

There was no need for the Fae on Skye. There never had been. It was the first thing she would reverse once she took over.

It was getting harder to wait. Kerry wished she could strike out at all the Druids on her list with one attack, but there were simply too many. Her power had grown tremendously, but she couldn't yet do something that dramatic. The Ancients had told her how to remove the Druids that didn't belong so that she could gain power and respect. It might be slower than she wanted, but it worked.

After all the years of sitting back and waiting to be acknowledged, for someone to see who she was, it had finally come to pass. No more would she fade into the background. No more would she put others' needs ahead of hers. Look what that had gotten her. Exactly nowhere. And stripped of the only thing that had ever mattered to her.

She couldn't wait to see Rhona's expression when Kerry finally revealed everything.

Kerry lifted her face to the sky. The chilly wind brushed against her cheeks. She felt them redden in response. She took a deep breath, letting her lungs expand as far as they could before slowly releasing it. For years, she would sit quietly with her eyes closed and silently beg for the Ancients to speak to her.

Now, they spoke without her having to take such extreme measures. Each time she thought about how they had chosen her, how they had picked her out of thousands of Druids, her entire body tingled with delight.

"It's going to be a good night," she told the Ancients.

They were listening. They were *always* watching and listening. They had seen the Druids' downfall and had begun planning. Soon, everyone would be reminded who the Druids were. Then, the fear and respect would come.

Just as it always should have.

"Your target is waiting," the Ancients said.

Kerry rubbed her hands together. There was no need to delay this time. Besides, it would be over before anyone even realized what had happened.

The spell fell from her lips as the mist formed and started to slip toward its objective. The dark night hid the mist, masking it from those who might be looking. They would be out of the way soon. To think they had fought her—and won. That was the last time that would happen.

The mist moved quickly, keeping low as it slithered over the mountain to the other side of the island. It found its destination and slowed. Kerry closed her eyes, watching it play out in her mind's eye. The mist went to the door and tried to slip underneath, but it couldn't. It then moved to several windows with the same outcome. Anger tightened Kerry's lips as the mist slid to the back door, but its entry was barred there, also.

"The Reaper worked quickly to ward houses," the Ancients said.

Kerry shrugged. "I doubt he got all of them."

She turned the mist on the next name on her target list. Just as she suspected, the Reaper hadn't yet reached this home. The mist entered easily. It went room to room, pausing when it reached the first bedroom. It rose before leaning over to look at the adolescent who slept peacefully.

"Young minds are easily swayed," the Ancients reminded her.

Kerry turned the mist away from the three children in the home to focus on the parents. Their door was closed, but that didn't stop her. The mist filled the room and hovered on the ceiling. The couple slept soundly. They wouldn't for long. She gave the silent order.

The mist formed a long column and dropped to the floor to encircle the bed. The brush of air soon stirred the couple, but by then, it was too late. The mist had them in its grip. The mother opened her mouth to scream. The father's eyes bugged when he saw the mist enter her before bursting from her chest. He tried to shout to the children, but he quickly followed his wife into death.

Elodie woke, choking. She grabbed her throat and tumbled out of bed to land hard on the floor. Her eyes watered as she continued coughing. She kicked her legs free of the covers and scooted as far from her bed as she could get. With her back pressed against the dresser, she eyed her mattress. She could've sworn something had been pinning her down and trying to choke her. Not around her neck but *inside*.

A shiver went through her. She suddenly needed to get out of her room. Elodie scrambled to her feet and fled. She tripped in her haste and slammed her shoulder against the corridor wall. She swallowed, but that only brought on another fit of coughing.

She made it to the kitchen and flipped on the lights. Her hands shook as she filled a glass with water. She turned to face the hallway as she drank some of the liquid. Her mind was trying to sort out what had happened. Another nightmare, to be sure. But this one felt real.

Very, *very* real.

The sweat that covered her soon had her shaking. She wished that Scott were here. She could use his solid embrace. His calm voice. But he wasn't. She was alone. Elodie lifted her chin and walked to the front room. Thankfully, the fire still roared, proof that either Scott or Filip had spelled it. She should thank them. And she would.

She walked to the sofa and grabbed the throw to huddle beneath it. There was no way she was going back to her room. Maybe Elias had been right. Perhaps she shouldn't be at the cottage alone.

CHAPTER THIRTY-FOUR

SKYE DRUIDS

Scott saw the light beam from the kitchen window land on the ground, drawing his attention. He couldn't see the window itself or inside, but he knew Elodie was up. Did she have another nightmare? Was it as bad as the others? Was she okay? He wanted to go to her, to offer her comfort.

But she wouldn't take it.

Not that he blamed her. He had no excuse. She was right. He should've been upfront with her from the beginning. Why hadn't he? It was too late to think about that. What was done, was done. He glanced at Filip, who was sleeping on top of some boards. Filip had surprised him by staying, but perhaps Scott shouldn't have been shocked. Kevin certainly wouldn't have left. Filip was more like his brother than he knew.

Scott wished Kevin were here. He'd always been the voice of reason. Scott had friends, but he allowed few as close as he had Kevin. Scott looked back at the house. Elodie had gotten that close without even knowing it. But *he* had known. He had *felt* it. And he'd been unprepared for it. Worse, he'd been ill-equipped to handle it, which was why he was in his current predicament.

He would make it up to Elodie. Somehow. No matter how long it took. She might never trust him again or reach for him, but he would ensure she was safe. He looked at the sky, wondering when the mist would return. It wanted Elodie, and he didn't think it would give up so easily. Was that what had been killing the Druids on Skye?

It certainly moved quickly enough. Not to mention, it could easily gain entry. The real dilemma was figuring out who controlled it. It could be anyone. They could be on Skye, or Edinburgh, or the other side of the globe.

He would find out. The murderers needed to be stopped.

Scott ran a hand through his hair. It was cold in the garage. He imagined himself lying before the fire next to Elodie, holding her in his arms. That night had been perfect in every way. There had been no hiding from her beautiful, pale blue gaze. And he hadn't wanted to. He had bared himself to her as he had never done before.

She had seen him. All of him. And still wanted him.

A woman of stunning beauty had chosen him. She had left him breathless and wishing for a spell to halt time. Perhaps he'd known what was coming. Maybe he'd realized that night would be the first and only one he'd have like that.

Filip wanted him to tell Elodie about his feelings. Scott wasn't sure he could. What he felt for her was more than love. It was…everything. In her anger, she would likely reject his words—whether he deserved it or not. That wasn't something he could handle. Not from her.

He searched the sky again through the small slit in the door. He didn't see anything. Scott yawned and rubbed his cold hands together to create heat. He pulled out his mobile and thought about texting Elodie to check on her but he didn't want to find out if she had blocked him.

His phone buzzed to alert him that he had received a text. It was from George. She wanted an update. This was her fourth text today. She was getting irritated by his silence. Scott couldn't put her off much longer. He had already decided that he would stay on Skye for as long as he could. Until Rhona and Balladyn forced him to leave, anyway. He hadn't been able to save Kevin, but he would Elodie.

He returned his mobile to his back pocket with a sigh and folded his arms across his chest. His thoughts slid to the woman who held his heart. He wondered what she was doing. Had she called someone? Was she scared? He searched the few windows he could see from his vantage point, but he hadn't spotted any shadows moving across them. The light was on in the kitchen, which meant she was still up.

The sound of Filip's phone buzzing drew Scott's attention. Filip stirred and reached for his mobile in his coat pocket. He pulled it out and looked at the screen before lifting his gaze to Scott. "It's George."

"Bloody hell. I was hoping to put her off for another day."

Filip shook his head. "She's pretty pissed. We have to tell her something."

Scott blew out a breath and palmed his mobile. "I'll do it."

"I doona mind."

Scott was already typing.

Filip sat up and swung his legs over the side of the stack of lumber he'd bought earlier that day. "What are you saying?"

"I'm telling her that things are taking longer than we'd hoped. I'm also filling her in on the deaths here."

Filip yawned and scratched his head. "That should buy us the time we need."

George's answer was quick. Scott looked up at Filip and shrugged. "She wants an update on Elodie."

"What are you going to tell her?"

Scott shrugged. "I still believe in George's mission."

"Just no' that it involves Elodie."

"It can no'," Scott stated. "She doesna have magic."

Filip placed his hands on either side of his legs on the lumber. "You'll have to tell George sooner or later. Would it no' be better to get it over with now?"

"Maybe."

"Tell her," Filip urged. "If she tells us to come home, doona reply. We'll go when we feel like it."

Scott eyed Filip. "You doona have to follow what I do."

"We're in this together."

Scott smiled and nodded. He typed out the text to George and hit send. Scott watched for the bubbles that would alert him to George responding, but there was nothing. "That isna good."

"No reply?"

"No' yet."

Filip pushed to his feet. "Doona worry. We'll get a response."

No sooner had he said that than Filip's phone vibrated. He and Scott exchanged a look.

Filip read the message. "She's asking me if Elodie has magic."

"She thinks I'm lying." For some reason, that offended Scott deeply. He'd never been anything but honest with George.

Filip tapped on his phone screen. "I'm letting her know that Elodie told us both about it."

Shortly after he sent the reply, there was another ding.

Filip tucked the phone into his pocket again. "She wants us back."

"You'd better go."

"I told you, I'm no' leaving," Filip stated.

Scott shook his head. "You doona want George as an enemy."

"I'll return to Edinburgh when it suits me. No' a moment before."

Scott nodded once to Filip before turning back to Elodie's house. George would send more people to make sure Elodie had really lost her magic. Scott needed to prepare Elodie for that—*if* she listened.

But he knew someone who would: Rhona.

"I know that look," Filip said. "What are you planning?"

"George willna give up so easily. Elodie probably willna listen to either of us, but she would Rhona."

Filip's lips flattened. "If you tell Rhona and Balladyn everything, it'll prevent anyone from bothering Elodie again."

"And make you leave your home."

Filip shrugged. "I came here despising Skye and my past here. I see it differently now. I also came thinking black and white lines had been drawn, and that I'd be able to see where everyone fit in. That was naïve. Kevin's death changed a lot for me. I see Skye with different eyes. I feel it now."

"Druids are still dying."

"They are, and George saw a way." Filip shrugged. "Who's to say George's way is the only one, though?"

"Good point."

"So…Rhona?"

Scott nodded slowly. "Looks like it." He parted his lips to call Balladyn's name when the entire garage shuddered.

He and Filip stilled, listening.

"Was that…drums?" Filip whispered, fear and shock coloring his voice.

"The Ancients," Scott murmured as he turned to Elodie's cottage.

Kerry's power surged with the death of the two Druids. She wished she could be nearby when Rhona saw what was left of them. It made her smile, thinking of the horror and shock Rhona and Balladyn would feel. If they were as powerful as everyone thought, they would know it was her. The fact that they didn't, proved she was the one with the real power.

The ground beneath her shook for a heartbeat, followed by one deafening drumbeat. Then it was gone. Kerry kept perfectly still as she looked around. But nothing else happened.

"Ancients?" she called.

Two full minutes passed before she heard the voice.

"Someone's coming to Skye that doesn't belong anymore. Stop Elias."

Kerry immediately split the mist in two. One would be at the ferry port, and the other at the base of the bridge from the mainland. One way or another, she would stop him.

Rhona gasped at the deafening sound of the single drumbeat. It had been some time since she'd heard the Ancients, but she hadn't thought anything of it. It wasn't as if she had a direct line to them. They spoke if and when they wished. Not one second before.

"What is it?" Balladyn asked from beside her.

She shook her head, her heart still pounding. "I don't know. It was the Ancients."

"What did they say?"

"Nothing. It was just a drumbeat."

He made a sound in the back of his throat. "That shook the house?"

Yeah, she didn't understand that either. If the Ancients wanted her attention, all they had to do was speak to her. She'd never heard about them shaking buildings before. Yet it showed her how powerful they truly were.

The knock on her door startled her. Balladyn gave her a look before he disappeared. A second later, he reappeared and opened the door at the same time he said, "Ulrik, Eilish."

Rhona went to greet the Dragon King and his Druid mate. "What brings you two here?"

"Did you feel it?" Eilish asked, her eyes wide.

Rhona nodded. Before she could say anything else, someone cleared their throat behind the couple. Ulrik ushered Eilish inside so Rhona could see Broc's indigo Warrior wings folding as he tamped down the primeval god inside him. Beside him was his wife and Druid, Sonya.

Sonya's amber eyes looked at Eilish, and she said, "We came for the same reason."

"One drumbeat," Rhona said as unease filled her.

Sonya and Eilish nodded. For those from Dreagan and MacLeod Castle to have felt the same thing that she had on Skye wasn't a coincidence.

"The Ancients are trying to tell us something," Sonya said.

Eilish rubbed her hands together. "Do either of you have any idea what it is?"

Rhona glanced at Balladyn before nodding. "I might. Someone is killing Druids."

"When did this start?" Ulrik demanded, his gold eyes blazing with anger.

Broc nodded his head of blond hair. "Point us in the direction of whoever's responsible. We'll take care of it."

"If only it were that easy," Balladyn said.

Elias rubbed his eyes. Shite, he was weary. He'd had little sleep for the past three nights. All he had planned for tonight was to catch up on some rest. He wished he would've had time to talk to his mum, but he didn't want to chance waiting another moment to get to Elodie.

He drove over the bridge to Skye and adjusted in his seat. He tilted his head to the side and popped his neck before turning it to the other side. His body wouldn't be able to take much more. If he weren't careful, he would find himself in a battle he couldn't win. That wouldn't be tonight, though.

"Hold on, little sis. I'm coming," he murmured.

Elias hoped Edie had gone to the cottage, but he knew she hadn't. She didn't have any idea what was going on. Neither of his sisters did. He'd kept it that way on purpose, but now he realized that had put them in danger. Elodie was never meant to return to Skye.

He increased his speed when he saw the end of the bridge approaching. Finally, he'd reached the isle. If he drove the speed limit, it would take exactly twenty-six minutes to get to the cottage. At this hour, no one was on the road, and he had every intention of speeding.

The instant his wheels touched the island, he saw something out of the corner of his eye. Elias barely had time to react before it slammed into the side of his SUV and flipped it.

CHAPTER THIRTY-FIVE

SKYE DRUIDS

Elodie stood in the hall, looking at the door to her parents' room. Others had walked into the space without a problem. Why did bone-chilling fear keep her rooted and stop her from doing the same?

"It's just a room," she told herself. "A place where Da died. Somewhere Mum killed him. But just a room."

The words didn't make her feel any better.

She lowered herself to the floor, never taking her eyes off the door. She was a grown woman. It was irrational for her to be so terrified. It wasn't as if she had seen anything that day. The only one who knew what'd happened was her mother and father, and her da wasn't there to tell his side of the story.

But her mum was.

Elodie pressed her lips together. Maybe she should visit her mother and have that conversation. It couldn't be any more difficult than her current situation. As a matter of fact, she felt better about going to see her mother than walking into her parents' bedroom.

"It's just a room," she said again.

It didn't matter how many times she said the words, they didn't help. It was more than just a room. It was the place where her family had fallen apart. It was the epicenter of change for her siblings and her.

Elodie brought her knees up to her chest and wrapped her arms around them. She let her mind drift back to the past. The ghosts of the house had hounded her ever since she'd arrived. She'd thought she could keep the memories away, but they rose even in her dreams. There was no escaping them. She had deceived herself for years, thinking she could close the door on the past and forget.

Returning to Skye had proven how naïve she was. Scott had been right. The only way to go forward was to face the past. It was such simple advice. Something a person should inherently know. But things were never that clear when trying to forget or ignore.

"It's just a damn room." She put more conviction in her tone.

Maybe if she said it enough, she might start to believe it.

As she sat there, dozens of memories filled her head. She saw quick glimpses of arguments she'd had with Edie, swimming with Elias, running along the beach with her mum. It was the recollection of her da making waffles one morning that her mind latched onto, though.

She had been about ten. She, Edie, and Elias were in the kitchen with their father as he sang along with a song on the radio. They joined in, each trying to out sing the other. There was lots of laughter as their da placed waffles before them. But someone had been missing—her mother.

Where had she been? Elodie had been sure she was there.

She closed her eyes as she went deeper into her memories. Most of her recollections about her father were filled with laughter, though she *did* recall a few times when he had lost his temper with them. And some others when he and her mother had fought.

That was normal, though. People argued. Parents got frustrated and angry with their children. There was nothing wrong with that.

Except the more Elodie began pulling up memories of her father, she discovered there were times her mother hadn't been with them. Again, though, that wasn't abnormal. She and her siblings had been alone with their mother often.

Why then did it unsettle Elodie?

But she knew the answer. Because she'd learned of her father's abuse. She was looking back on this with an adult's perspective, not that of a child.

Elodie went even deeper into her memories. There were more there. She was sure of it.

"You took my headband, didn't you?" Edie demanded as she stormed into their room.

Elodie rolled her eyes as she finished brushing her hair. "No, I didn't."

"Just hand it over."

"I didn't take it!" Elodie stated angrily and faced her sister.

Edie glared at her. "Ugh. I'm so tired of sharing a room with you. You take everything."

"Me?" Elodie replied, fury coursing through her. "That's my shirt you're wearing."

Edie smiled and shrugged. "And it'll be mine until you return my headband."

"Maybe if you stopped blaming me for everything, you might remember what you did with it."

"Whatever," Edie said and turned on her heel. "I need to get Mum to sign that paper for school. Where is it? Oh, in the car. I can't forget that."

Elodie shook her head as Edie ran outside. A crash down the hall made her still. Elodie slowly straightened and moved to her doorway. Elias stood in the corridor, his eyes wide. Then he turned to face their parents' room.

"You heard that, right?" he whispered.

The water was freezing, but Elias barely felt it. Instead, adrenaline pumped through him, keeping him alert and aware. He'd had enough time to raise a shield before hitting the water. It'd saved him from the rocks, but not the shards of glass from his window exploding.

Elias had no idea how many times his vehicle had flipped. His head pounded. He unbuckled the seat belt as water rapidly filled the car's interior. He suspected that whatever had attacked him waited to see if he would surface. The SUV was sinking to the bottom of the sea quickly. He sucked in a breath as water covered him and waited for the vehicle to come to rest.

As the SUV drifted down, he looked around the interior. The window was shattered, giving him a way out. But he couldn't just swim to the surface, and his lungs already burned for air. To take his mind off that, he tried to think about what he'd seen as he'd gone off the bridge. It had come at him fast. His eyes snapped open when he remembered catching a glimpse of what looked like mist form into a long, cylindrical shape before ramming him.

The slight jarring as his SUV settled on the bottom of the sea got him moving. He turned and pushed off the seat with his hands and the dash with his feet, propelling him to the back, where a small air pocket had formed. Elias turned onto his back, his face pressed against the roof of the vehicle as he sucked in mouthfuls of air. He got in two before water filled his mouth.

Elias then went back to the front of his SUV and slipped out the window. He swam as far as his lungs would allow and then began to ascend. His head broke the surface just as his lungs felt as if they might burst. He treaded water as he looked toward shore.

There, he saw the mist hovering near the waterline next to the bridge. It was waiting for him, just as he'd thought it would be. Though it wouldn't come into the water for him. He kept an eye on the mist as he swam diagonally away from it to the shore. When his feet finally struck ground, Elias had to use his hands to pull himself out of the sea.

He shook water from his face and waited, but the mist didn't come his way. He crept up to the road and peeked around the bridge. The mist appeared to be gone. For now.

He dripped as he traveled the road. It would take him

much too long to reach Elodie on foot. He couldn't even call Edie to come and get him since his phone was in the SUV with the rest of his belongings. But there was nothing around him.

Elias started to run, each beat of his heart urging him to go faster. It was just over a mile to Kyleakin. Once there, he hoped to find someone to help him. He was out of breath when he finally reached the city. Elias passed several cars. He stopped beside one to see if it was unlocked.

"Mate, you're soaked."

Elias halted at the slurred voice behind him. He turned to see a thirty-something man swaying slightly from too much drink. "I went for a swim."

The man frowned in confusion. "Why would you do that?"

"I doona know."

"Marty is never gonna to believe this," he said.

Elias walked to the man. "You've had a few too many, my friend. This never happened. It was just a dream."

"Same with that mist I saw hit a vehicle?"

"Aye. An illusion."

The man wrinkled his nose and let out a burp. "That's what I get for drinkin' vodka."

"Do you have a car?"

"A car? I can no' drive now."

Elias prayed for patience. "I can drive you."

"Oh." The man swayed back so far that Elias had to catch him to keep him upright. "Wait. I just live there." He pointed.

Elias looked across the road at the flat. Then he faced the man. "I need to borrow your car."

"Sure," the man said and pulled a set of keys from his pocket.

Without another word, the drunk stumbled home. Elias watched to make sure he made it inside before Elias pressed the unlock button on the key fob. When lights blinked, Elias rushed to the vehicle.

"What the bloody hell was that?" Filip asked.

Scott shook his head and dashed from the garage. He didn't care if Elodie was pissed at him for being there, but he had to see if she was safe. He went to the door and banged on it.

"Elodie? Are you all right? Please," he called. "I just need to know you're okay."

There was no answer.

"I'll look around the front," Filip said and ran around the house.

Scott hadn't even heard Filip follow him. Scott's heart pounded wildly. He leaned to the side and looked through the window, but the curtains were tightly shut. "Elodie!" he shouted and banged on the door again.

"I can no' see her," Filip yelled.

Scott looked at the door. They couldn't break it down. It had been warded against just that.

"What do you want to do?" Filip asked as he returned.

Scott shoved his hands into his hair. His gut told him that he had to get to Elodie and quickly. He dropped his arms and glared at the door. He was getting in one way or another.

It didn't take Rhona and Balladyn long to fill Ulrik, Eilish, Broc, and Sonya in on what had been happening on Skye.

"No one at MacLeod has heard the Ancients in a while," Sonya said.

Eilish shook her head. "Same with at Dreagan. We were just talking about that yesterday."

"Seems the Ancients wanted to get everyone's attention," Ulrik replied.

Balladyn nodded. "What do we do?"

Rhona turned to Balladyn. "I need to talk to Emily MacLean."

"Where is she? We'll get her," Ulrik said.

Broc quirked a brow, his brown eyes meeting hers. "She's in prison."

"So?" Balladyn asked.

Ulrik shrugged. "I'm game."

"Me, too," Balladyn added.

Broc's lips thinned into a flat line. He closed his eyes for a moment, using his power to find anyone, anywhere. When he opened his eyes, he nodded at Rhona. "I found her."

"We'll go," Ulrik told Balladyn. "You need to stay on Skye."

Balladyn's nostrils flared, but he bowed his head in agreement. Rhona watched as Broc told Ulrik Emily's exact location. Then Ulrik placed a hand on Broc's shoulder and touched the silver cuff on his wrist, which allowed him to teleport.

"Do we have time for this?" Sonya asked.

Rhona battled a wave of anxiousness. "We have to make time."

Suddenly, Broc and Ulrik were back, along with a woman. Emily MacLean didn't look like a woman in her mid-fifties. Her blond hair was in a plait that fell to the middle of her back. It was nearly the same shade as Elodie's. Emily's blue eyes matched Elodie's perfectly, and the resemblance didn't end there.

"What's going on?" Emily asked.

Rhona took a breath. "I'm sorry we've gone to such extremes, but I need to know about the day your husband was killed."

"Why?" Emily demanded warily.

Rhona held her gaze. "It's about Elodie."

Emily's face drained of color. "Where is she?"

"Your cottage," Balladyn answered.

Emily grabbed Rhona's arm. "Take me to her immediately."

"No' until you tell us what's going on," Ulrik stated.

Rhona felt the woman's apprehension, but she stood her ground. "Quickly. Please," she urged Emily.

"There isn't time," Emily replied. "Take me to her now!"

CHAPTER THIRTY-SIX

SKYE DRUIDS

Elodie didn't remember getting up. She didn't remember walking to the door. She looked down to find her hand on the knob. All she had to do was turn it. A single piece of wood stood between her and the past.

She just had to turn. Once she faced the past, she could have the life she'd always dreamed of. She would no longer feel as if she carried the burdens of the world on her shoulders. She would be free.

Her heart beat a slow thump in her chest, banging against her ribs.

"It's just a door," she whispered. "It's only the past. I know what happened."

Even if she hadn't looked inside the room, she knew the truth. Why was it so hard to face it?

Scott tried to use magic to flip the lock. When that didn't work, he attempted to pick it himself. Still, the door held.

"Fuck!" he bellowed to the sky.

He got to his feet and paced away. Filip took his place and tried, as well. Each time they failed, it felt as if Scott were losing Elodie. That was silly because he had already lost her.

"Elodie!" he shouted and banged on the door again. "Elodie!"

The sound of tires squealing made Scott's head turn in the direction of the drive. A car barreled toward the house and came to a stop, sliding on the dirt. The vehicle's door flew open, and a man jumped out without shutting off the engine.

"Get out of my way," he demanded.

Scott blocked his path, noting the man's wet clothes and the blood running down his face from a gash on his temple and several cuts on his face. "You're no' getting anywhere near her."

The man halted and looked from Scott to Filip, then back to Scott. "Who are you?"

"Who are *you*?"

"I doona have time for this," the man stated angrily, his fists clenched.

Scott didn't budge. "Make time."

"Elias?" Filip called as he walked around Scott. "Is that you?"

Elias squinted at Filip and nodded. "Aye. Now get out of my way so I can get to my sister."

"That's what we've been trying to do," Scott told him. "The house is warded, and we doona have a key."

Elias searched the flowerpots and lifted a key. "Move," he all but shouted.

Scott watched Elias in the porch light. The hair color was similar to Elodie's, and Scott supposed he saw a resemblance. His thoughts halted when the door swung open. Elias was the first one through, followed by Scott and then Filip.

"Elodie!" Elias called as he hurried through the cottage.

Elias suddenly stopped in the kitchen. Scott looked over his shoulder and saw Elodie with her hand on the doorknob to her parents' room.

"Elodie," her brother called. "You doona want to do that."

Scott frowned, wondering what the big deal was. He'd been in that room. Nothing in there could harm Elodie.

"Hey, lil sis. I'm home," Elias coaxed. "Just like I said I would be. We've got a lot of catching up to do. Come away from the door."

But Elodie didn't seem to hear him.

"Bloody hell," Elias whispered.

Scott moved closer to him. "What's going on?"

"She can no' go into that room, that's what," Elias stated without taking his eyes off his sister.

Scott took a breath, fear clutching him firmly. The panic in Elias's voice told him all he needed to know. "Elodie?"

Scott. The sound of his voice reached her as if from a distance. She slowly turned her head and saw him with Elias and Filip.

What was her brother doing here? She wanted to ask, but she had something to do first.

"Look who's come to see you," Scott continued. "Come greet your brother."

Elodie remembered the taste of Scott's kiss. How he had made her feel again. She didn't want to go back to the way things were, but she wasn't sure she could be with him. He had betrayed her, used her. And for what? She had no magic to help him.

"Elodie," Scott called again. "Doona open that door."

She looked down at her hand that gripped the knob. "I have to."

"You doona," he told her, his voice growing closer. "Let go of it. That's all you have to do."

"You told me to face my past."

"Look at me," Scott beseeched her.

Elodie found herself gazing into his dark blue eyes. She saw him reaching for her hand. He was going to stop her, and she couldn't allow him to do that. Elodie twisted the knob, and the door opened as if on its own.

"NOOOO!" Elias bellowed.

Elodie looked inside the room. In an instant, she was taken back in time.

"You heard that, right?" Elias whispered.

She nodded. "Is Mum hurt?"

"Da's with her."

There was another grunt, this one followed by soft crying. It was Mum, Elodie knew it. She raced to the door to help. Elias tried to stop her.

"You doona want to know what's happening. Trust me," he

said as he yanked her away.

But she slipped free of his grasp and threw open the door. There, she saw her mother on the floor between the bed and the wall. Blood poured from her nose and trickled from her lip. There was a red mark on her cheek. But worst of all, her father had his hands around her neck and was squeezing.

Elodie was immobilized by the rage she saw on her father's face. She didn't recognize the man who always sang to her. His skin was blotchy and red, his eyes wide as he glared at his wife, his hands gripping her firmly.

Elodie's mother's gaze met hers, pleading with her to leave. But there was no way she could do that. Fear got her moving. Everything she loved and held dear was on the verge of shattering. She had to stop it.

"Get off her," Elodie shouted as she ran at her father, shoving him as hard as she could.

He backhanded her so violently, she slammed against the opposite wall, momentarily stunned when her head banged against it. She blinked at the lights dotting the edges of her vision. All she wanted to do was stay there, but she couldn't.

"Well, well, well," her father said as he straightened and turned to Elias. His voice was cold and cruel, nothing like the teasing man she knew. "Look what we have here. Come back to learn more?"

Elias lifted his chin, but Elodie saw his fisted hands tremble. "Get away from her."

"Think you're a man now, aye? I told you before that what happens between a man and his wife is no one's business," her father stated, spittle flying from his lips.

Elodie pushed herself into a sitting position. Her head

throbbed; her stomach knotted in fear. She didn't know what was happening. Who was the man standing before her? Because he wasn't the father she knew and loved.

"Did the lesson I gave you last week no' sink in?" her father demanded as he moved closer to Elias.

Elodie watched in horror as her father struck her brother. Elias tried to raise his hand to deflect the hits, but it did little to hinder the blows. Elodie glanced at her mother, who was struggling to get to her feet. That's when Elodie saw the ripped nightgown and the bruises along her mother's ribs and arms.

Suddenly, her father flew through the air. He crashed into the dresser, toppling everything off as he dropped to the floor. Elias stood with his hands clenched at his sides, breathing hard, his face bloody and already swelling.

"Magic?" her father bellowed as he pushed himself up. "You dare to use magic on me!?"

When he regained his feet, Edward MacLean had a knife. Elodie had no idea where it had come from. She rushed to Elias to protect him, but he wasn't her father's target—her mother was.

Something snapped inside Elodie when she saw the knife raised over Edward's head as he went to plunge it into her mother's chest. The horror that had kept her motionless vanished, replaced by a calm she'd never experienced before.

Her power rose so quickly, she stumbled with the force of it before finding her footing. The magic pooled in her hands without her even calling to it. She felt as if she might explode with the force of the magic inside her. Elodie tried to think of a spell, something, but there wasn't time. She could do nothing but throw out her arms and release what had built inside her.

The magic that flew from her felt foreign, and yet she knew it was hers. She watched as it wrapped around her father, stopping him just as the point of the knife pierced her mother's chest. The magic lifted him into the air as it sparked and hissed, forming a circle around him. He struggled against it, but there was no getting away.

"Elodie!" he shouted. "You know me. You know how much I love you. I'd never hurt you."

"No."

One word. That's all she said, and her magic curled in on itself, taking him with it until there was nothing left of her father.

Scott knelt on the floor and cradled Elodie in his arms. "Open your eyes, sweetheart. Open your eyes and look at me. You have to come back to me. Please."

"Nay!" a woman's voice behind him wailed.

Scott glanced over his shoulder. Elias had stopped just inside the room, Filip behind him. Beyond them was an older woman, who came running down the hall. She dropped to her knees on the other side of Elodie, tears streaming down her face.

Scott then found himself looking into Rhona's eyes. Balladyn and others he didn't recognize stood behind her, but he didn't care who they were. He gazed down at Elodie and gently tugged a strand of hair from her lashes.

"How?" the woman demanded. "How did this happen?"

Elias walked to her and knelt beside her, an arm around her shoulders. "I'm sorry, Mum. I tried to get here in time."

Emily MacLean leaned her head against her son and sobbed uncontrollably.

"Someone tell me what just happened," Scott demanded in a voice thick with fear and anger—for what, he didn't understand.

Emily sniffed and folded her hands around one of Elodie's. "The spell I used only worked if she never returned."

"I don't understand," Rhona said. "You spelled your daughter?"

Elias sighed. "Mum didna have a choice."

"Elodie saved me," Emily said. "Edward was always careful about when he…beat me. We both went to great lengths to keep it from the children. He liked that the kids thought him cool and funny. He also liked having them to himself. But that morning, I told him I wanted a divorce. He began hitting me while the kids were still here. Elias and Elodie heard."

Elias swallowed loudly. "Da had begun hitting me a few weeks before. Told me it was to toughen me up. I tried to stop Elodie. I didna want her to walk in on that, but she did anyway. Da was in a rage. He was choking Mum. Elodie tried to pull him away. He backhanded her. Then he came after me. I tried to get away, but I knew he was intent on harming someone. So, I used magic to get him off me."

"That set him off," Emily said and sniffed. She looked up

at Scott, then at the others. "He knew then that I'd kept my magic from him. I don't know where the knife came from, but it was suddenly in his hand and aimed at me."

Elias squeezed his mother's shoulder. "That's when Elodie used her magic."

"How?" Scott asked softly.

Emily shrugged. "I would say it was a spell, but she didn't move her lips. She was gifted with her abilities, but the force of the magic that came from her then was unlike anything I'd ever seen before. She caught Edward up in it, held him in midair. And then it...it..."

"It was like it ate him," Elias finished for her. "There was nothing left of him."

Rhona's brows drew together. "I saw the police report. There was blood everywhere."

"Magic," Emily answered with a shrug. "Elodie was hysterical after it happened. There was nothing I could do to calm her. Edie was on her way back into the house at that time. I had to think fast. I sent Elias to occupy Edie, and then I did what a mother does best, I protected my children. I promised Elodie that she would never remember any of it. I told her I was taking the blame and that she would be free to live her life." Emily smoothed Elodie's hair back. "That wasn't enough, though. She feared herself. Her magic. So, I bound it for her. With my spell, I put a thread of fear in her anytime Elodie thought of this room. I thought it would keep her away."

Scott felt like a fool for pushing Elodie to go inside. "It did."

"No' enough," Elias declared.

Rhona shook her head. "But her magic? She should've learned to control it, not run from using it."

"Mum made her decision," Elias answered.

Emily brushed away her tears. "Elodie asked me to. What she did had terrified her. I tried to tell her that she was only protecting me, but she wouldn't listen. So, I did what she asked. After Elodie left the room, I staged it. Then I screamed. Elias and the girls came running. The police were called, and they took me away."

"For a crime you didna commit," Filip said.

Emily shrugged. "I should've stopped Edward earlier. I thought as long as he was just hitting me, then I could endure it. When I found out he had begun abusing Elias, I made plans to leave with the kids. Just not soon enough."

"What now?" Scott asked into the silence the followed.

Emily shrugged. "I don't know. I did the spell in haste. I don't know what's happening to Elodie now."

"Let us figure it out," Rhona said as she and two other women came forward.

Scott didn't want to loosen his hold on Elodie, but Rhona laid a gentle hand on his shoulder. He reluctantly lay Elodie on the floor and moved back as the three Druids stood around her, their hands outstretched and palms-down over the woman he loved.

CHAPTER THIRTY-SEVEN

SKYE DRUIDS

Elodie knew she had to wake up, but she resisted. She remembered everything now. All the horrific, sordid details of what she had done. *She*. Not her mother. Elodie couldn't believe her sweet mum had allowed herself to be prosecuted and locked away for a crime she hadn't committed.

Shame rocked Elodie. She had blamed her mother for everything when the culpability fell on her shoulders. Elodie wrapped the darkness around her, shying away from the light that attempted to reach her. Magic surrounded her, but she pushed it away, also. She didn't care whose it was. How would she ever face her mother again? Or Elias?

Or anyone.

What she had done was criminal. Worse, she had allowed her mother to be convicted and put away for it. Would her mother ever forgive her?

Then Elodie felt a familiar hand take hers. Scott's callused palm was comforting. His presence soothed her frayed nerves.

She could only run for so long, and she had done it for too
many years to continue. She had come to Skye to put the past
to rest so she could have a future. It was time to face that, as
tragic and ghastly as it was—despite her fears and shame.

Magic swarmed her. She knew the feel of it. Her powers. It
had been there all the time, waiting. Her eyes burned with
tears. The sensation of her magic made her dizzy, and yet at
the same time, it comforted her, reassured her.

Elodie squeezed Scott's hand. He returned the gesture. She
didn't know what would happen when she opened her eyes,
but she would never know unless she did it. Growing up, she
had never been afraid of anything. She missed that about
herself. Yet it was within her grasp to change and be the
person she had once been. And she wanted to shake off the
past fifteen years and remember the dreams and ambition
she'd once held so fervently.

She took another breath. Then, she opened her eyes. She
found herself on the floor with Rhona and two other women
over her. Scott was on her right. When Elodie looked to the
left, her gaze clashed with her mother's.

"My sweet girl," Emily said with tears running down her
face.

Elodie sat up and embraced her mum as she wept. Emily
held her tightly. Elodie needed to say so much, but she
couldn't get any words out. Not yet. But soon.

The room was quiet. She knew that Scott was there,
watching. Others were, too, but she didn't pay them any heed.

"I'm so sorry," Elodie finally whispered to her mother.

Emily leaned back and gave her a watery smile.
"Don't be."

"You confessed to something you didn't do."

"It was my fault that things went as far as they did with your father," Emily argued. "I knew what Edward was, but I loved him anyway. I told myself that as long as it was only me he abused, that I could handle it. When I found out about Elias, I ended it. It was the reason your father was in such a rage that morning."

When Emily turned her head to the side, Elodie followed her gaze and found Elias. Elodie's tears started again.

Her brother shot her a lopsided grin as he brushed away a tear. "It's good to see you, too, sis."

"I hate to break up the reunion," a man said from behind her. "But could the drumbeat you Druids heard have been caused when Elodie walked into this room?"

Scott said, "No."

Elodie turned to face him. Their gazes clashed. He knew everything now. Every wretched detail of her past. "He's right," she answered. "I felt the house shake and heard the drum before I opened the door."

Scott got to his feet and held out a hand. Elodie took it, allowing him to help her stand. He linked their fingers. Things needed to be said between them, but right now, she wanted to feel him beside her. She didn't know what the future held. That seemed too distant to imagine with everything else going on.

Elias and Emily got to their feet. Elodie took the moment to look at the others in the room. She wasn't surprised to see Balladyn and Filip, but she didn't know the other two men. Both were handsome in their own right, but they didn't compare to Scott in her mind.

Rhona made the introductions. Elodie was at a loss for words to discover a Dragon King and a Warrior in the cottage with their powerful Druid mates. She was about to ask what they were doing there when she noticed the blood on her brother. "What happened?" she asked Elias, nodding at his wound.

Elias tenderly touched the cut on his brow. "I was attacked as I drove over the bridge, headed onto Skye."

"Attacked?" Balladyn asked, his eyes narrowed, and his body tense. "By whom?"

Her brother shrugged. "I can no' say. All I saw was mist that slammed into my SUV. The vehicle's in the sea."

"It has to be the same mist that's been after Elodie," Scott stated.

Filip nodded as a shiver ran down Elodie's spine.

"Why is it after Elodie?" Sonya asked.

Emily caught Elodie's gaze. "I think I know."

"You mean because of what I did to Da?" Elodie asked.

Rhona frowned as she shook her head. "Wait. Are we saying the mist wants to kill Elodie? Or take her?"

"I'm no' sure we want to find out," Filip said.

Neither did she, but Elodie suspected she wouldn't have that option.

"I know it wanted me dead," Elias said.

Scott nodded. "And me."

"Two Druids on Skye have been killed in two days," Balladyn said. "No one mentioned any mist, but no one was left alive to say anything."

Rhona grabbed her phone and glanced at the screen. Her face tightened as she looked at Balladyn. "Make that four dead. Frasier just texted. A kid called the police. Said they didn't feel well and went to wake their parents but found them dead. It's a family of Druids."

"The children were no' harmed?" Broc asked.

Rhona shook her head. "According to the DI here, it was only the parents."

"Were any other kids left alone?" Eilish asked.

Balladyn crossed his arms over his chest. "No children were at the previous crime scenes."

"There's a reason the children were left unscathed," Ulrik stated.

Elodie's stomach turned violently as she realized the answer. "Adults aren't likely to change their views, while kids can be molded."

"What about in Edinburgh?" Rhona asked Scott.

He and Filip exchanged a look. "Only adults were slain. No one mentioned anything about any bairns."

Emily cleared her throat. "I wish I could stay and help, but I must get back."

"No," Elodie said as she grabbed her mother's arm.

Elias said, "She'll get out in a few months. She's served her time."

Ulrik stepped forward. "I'll return Emily."

"I love you," Emily said as she hugged Elodie once more.

Elodie squeezed her eyes closed. "I'll see you soon."

Then, Emily was gone. Elodie felt a fresh wave of tears well, but she held them back. Now wasn't the time to give in to that emotion.

"This is connected to the drumbeat," Eilish stated. "It has to be."

Sonya nodded in agreement. "A warning of some kind."

"Can one of you ask the Ancients what they want?" Balladyn inquired.

Rhona grunted. "If only it were that easy."

"It wasn't the Ancients I heard, it was the trees," Sonya said.

Broc glanced at Sonya as he nodded. "If there's been trouble, the Ancients usually speak to one of the Druids at the castle."

"Isla mostly," Sonya added. "She has a strong connection to them."

"Have the Ancients said anything?" Scott asked her.

Eilish shook her head as Ulrik returned. "Not to them, and not to anyone at Dreagan."

Elodie looked at the window where the branch had smashed through the glass.

"What?" Elias asked her.

She hesitated before she said, "When I first arrived, there was a storm."

"An unnatural storm," Filip interjected.

Rhona added, "Created by magic."

"A sizable limb came through this window," Elodie continued and pointed. "Did someone want to hurt me? Because that limb could've struck any of the windows."

Scott's lips pressed into a line. "Or were they trying to get you to come inside?"

Elodie's gaze met his. "Exactly."

"And by doing so, revealing your memories as well as your magic," Elias said.

Filip grunted as he crossed his arms over his chest. "Let's no' forget it was coated in *drough* magic."

"Which would've hurt Elodie if not outright killed her," Balladyn stated.

Sonya's lips twisted. "Maybe someone wanted Elodie to walk into this room, and by using *drough* magic on the limb, ensure that she had to use her magic to get rid of it."

"That's a possibility," Broc said.

Rhona blew out a breath. "I don't like any of this happening on Skye. Whoever this is must be stopped."

"Everywhere," Filip added.

Balladyn slid his gaze to Filip. "That's the plan."

"How can we help?" Ulrik asked.

Before anyone could reply, Scott said, "We keep Elodie out of anyone's grasp. Whether they want to harm her or use her."

"Agreed," Elias and Filip said at the same time.

Elodie felt everyone's eyes on her. She thought about the last fifteen years. Everything made sense now. She hadn't been herself. Her magic had been bound, and her memories wiped. It should have given her freedom. Instead, it had trapped her. She loathed what she had done, but she hated that her father had become someone she had no choice but to stop.

Yet she hadn't needed to go to those extremes. She could've hindered him and fled with the rest of her family. It was a nice thought, but Elodie knew that the chances of any of that happening had been slim. He never would've let them go. Her young mind must have come to that conclusion, too.

Or, it was simply seeing her father with a knife, attempting to kill her mother after trying to strangle her that made the decision for her. He wouldn't have stopped. He would've tried again. He might even have gone after Elias. Or her. Or Edie.

Edie. Her sister didn't know anything. She'd been kept completely in the dark. It was no wonder Edie had gotten on with her life better than either her or Elias. Elodie's gaze met her brother's.

As if knowing where her thoughts were, he mouthed, "*Later*."

Beside her, Scott stood strong and unyielding. She had her magic now, just as he had sought. His organization wanted to use her. Would she let them? She wanted to hate him for what he had done, but she couldn't. She was hurt. Deeply. But the feelings he stirred within her weren't so easily forgotten or dismissed.

She felt his warm gaze and turned to him. His deep blue eyes searched hers. He looked for forgiveness. Did she dare give it? Could she?

"I'm not going to make decisions for someone else," Rhona said, returning Elodie's attention to the present. "This is about Elodie. She gets to decide what she wants to do."

Elodie looked at the spot where her magic had made her father disappear. She thought about the intensity of the magic that had erupted from her, the anger and fear that had swept through her. If put into a similar situation, would she react the same way? She was older and wiser now. She knew how to better control her emotions instead of simply reacting.

She returned her attention to her brother. Then she looked at Filip, and then finally at Scott. She thought about her mother, Edie, and her sister's children. If any of them were in danger, if their lives were on the line, Elodie wouldn't stand by and do nothing. Would she kill? Maybe. It depended on the situation.

Perhaps that was why someone wanted to harm her. They might want to make sure a murderer who had escaped punishment received the justice they deserved.

Elodie looked at Rhona. "I'm not running or hiding anymore."

Then she released Scott's hand and walked away.

CHAPTER THIRTY-EIGHT

SKYE DRUIDS

Scott watched Elodie go. His gut twisted at the thought of her putting herself in danger, but at the same time, he understood. She wanted to uncover who was after her. He'd want the same if in her shoes.

"We'll stay to help," Broc replied.

Scott didn't pay the Warrior any mind as he walked after Elodie. He needed to talk to her. She hadn't pulled away from him. In fact, it seemed as if she had wanted his touch. Did that mean she had forgiven him? He needed to know.

He reached the kitchen, but Balladyn suddenly materialized, blocking his way. Scott drew up short just before he ran into the Reaper. "Bloody hell," he murmured and took a step back. "Did you have to appear right before me?"

"Aye."

Scott glared. "What do you want?"

"You know what I want."

Scott raked a hand through his hair. It made sense to tell

Balladyn everything. If there wasn't such a history about the Others, then their two groups might have been able to work together. But Scott knew that wouldn't happen. Neither Balladyn nor Rhona would take kindly to hearing about his connections.

It wasn't just him either. This was Filip's home. He might have hated it when he was younger, but it was the only tie he had to his family. Scott couldn't let anyone take that from him, and that would happen if he shared what he knew with Balladyn.

"I can no'," Scott finally said.

There was no gruff demand from the Reaper. Instead, Balladyn replied, "Your honor is commendable, but you need to choose between it and Elodie."

Scott met his gaze. He didn't tell Balladyn that his time with the beautiful Druid had already come and gone.

"You've seen a lot in Edinburgh," the Reaper continued. "Lost friends. We're losing Druids here. Friends. Family. Can you look any of them in the eye and continue keeping your secret?"

"We're trying to help," Scott argued.

"Ah. Keeping secrets is aiding others, is it?"

Scott glanced over his shoulder to the room down the hall where the others remained. "How many secrets do you have?"

"This isn't about me. You've put your life on the line for Elodie. I suspect you'll continue to do that."

"I will."

Balladyn eyed him. "You're a warrior. I've known some of the best, so I know what to look for. You're not afraid to stand for those you care about. You risk your life again and again because it's the right thing to do, not because you're looking for glory. That kind of man keeps secrets because he thinks he's protecting others. Not to safeguard himself." Balladyn took a step toward him. "Is it Filip or Elodie?"

Scott pivoted to pace the small area. How much longer would it take for Balladyn to figure things out? Who was to say the Reaper hadn't already? The way he looked at Scott and Filip made him think that Balladyn knew everything. Scott paused behind a chair and placed his hands on the back as he dropped his chin to his chest.

"Filip, then," Balladyn stated.

Scott closed his eyes for a heartbeat before lifting his head and meeting the Reaper's gaze. "If I tell you, will you promise to allow Filip to remain on Skye? It's his home."

"It's not my call to make. Rhona leads the Druids."

Balladyn knew everything. The surety of it slammed into Scott. Why hadn't Rhona forced him and Filip from the island? Could it mean that Rhona might be interested in working together? Scott wouldn't know unless he told Balladyn everything. "The organization I'm a part of is a group of Druid Others. It's been active for over a year, and we've never sought power like the Fae Others did. Our leader, Georgina, is a seer. George had a vision that indicated that Elodie was the answer to stopping the Druid killings."

"And you believe George?" Balladyn asked calmly.

Scott straightened. "Her visions doona come often, but they're usually spot-on."

"But not always?"

Scott couldn't deny that. "No' always."

"Why did she send you and Filip?"

"She sent Filip because he's from here. Figured he could help me navigate the tight community of Druids. And she sent me because I can talk anyone into anything."

Balladyn raised a black brow. "Can you now? Because I sense tension between you and Elodie."

"I didn't use my…skills…on her."

"But she knows what you came for?"

Scott blew out a breath as he nodded. "She does. How long have you known?"

"After you brought Elodie to see Rhona, I knew there could only be a few reasons you'd keep a secret. You were adamant about wanting to stop the killings, and you were willing to work with us, but only to a point. I then worked out that there were two probable reasons you would hold back. The first was because you were scared of me and Rhona. And the second was because you were part of an Other group. Since you never once backed down from me, I deduced it was the latter."

"We're no' the same as the Fae Others," Scott hurried to add. "We're trying to save the Druids."

Balladyn raised a hand to silence him. "You've not fought the Others as we have. Talk to the Dragon Kings. Talk to Druids here. Talk to any Reapers or Fae whose loved ones were killed for their magic and see if it makes a difference. A group of Others has one agenda. Power. Can you say your leader doesn't want that?"

"George wants to halt the murders. That's her main goal."

"And after?" Balladyn asked.

Unfortunately, Scott didn't have an answer. "No one talks about it. We're too focused on what's happening now."

"There are Druid Others out there. We're aware. And all of them came about because they want to have power over others. They don't want another group dominating them."

Scott shook his head. "I can no' speak about any other groups. All I know is mine."

"How long ago was it formed?"

Scott licked his lips and widened his stance. "The group itself has been around for years, but the formation as a Druid Other group only happened about a year ago."

"Who suggested it?"

"George. The goal was for the Druids in the city to have a place to be themselves, to know that others like us are walking the streets. That we're no' alone."

Balladyn's shoulders rose as he took a deep breath. "An admirable undertaking."

"But you still see us as evil?"

"As I said, you've not battled the Others."

Scott sighed. "This is why I didna want to tell you. I knew you would be too narrowminded to see the difference."

Balladyn's brows shot up on his forehead. "Narrowminded? Tell me, Druid, did I lie about my intentions while going into your area to convince someone to help me?"

Scott bit back his anger, mainly because the Reaper spoke the truth. Scott's ire was directed at himself. "No."

"You didn't tell us because you knew what our reaction would be."

"Narrowminded."

He and the Reaper eyed each other. Finally, Balladyn said, "From what I've seen, there isn't much difference between your group and the others out there. You keep to the shadows, you lie—and before you say anything, an omission is a lie any way you want to look at it. You seem like an honorable Druid. You should act like one."

Scott said nothing as Balladyn made his way down the hall to the bedroom. He didn't like the truth in Balladyn's words. He should've been honest with everyone. He'd done everything the Reaper had said, and it left a sour taste in his mouth. Before this, Scott had contemplated staying on Skye. He doubted that was an option now, and that saddened him greatly. The isle was special. And not just because it was home to the Skye Druids, but because of the island's beauty and peacefulness that Scott hadn't found anywhere else.

And because of Elodie.

He shoved aside those thoughts and went in search of her. He found her on the back deck, standing huddled in her coat and staring at the sea.

"You won't change my mind," she stated.

He softly closed the door behind him. "I didna intend to try."

"You know everything now. That I'm a…a killer."

"You protected yourself, your mother, and your brother."

She snorted at his comment. "Protected," she said as if the word were acidic on her tongue. "I obliterated him. My *father*." She shook her head, her long, blond locks lifting in the soft sea breeze. "I didn't restrain him. I didn't knock him out. I killed him."

Scott came up beside her. He could see her shaking, and he didn't think it had anything to do with the cold. "You know as well as I do that if you had restrained him or knocked him out, it would've only prolonged the inevitable."

"I know." She turned her head to him.

He looked into her light blue eyes, seeing the porch light reflecting in them. "He would've tried to win all of you back."

Elodie nodded once.

"When that didna work, do you think he would've tried to force your mother to return? What about you and your siblings?"

Elodie swallowed loudly and looked back at the cove. "He used to tell us all the time that family was everything. I've been looking back at memories tonight, and I wonder why I didn't notice how often Mum was missing from things. Because he had hit her, and she didn't want us to see his handiwork."

"The truth is that your father tried to kill your mother. He choked her. He punched Elias. He backhanded you. Then he went after your mother with a knife. His intent was to do as much damage as he could. You stopped him."

"With magic I still don't understand." She looked at him again. "If that's what you want me to use in Edinburgh, I won't. I don't know how, and I don't want to find out."

"I doona want you to do anything in Edinburgh." The instant the words were out, Scott realized how true they were.

She frowned in confusion. "Isn't that why you were sent here?"

"It was. But things have changed."

"Like what?"

He swept his gaze around him. "Look at the island. I've seen pictures of Skye, but they doona do this place justice. Being here brings everything to life. The beauty, the history, the magic. It's all rolled into one incredible place."

"You found peace."

He smiled as he looked at her. "I did. It surprised me since I wasna looking for it. I was happy in the city, but here…here, I feel like it's…"

"Home."

Scott nodded as he grinned. "Exactly. Home."

"You plan on staying, then?"

"I want to, but I doona think that's an option."

Her lips formed an *O*. "You told Balladyn and Rhona."

"I did, but Balladyn had already figured it out. He doesna understand that our group is different."

"Have you looked at it from his perspective?" she asked.

Scott started to reply, then paused. He had been so adamant about the Reaper understanding him that he hadn't taken the time to do the same with Balladyn. "I have no'."

"Maybe you should."

"I will." He faced Elodie. "I'm sorry about no' being honest with you from the beginning. You deserved better."

"Yes, I did."

Scott searched her face. "Do you think you would consider giving me a second chance?"

Elodie smiled and walked away without answering.

He watched her return to the house. Scott moved to the railing and braced his hands on the wood. He sighed, thinking back to what Balladyn had said. George had urged them to be cautious and not to trust anyone. After all the Druid deaths, Scott had agreed with her. George was fiercely protective of Druids, and single-minded in her focus to find the culprit who was killing their kind. That meant she needed more power.

Forming a Druid Other group had given her that. George's

vision about Elodie had been clearer than any before. That was because the three *droughs* and two *mies* who'd joined George had gathered their magic together so she could use it to heighten her power.

Scott knew about the Fae Others. He doubted many Druids hadn't heard about the battle on Skye. So, he understood why everyone was leery about any Other groups. He'd thought it easier—safer, even—if no one knew who he and Filip really were. Or why they were on Skye.

Now, he thought back and wondered about his reasoning. If he were in Rhona's or Balladyn's shoes, he would've been wary of any newcomers, and he would've confronted the first person he deemed an enemy.

Just as Balladyn had.

Scott didn't want to leave Skye, but he would. He owed it to George to return to Edinburgh and share what he had learned with her and the rest of the organization. Then, he would come back. If Rhona didn't permit it, Scott would find somewhere else to live, but Edinburgh was no longer the place for him.

He'd truly believed their organization was the only way to end the Druid murders. His eyes had been opened to many things in his time on Skye. Not the least of which was the fact that there was always another way.

Scott straightened. As he turned to go back inside, a sound drew his attention upward. He lifted his head just as the mist dove from the sky.

CHAPTER THIRTY-NINE

SKYE DRUIDS

Elodie collapsed onto the sofa. Exhaustion pulled at her. She wanted to sleep for a week. She tucked her cold, bare feet up as she tugged the throw around her. She stared into the fire as she went over her conversation with Scott. Elodie wasn't sure what to do. Her heart and body urged her to give Scott a second chance, but her head cautioned her. It didn't matter how deeply she cared about Scott; she didn't know if she could trust him. And without trust, there wasn't a relationship.

Movement near the doorway grabbed her attention. She smiled when she saw her brother. Elias had changed into dry clothes. For the first time since he returned, she got a really good look at him. He was taller than she remembered. His shoulders were broader, and his body had filled out. He moved like a man who had seen—and experienced—a lot. Strong jaw. A nose that had been broken at least once. Blue eyes that saw everything. Dark blond hair that would appear shaggy on others but worked for him.

"Hey," he said with a crooked grin.

"Hey."

He strode into the room and sat beside her. "How are you doing?"

"On the one hand, I got my magic back. So, there's that. I feel more like myself. But on the other, I remembered that I killed our father."

"Who was about to take Mum's life."

Elodie met his gaze. "I know."

"You saved her. You saved all of us."

She worried her lip. "He never hit me until that day."

"He would have eventually. Trust me." Elias looked away, but not before she saw the pain he had buried deep. "He deserved what he got. I wished I would've been the one to do it."

"No, you don't."

Elias sat still—too still. "Aye, I do."

"Why didn't you do something?"

"He told me that he would kill one of you if I said anything to Mum, you, or Edie."

Elodie's stomach clenched painfully as she thought about what her brother had endured. "You kept quiet. I would've, too." She swallowed, telling herself that she shouldn't ask the next question. But she had to know. "How many times…?"

"Does it matter?" he asked tightly. "He controlled me as he did Mum."

She leaned toward him, resting her head on his shoulder. "Why did you leave? I needed you."

"I know." His shoulders moved as he took a breath, then he rested his head atop hers. "I had to. I couldna be the brother you or Edie needed by staying here. I had too much anger. Mum worried that I would slip and say something around you, breaking her spell."

"I would've been all right."

He turned, his chin brushing the top of her head. He stayed there for a moment. "You forget, I was in the room. I saw how distraught you were. We were trying to get you to lower your voice so Edie wouldna hear, but we couldna. No' until Mum agreed to bind your magic."

"She knew that wouldn't be enough," Elodie whispered.

Elias shook his head. "What he made you do...it broke you, sis. Mum knew if she couldna be there to help you, there was only one alternative."

"She never should've been prosecuted for Da's death."

"She made that decision before I could talk to her. The thing is, that day broke all three of us. I think Mum had been broken for some time. She told me years later that the only reason she was able to keep going was because of us. She did what she did to protect us—but you, especially."

Elodie lifted her head to meet his gaze. "And because he had begun abusing you."

"She still hasna forgiven herself for no' realizing sooner. I never faulted her for that. I've only ever blamed him."

Elodie rubbed her hand up and down his arm, sensing the deep anguish that had yet to heal within her brother. "I've lost fifteen years with my family."

"Because of him."

She nodded slowly. "I'm sorry he did that to you."

Elias looked at her solemnly. "I'm sorry you had to be the one to kill him. But you saved us, Elodie. You may no' believe it, but I do. With every fiber of my being. So, thank you."

Her eyes teared, making his face go blurry. She looked away in an effort to regain some control. She had cried enough tonight. "Did you ever tell Edie? That I was the reason Da's gone?"

"She knows nothing about what transpired in that room with us."

"Should we tell her?"

He shrugged. "Would you want to know?"

"She seems content with how things are. It might not be wise to upend her world like that."

"I agree. It's why I never told her anything." Elias cleared his throat. "I'll talk about it all you want tonight, but after this, let's not discuss it again."

She returned her head to his shoulder. "It feels wrong to leave her out, though."

They sat in silence for several moments before he said, "Want to tell me about Scott?"

"I'm not sure there's anything to tell."

"That wasna what I saw."

The teasing note to his voice brought a soft smile to her lips. "He was the first person who made me feel anything in years. I thought something was developing between us."

"Looks to me there *is* something."

"He came to Skye for me."

"What?" All the humor vanished from Elias's voice.

Elodie sighed, her heart heavy. "He's part of a Druid Other group. Their leader is a seer, and she told him that I was the answer to stopping the Druid killings."

"I think I'm changing my opinion of him," Elias stated tightly.

She hadn't realized how much she had missed her brother until then. Elodie watched the flames dance. "He told me everything after he knew that I didn't have magic. He said they would find another way."

"And now that your magic has returned?"

Elodie shrugged. "Everything happened today. I told him I didn't want to see him again."

"He was here when I arrived. He was trying to break the door down to get to you."

Her throat tightened at Elias's words.

"He cares about you," Elias stated. "Deeply."

"He asked for a second chance."

Elias let out a long breath. "Are you going to help him and his organization?"

"No. I told him that a few moments ago. I might have my magic again, but I won't use it the way I did with Da. I refuse to allow myself to be put in that position. I can't imagine any other reason they would want my help."

"You always did have the strongest magic in the family. Maybe there's more you can do."

She squeezed her eyes closed. "I don't want to know. I don't know how I did what I did with Da. It was pure reaction."

"Exactly. That's the kind of inherent power you have, sis."

"It scares me."

Elias's hair brushed her forehead as he turned his head to the door. "You've some powerful friends that could help you."

"I only know Rhona and Balladyn. The others I met with you."

"Still. A Dragon King, a Warrior, and their Druid mates?" Elias let out a low whistle. "As for Balladyn, word has spread quickly through the Druids about his and Rhona's connection."

Elodie sat up, her stomach dropping to her feet. "What do you mean word has spread?"

"It's no' like we have a newsletter or anything, but there are some groups and chat rooms. That's how we share information. Skye is on everyone's radar."

She changed the position of her legs because they had begun to cramp. "Is there talk about the Druids being killed?"

"Absolutely."

"Does anyone have any theories?"

"There are thousands of them."

"Are the killings here like those in Edinburgh and elsewhere?"

"Nay."

"So this is someone different?"

Elias shrugged. "Your guess is as good as mine."

Elodie thought about Scott and then about the group in her parents' room still talking. "You should tell Rhona about the Druid chat rooms."

"I will. I wanted to spend some time with you first."

"Four Skye Druids are dead." Elodie shoved the blanket away and got to her feet. "Maybe Rhona knows about the chat rooms and such. But, regardless, you need to tell her."

Elias lifted his hands, palms up. "Okay. Okay."

"You were attacked," she said with a shake of her head.

"Something has been after me. I don't want it to return for either of us."

His nostrils flared as he pushed to his feet. "I dare it to take another go at me."

"No. I just got you back."

"I'm no' in the habit of hiding, sis."

"To hell with that," she stated. "This is about keeping our family together."

He flattened his lips before they softened. "True."

"I'll get Scott and meet you with the others."

Elodie leaned out the back door, her gaze sweeping around the deck. "Scott!" When she didn't see him, she went back inside and tried the front door. "Scott?"

No answer. She thought maybe he might have come inside without her knowing. Elodie made her way to her parents' room, detouring briefly to get a cardigan and some slippers. But when she reached the others, there was still no sign of Scott.

"Where's Scott?" she asked, talking over Ulrik.

Every head turned to her. Filip's brows snapped together. "He went after you."

"I spoke to him outside, but I came back in," she told them. "Now, I can't find him."

Elias spun on his heel and retraced his steps. "We'll find him."

Elodie followed everyone out, but she had a feeling they wouldn't find Scott. Ten minutes later, they confirmed her fears. Their small group stood looking at each other as if someone had the answer and would give it at any moment.

"He wouldna leave like that," Filip said into the silence.

Sonya looked at Broc. "Honey."

The Warrior nodded, his gaze going distant.

Balladyn said nothing as he stalked from the house to the back deck. Everyone followed. Elodie twisted her hands as she fought for some semblance of calm instead of screaming as she longed to do. Because what good would that do?

The Reaper said nothing as he turned slowly, his gaze moving over everything. He paused and knelt to touch something. Ulrik went to see what it was. The two spoke quietly. It was on the tip of Elodie's tongue to demand that they share what they'd discovered.

"I found him," Broc suddenly said as he walked onto the deck.

Elodie jerked her head to him. "Where? Tell me where he is."

But Broc's gaze was on Ulrik and Balladyn. An unspoken message passed between them. The scream of frustration and panic that Elodie fought was ever closer to being released.

"Let's go back inside," Rhona said calmly into the silence.

Elodie whirled on her. "If you tell me I have to stay out of it, I won't be responsible for what I do to you."

"I'm going, too," Filip stated.

Elias crossed his arms. "We're all fucking going. This is our fight. He's a Druid. On Skye."

Elodie stared down Rhona, silently demanding the Druid leader give in.

The Druid's green eyes were firm, but she finally gave a single nod. "Fine."

"Doona make it sound like you had a choice," Filip stated. "We all know Scott was taken because of Elodie."

Was that true? Elodie felt the world begin to spin. She put out a hand and grabbed hold of the closest thing to her. Elias. He kept her steady.

"Which is why she shouldn't go," Balladyn said.

Elodie looked at the Reaper. "I have to."

"I doona think you're ready," Ulrik told her.

Eilish made a sound as she eyed Elodie up and down with a smile. "She's a Druid. She's ready."

Elodie was glad that someone had faith in her because she didn't. It had been so long since she'd used her magic. She feared she'd forgotten how.

"I'll be with you," Elias said near her ear.

Sonya stepped forward. "We all will."

CHAPTER FORTY

SKYE DRUIDS

Scott grabbed his head. The pain was excruciating. He gingerly felt along the back of his skull and found the wound. Even that soft touch made him nearly pass out and gag with nausea. It took several minutes of breathing through his mouth before he attempted to open his eyes. The place was dark and frigid.

Shrill wind sounded all around him as he shivered. He touched the ground beneath him. Hard stone. He tried to use magic to create some light, but nothing happened. That was when he realized he could no longer feel his magic.

"Bloody hell," he murmured.

The soft, maniacal laugh that greeted his words immobilized him. He couldn't tell if the person was male or female. He squinted into the darkness but couldn't make out a form, no matter how hard he tried.

"Who's there?" he demanded.

The silence was worse than the laugh. He knew that

whoever it was observed him. Without his magic, he was defenseless. Exposed. He could deliver a solid punch, but even that would be hard to do when he couldn't see past his hand in front of his face.

Scott crawled, feeling with his hands to find a wall. The cold seeped through his clothes and into his body, causing him to shake. He clenched his teeth together to keep them from chattering. He didn't know how long he'd been unconscious and on the frosty stone floor. But he knew that the kind of cold that surrounded him wasn't something he could survive without proper clothing and heat.

Finally, he found the edge of a wall. It gave him something else to think about rather than how cold he was. Scott rose to his knees and then to his feet, all the while learning the uneven rock that made up the wall—a support that curved toward him. He was in a fucking cave. Was he still on Skye? Or had the mist taken him elsewhere?

Scott kept still and willed his eyes to adjust to the darkness. No matter how he strained, he couldn't see any farther. At times, the wind became so loud that it sounded like a train barreling toward him. Other times, Scott heard soft dripping coming from somewhere. He needed to know the size of the area around him. He lifted his hands to see if he could touch the ceiling. When he couldn't, he kept his hands raised and returned to the wall that he'd found earlier. In three steps, his palms felt the stone.

He slowly moved his hands over the undulations of rock as the ceiling curved down to the wall. The hairs on the back of Scott's neck rose, reminding him that someone was there. He wanted to call the bastard out, but whoever it was liked this game they played. Well, Scott didn't intend to play. Not in the way his captor might want.

Scott braced his hands on the wall and gradually walked to one side, counting each step. At ten, he reached the back wall. He repeated the process. Thirteen steps until he reached the other side, though he hadn't moved in a straight line. It was more of an inward progression, then back out. He tried to put the image in his head in case he needed to move quickly. The second wall was eleven steps. When his hand touched bars instead of a wall, he stilled, incredulity settling over him.

The laugh sounded again. This time louder, longer. His captor was enjoying this. The bastard.

A multitude of retorts filled Scott's head, but he didn't utter any of them. Scott wouldn't give the wanker the satisfaction of knowing how unsettled he was. If only Scott could see a face or hear a voice. Something. Anything!

He squared his shoulders and counted his steps across the bars—fourteen and a half. So, the front of his prison was wider than the back. Scott wasn't finished, though. He walked seven and a quarter steps to the middle of the wall of bars. Then pivoted and walked straight to the back wall—just over ten steps. Scott now had a mental picture of his jail. He just hoped it would be enough if and when the time came.

Scott moved to the farthest back corner and pressed himself against the stone, hoping his captor couldn't see him. It was colder here. He wrapped his arms around himself and clamped his teeth together. He thought of his da, his sister, and Filip. Elodie. Beautiful, brave Elodie.

There were so many things he wished he would've done and said. But wasn't that what everyone thought when they found themselves in a situation that could potentially lead to their deaths? People always wished they had hugged their loved ones more. Said, "*I love you*" more often. Told those who mattered that they meant something.

The problem was that no one ever thought their last day would be their last day. Scott certainly hadn't. He'd foolishly believed that Elodie's cottage was safe. And it was. On the inside. He'd been outside, though. He hadn't even had time to shout a warning or use magic before the mist consumed him.

He shuddered as he recalled the revolting feel of it consuming him. Yes. *Consumed* was the right word. It had devoured him. He'd thought he was dead. The entire event had occurred so quickly. Too quickly. He was just thankful that Elodie hadn't been with him. Though, why *wasn't* he dead?

Scott's lungs locked as the truth slammed into him. He was alive because his captor wanted something—Elodie.

He squeezed his eyes closed, fighting against the powerlessness that gripped him. He couldn't warn her. He couldn't even protect himself. Scott fisted his hands in fury. Elodie and Filip would look for him. Elias would join his sister. No doubt Rhona and Balladyn would, as well. What about Ulrik, Eilish, Broc, and Sonya? They had a tremendous amount of power between them.

Scott forced his screaming lungs to unseize so he could suck in a breath. He gulped in the air as his mind realized the enormity of the people who had been at the cottage. Was it just Elodie that his captor wanted? Or was it Rhona? Balladyn? Could it be Ulrik? Maybe Broc? Eilish or Sonya? What about Elias?

No, not Elodie's brother. The mist had tried to kill him.

Scott's heart thudded painfully. There were so many potentially awful outcomes if they came looking for him. *If?* They would come. Scott just hoped that he had enough time to shout a warning. It might be all he could give them.

It had been too easy. Kerry had anticipated more of a struggle from Scott. It maddened her how effortlessly she'd taken him. Especially after he had battled her mist so effectively before.

She stood in the cold, dark caves of the Red Hills. One Rhona had put her in a short time ago. Kerry knew everything there was to know about the cell. The width and breadth. The blast of cold air that came from one of the back corners. The undulating ground.

The unforgiving bars that impeded her magic.

She had expected to be locked inside the cell until she died of old age—or Rhona killed her. Instead, the Druid leader had released her. That hadn't been the first of Rhona's mistakes, but it was the gravest.

Kerry couldn't wait to show Rhona just how stupid she had been, but it wasn't time yet. Kerry had made good headway over the last few days. Yet there was more to do. Rhona had to suffer, and with her, the Reaper who had dared to interfere with Druid business. Kerry hadn't intended to involve the Warriors from MacLeod Castle yet, but as one of them was here, she could test her strength on them.

Same with the Dragon King.

They were all meddlers. Intruders who had no business on Skye.

As for the two Druids, the one from Dreagan and the other from MacLeod Castle, she could use them. They were just the sort of Druids she wanted on Skye. She needed powerful leaders like that. Unfortunately, she wasn't sure if they would follow her. Not now, at least.

They only listened to Rhona because of her position. One that Rhona wouldn't always have. Once Kerry took over, those Druids—like everyone else around the world—would heed every word she voiced. As well as beg to come to Skye.

"Aye," the Ancients whispered.

Kerry smiled. If anyone ever doubted her, all she had to do was tell them that the Ancients guided her. Of course, she could do that now, but it wouldn't be as impactful as what she planned. There wasn't time to take the long way to her goal. To debate Rhona in front of others. To have an all-out battle with the current Druid leader—because that's what would happen.

The Ancients had shown her all of it. Including the path she was on now. This would be the one that turned the tide for the Druids forevermore. Everything she did was for her people—at least the ones who lived through it.

She had been startled to discern how easy killing was—and how little she felt after. She'd assumed she might be remorseful and be unable to carry on with the plan, but that hadn't been the case. In fact, it had been the opposite. Removing the Druids who could pervert her cause for justice rejuvenated her.

The addition of the magic of those she had slain had been

a surprise from the Ancients. And that made ending the Druids' lives that much easier.

Kerry whispered to the mist that hung high against the cavern's ceiling. It would wait for the others to enter before it moved again. Then she turned on her heel and went out the secret tunnel.

CHAPTER FORTY-ONE

SKYE DRUIDS

Teleportation wasn't at all what Elodie expected. She didn't feel herself moving from one place to another. And yet, she did. Everywhere. Her body buzzed as if every nerve ending were vibrating from the magic.

She didn't have long to think about that as freezing air blasted her. Rhona had warned her, but experiencing it was altogether different. A rush of wind sucked Elodie's breath away. She clung to Elias, who had a hold of her hand as the wind battered her. No matter how many times she'd begged him to remain at the cottage, he had blatantly refused. He had nearly been killed earlier, and the thought of losing him was too much.

"I go where you go," Elias had stated calmly.

Elodie blinked against the force of the wind that was doing its best to knock her on her arse. It would've succeeded if her brother and Filip hadn't been keeping her upright. Her mind traveled back to the conversation from before they'd arrived at the Red Hills.

"It's a trap. You all understand that, right?" Eilish stated.

Filip nodded once. "We do."

"Only a few know of the prison," Rhona said, her mouth tight.

Ulrik raised a black brow. "How many?"

"My five deputies," Rhona answered.

Balladyn crossed his arms over his chest. "And Kerry."

"Should we be concerned about her?" Broc asked.

Rhona said, "No."

At the same time, Balladyn replied, "Aye."

"Maybe," Rhona amended with a sigh.

"I can see her using this place against us," Balladyn said.

Rhona wrinkled her nose. "She was terrified here."

Filip ran a hand through his hair. "Perhaps we should be cautious about her."

"Agreed," Sonya said.

"And talk to her later," Eilish added.

Rhona nodded in agreement. "We definitely will."

Elodie felt Balladyn's gaze on her. She looked at the Reaper as his unusual, red-ringed silver eyes observed her.

"Are you ready for this?" he asked.

She knew what he meant. She was the bait. The last thing she wanted to do was go into some mountain to be pitted against an unknown enemy, but she would do it. Because Scott wouldn't hesitate to march himself there for her. Despite the betrayal she felt, she cared deeply for him—more than she had believed possible. It might even be love. "Yes."

"You willna be alone," Elias told her.

Ulrik's lips flattened. "I think she has to go in alone."

"What? No," Filip answered as he shook his head.

Elodie's stomach dropped to her feet. Alone? They couldn't be serious.

"He's right." Rhona's green gaze held Elodie's. "We need them to think you're by yourself."

Balladyn gave her a single nod. "I'll be veiled with you so they can't see me."

That made Elodie feel a little better. Then something occurred to her. "They'll expect that." Her gut twisted as she realized the truth of her words. "They know you're the Warden. A Reaper. They'll plan on you and Rhona helping me."

"Bloody hell," Broc mumbled. "She's right."

Eilish threw up her hands. "Someone needs to be in there with Elodie."

"No," Elodie said firmly as she realized just what she had to do. "I have to go alone. If I get into trouble, I'll call for Balladyn. But...we all know I'm a killer."

Elias shook his head. "You did what had to be done, sis. That was different."

It wasn't, but she wouldn't get into another debate about it. "If they want me, then they'll get me." If she said it convincingly enough, would it be true? She had to do something to help Scott.

Now, she stood outside in the bitter cold, the wind whipping furiously. Her blood ran like ice in her veins. She was numb. From the freezing temperatures, trepidation, and the ghastly situation. How had she found herself here? More importantly, was there a way for her and Scott to get out alive?

She wasn't so sure. She would do everything possible to make sure Scott was freed and remained unharmed. As for her? If someone went to such trouble to bring her here, Elodie didn't think that what they'd planned would be a warm and cozy welcome.

The thought of taking another life made her sick to her stomach, but if she were defending herself or someone she cared about, she would do it without hesitation. She wished with all her might that she wouldn't find herself in that predicament, though. Even as she sent up the silent prayer, she knew it was useless. Facts were facts, and there was no getting around them.

Elias squeezed her hand. Words were useless in the gusting wind. Besides, they didn't want to alert anyone to their presence. Elodie had never been brave. Not really. Edie had often teased that she ran headlong into anything, but that wasn't true. Elodie was all about self-preservation. Except this time, she had to ignore her brain shouting at her to flee.

Fight or flight. She'd been in that kind of situation once before and had chosen fight. This time, she wished she had the option. Unfortunately, Scott's life was on the line. He had stood with her against the thunderstorm and the mist without a second's thought for his safety. He deserved the same from her.

Elodie nodded at her brother before squaring her shoulders. She pulled her hand from Elias's and squeezed both into fists, hoping to draw some heat into her palms. The gloves didn't seem to be doing anything to keep her fingers warm. She felt everyone's gaze on her. She stepped through the few inches of snow. Her feet were like blocks of ice, which matched her insides.

Life didn't teach you how to manage having someone's life in your hands. There was no manual instructing you how to talk or act. You were simply thrown into the lion's den and expected to come out the victor. Nothing in Elodie's past could have prepared her for this moment. No revelations. Nothing but her lack of knowledge.

And Scott's very life rested on her.

She started toward the narrow entrance that Rhona had pointed out. It felt like an eternity before Elodie reached it. She wanted to turn around and look at the group, but she was afraid she'd lose her nerve if she did. So, she stepped into the mountain.

Her ears rang from the wind. She could still hear it howling outside, but it wasn't nearly as thunderous inside. She strove to hear anyone in the mountain, but the ringing didn't give her a chance. Rhona had warned her that the tunnel to the cells was long.

Cells. Elodie shouldn't be surprised that someone had erected a place to put out-of-control Druids. They were still human, only they had magic. That didn't make them saints. They still did cruel and wicked things. Still harmed others. It'd never dawned on Elodie that they had a place like this, though. She hadn't really thought about what happened to those who broke the law. And not just human laws but also Druid laws.

The mountain swallowed her from her first step inside. The darkness was so great that it gave Elodie pause. It was marginally warmer inside the mountain than outside, but not enough to make a real difference. She shivered and stuffed her hands into her pockets. She needed to be able to feel her hands if she were to do any magic.

Just thinking about her magic sent a rush through her as if it wanted to let her know it was there and waiting. With the return of her memories and power, it felt as if a curtain had been lifted. As if she could see the world clearly again. No wonder she had walked around in a fog all those years. Her true self had been bound, restricted. But no longer.

She removed her hands from her pockets and let the magic pool in her palms. It wasn't as if she could be too careful. She was in a tunnel leading to prison cells, where someone had taken Scott. This person was her enemy— however many there were. They had killed Druids. They had tried to kill her brother. There was no other way to look at them than as adversaries—not that she would tell them that, of course.

Elodie walked a few paces, only to pause because it was pitch-black. She took out her mobile and turned on the flashlight. She could use magic, but she was waiting. It had been a long time since she'd used her power, and she didn't want to waste it on a light when she had another option. She blew out a breath and continued onward.

She wondered what the others outside were doing. Did they question her ability to free Scott? They should, because she certainly did. She really hoped Scott's organization was involved in his kidnapping, because at least then she knew they wanted her to help them. She could use that. That could also explain why they had taken Scott instead of killing him.

On the other hand, whoever this wanker was, they knew that she and Scott had gotten close. Anyone with a brain would've realized they could use him as bait when they couldn't get to her in the cottage.

Elodie was leaning toward the latter option. If it were the Others in Edinburgh, they wouldn't have used mist to kill the Druids on Skye. They were trying to *stop* the deaths. So, yeah. She would soon come face-to-face with a murderer. If she got out of this alive, she would mention to Rhona that the Druids should be taught how to handle such situations. Maybe even put together a manual because could there really ever be too much information for these circumstances?

The tunnel suddenly widened. Elodie paused, her thoughts skidding to a halt. She leaned to the right and peered around the side of the wall. It was the cavern Rhona had described. A large, blackened area where fires burned when someone was imprisoned sat in the middle. It wasn't lit now, though. Beyond that, she saw five individual sets of bars for the cells. Scott wasn't in any of them.

Her heart thudded against her ribs so violently that she expected it to launch from her chest at any moment. Fight or flight. She shoved aside the voice screaming in her head to run. She thought about Scott, of how he had always been there for her. She thought about the way he had held her, of how he had felt inside her.

Elodie walked slowly from the tunnel, her gaze moving from one area to another as she scanned her light to see. There were so many shadows and crevices where someone could be hiding. She half expected someone to jump out at her—but no one did.

Rhona had warned that there was only one way in and out. That meant if anyone was in there, they had to get past her to leave. And then run into the very formidable group waiting outside. One way or another, whoever had abducted Scott would soon be stopped.

That thought didn't calm Elodie as she hoped it would. Her mind raced with things she could possibly say to get Scott released, which meant nothing because she didn't know what they wanted her for.

"Leave. Now!" Scott shouted.

Her head jerked toward the sound of his voice. She tried to see inside the middle cell. "Scott?"

"Elodie, goddamn it. Run!"

She ignored him and rushed to the bars. "Are you hurt? Let me see you."

The words were barely out before he shouted her name. She felt something behind her. Elodie spun to see mist coalescing into a giant ball as it dropped menacingly from the ceiling. Her mobile slipped from her fingers, diminishing the light before extinguishing entirely as it landed screen-up against the floor before the impact flipped it again. The beam shone right on the mist.

Terror gripped Elodie. Her stomach dropped to her feet as the mist twisted and formed a huge hand that reached for her. Elodie threw up her arms and hoped her magic answered. She wanted to shout with joy when her movements cut the mist in two. But her elation didn't last long as it reformed in an instant.

She called to her magic, and it pooled in her hands. She felt the power and the intensity of it. Elodie let out a yell as she released it, imagining it enveloping the mist. She watched in awe as it did just that.

In the next second, a second bundle of mist slammed her against the bars. It seemed to have come out of nowhere. It pushed her so viciously that she almost felt her bones shuddering. For just a moment, she had thought she could take on the mist and free Scott. She hadn't expected there to be more. But villains never fought fair—another lesson Druids should be taught.

"Elodie," Scott called, his voice sounding far away.

She tried to answer him. She couldn't see her flashlight anymore. The mist had enveloped her. She felt it trying to enter her nose. Elodie blew out some air, but she would have to take a breath eventually. It didn't take her long to realize that she should've called for her friends as soon as she entered the cavern. She hoped it wasn't too late now.

"Balladyn!" she yelled.

She didn't get to finish the word as the mist flew into her mouth, choking her.

CHAPTER FORTY-TWO

SKYE DRUIDS

"Noooo!" Scott roared as he desperately fought to hang onto Elodie.

He knew the cloying feeling of the mist. Knew how difficult it was to breathe or see or even hear. Elodie's arm jerked in his hold. Then she was still. So very still.

"Elodie," he called.

The mist had moved over his hands, wrapping itself around Elodie so no part of her showed. If Scott hadn't had a hold of her, he wouldn't have been able to reach her now. And nothing would make him release her.

He peeled back his lips as his skin started to sting. That sensation soon turned into burning. He looked down to see that the mist encased his hands from the wrists down. Beneath his skin, his veins appeared to glow. The pain brought him to his knees. With his teeth clenched, he tried to will Elodie to use her magic.

Then, suddenly, she was gone. Vanished as if she had

never been there. Scott fell forward, his head slamming into the bars since he no longer held Elodie. He heard footsteps. He tried to lift his head, but the fire in his arms was spreading.

Dimly, he heard voices. He tried to focus his eyes as he slumped to the ground. His gaze landed on Elodie's phone—the only proof that she had been there. The fire in his veins had reached his shoulders and neck. He felt it spreading to his face and across his chest.

"Scott," Filip called. "Scott, stay with us. Keep your eyes open."

He tried. He really did, but it was too much—the pain and losing Elodie.

"What the bloody hell?" someone asked.

There was the loud squeak of metal against metal. Then hands were on him. Someone spoke, but Scott couldn't really hear them. He was sinking beneath the waves of unconsciousness. He kept thinking about Elodie as she'd rushed into the cavern. He'd known that she would, even as he hoped that she wouldn't. He'd failed her. If only she had listened when he'd told her to leave.

He felt something or someone tug at him. Scott turned away from it. He didn't want to go back to a world without Elodie in it. How would he look her brother and sister in the eye? How could he tell them that he hadn't been able to save her?

"Scott?"

The feminine voice was soft and one he recognized. It would be easy never to wake, to hide beneath his shame and grief. Then he thought about Kevin. Both he and Elodie had died because they were Druids. He'd vowed to find whoever was targeting their kind and stop their reign of terror. Would he give up now? He couldn't. He had more reason than ever before to keep going.

He opened his eyes to find a sea of faces looking down at him.

"Fuck. You scared the hell out of me," Filip said in a voice raw with emotion.

Rhona was near his head. Hers had been the voice he'd heard. She smiled wanly at him. "There you are. I thought we'd lost you for a second."

They nearly had. Scott realized there was some kind of light in the cavern now. Not only did a ball of magic hang in the air above them, but a fire also blazed in the middle, blanketing the room in warmth. He started to sit up, helped by Rhona and Sonya. He rubbed his icy hands together as anger festered.

"Ready to tell us what happened?" This came from Ulrik.

Scott got to his feet and looked around, hoping against hope that Elodie was there somewhere. Then he looked up. The ceiling above had hidden the mist. He hadn't seen it because it had been dark. "It waited for her."

"What did?" Broc asked.

Scott swallowed around a painful lump in his throat. "The mist."

"Was anyone else here?" Eilish prompted.

Scott drew in a shuddering breath. "There was, but I didna see them. They kept everything dark."

"Fek," Balladyn mumbled as he and Rhona shared a look.

Filip shook his head. "Where is Elodie?"

Scott went to retrieve her mobile from where it lay. He

turned off the flashlight and pocketed the device. "The mist took her."

"Taken and no' killed?" Elias asked hopefully.

Scott nodded.

Sonya tugged her gloves back on. "That's good news."

"Is it?" Rhona asked doubtfully. "Whoever this person is, has randomly killed around Skye. We don't have any clue how he's targeting his victims. And now he's taken Elodie? I don't see that as good."

But Scott did. "She's alive. We can find her."

"We may not want to," Balladyn replied.

Scott looked the Reaper in the eye. "I willna stop until I locate her."

"She's a fighter," Elias stated firmly. "If anyone can survive this, my sister can."

Rhona's gaze slid back to Scott. "Did you get anything from your kidnapper? Did you hear anything to let us know if it was a man or a woman?"

"Are they working alone or with someone?" Broc added.

Scott shrugged. "I didna see or hear anything other than a laugh, which I couldn't discern as being male or female. I knew they were near, but it was just a feeling."

Eilish tapped the top of her boot. "Do you know why they didn't stick around?"

"I think because they knew we would be here." Elias let out a string of curses.

Ulrik grinned. "Because they doona wish to fight all of us."

"We can sort all of this out later," Scott said before anyone could speak again. "We need to find Elodie."

Broc's lips twisted. "I've been trying. I can no' locate her."

"Then we do this another way," Rhona said.

Sonya yanked back off her gloves and smiled. "I'm game."

"You know it," Eilish replied.

Rhona raised her brows to Elias. "Join us?"

Elodie's brother stepped forward without a word.

Rhona then looked at Scott. "What about you?"

"Whatever you need," he told her.

Rhona's head swung to Filip. "We're going to need you, too."

"Like Scott said, whatever you need," Filip replied as he came up beside Scott.

The six of them stood in a circle with Balladyn, Ulrik, and Broc guarding. Rhona was the first to start the chant. By the second utterance, the rest of them joined in. Scott had never heard this spell, but he suspected there was a lot he didn't know—which was a pity. The Skye Druids were trained, but Druids elsewhere had to get by by picking up what they could and winging the rest.

His thoughts halted as their magic began swirling around them. It wasn't just any locator spell, but one imbued with strength for Elodie, helping her to shake off whatever magic shielded her, stopping her from being found.

Minutes ticked by. Scott pushed more of his magic into the spell. They had to find Elodie. She could've been taken anywhere, and if she were to be found, it had to be because of the people around him now.

"I found her," Broc announced.

Sonya asked him, "Do you have a good lock?"

"Aye," Broc replied.

With that, they ended the spell. It felt good to have his magic back. Scott never wanted to be in a situation where he couldn't access it again. "Come on," he hurried them. He didn't want to waste any more time.

They split into two groups. Balladyn teleported Rhona, Scott, Elias, and Filip. Ulrik took Eilish, Broc, and Sonya. In a matter of seconds, they were outside a building. No one said a word. Suddenly, Broc released his dark blue leather-like wings, and his skin turned indigo. The light from a nearby post showed that the same blue spread across Broc's eyes from corner to corner, but it was the fangs and the long blue claws that gave Scott pause. Broc nodded to Sonya before jumping into the air, his wings beating softly as he quickly rose.

Scott wondered if Ulrik would shift into his true form. He wanted to see a dragon, but in the middle of town might not be the best idea. Ulrik faded into the shadows on the right and disappeared along with Eilish. Sonya and Elias remained at the front. Balladyn took Rhona's hand just as the Reaper caught Scott's eye and jerked his chin to the left. Scott motioned to Filip, and the two of them went to the left of the building as Balladyn and Rhona teleported to the back.

The three-story structure was vacant, its years of unuse evident in the chipped paint and broken windows. Some were boarded, but even that wood was rotting. Scott saw a door on the side. He walked to it. Before he touched it, he tested it with magic.

"Shite," he murmured when he felt magic push back against him.

Scott hoped the others tested, as well. Then he remembered who he was with. Of course, they would. He was trying to figure out a way to bypass the magic when Filip tapped him on the shoulder. Elias was at the corner of the building, motioning to them. Scott and Filip hurried over to find the others waiting in the shadows.

"It needs to be a coordinated attack," Balladyn whispered.

Ulrik nodded. "Windows and doors. It's the only way we'll get past the magic."

"And the roof," Broc added.

Rhona looked at each of them. "We won't know what's inside. There could be one or a hundred of them waiting for us."

"Their killing spree needs to be stopped," Filip replied.

Eilish nodded. "They stayed on Skye when they could've left. That benefits us. Let's use it."

"Should you call the deputies?" Balladyn asked Rhona.

She shook her head. "I don't know which of them is involved. Again," she said with a sigh.

"Everyone get into place. We go in together," Balladyn said.

Scott frowned. "When do we go?"

"You'll know the signal," Rhona told him.

Scott and Filip returned to the left side of the building. Scott glanced at Filip to find him at the ready, his gaze locked on the windows nearest him. Scott called to his magic. His palms tingled with it. He thought about Skye, the wild island that had swept him up in its beauty and mystery. He thought of the many generations of Druids who had lived and trained on the isle. He thought of the magic that made it special.

He'd found his home here, just as he'd found the woman he loved. He wouldn't lose either of them. He couldn't.

To his surprise, Scott felt magic below him. Skye. It was the island; he knew it. The magic came up from the ground to seep into his shoes and then his feet. He couldn't see it, but he felt it as it wound around him. His magic answered immediately, pulsing and racing. The power that met his made Scott sway. He'd never experienced anything like it before. He knew Druids could strengthen their magic in different places. It appeared he had found his — Skye.

A loud boom sounded from the roof, shaking the building. Scott unleashed his magic along with the others. Windows blew in, and doors buckled under the onslaught of Druid, Dragon King, and Warrior magic.

Scott strode to the collapsed door and tested it. The magic was gone. He glanced at Filip to see him on his heels. Their gazes met before Scott entered the building.

CHAPTER FORTY-THREE

SKYE DRUIDS

"Yes. That's it. Go inside," Kerry said gleefully as she watched the group enter the building. She could barely contain her excitement.

She wished she was inside to see their faces, but that was fine. It was enough that they were doing exactly what she wanted. For beings with such authority, they were so easily manipulated. If she had known this, she would've done something sooner. But she had never dared to even allow herself to think the things she was now.

Kerry rubbed her hands together as she watched from inside her vehicle. She took a deep breath and smiled. Throughout all the years of her life, she had thought she knew what confidence felt like, but she hadn't a clue. Not until recently. Now, she fully embodied the sentiment. She *was* self-assurance. She had to give credit to the Ancients. Had they not spoken to her, she never would've had the courage to do anything.

Her smile grew as she spotted Elodie through a shattered window. Kerry started her engine and put the car in drive. There was no need to stay. The mist knew exactly what to do.

Elodie shook her head. This couldn't be happening. She stared at those coming at her, each wearing her father's face, each holding the same knife he'd brandished when he attempted to take her mother's life.

"No," she said and gathered her magic. "I stopped you once. I'll do it again."

One of her fathers paused and tilted his head to the side. "Elodie," he said in a voice that took her back to her childhood. "I'd never hurt you."

"You hurt me. You hurt us all. You were a monster," she proclaimed.

His forehead wrinkled in a frown. "What are you talking about?"

She shook her head. She wasn't going to get into a debate. A sound behind her drew her attention. She glanced over her shoulder. There were more of him. Dread churned in her stomach. This was a nightmare. She'd had plenty of them since arriving on Skye. She had survived them. She would endure this one, as well. Just as soon as she killed each and every incarnation of her father.

Emotion caught in her throat. She had loved him deeply. She couldn't stop thinking about how he used to tease her and her siblings. How loudly he'd sung off-key while making breakfast on Saturday mornings. How he always found fun things for them to do as a family. She faltered, her magic dimming. Their family had been close, their love strong.

Her father's smiling face shifted in her mind, replaced by the monster who had choked her mother, punched Elias, struck her, and then tried to stab her mum. That was her father. He had carefully hidden his true self from all of them. And his blood ran through her veins. His tainted, evil essence. Maybe that was why she hadn't hesitated to take his life. She was a monster, too.

She would show him again.

She would kill him however many times he entered her nightmares. He had no business in her life. If she could remove every memory of him, she'd do it in a heartbeat. Elodie felt her magic rushing through her. It collected in her palms.

"No more," she whispered as she threw out her hands.

Scott dove out of the way just as Elodie released her magic. He heard someone curse behind him as the others quickly moved.

"What the bloody hell?" Elias shouted.

Scott was closest to Elodie. He'd heard her words, seen her face. "She thinks we're her father."

"All of us?" Balladyn asked, veiled somewhere behind Elodie.

Rage colored her face as she shouted, "Stop talking! You mean nothing to me!"

This didn't make any sense. Why had he been kidnapped so Elodie was brought to the mountain? Scott had thought that whoever was behind this wanted to kill Elodie. Seemed he had been wrong. But he couldn't work out why they were using her in such a way. Not that he wasn't thrilled that Elodie was alive and well. Well, as good as someone could be with her mind playing tricks on her.

Scott suddenly got a sick feeling in his stomach. Something wasn't right. Not at all. The building had been too easy to get into. At first, he'd thought it was because of the combined strength of those with him, but now he wondered if it had been something else entirely.

"Someone do something," Sonya whispered.

No one moved. Elodie stood in the middle of the ground floor, her blue eyes blazing with anger and hatred. Scott didn't need to see her magic to know that she had it gathered around her, waiting to strike.

Scott slowly got to his feet, and Elodie's gaze fastened on him.

There was a soft sound behind him, and then Balladyn's voice whispered in his ear, "We need to attack her together to subdue her and figure out who messed with her mind. Keep her focused on you."

Scott nodded once to let the Reaper know that he'd heard and agreed.

"What?" Elodie asked Scott. "Why did you nod? Do you think I care about you? After what you did to Mum? To Elias?"

"I'm no' your father," Scott told her.

She snorted. "I wish that were true. I'm tainted with your blood and your sick nature. That's why it was so easy to take your life."

"Elodie," Scott said as the others gradually closed in on her. "Look at me. *Really* look at *me*. I'm no' your father. I'm Scott."

"More lies. How many did you tell us? Was anything you said true? What was it that broke inside you that made you want to hit your wife and your kids? Would you have eventually struck Edie? Don't worry about answering. I know the answer. I did everyone a favor by ridding the world of your sickness."

Scott swallowed, his heart aching for the woman he loved. She probably never would've said anything of this to him or anyone else. It was good that she was getting it out. He just wished she didn't believe that he was her father. Scott glanced at her hands. She hadn't known the amount of power she had at fifteen, but she did now. She had killed her father as easily as snuffing out a candle—and she could do it to him. To all of them.

But Scott wasn't afraid. He didn't want to die, but if he lost his life in an effort to save Elodie, then that was fine with him.

"Look into my eyes, Elodie," he told her as he took a step to her. "Look deep. See *me*."

Elodie didn't want her father anywhere near her. She held up her hands, her magic eager to be released. "Don't come any closer. The mask you wore for our benefit is gone. I see the real you, and it's twisted and grotesque, just like your soul."

"I'm Scott," he said again. "You'll see that when you look at me."

She shook her head. "More tricks. I've had enough to last a dozen lifetimes."

"No trick. Just me," he replied.

Elodie saw him take two more steps. They were measured, controlled, but she wasn't fooled. He wanted to get close to her. She noticed that the other incarnations of her father had also begun to close in around her.

"Time for you all to die, once and for all," she declared.

As she released her magic, someone jerked her arms to the side, causing the magic to crash into a wall. Elodie screamed her frustration, but it didn't do any good. They had her—all of them.

All except the one who had been speaking to her.

She tried once more to rid the room of the manifestations of her father when suddenly, everything went black.

"What the fuck?" Elias murmured as he stared down at his sister, who he'd carefully lowered to the floor when she fell unconscious.

Scott ran a hand down his face, sweat beading on his

forehead because of how close he'd come to dying. Everyone in the room had been affected by what'd just occurred.

"It has to be a spell," Eilish said.

Rhona nodded. "Let's find out."

Scott's heart still pounded erratically as he joined the other Druids in a circle around Elodie. He tried to concentrate on the spell they were casting, but his mind kept drifting to the things Elodie had said. He felt Rhona's gaze and looked across the way at her. Worry filled her face. He didn't know if it was for him or Elodie. Scott then cleared his mind and focused on the spell.

"There," Sonya suddenly said. "I feel it."

Eilish winced. "Me, too. It's…"

"Sickening," Elias finished.

Scott sucked in a breath when it slammed into him. His stomach roiled in response. "It isna a spell. It's a curse."

"Bloody hell," Filip murmured tightly.

Rhona squeezed her eyes closed. "It's staying just out of reach."

Balladyn came up behind her and put his hand on her shoulder. The surge of his magic joining theirs made Scott lightheaded, and he wasn't the only one. The curse didn't stand a chance now. They stripped it from Elodie in seconds.

When it was gone, Scott bent at the waist, his hands on his knees as he tried to shake the feeling of the curse. Sonya coughed. Eilish gagged. Filip sank heavily to the floor. Elias dropped to one knee. Rhona slumped back against Balladyn. Each of them had felt the wrongness of it, the malevolence.

"Something doesna feel right about any of this," Ulrik said.

Scott lifted his head. "Because *nothing's* right about it. I thought I had been abducted to set a trap for Elodie."

"We all did," Eilish said and swallowed loudly, her skin ashen.

Elias got to his feet and swayed slightly. "I expected to find Elodie dead, or at the verra least, injured. No' ready to attack us."

"I wasna the trap," Scott said as the truth hit him. His gaze then dropped to the floor where Elodie remained unconscious. "She was."

Balladyn's eyes flashed with fury. "For us."

"Aye, but which one of us?" Broc asked as he tamped down his god, his blue skin and wings disappearing.

Sonya shrugged. "Maybe all of us."

"Nay." Filip shook his head as he awkwardly gained his feet. "They couldna have known a Dragon King, Warrior, or other Druids would come."

Rhona glanced at Balladyn. "Which means it was either you or me."

"Doona forget, they knew I was here," Elias added.

Scott sighed. "As well as Filip and me."

"But we stopped Elodie and the curse," Broc said. "It's over."

Scott remembered how the mist had come from the top of the cavern. He lifted his head and saw nothing but darkness. A flare of light shot up from Ulrik to the ceiling, where they spotted the mist roiling violently.

That was the only warning they got before it barreled down at them.

Elodie's eyes snapped open. She gagged as she recalled how the mist had been in her throat. She rolled to the side and dry heaved. It was then that she heard the shouts. Her head jerked up as she saw her friends battling the mist.

She didn't know how she had gotten to this place or even where she was. She didn't know how her friends had found her. But none of that mattered. Elodie jumped to her feet and immediately began pummeling the mist with magic.

"Together!" Rhona shouted.

The Druids made a circle as Ulrik, Balladyn, and Broc continued battling the mist with their magic. Then the Druids locked hands, the strength of their magic swirling around them. Elodie found Scott to her left and met his gaze. He winked at her, and she wanted to cry at the sight of him. He had gotten free, but she didn't know how. She would find out, though. First, however, they had to eradicate the mist.

The mist slithered between them. It locked onto Elodie's legs and began crawling up her body. She ignored it and instead concentrated on her magic. When it reached up to wrap around her neck, she remembered how it had choked her in the mountain. Her magic faltered. That gave the mist an advantage. Balladyn blasted it with an orb, and the mist reared back. The reprieve was all Elodie needed to return her attention to the circle of magic.

The Druids' voices rose as their power grew and swelled. Together with Ulrik's, Balladyn's, and Broc's magic, the mist continued shrinking until only a sliver of it slithered out a window and into the night.

CHAPTER FORTY-FOUR

SKYE DRUIDS

It was over. Elodie had never felt so emotionally, physically, and mentally drained in her life. She wanted to collapse and forget that all of this had happened. Instead, her brother enfolded her in his embrace.

"I thought I'd lost you," he whispered.

Elodie hugged him tightly. "I'm here."

Elias pulled back and smiled at her. "I'm going to stay on Skye for a wee bit. I'd like to catch up with my sisters. Besides, there's someone who is waiting to speak to you."

Elodie looked around her brother to Scott. Filip was talking to him, but she didn't think Scott heard since he was staring at her. Scott walked away from Filip without a word. She moved around her brother and met Scott halfway. "I'm sorry I didn't get you out of the mountain."

"We're alive. That's what matters." He gave her a crooked smile that made her stomach flutter at the sexiness of it.

She glanced at the ground. "You asked for a second chance."

"I did."

"I'd like to start over instead."

He quirked a brow. "Oh?"

"Well, there were things I didn't know about myself. That might change us."

She barely got the words out before he pulled her against him, his mouth covering hers in a kiss that stole her breath. Elodie leaned against him as the flames of desire sparked and soared. When he eventually ended the kiss, she was breathless and needy.

"Does that feel as if things are different?" he asked in a voice roughened with need.

Elodie shook her head. "No."

Scott smoothed a strand of hair back from her face. "I love you. It might be too soon to tell you that, but I doona care. I knew it before I thought you'd been taken from me. And when you vanished with the mist..." He paused and shook his head as if the words were too terrible to say. "We're here now. That's all I need."

"You love me?" The joy inside her was so immense that she thought she might burst with it.

His face split into a smile. "I do, lass. Verra, verra much."

"Good. Because I love you."

He linked his hands behind her as they stood together. "I'm no' sure the day could get any better."

She grinned. "Oh, I think it could."

"I hate to break this up because it's all kinds of awesome," Elias told them, "but we need to talk."

Elodie reluctantly released Scott and faced everyone. She didn't care that the others had heard her declaration to Scott and his to her. For the first time in years, she felt free and whole. Complete.

Balladyn, Ulrik, and Broc walked in through an outside door. "The area is clear," Balladyn said. "No sign of anyone suspicious here or nearby."

Then everyone looked at her.

"Do you remember what happened in the mountain?" Rhona asked.

Elodie frowned as she shook her head. "Not really. I remember hearing Scott and then seeing the mist. I do recall how it went down my throat to choke me."

"It took you," Scott told her. "You disappeared right before my eyes."

Sonya frowned. "What do you remember next?"

"Waking up to see all of you fighting the mist," Elodie answered. The way the others glanced at each other told her that she was missing something. "Tell me," she insisted.

For the next few minutes, she listened as they told her about freeing Scott from the mountain until they found her here, trying to kill them. Elodie was staggered to learn that she had been cursed. It wasn't that Druids didn't use curses, but *droughs* usually did them. Which made sense with all the Druids being murdered. Only a *drough* would take life so callously.

"Thank you," she told them, shocked and stunned by what had been done to her. "I'm glad I didn't hurt anyone."

Scott's arm wound around her shoulders. "We were no' going to let anything happen to you."

But they all knew it had been a miracle that she had been freed.

"We're no closer to learning who the culprit is," Elias stated.

Scott swallowed. "I doona think it's the same killer that's in Edinburgh."

"This does feel different," Filip agreed.

Eilish's lips pressed into a line before she said, "Unfortunately, I think we're just getting started with this foe."

"Aye. They'll keep pursuing Druids," Broc said.

Rhona lifted one shoulder in a shrug. "Or whoever was their intended target tonight."

"Which is why we all need to be vigilant," Filip replied.

Balladyn stood as still as granite. "Aye."

"We're always available to help," Ulrik told the group.

Sonya was pensive. "Druids everywhere are at risk. There needs to be a way to reach them."

"There is," Elodie said and looked at Scott.

He squeezed her shoulder. "There are some chat rooms where Druids stay in contact. It's one way to get to them. I can share them with whoever wants the links."

"Thanks. It's a start," Rhona said. "We'll need to find a better way, though."

Eilish nodded in agreement. "We will. For now, let's just get the word out about what has happened here as well as elsewhere. The number of Druid deaths are concerning."

"I can start sharing," Filip said.

Rhona smiled at him. "We'd appreciate that."

Balladyn looked around the building. "Let's get to our homes to rest. We'll reconvene later to come up with a plan."

In a heartbeat, Elodie, Scott, Filip, and Elias stood in her cottage's kitchen. Balladyn and Rhona didn't stick around. Elodie couldn't stop grinning at Scott. He loved her. She couldn't believe the man she had fallen for really loved her.

"Ah…we're going to head to my place," Filip said after he cleared his throat.

Scott nodded without taking his eyes from Elodie. "Sounds good."

"We'll catch up tomorrow, sis," her brother said.

She waved. "Be careful."

The door closed behind them. Scott lifted her into his arms, cradling her body against his as he stalked into the front room. He lowered her feet to the floor as the fire roared to life behind him. Dawn streaked the sky, but neither noticed as they hastily removed their clothes and reached for each other, their lips and bodies melding.

He kissed down the length of her throat. "My heart is yours for eternity."

"And mine yours." Her fingers slid into his hair as he lifted his head. Their gazes met.

Scott grinned up at her. There was so much horror that had happened in the cottage but finding love with Scott within its walls banished all of the evil. Their love would continue to wash away any darkness that lingered. She had found the future she had dreamed of with a man who would stand strong and solid beside her.

He lifted her to lay her on the rug before the fire, the light from the flames reflecting in his dark blue eyes. The love she saw there made her breath catch.

"Och, lass," he murmured before finding her lips with his.

Her thoughts evaporated as desire filled her. Pleasure awaited them, and she wouldn't deny either of them a second longer.

EPILOGUE

SKYE DRUIDS

Three days later...

When a knock sounded on the door, Scott lowered his book. Elodie put aside her magazine and rose to answer it. He'd been dreading this meeting for the past day. Mostly because he knew their time of peace was coming to an end.

The past couple of days had been locked in meetings for hours with everyone from the other night. They were no closer to finding answers, but with Druids, a Reaper, the Dragon Kings, and the Warriors, they would uncover everything eventually. Scott hoped it was sooner rather than later.

He and Elodie also had a lot of time alone. She discovered that her fear of Rhona earlier stemmed from her mother's spell. Rhona's station and power could have removed it, and it triggered Elodie to be frightened of Rhona. It seemed everything that touched her magically while her powers were bound affected her adversely.

Elodie had been testing and relearning her magic, as well. He had seen her power firsthand, and Scott suspected the dreams she'd had that coincided with the Druid deaths was her magic trying to tell her there was someone dangerous on Skye. He couldn't test that theory, but it was the only one that made sense to him.

Scott had taken the opportunity and already began to expand his knowledge of spells. There was so much to learn, and he could barely keep up with everything Elodie taught him. But he wouldn't want it any other way.

These few days had given him a peek into what his life would be like on Skye. Scott had never been happier before. The last thing he wanted was to have his past intrude, but it would until he found Kevin's killer. He needed that closure for himself and for Filip. Which was one reason for their guest.

"Are you ready for this?" Elodie asked.

Scott shook his head. "Nay, but I'd rather get it over with."

He pushed to his feet and followed Elodie to the door. She swung it open, her smile not as wide as it would've been had she greeted a friend. Not that Scott blamed her. He stepped up beside her and nodded at George. "Elodie, let me introduce you to Georgina Miller. George, this is Elodie MacLeod."

"I thought our meeting would've been in Edinburgh," George stated with a slight bite to her words.

Scott parted his lips to reply, but Elodie beat him to it. "Things change."

"What of your father and sister?" George asked him.

Ire rankled Scott, but he held it in check. "I've already spoken to them."

George's attention shifted to Elodie, where the two stared

at each other for a long minute. This was Elodie's home, after all. She would decide whether George would be invited inside or not. And at the moment, Scott was inclined to shut the door in George's face. But Rhona had wanted to meet her. It was a step Scott had never thought would happen. The fact that George didn't seem to understand the importance—or relevance—of any of it wasn't lost on him.

Finally, George's deep brown eyes returned to Scott. "You seem to have come out the other side of this just fine."

"If you consider being attacked, kidnapped, and held in a frozen mountain fine, then I suppose I have," he replied coolly.

She blinked, surprise flickering in her eyes. "You've never spoken to me like that before."

"Perhaps it's because of the way you're speaking to us right now."

George had the good grace to look ashamed. "I apologize. I expected things to be one way, and instead, it's been flipped around completely."

"Par for the course," Scott replied.

George nodded, silently waiting.

"Please, come in," Elodie said as she opened the door wider.

After George had walked past, Scott glanced at Elodie. She shot him a small smile, letting him know she was good. They brought George to the front room, and Elodie parted her lips to speak, only George beat her to it.

"I know who's been killing the Druids in Edinburgh," she stated.

Scott was taken aback by the news. "Have you told Rhona yet?"

"I stopped here first." George's dark eyes then landed on Elodie.

Scott frowned. Something was amiss. "Who is it?"

George never took her eyes off Elodie as she said, "Elias."

"I don't like it," Balladyn replied heatedly.

Rhona sat with him on the sofa, their legs and feet intertwined. A movie played on the television, but neither paid it any attention. "I know. Me, either."

"Then why do this?"

"Because it's time the Druids stop being a hundred different factions. We need to band together. We have to learn from history. The only way we'll survive is by becoming one group."

Balladyn snorted as he ran his fingers through the length of her hair. "And this George is the answer?"

"Maybe. I don't know." This was the same conversation she'd had with herself. "Scott and Filip both think a lot of her. You're the one who told me to give her organization a chance."

"Nay, I didn't," Balladyn corrected her. "I said *Scott* wanted us to give them a chance."

She shifted her head to look at him. "You like Scott."

"I do. That doesn't mean every decision he makes is a good one."

Rhona sighed as she took his large hand in hers. "Druids are dying. I have to do something."

"We agree on that."

"You've not even met George yet."

Balladyn raised a black brow. "Tell me you're not irked that she rescheduled."

"She probably had a valid reason."

"Putting off meeting the leader of the most powerful group of Druids on this realm doesn't ingratiate someone."

Rhona *was* a little irritated, but she was trying not to let it color her view of George, which was already stained by the fact that she led a group of Druid Others.

"That's what I thought," Balladyn replied.

Rhona teasingly elbowed him. "We're going to keep an open mind. We've gotten nowhere over the past few days trying to figure out who could've used the Red Hills."

"I really thought it was Kerry."

She grunted. "I admit, I did, too. It would make sense that she'd want revenge. But…we went straight to her. Like she said, if it was her, she would've used somewhere different."

"I'm not convinced she's not somehow involved."

"Which is why she's being monitored." Rhona winked at him.

Balladyn grinned. "Aye."

Rhona sobered as her thoughts turned to what kept her up at night. "You and I both know it's only a matter of time before more Druids die."

"Unfortunately, you're right."

"I wish Corann were still leading us."

Balladyn pulled her against him as he kissed her temple.

"You're doing a great job, sweetheart. You should believe in yourself as much as I do."

Rhona wished she could, but she constantly second-guessed herself. It wasn't just her life on the line—it was everyone on Skye. And that was a tremendous amount of pressure.

"We'll figure it out," he told her.

"And?" she pushed.

He sighed dramatically. "And I promise to give George a chance."

She settled her head back on his shoulder, but her smile quickly faded. Balladyn's words carried weight, but also because she had a bad feeling in the pit of her stomach that had only grown larger with every passing minute since George's arrival.

Edie stared at her reflection in the bathroom mirror. Outside the door, the kids argued over something trivial. Trevor was on his computer, ignoring them. She gripped the counter tightly, the urge to throw her head back and scream tempting. She tried to drown out the children. Everything irritated her lately. But she knew the reason—her siblings.

Since Elias's arrival, Edie had noticed a marked change in Elodie. The biggest being that her sister's magic had returned. No matter how many times she asked, Elodie wouldn't give her a straight answer as to how or when it had returned. She simply kept saying that it'd just come back. But Edie knew that was shite.

Something had happened between her siblings that neither would admit to. And Edie wasn't stupid. She saw it. But this wasn't the first time her brother and sister had thought they were keeping a secret from her.

Dreagan

"I have to go," Esther told Nikolai.

He held her gaze. "Henry isna here. You and your brother are a team."

"I know that," she snapped. Esther paused and blew out a breath. "I'm sorry for my tone, but he's the one who left for Zora. He said something was drawing him there. Nothing I said could have stopped him. We work in tandem, but he doesn't seem to care."

Nikolai took her hands in his. "You willna be going to Skye alone."

She didn't argue with him. Not because it was futile, but because she wanted him with her. She and Henry were from a long line of Druid enforcers. There were always two. A TruthSeeker and a JusticeBringer. She was the TruthSeeker. Esther didn't know how things would work with only one of them, but she knew something big was happening with the Druids. She had felt it right after Henry had gone through the Fae doorway to Zora.

At first, she'd thought she'd just imagined it because Henry had left. Now, she could no longer ignore what her instincts were telling her. As someone who could track down and stop dangerous Druids, she had no choice but to do her duty.

"I can have someone alert Henry," Nikolai offered.

Esther smiled up at her Dragon King. "That won't be necessary. I can handle this."

MacLeod Castle

Sonya paced the great hall. Every Druid at the castle had tried to reach out to the Ancients, but no one had gotten a response. The trees kept repeating the same warning to Sonya
—*Danger*.

Evangeline and Gwynn entered the castle. Sonya halted and looked at them expectantly.

"The stones just told me to be careful," Evie said.

Gwynn sighed. "There's an urgency to the wind, but I can't get anything else from it."

Sonya turned to look at the other Druids sitting in the hall. "Someone's targeting our people, and we're no closer to discovering who it is. The Ancients sent that one-drum warning, which only raised more questions."

"I think we only have one alternative," Cara said. She looked around at the others. "But we can't do it and stay hidden here at the same time."

Saffron shrugged. "In my opinion, we only have one choice."

"We fight," Marcail replied.

The others nodded in agreement.

Thank you for reading **IRON EMBER**! I hope you loved Scott and Elodie's story as much as I loved writing it. Next in the Skye Druids series is SHOULDER THE SKYE.

A desire this powerful is a war worth fighting for.

BUY SHOULDER THE SKYE now at www.DonnaGrant.com

If you love the Skye Druid series, you'll love the next Dark Universe book set in the Dragon Kings series, DRAGON LOVER...

Can she learn to love the man—as well as the dragon within?

BUY DRAGON LOVER today at www.DonnaGrant.com

To find out when new books release
SIGN UP FOR MY NEWSLETTER today at
http://www.tinyurl.com/DonnaGrantNews.

Join my Facebook group, Donna Grant Groupies, for
exclusive giveaways and sneak peeks of future books.

Keep reading for an excerpt from SHOULDER THE SKYE
and a glimpse at DRAGON LOVER...

EXCERPT OF THE NEXT SKYE DRUID BOOK

SHOULDER THE SKYE, SKYE DRUIDS SERIES, BOOK 2

COMING SOON

NEW YORK TIMES BESTSELLING AUTHOR
DONNA GRANT

Bronwyn hated when she had to make a trip into town. She parked and shut off the engine to the old SUV, but she didn't get out. She watched the rain pelt the windshield until it completely distorted the outside world.

She felt like the glass. Bombarded. Flooded. Engulfed. She stared at the building before her. The only place within miles to get grocery items. It also doubled as a post office. The co-op didn't have much of a variety but made up for it by stocking a little of everything.

Bronwyn drew in a deep breath as she steeled herself. Maybe she'd get lucky and there wouldn't be many inside.

The longer she waited, the more she tried to talk herself into coming back another time.

"For fuck's sake. I'm an adult," she mumbled and shoved open the vehicle door.

It creaked loudly, metal rubbing against metal. As soon as she stepped out, the rain drenched her. Bronwyn pulled up the hood to her raincoat and slammed the door closed. She walked toward the door, her Wellies splashing in the puddles.

A small bell chimed when she walked into the co-op. Almost immediately, her gaze landed on four people toward the back. They didn't look her way, but they didn't need to in order for her to recognize them. The fight or flight response wavered as she contemplated leaving. It was the sound of the cash register drawer closing that drew her attention. Her gaze met the pale green eyes of the cashier, Kirsi.

They had never been enemies, but Bronwyn wouldn't call her a friend either. Kirsi thanked the customers who had just paid, but her eyes never left Bronwyn. No way Bronwyn was going to leave now. She shoved back the hood of her coat. She lifted her chin and grabbed a basket as she started down the aisle.

She pulled out her mobile phone and opened it to the list. Coming into town for necessities was always the worst days for Bronwyn. She was determined to buy enough that she wouldn't have to come for at least a month. It made her contemplate having deliveries again, but that meant spending extra, and she was stretching money as far as she could at the moment.

The only way to make things better would be if she could disappear altogether.

Unfortunately, that wasn't an option. Well, it was, but she couldn't do that quite yet. So, that left her right back in her current predicament. The despised errand day.

It wasn't as if she particularly liked food. She'd be fine not eating, if it was an option.

Sadly, it wasn't. Food was there to keep her alive. Nothing more. Nothing less. She didn't understand people who called themselves foodies. What even was that? She certainly didn't understand those who loved to cook.

Bronwyn gathered the items she needed and moved to the next aisle. She inwardly berated herself for not paying attention to others and ending up on the aisle with the group she'd seen when she first entered. There was no escape either, because Sarah, the leader of the pack had caught sight of her.

"Well, well, well," Sarah said as she put back the can she'd been looking at. "What do we have here?"

"A drowned rat," Lizzie said with a snooty laugh.

Sarah grinned, her malicious intent clear. "A drowned rat indeed. Bronwyn, you look worse for wear. I mean, that hair. Really."

Bronwyn felt her wet hair sticking to the sides of her damp face. She fought the urge not to reach up and shove it away. Sarah was a bully. Had been since they were children. And she hadn't grown out of it in the years since. Nor had the others who ran around with her.

Bronwyn usually ignored the snippy comments. Normally, people left her alone for the most part. They were afraid of her. But not Sarah and her crowd. Bronwyn hated that people crossed the street to get away from her. Though, she could do without Sarah. Maybe it was time to put a little fear in her old frenemy.

The bell over the door dinged as someone entered the building. Bronwyn kept her gaze on Sarah as she closed the distance between them. The fear that flashed on Sarah's face almost made Bronwyn smile. That was always the case when someone stood up to a bully.

"You have something to say about my hair?" Bronwyn asked her in a soft voice.

Sarah swallowed nervously and tried to back up, but the shelves and her friends blocked her way. "It's…it's wet."

"Very perceptive." Bronwyn looked her over slowly. "Perhaps I should say something about you. I know just the words."

"No need."

The fear that rolled off Sarah was palpable. Bronwyn held Sarah's gaze as she muttered something unintelligible and walked away. When Bronwyn blew out a breath only to discover other customers staring at her. As soon as she met their gazes, they hurriedly looked away partly in fear and partly in disgust.

All but one person, that is.

The man stood on the next aisle watching her over the short shelves. He shoved his wet, dark blond hair away from his face. A thick lock fell back over his forehead. But it was his bright blue eyes that held her entranced, utterly enthralled. It felt as if he saw through all her defense straight to her soul —all her secrets laid bare.

He didn't stare at her with contempt or quickly lower his eyes, hoping that she didn't notice him. No, he looked at her.

Unable to help herself, she studied him, noting the handsome face and square jaw dusted with a shadow of a beard that made him even more appealing. His eyes crinkled in the corners, and she realized that his lips had curved up in a smile. That's when she noticed his mouth. Surely a man shouldn't have such full lips, lips that made her think of his mouth against hers. Slow, wet kisses.

And deep, scorching, hungry kisses.

Her heart pounded, her breaths came faster, harsher, and her blood heated. Desire.

Sizzling, brazen, beautiful desire.

It had been so long since she had experienced it. The dull memories of the past couldn't compare to the spine-tingling intensity that found her now. She pulled her eyes from his mouth and found herself caught in his gaze again. It was a mistake, but even as she realized it, she couldn't stop herself from drowning in the incredible blue shade.

Time paused. The world ceased. It was only her.

And him.

BUY SHOULDER THE SKYE now at
www.DonnaGrant.com

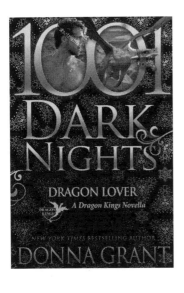

*Can she learn to love the man—
as well as the dragon within?*

Sensual. Clever. Daring. There's only one thing Kendrick yearns for—peace that has eluded the Dragon Kings. Zora may have been made in the image of Earth, but it's a far cry from home. For too long the Kings have been on the defensive, betrayed time and again. When Kendrick has an opportunity to stop a foe, he takes it. Except he isn't the only one tracking it. Soon, he finds himself face-to-face with an exquisite swordswoman who holds him enthralled...and sparks passion within his cold heart.

As an Asavori Ranger, Esha has dedicated her life to protecting her people. She trains relentlessly to become one of their best warriors, forsaking everything else. When a treacherous new enemy invades their lands, she vows to destroy it. Esha's rash decision has her crossing paths with that of a mysterious, handsome outsider. He's trouble the Rangers don't need, but she can't walk away. He awakens desires long buried and dreams neglected. The temptation of their forbidden union is more than she can resist. She's soon walking a treacherous path—one that could be the downfall for them both.

BUY DRAGON LOVER today at
www.DonnaGrant.com

ABOUT THE AUTHOR

New York Times and *USA Today* bestselling author Donna Grant® has been praised for her "totally addictive" and "unique and sensual" stories.

She's written more than one hundred novels spanning multiple genres of romance including the bestselling Dragon Kings® series that features a thrilling combination of Druids, Fae, and immortal Highlanders who are dark, dangerous, and irresistible. She lives in Texas with her dog and a cat.

www.DonnaGrant.com
www.MotherofDragonsBooks.com

facebook.com/AuthorDonnaGrant
instagram.com/dgauthor
bookbub.com/authors/donna-grant
amazon.com/Donna-Grant/e/B00279DJGE
pinterest.com/donnagrant1